"When war took their me[n]___ ___ ___ ___ [Cher]ukee women and children hac[d to survive in t]___ ___ [l]and. I tried to show their courage and fortitude."

LUCIA ST. CLAIR ROBSON

Fighting in a Line saves her young grandson Osceola from death when Andrew Jackson attacks their village—by calling him a child. And though he rages, humiliated, Fighting in a Line knows that her people will need tomorrow's warriors to fight tomorrow's battles...

Morning Dew is the woman for Osceola, a woman who can beat him at ball-play, a woman who can feed their children from the wilderness of swamp, a woman who will give him strength through long years of war...

Dahomey Woman survives the unspeakable passage from Africa with the fighting courage of her people intact. Then she finds a new people, a new home worth defending, with the free Seminole...

Mink is only a child when Osceola rescues her from a slaver's coffle. For seven years she worships him silently from her place on the other side of the evening fire—longing to be part of his family and his vision...

Little Warrior's beloved father Osceola tells her hundreds of stories and teaches her the way of the hunt and the magic of the forest. And he charges this child of his heart to carry the fire for their people's future.

LIGHT A DISTANT FIRE

Lucia St. Clair Robson

BALLANTINE BOOKS
NEW YORK

Library of Congress Catalog Card Number: 87-91861

ISBN: 0-345-32548-6

Text design by Debby Jay
Cover design by James R. Harris
Cover illustration by Judith York

Manufactured in the United States of America

First Edition: October 1988

10 9 8 7 6 5 4 3 2 1

I dedicate this book to Buddy, Randi, and Mark,
who are my friends, my siblings, and members
of a rare breed—
native Floridians.

It is a land of swamps, of quagmires, of frogs and alligators and mosquitoes! A man, sir, would not immigrate into Florida. No, sir! No man would immigrate into Florida—not from hell itself!

—JOHN RANDOLPH OF ROANOKE
1773–1833

ACKNOWLEDGMENTS

I would like to thank Ken and Ginny Stibolt for the myriad ways in which they've been of help in the writing of this book. I'm also indebted to Dr. Stephen R. Humphrey of the Florida State Museum; Dr. Daniel Austin, professor of Biological Sciences at Florida Atlantic University; Bob Ellis of the Florida Fresh Water Fish and Game Commission; Connie Haas of Lake Worth Public Library; Gene Joyner and Tom Teets, Urban Horticulturists with the Palm Beach Country Extension Service; Patsy West, historian and archivist; and Pat and Guy LaBree, artist and longtime student of Seminole history.

I owe special thanks to James Billie, Chairman of the Seminole Tribe; Naomi Wilson, whose "other" name created a link with the past; O.B. Osceola, Jr., who was willing to answer a stranger's questions graciously and thoroughly; and to the Seminole and Mikasukee, living and gone, whose courage indelibly affected the author when she was a child.

The Seminole War may now be considered at a close.

> GENERAL ANDREW JACKSON
> 1818

I cannot see that any danger can be apprehended from the miserable Indians who inhabit the peninsula of Florida.

> GENERAL ALEXANDER MACOMB
> 1829

The enemy has been met, beaten, and forced to sue for peace.

> GENERAL EDMUND PENDLETON GAINES
> (March) 1836

In less than twelve days from the time I leave Fort Drane, I will have the pleasure of shipping off the hostiles and disbanding his [sic] army.

> GENERAL WINFIELD SCOTT
> (April) 1836

I promise you that I will soon put an end to the war in Florida, or perish in the attempt.

> GENERAL RICHARD KEITH CALL
> (May) 1836

The war I believe to be over. . . .

> GENERAL THOMAS SIDNEY JESUP
> 1837

ALABAMA

Horseshoe Bend ✕

Tukabachee ▲ Talasee

Tukabachee-Pensacola Trade Road

GEORGIA

Tallapoosa R.

Alabama R.

Escambia R.

Apalachicola R.

ATLANTIC OCEAN

0   50   100
MILES

Ft. Mims ✕

Pensacola ●

Ft. San Carlos ✕

Black Villages ▲

(San Marcos) ▲ St. Marks

Tallahassee ▲

Econfina R.

(Gainesville) ● Hog Town

(Ft. Marion) Castillo de San Marcos ✕
St. Augustine ●

Ft. Peyton ✕

St. John's R.

Negro Fort ✕
Arbuthnot's Store ▲

Suwanee Village ▲
Suwanee Village ▲

Suwanee R.

Ft. King ✕

Bulowville 🏠

New Smyrna ●

Gulf of Mexico

FLORIDA TERRITORY

Ft. Mellon ✕

SEE DETAIL MAP BELOW

Wococoi ● Clark's Store 🏠
Tampa Bay

Ft. Brooke ✕

Pease R.

Lake Okeechobee

Caloosahatchee R.

EVERGLADES

Cape Florida Lighthouse 🏠

Detail map (inset):

Suwanee R.

(Ft. Marion) Castillo de San Marcos ✕
St. Augustine ●

(Gainesville) Hog Town ●

Moultrie Creek 🏠

Alachua Savanna

Ft. Peyton ✕

Suwanee Villages ▲

Ft. Drane ✕

Ft. King ✕

Payne's Landing 📜

Gaines's Battle ✕

Talasee Old Fields ▲

Oklawaha R.

Clinch's Battle ✕

Wahoo Swamp ✕

Withlacoochee R.

Dade's Battle ✕

Chukachattee ▲

Mad New Town's ▲ Village

✕ Forts

✕ Battles

● Towns

▲ Villages

🏠 Trading Posts and Plantations

📜 Treaty Sites

LIGHT A DISTANT FIRE

PROLOGUE

"BAD LUCK AT THE HORSESHOE"

"I awoke facedown in the dirt." Osceola pinched tobacco from a leather pouch worn soft as satin by his touch. He stuffed the pungent brown powder into the bowl of his pipe. Little Warrior held a sliver of pitch-pine in the flames until it ignited, then lit her father's pipe with it.

"Then what happened?" When Little Warrior leaned forward, twin reflections of the fire's light danced in her huge dark eyes.

"My grandson slept through the battle at the Fort, that's what happened." Fighting in a Line shifted her bony haunches on the palm log radiating from the star-shaped fire. She squinted at the ruffle she was sewing onto a long calico skirt.

"A cold wind blew." Osceola ignored his grandmother's teasing. "But the smoke of the guns still hovered over the field. I heard the screams of Old Mad Jackson's wounded blue-jackets." He gazed into the flames and smiled sadly. "White men do not die well.

"I felt a sharp stone jabbing into my cheek." Strange how one remembers the details, he thought. Even after memories of the great causes fade. "I tasted blood mixed with the dirt in my mouth. My head felt as though the stock of the blue-jacket's musket had crushed it like a melon. My ankle was broken. It swelled until it throbbed against the lacing of my winter moccasins. My face, my hands, my chest, were crusted with blood."

"Was the blood yours, Papa?" A frisson of dread passed through Little Warrior. Her beloved father might have died that day, before he ever earned his war name. Before he ever sired her.

"Most of it came from the body lying on top of me." Now Osceola held his audience in his slender hands. To touch a corpse could bring terrible consequences. The dead could cause more trouble than the living. And the living had caused trouble enough at the fortifications the Maskokee called the Fort and the Americans called Horseshoe Bend.

Osceola paused to relight his pipe. "I listened for the Red Sticks' war cries, but I heard only Jackson's blue-jackets. They were scalping the fallen Red Sticks. They were taking their weapons. They were stripping skin from their thighs, to make into moccasins. I pretended to be dead. They passed me by."

"He's lucky the blue-jackets didn't make a tobacco pouch of his testicles," Fighting in a Line observed. "Of course, he was only eleven. His pebbles would have made a very small pouch."

"When I could hear only the cries of the dying, I crawled from under the body. I slithered on my belly across the rough ground of the battlefield. It had been harrowed by cannon shot. It had been sown with bodies. It had been soaked with blood.

"The sun was dying, but still the crows, the buzzards, circled. The winter had been hard on us. Our starving dogs were already quarreling over the dead." When Osceola paused to light his pipe again, his family was silent. He had carried them back to the place and time that still harried his dreams after fifteen years. They all listened to the gunshots in the crackle of the fire. The eerie screams of the limpkins in the jungle around them sounded like the voices of dying men.

"Shreds of blue smoke drifted across the field like homeless ghosts." Osceola's soft, resonant voice went on hypnotically. "Breechclouts, coattails, fluttered in the wind. I whispered the blessing, 'Ni'tak intaha, the days allowed him were finished,' to each Red Stick brother I passed."

"Were they avenged?" The thought of hundreds of un-avenged spirits haunting the eaves of their families' homes drew Little Warrior closer to the comfort of her mother's warm body.

"No, daughter. That day, Old Mad Jackson killed almost

all the warriors the Red Sticks could gather. He extinguished the fire of the Maskokee nation in the north country."

"We escaped by swimming the river." Night-shadow and remembering etched the stark planes of Fighting in a Line's face more deeply than usual. Her eyes were large and luminescent in her severe face. "The water was full of corpses," she said. "The bank was lined with Old Mad Jackson's Cherokee dogs. They were shooting at those in the river, but they missed us. Cherokee can't hit their own feet."

"I'm grateful to Old Mad Jackson," Morning Dew murmured.

"Why, Mother?" asked Little Warrior.

"Because of him your father came south, to our country."

Little Warrior glowered into the dark, vine-choked woods as though General Andrew Jackson lurked there. "If I ever meet Old Mad Jackson, I'll kill him."

Ah, my precious Little Warrior, Osceola thought. I've sworn to do that more times than I can count.

CHAPTER 1

"I'm a charmer," fifteen-year-old Cricket chanted at the bull. "I can charm my enemies at a distance."

When the bull stamped, Cricket could feel the vibration through the soles of his bare feet. The bull lowered his grizzled muzzle and charged, but Cricket dodged behind an oak, then waded into the Econfina and splashed across. The bull stood in the shallows and bellowed after him. The cows in the dense palmetto thicket took up the call.

Cricket was supposed to guard the cows, not annoy them, but he didn't worry about their escaping. The large hammock where the Red Stick refugees camped was surrounded by miles of boggy ravines. The thigh-high mud underneath the black water was spiked with rotting logs and sharp cypress knees that made it difficult for animals to stray. Cricket's main duty was to chase away alligators. He carried a stout oaken club for the purpose.

Even Old Mad Jackson couldn't drag wagons and cannon through the morass around the Econfina River. The hammock was so well protected that Cricket's great-uncle, Mad New Town, was considering it as the site of his village. After three years of fleeing from the Americans and their Creek allies, Cricket dared hope he would have a home at last.

He sauntered into a clearing crowded with palmetto shelters and piles of belongings and firewood. He dodged through the clutter until he reached his family's fire. Mad New Town dipped the ladle into the kettle of thin corn gruel called *sofkee* and handed it to his nephew.

"The cows are restless." Mad New Town listened to the herd still crashing and lowing in the dry palmettos. "Were you teasing them, nephew?"

"Yes, Uncle."

"I'm proud of my nephew," Mad New Town announced to those camped around him. "He knows our enemies might be nearby. He knows childish pranks might endanger everyone. He's careful not to call attention to our position."

Cricket ate in silence, his face burning with shame. The uncles would bring this up in their daily council and humiliate him again. And again. And again.

The women's screams started at the edge of the clearing. "*Istee chatalgee!* Red men!" The cries spread toward the center of camp as people rushed to gather their weapons, their children, and their belongings. The vanguard of McIntosh's two thousand Creek warriors opened fire from the trees.

Mad New Town's men defended their families as best they could. People hid behind bushes and heaps of gear. Before long they were using dead bodies as cover. Children wailed for their mothers.

Cricket knelt behind a pile of brush and, with shaking fingers, loaded his musket. He spilled precious priming powder. More powder stuck to his sweaty palm when he emptied it into the barrel. Then he couldn't separate the tiny greased squares of cloth in the patch box.

He finally seated the ball, rammed it home, and shouldered his piece. He squinted through the smoke and the dust raised by the terrified horses and cows and chickens, but he saw only the tongues of fire flashing from the wall of bushes and vines and trees around the clearing. He picked a flame and aimed above and to the left of it as Mad New Town had taught him. But he couldn't be sure he had hit anyone.

Mad New Town seemed to be everywhere, encouraging his men and distributing what little powder and shot he had. As he ran he shouted assessments of McIntosh's anatomy, intelligence, lineage, and sexual proclivities. Defamation was an art Mad New Town had learned from his Scottish father, James McQueen.

McIntosh was part Scot, too, and both men were Maskokee, one tribe of the vast Creek confederation. The Red Stick faction had broken away from the rest of the Creek nation in Alabama five years earlier. The ensuing hostilities were of the bitterest sort, as warfare between brothers usually was.

For an hour Mad New Town's Red Sticks fought Mc-

Intosh's Creeks. Cricket poured the last of his water onto his fusil, but the hot brass had already burned large blisters on his hands. His mouth and nose were so dry, breathing was painful.

Cricket ran out of ammunition about the same time the other Red Sticks did. Their return fire dwindled, then stilled. Cricket heard the sound of his blood thumping in his temples. The Creek war cries grew more triumphant. Above the serrated fans of the palmettos Cricket could see his enemies' red-and-white plumes closing in.

"*Hobuk waksi.*" Mad New Town threw up his arms as though to present as large a target as possible and turned slowly. "Effeminate cowards who play with your own cocks." This was the signal for his men to draw the Creeks' fire so the women and children could escape. But someone panicked.

Her screams stampeded the others, and they began running blindly toward the swamp. When their men tried to cover their families' flight, the arrows wounded many of the women and children. Cricket dodged through the confusion as he searched for his mother and grandmother.

"Dog excrement! Skunk breath!"

Cricket heard Fighting in a Line's shrill voice over the din.

"Cowbirds! Did your parents leave you in the filthy nests of white people that you would betray your own?"

As Cricket ran through the rustling palmettos, he followed his grandmother's voice. In the middle of a small clearing six Creeks lounged on their muskets. They were laughing at two others who were trying to subdue Fighting in a Line.

"Filth! Toad turds! Buzzard vomit! May ants nest in your eye sockets. May vultures dine in your anus!" Fighting in a Line saw one advantage in having her own people as enemies. They understood her invective.

With a shrill whoop Cricket brandished his empty musket and charged, but he tripped over a knobby palmetto root and fell sprawling. The firelock clattered from his outstretched hand, and a grinning Creek picked it up. Fighting in a Line turned on Cricket.

"*Nuk'uh-ilio'me!* Stupid! Stupid, clumsy child! It's fitting you're named Cricket. You have a cricket's intelligence." She tried to kick him, but the two warriors holding her arms lifted her off the ground at the same time. She was so tiny that she swung between them like a bell.

"Do you think you're a warrior, then, little Cricket?" she went on shouting in midair. "You who still bear your child's name? You who soil your bed at night?" *Do not kill him,* she pleaded silently. *Do not kill this child of my heart.*

"I never . . . How can you . . . ?" Cricket burned with shame. "You lie!" he finally managed to shout. "*Tsatsap-a'kida ma'his.* I am very angry!" he screamed as two large warriors dragged him away.

Cricket was more than angry; he was blind with rage. Two more men had to help subdue him. Fighting in a Line went limp with relief. The Creeks thought him a child. They weren't going to kill him. At least, not yet.

Cricket hated Old Mad Jackson's traitorous henchman, McIntosh. He hated the Creek who casually inspected Cricket's beautiful, slender new trade fusil. He hated himself for stirring up the cattle and maybe giving away his people's position. Most of all, he hated his grandmother.

"Stop sulking." With her ragged fingernails, Fighting in a Line tore apart her ration of dry wheaten bread. "Pooh!" She pretended to spit out the crumbs. "This tastes like powdered mouse turds." She turned to Cricket. "If you aren't going to eat yours, give it to me."

Clutching his chunk of bread, Cricket turned his back on his grandmother and the small comfort of the flames. In the darkness beyond, someone was sobbing inconsolably. Her man must have been among the dead still lying where they fell along the Econfina.

Cricket's bare feet were numb with cold. The weather was far more frigid than anyone remembered it being in April. Frost had tatted lace around the leaves and twigs on the ground. The women were whispering that Mad New Town had angered the spirits somehow and turned them against him and his followers. The bitter cold was just another sign of their displeasure.

Cricket stared into the icy night. Somewhere out there Mad

New Town and his men were hiding and tending their wounded while Old Mad Jackson held their families prisoner.

As she searched for crumbs in the ruffle of her blouse, Fighting in a Line considered their situation. She doubted the warriors would try to rescue them. Old Mad Jackson had arrived with a thousand men to add to McIntosh's two thousand. The hundred women and children and six hundred head of cattle captured in the raid were ringed now by blue-jacket guards. Beyond the guards, Fighting in a Line could see the rows of waxen tents and the flares of towering bivouac fires among the pines.

Cricket's mother, Peeping, stood ponderously. She was exhausted from the day's long march. She didn't know where her new husband was, and she was carrying his child. With one hand she held her full skirts against her legs, away from the flames, as she stirred the small amount of *sofkee* in the kettle.

"You should thank your grandmother." Peeping spoke to her son's back. She had been making peace in this family for years.

"Thank her for what? For saying that I . . ." The affront was too egregious to voice.

"Thank her for saving your life. They would have killed you as a warrior if she hadn't treated you as a child."

"At least I would have died with honor."

"We need tomorrow's warriors to fight tomorrow's battles," said Fighting in a Line. "We can't squander them today."

"Why couldn't I have a dignified grandmother?" Cricket said it loudly enough for both women to hear. Peeping was horrified, as though her rearing of him were responsible for the disrespect.

Fighting in a Line only chuckled. "I used to be dignified. Ask anyone from Talasee, from the north country." She waved a freckled, knobby hand toward the dark forms huddled around their tiny fires. Most of the people in Mad New Town's band were from his old town of Talasee.

"I was a good mother. I was a dutiful wife to three husbands." Fighting in a Line mimicked the sweet tones of a new bride. "Yes, my husband. Whatever you say, my husband. What pleases you, my husband?

"Now they're all gone. Poof." She blew a cloud of vapor that hung a moment in the air, then vanished. "All gone. Now there is no one to order me. I do as I please. I say what I please.

"When you're old you can do the same. Until then you must do your duty. Your duty is to stay alive, to take over when my brother can no longer lead."

"How can I lead when we are penned here like Old Mad Jackson's cattle?"

With her tongue, Fighting in a Line excavated a bit of stone baked into the bread. "Tspeek Eeng-glis, I, li'l bit." To prove it, she said it in the language of her father, old James McQueen: "I have a plan."

Just after dawn the next day, Peeping used the fat from their ration of salty army bacon to oil her mother's hair. With clam shells she plucked the few wiry hairs from Fighting in a Line's chin. Fighting in a Line shook as much dust and mud as she could from the hem of her long skirt. She borrowed all of Peeping's strands of beads to add to the pile on her own neck. She took even longer than usual to arrange and knot them so they formed a neat cone from her shoulders to her chin.

She tried to see the results in the film of ice on the surface of the water basin. Then, flapping her skinny arms to warm herself, she set out for the nearest sentry. With anxiety pooled in her brown eyes, Peeping watched her go.

Fighting in a Line spoke loudly to the pale-eyes and stared him in the face, a mannerism she had noted in her Scottish father. She stabbed her own hard chest with her finger, then pointed toward General Jackson's gaily striped marquee.

"Tsee Tsek-sin, I. Tspeek Eeng-glis him, I."

Word that Mad New Town's sister had gone to talk to Old Mad Jackson spread quickly among the captives. The women and children moved closer to Peeping's fire, as though drawn there by fragile strands of hope. Cricket didn't indulge in hoping. He stared toward the blue-jackets' camp and brooded about his grandmother's latest folly.

When the sun had risen halfway to the apex of its course,

Cricket began to be alarmed. Peeping paced, her path circumscribed by the women who crowded close now. All of them stared toward the bivouac area. They had draped the thin gray army blankets over their heads for protection against the bitter wind, and they looked like the mourners they were. They shifted their babies from one hip to another, while their older children squatted at their feet.

When the pallid sun was straight overhead, Cricket could stand it no longer. He rose and walked toward the sentry. He was wondering how to ask about his grandmother when she appeared.

She stared stolidly ahead of her. A pale-eyes would not have been able to tell if she had been successful or not, but Cricket and Peeping knew. She had talked to Old Mad Jackson.

Cricket forgot his resolve to keep silent. As they walked back to the fire he danced around her and rained questions down on her. The crowd of women parted to make way for them.

"Did you see him? What does he look like? Did you speak to him? Does he know where Uncle is? Will he send us back north? Will he kill us?"

Fighting in a Line leaned over the almost empty kettle and dug into the congealed mass of *sofkee* in the bottom.

"*Hauha'kis*. I am hollow," she said. "Old Mad Jackson is rude. I visited his lodge, but he offered me no food." She scooped out a gray lump of hominy and ate if off her fingers.

"Grandmother, tell us of Tsek-sin Chulee Hadjo."

"Ah, my grandson has found his tongue. I thought you were too angry with your poor, weak old grandmother ever to speak to her again."

Cricket controlled his anger. She was having fun with him, but she must have spoken to the pale-eyes' *Hobayee Tastanagee*, the One Who Understands All the Arts of War. Her love of drama would force her to tell her story soon.

"I held council with Tsek-sin Chulee Hadjo, Old Mad Jackson." She spoke as though what she had to say were of no great moment. The women murmured in awe.

"As I passed through the blue-jackets' camp, I could see there was little food there. Old Mad Jackson is not going to kill us, or he would have already. Now he must feed us, when he barely has enough for his warriors, so I told him to let us go.

"I told him my brother, whom the pale-eyes call Peetuh Mahkwee, will never surrender, not even to ransom us. A Red Stick doesn't surrender. Old Mad Jackson was at the battle of the Horseshoe. He knows Red Sticks don't surrender. I told him I would try to find my brother, the great war leader. I would try to bring him in."

"You didn't!" Cricket was outraged, but Fighting in a Line only looked shrewdly up at him.

"I said I would *try* to bring him in. I didn't say how hard I would try. Old Mad Jackson believed a toothless old woman. He believed I could make a *tastanagee*, a war leader, surrender.

"He also says when all we Red Sticks are together, he will send us to live with our Maskokee brothers in the north country. Our Creek brothers have been killing us for five years, yet Jackson still thinks we can live in peace with them. A river of blood flows between us now. We can never cross it."

From the waistband of her skirt Fighting in a Line produced the most astonishing surprise of all. She grandly waved a folded letter, already smudged and wrinkled. "This is marked by Old Mad Jackson himself." She held it in front of Cricket's nose as though he could read it. "Its medicine gives us safe passage through the territory where the blue-jackets are."

"*Tche'*," she said, to inform those standing farther back that she had finished her speech. She waved the letter again, this time to shoo the women and children away.

"Gather your belongings. We must leave before he changes his mind. Before he realizes what a fool he's been."

"Yes, *adsulei'dshi-tut*, most ancient one."

Less than an hour later Old Mad Jackson himself, seated on his gaunt gray horse, watched Fighting in a Line lead a slow procession of women and children away from camp. Cricket stared up at him as he passed and felt a chill of dread and of awe mixed with his hatred. This was the *tastanagee thloko*, the great war leader who had destroyed the powerful Creek nation and humiliated Mad New Town. This was the man who had driven Cricket from his home, destroyed his past, and put his future in jeopardy.

Jackson reminded Cricket of some alien, predatory bird. His scythe of a nose cast a shadow across his long, pale face. A shock of wiry hair sprouted like pinfeathers above his high forehead. His small, piercing gray eyes seemed to bore into Cricket's soul and despoil it, too.

When they were out of sight Cricket's legs wobbled. He realized how much he had expected Jackson to change his mind at the last moment. Fighting in a Line had the same thought. She picked up the pace considerably when the last of the blue-jackets' wood details and horse pickets were behind them. Cricket eyed the horses longingly as he passed them.

"I'm going back to steal a few horses, Grandmother," he said. "The sick, the wounded, can ride."

"You're the man." Fighting in a Line was trying to make amends for shaming him. "You must do what you think right. A *tasikaya*, an ordinary warrior, would steal those horses. A *tastanagee*, a war leader, would not."

"Why?"

"The horses will be of little use in the swamp. The loss of them will bring the blue-jackets after us." She glanced fondly up at him. "Do not concentrate so hard on the ground under your feet that you miss the trail ahead."

"Grandmother, how did you fool Old Mad Jackson?"

"I think that like the alligator, he has a tiny soft spot in his thick hide. A spot where he's vulnerable. I think his soft spot is that he believes women, especially old red women, are weak in mind as well as body. He thinks we're incapable of gulling him." She chortled softly to herself as she clambered through the vine-tangled bushes and wheezed over the rough, swampy ground.

CHAPTER 2

Everyone agreed the sister of Talasee *tastanagee* had pig magic. After she gulled Old Mad Jackson, Fighting in a Line and her column of barefoot refugees walked a hundred and fifty miles south, following the convex curve of Florida's western coastline. Somewhere along the way she acquired a pair of shoats.

In the year since then, the hogs had rooted in the vast live-oak forests along the Hillsborough River. The rich acorn mast had fattened the original pair of pigs to the size of calves. The spotted matriarch was constantly with farrow, and her litters usually numbered around ten.

Fighting in a Line's sounder of swine had grown to impressive size and considerable inconvenience. All the gardens were enclosed by stout paling fences. Sometimes the fences kept the pigs out, and sometimes they didn't.

During the day, most of Fighting in a Line's immense wealth had the wisdom to be heard but not seen. The hogs snuffled and grunted and crashed about in the surrounding jungle of the hardwood hammock. But each night, as soon as the last group of men had knocked the dottle from their pipes and left the town square for their cabins, the pigs invaded the village with a great chorus of squealing and honking and snorting. Early risers had to watch where they walked until the pigs' nightly deposits were collected and spread on the gardens.

When Mad New Town and his men reunited with their families, they built the women's log houses here, about ten miles from the large, ceremonial town of Chukachattee, Red House. General Jackson's sweep through the northern part of the Florida peninsula had left destruction in its wake. Refugees from the burned villages along the Suwanee River had fled south and rebuilt here. Their small settlements were scattered for miles through the dense, tall, live-oak forests along the river.

Old Mad Jackson had finally withdrawn his troops while his government dickered with the Spanish for Florida. When the Senate began an inquiry into Jackson's unauthorized invasion of Spanish territory, Old Hickory threatened to cut off the ears of anyone who censured him. In the end, the House sustained Andrew Jackson's illegal campaign, the Senate tabled the motion against him, and things quieted down.

Now, corn was chest-high among the charred tree stumps in the new communal fields. Mad New Town had insisted his people plant their meager supply of seed, although many hadn't wanted to bother. They all had heard that the Spanish had sold the entire peninsula to the Americans. They lived with the fear Old Mad Jackson would swoop down on them again and they would have to abandon what they'd planted.

They had a point. The United States government planned to recoup the cost of the purchase by selling Florida land. They also intended to capture and sell the runaway slaves who had taken refuge with the Indians.

It was June 1819, time for Fighting in a Line to notch the ears of the latest litter of pigs and castrate half the males. She stood on a crate to reach one of the beams supporting the steeply pitched roof of the cabin. She slid the five-foot handle of her pig net from among the hoes and digging sticks and alligator poles stored there. A scorpion with its barbed tail curled over its head scuttled from among the tools.

The handle of the net was longer than Fighting in a Line. She maneuvered it down out of the door, set its butt end on the ground, and leaned it against the front wall. She took down a coil of palm fiber cord and threaded her arm through it so it hung from her knobby shoulder.

She gave the blade of her knife a few deft swipes on her whetstone and stuck it into the sheath on her belt. She tugged the hem of her short blouse down to meet the waistband of her skirt. She straightened the twenty pounds of beads around her neck and tucked a few stray wisps into the conical bun above her forehead. She shouldered the net and headed, barefoot, for the woods.

The huge live-oak hammock wasn't far away, but Fighting in a Line took considerable time reaching it. Most of the women were members of her clan, the Snakes. They were mending clothes or stirring *sofkee* in the kettles, hoeing their gardens or pounding *koontee* roots in their log mortars. As she passed each one, Fighting in a Line stopped to inquire at length about her family.

The usual morning chatter and laughter were subdued here. Mad New Town's village wasn't a happy one. Most of the inhabitants were still mourning the thirty-seven men killed in Jackson's raid on the Econfina. Like most Maskokee towns, this one centered around the women of one or two clans. The entire village was almost one extended family. The loss of a single member affected them all.

Peeping's new husband and the father of her infant daughter had died at the Econfina. Like the other widows, Peeping had taken off her beads and jewelry. She wore the same ragged skirt and blouse every day. She left her hair unwashed and uncombed. She had always been quiet and unassuming, but now even the shy laughter had left her brown eyes. Each sundown she went to the edge of the village to mourn.

When Fighting in a Line passed the last of the women's compounds, she paused to stare toward the river. Her grandson was out there somewhere, fasting and studying to be a warrior. Today he was seeking the vision that would reveal his guardian spirit. Fighting in a Line had already chewed a bit of ginseng and blown toward the river to influence Cricket's thoughts in the right direction.

From the corner of her eye she saw the man who had been lurking around the village for days. Neither of them had spoken to each other, but they didn't need to. Between them they had almost a century of experience playing this game. Their signals were too subtle to be noticed by the casual observer, but they were as obvious to Fighting in a Line and her suitor as the elaborate elegance of the cranes' courtship dance. With a sly smile on his face and a bounce to his step, the old man followed her like a hound in hot ashes.

The ground below the maze of aerial mangrove roots heaved and twitched. It advanced with a curious rippling motion to-

ward Cricket. Thousands of tiny serrated claws waved and
snapped above the beige-and-red-tippled surface. The clicks
and the rubbing of chitinous carapaces sounded like wind
rustling dry leaves. But no breeze stirred the dark green canopy of the mangroves or rippled the black water beyond them.

Not much else moved within the mad basketry of prop roots
that rose fifteen feet to connect with the mangrove trunks.
No raccoons harvested the oysters clinging to the roots exposed by low tide. The ibis and herons and anhingas had left
their rookeries here to fish the teeming estuaries of Tampa
Bay. A gaudy orange-and-yellow corn snake lay curled, tranquil as a cat, in the crotch of a mangrove. The snake's stomach bulged with the swamp rat it was digesting.

In the still, humid air of the clearing where Cricket sat,
dragonflies stitched erratic courses after mosquitoes. The sun
struck iridescent green and blue and purple and gold sparks
from the dragonflies' slender bodies. The air thrummed with
the shrill crepitation of insects. Katydids rocked on the tips
of grass blades.

Cricket stared, hypnotized, at the seething current of fiddler crabs advancing toward him. He was naked and vulnerable. The crabs would swarm over him. They would perch
on the ridges of his brows and cheekbones. With their small
pincers they would daintily pluck his eyes from their sockets.
Cricket imagined his glistening eyeballs waving in their claws
before being shoved into the opening between fluttering man-
dibles.

The crabs would strip the flesh from him. His dry, clean
bones would rest in the sparse turtle grass. Mice would nest
in his skull. Flowers would grow through the curved bars of
his ribs. The idea of getting up and walking away flashed
through Cricket's mind, but he couldn't move. His wandering
soul had left his body as helpless as the brittle, papery husk
shed by a cicada.

For twelve days Cricket had been studying under Abihka's
stern tutelage. Now, hunger and the sun on his shaved head,
the exhaustion of his vigil and the intoxicating effects of the
sowatchko root, were playing with his senses. In the shimmering waves of heat, the mangrove trees began to shimmy
and bob on their ungainly stilts. They seemed to be trying to

tug free of the black muck that held them. Like enormous, dancing centipedes, they swayed in time to the pulse of the insects' song.

In the moist oven of mid-June, Cricket's teeth began to chatter. The sound blended with the growing susurrus of the crabs whose first rank had reached the edge of the clearing. Behind them, the mangroves were working themselves into a frenzy, as though whipped by a hurricane.

Cricket wondered if the crabs were a dream, or if they were a prank of his inner demons, released by the root whose bitter taste coated his dry mouth. If they were a vision, Cricket was disappointed. He had come here to meet the spirit that would guide him along life's path. A warrior's spirit should take the form of a fierce, skillful predator like the wolf or panther or alligator. Cricket hadn't expected enlightenment to appear as a migration of fiddler crabs.

Overhead, gulls gathered in a roiling, strident cloud. Their skirling was an eerie mix of lamentation and laughter. Cricket knew with a chilling certainty they were going to join the crabs' attack on him. He tried to shake his head to dispel the hysteria, but his muscles failed to obey even that simple command.

A single thought, shimmery and tenuous as a water drop, condensed in the swirling mists of his mind. *Use what you can of fear,* Mad New Town once had told him. *Ignore the rest.*

Cricket had to tread the narrow high ground between the swamp of his fear and the deep, tranquil lake of reason. In the ordinary world reason organized events into orderly progressions. Reason allowed one to plan for the future and remember the past. But this was the country of dreams and of the soul, where past and future didn't exist.

Cricket's face muscles cooperated enough to twitch into a smile before he surrendered to his vision. If the crabs ate him, he would become part of the great circle that was life. His flesh would be divided into thousands of bits and would grow as part of the crabs, then part of whatever ate them.

For an instant he saw the world as did every living creature in it. The answers to every question were almost in his grasp. For the length of time a dragonfly took to beat its wings,

Cricket weighed nothing. His spirit spread like smoke through time.

The sun fractured into golden arrows that shot into him. From a spot on the crown of his head, heat flowed like syrup through his body. The dragonflies laced a veil of iridescent color around him. He felt the radiant sapphire and emerald and amethyst light drift languidly around him like spiderwebs.

The first crab sidled up to Cricket's bare feet. Peevishly it waved its claw at him, as though ordering him out of the way. It measured about the length of two knuckles across, and it looked ready to take on anything that blocked it.

Will you try to devour all of me, Brother Crab? Cricket asked affectionately.

The crabs were not imaginary. The gulls dove into them and, with claws dangling from their beaks, flew in search of rocks on which to drop them and shatter the hard carapaces. The survivors skittered on, driven by whatever urge had started this curious migration in the first place. They parted at Cricket's feet and flowed around him. The rough edges of their shells tickled. The gulls' mockery filled the clearing until Cricket felt as though he were breathing in sound along with the heat and dust and iridescence.

Slowly at first, then faster and faster, the mangroves and the meadow began to spin in time to the wheeling gulls. The sun focused on top of Cricket's head like a burning glass. Then it exploded. From a point behind his closed eyes rays of light arced outward in a shower of meteors. He fell, spiraling into a well of blinding light. As he plummeted, he screamed like a gull.

The last he remembered were the words "Patience is knowledge." The sun itself had spoken to him. His spirit helper was to be a giver of life, not a taker of it.

An hour later Abihka found him pitched forward on his face. When the old man squatted next to the boy, the cartilage grated dryly across the flaky knobs of his knees. He hunkered there with his thin, muscular arms around his legs and watched his favorite pupil moan and twitch in his sleep.

Cricket woke to find Abihka staring intently into his face. He sat up and shook his head cautiously to clear the sparks of light that still sputtered behind his eyes, like green cedar needles on a fire. He stared at the ground and waited for *Kithla*, the Knower, to speak.

Abihka knew Cricket had journeyed to the other side. The guiding spirit, What Comes to Him in Sleep, had visited him. Abihka handed Cricket a stiff new pair of moccasins.

"These moccasins are made to run toward an enemy. They must never run away from one."

"Yes, Uncle." Cricket put on the moccasins and flexed his toes inside them. The word "uncle" pained him. Mad New Town should have given him his man's moccasins. Mad New Town had been more than a teacher and a hero to Cricket. He had been a father to him.

But at the Econfina something had changed in Mad New Town. He hadn't avenged the crying-blood of his followers who died. Now Talasee *Tastanagee* hunted enough to feed his family. He sat silently through the daily councils of the elders. The rest of the time he brooded in front of his sister's cabin. He smoked and stared into the past and barely acknowledged the men who greeted him politely. Old Mad Jackson had bewitched Mad New Town's soul.

Day after day Mad New Town refought the battle of the Econfina. The shame of his defeat there hovered around him. No one mentioned his disgrace, but no one talked of naming him *Tastanagee Thloko*, Great Warrior, either. It was a title and an honor a man of his age and talents could expect.

Abihka was a Mikasukee, the southernmost tribe of the far-flung Creek empire. His people had been in Florida a hundred years. And frankly there were those among the Mikasukee who resented the intrusion of the Red Stick Maskokee. There were those who blamed them for bringing Old Mad Jackson and the blue-jackets swarming like angry hornets after them.

Abihka's narrow chest was almost obscured by the huge, tarnished half-moons of his silver gorget and by the criss-crossed thongs and belts supporting various necessities. He looked like the pale-eyes peddlers who, with pots and pans clattering on their backs, used to stroll into Talasee to do business with James McQueen.

Cricket wasn't fooled by the old man's harmless appearance. *Abihka* meant Heap at the Root. It was an ancient name from the time when warriors piled scalps at the base of a tree to prove their town's superiority in warfare. Abihka was also called *Hobayee Tastanagee*, One Who Understands All the Arts of War.

He was a healer and a knower. He could heal all three types of wounds. He could divine the location of lost objects. He could make things dropped in the water rise to the surface. Even Fighting in a Line, who disdained the Mikasukee, regarded him with awe.

Abihka carried his holiest articles—his hollow cane medicine tube, his tobacco pouch of opossum skin, and his fox hide. The opossum and fox hides meant he could cure snakebites. The tobacco was a special type that protected him against the souls of the dead. Stuck in his scalplock was the buzzard feather he used to clean gunshot wounds.

Not all the articles dangling from him were holy. His small wooden *sofkee* bowl and spoon hung among the bulging leather pouches clustered like ticks at his waist. A moth-eaten raccoon skin was tucked under his breechclout belt. The raccoon's tail swung between his legs. Abihka sat on the hide when the ground was damp.

Abihka reached behind his back and separated a palm fiber sling from among the bow, the medicine tube, the long pipe for everyday smoking, and the quiver made from an alligator tail. The sling cradled a thick glass bottle that once had held Barbados rum. Abihka said a short prayer while he held the bottle up in one hand and in the other a large conch shell stained molasses brown inside. The black liquid in the bottle absorbed and nullified the rays of the setting sun.

"Now that you've finished the first course of instruction, you're qualified to be *tasikaya*, an ordinary warrior," Abihka said. "I've taught you more than I taught the other boys, because you have the fire that will make a great leader someday. You know many herbs. You know the songs that will release their powers. You've journeyed to the spirit world.

"The council has decided you'll serve the sacred *Asee*, the Black Drink, at the ceremony of the Green Corn. It's time to purge yourself."

When Abihka pulled the wooden stopper out of the bottle and poured the thick, opaque liquid into the shell, white foam formed on top of it. With his medicine tube Abihka bubbled his breath into the Black Drink to add special magic. Cricket could smell the brew's strong odor. He prepared himself for what he knew its effect would be.

CHAPTER 3

Old Squat, Mad Dog, and Swamp Singer had been in their customary places on the lower tier of the Panther clan's long, open-fronted shed since well before dawn. Each morning, after bathing and greeting the Breath Maker, they padded like arthritic panthers through the sleeping town. They met here in the town's ceremonial square to take up their reminiscences and discussions where they had left off only a few hours before.

Their clan shed faced east, and early arrivals for the daily councils found them basking under their fringed shawls like ancient gopher turtles in the morning sun. Swamp Singer's nephew always sent his daughter with a large bowl of *sofkee* and strips of roasted bear or venison or manatee meat for their breakfast. The three friends passed the wooden ladle from one to the other. They seasoned the bland *sofkee* with acrid tobacco smoke and spicy gossip. Over the years they had perfected the technique of telling the most outrageous stories with faces as solemn as owls'.

Today they were in their places even earlier than usual because as Beloved Men they were in charge of arranging Chukachattee's Green Corn ceremony. They were making sure all went as it should. They were also reserving their seats. For days people had been arriving from the outlying settlements to celebrate the annual time of renewal. More men than usual would be expecting to sit in the four long, three-sided clan shelters bordering the square.

Very little was done in Chukachattee without consulting

Mad Dog, Old Squat, and Swamp Singer. Their advice was considered infallible. Only Mad Dog recently had shown weakness in judgment. He had formed a strong and inexplicable attachment to the sister of Talasee *Tastanagee*. Given Mad Dog's stubborn disposition, his friends dreaded and anticipated the courtship. It would undoubtedly prove stormy and entertaining.

As near as Mad Dog could reckon, he was in his sixty-first season and the youngest of the three. The spikes of coarse black hair that poked from beneath the front of his best but frayed turban were threaded with gray. He had the bright, mischievous eyes of a crow. Time was beginning to etch delicate furrows around his eyes and his broad mouth. The bold planes of his lips and nose and cheeks looked as though they'd been chiseled from cypress wood and polished.

A tear in his hunting shirt was still unpatched. He lived alone, with no woman to cook or mend or tend his garden for him. That may have explained his fixation on Fighting in a Line. That and her awesome wealth in pigs.

"They say Old Mad Jackson is the cause of our troubles," Mad Dog said.

"You don't agree?" Old Squat could tell from the tone of his friend's voice what path this conversation would take. It was one they had traveled before, and he was in no hurry to reach the end of it. He was content to lounge here and smell the delicious aroma of the newly woven palmetto mats spread over the old ones on the platform.

Old Squat was tall and very thin. He had instructed the best weavers in the village to make the mats extra thick to cushion his bones. Chukachattee had been here five years, so only five layers were under this most recent one. It was not the soft cushion formed by the mats of a long-established town.

"We should be grateful to Old Mad Jackson," Mad Dog said.

"Tell that to the widows, the orphans, the starving, the homeless." Swamp Singer was short and stocky, and his head looked a little too big for his body. The effect was exaggerated by his elaborate turban and egret plumes.

"War is the only way to train our youth in the manly arts."

"I weary of Jackson's way of warring." Swamp Singer sat cross-legged and leaned against the partition separating the Panther clan's section from that of the Bear clan. He reached up and drew a small chamois packet from the paisley folds of his turban. His fingers trembled as he unwrapped it and pinched a bit of tobacco for his pipe.

In public his friends ignored the palsy that was creeping over Swamp Singer. In private each worked his own magic to dispel it. Despite their efforts, it had begun affecting his voice, which shook as though he were perpetually angry. In this case he was.

"Old Mad Jackson doesn't act from honorable motives of revenge, to quiet the ghosts of his dead. He has an insatiable lust to own Mother Earth. He's a greedy man. He's *istee fut-chigo*, a man who behaves perversely." After that worst of epithets, Swamp Singer subsided against the latticework partition. After the battle at the Horseshoe five years earlier, Andrew Jackson had wrested away not only the land of the defeated Red Sticks, but eight million acres belonging to his own Creek allies.

"The real problem is not Old Mad Jackson." Mad Dog was unperturbed by Swamp Singer's outburst. "It's that our people forget the old ways. This land is too warm, too easy. It makes us indolent. Look at them." Mad Dog pointed his pipe toward the line of boys approaching the public square. "They consider themselves trained in less than a month," he grumbled. "When I was a boy we spent a year studying."

"When you were a boy the earth was still a ball of worm shit," Old Squat said.

"When you were a boy the sister of Talasee *Tastanagee* was already wearing out her second husband." Swamp Singer hawked, spat a wad of phlegm into a corner of his bandanna, and tied it with shaking fingers. One didn't sully the holy grounds.

"My friend," said Old Squat, "you should raise a war party to woo that one."

"I hear she's had so many husbands they've worn all the hair off her nether scalp."

While Swamp Singer and Old Squat bedeviled Mad Dog, Cricket and the other initiates left their retinue of children at the back wall of the clan sheds. The children were fascinated by the young men about to become ordinary warriors. Only weeks before they had been boys like the rest, burdened with foolish names and the object of everyone's jokes. Now they were to be transformed into men. Each year the initiates proved to those waiting for manhood that it would come in time.

Cricket was afraid if he moved a muscle in his face, he would smudge the red-and-yellow stripes that angled from his high cheekbones to his mouth. Sweat collected under the armload of cassine branches he carried and caused his chest to itch agonizingly. More sweat dangled from the wavy fringe of black hair framing his face and from the three scalplock braids at the nape of his neck. His uncle had shaved the rest of his scalp for him this morning, so it would be done just right.

Cricket was afraid he would commit an error here that would dog him the rest of his life. If he made a mistake in this long, complex ceremony, misfortune would haunt those who called themselves *Kanyuksa Istichatee*, the People of the Peninsula. And Mad New Town would suffer more shame.

Abihka stood motionless in the center of the square and faced east, praying to the Breath Maker. He had left his usual commissary and tool kit in his wife's cabin. He wore clean white moccasins and leggings and a white deerskin draped over his shoulders. He had painted half his face red and the other half black.

Cricket knew the long clan sheds were filling with men. He heard the murmur of their moccasins across the new palmetto mats and the creak of the three-tiered platforms when they sat. The women were crowding onto the rough benches set beyond the square.

All day Cricket and the other initiates helped Abihka prepare the fire and the Black Drink while the women filed by. They brought their families' old clothes and utensils to be burned. They left baskets of corn to be blessed and added to the coming feast. All day boys with torches ran from the square to deliver the new fire to each household.

As darkness fell, the firelight distorted Abihka's sharp features, turning his painted face into a mask. Night faded the color from the men's bright turbans and ruffled hunting shirts, but the egret plumes in their turbans shone like white torches in the darkness of the sheds.

Foam rose over the rim of the huge brass kettle balanced on the four logs radiating out from the big fire in the center of the square. The time for the most important part of the ceremony had come.

"Remember to move out of the way," Abihka whispered as Cricket carried his gourd full of the Black Drink toward the Panther clan's shed.

Cricket clutched the gourd tightly to keep his hands from shaking as he handed it to Bolek, the headman of the Suwanee towns. As Bolek lifted it to his mouth, Cricket threw back his head and sang the shrill, descending note, the cry of the Black Drink. He held the note while Bolek drained the gourd.

Cricket was so fascinated by how much Bolek had drunk he almost forgot to step aside. He was warned by Bolek's huge belch as he brought up a mouthful of the Black Drink. Cricket dodged to avoid the stream Bolek spewed into the square. A dark stripe at least ten paces long soaked into the sand.

Two hours passed while the gourds made the rounds of the warriors and leaders. Finally, when the perimeter of the square was awash in Black Drink, Abihka approached the boys standing motionless in the center. When Abihka nodded to Cricket to step forward, Cricket's heart pounded so loudly he feared the men in the clan sheds would hear it.

"This man, who has seen sixteen winters, was in the battle at the Econfina where a scalp was taken," Abihka shouted. "He has earned the right to become an ordinary warrior. His war title shall be *Asee Yaholo*."

Abihka shouted the name three more times, but even after that it continued to echo in Cricket's head. Elation surged through him until he trembled with it. The event he had worked for and anticipated all his life had arrived. Moments ago he had been a child. Now he was a man.

He turned to the shed where the Snake clan sat, and he stared straight into his uncle's eyes. For a few heartbeats the defeat left Mad New Town's face. *I'll make you proud of me,*

Uncle, Cricket said silently. *You already have,* his uncle replied.

From now on Cricket would be known to his people as Asee Yaholo, Black Drink Singer. Those outside the nation would call him Osceola.

From the darkness beyond the fire's light, drums started. Three or four rhythms scuffled and merged, then separated again in a wild, bewitching pattern. A powerful bass voice chanted, and a chorus answered. The men's voices were low and pulsing. The women's soared in eerie ululations. The drums were neither Maskokee nor Mikasukee. The voices didn't belong to *istee chatalgee*, red people. More than a hundred blacks, in double lines, danced into the square.

Most of them were Mikasukee or Maskokee slaves, bought years ago, then allowed to live in their own villages nearby. Slavery here meant occasionally working for their masters and giving up a portion of the crops from their own fields and orchards. In return they received protection from those they considered more allies than owners. Many of these blacks had fled south with Bolek and his people when Old Mad Jackson attacked their settlements along the Suwanee River. Some of them were runaways from plantations in Georgia and Alabama.

Most of the time they lived as the Maskokee and Mikasukee did. They wore turbans and leggings and long, ruffled, calico shirts. They built cabins, met in council, elected leaders, tended their livestock, and cultivated neat gardens and fields. But now and then, during festivals like the Green Corn ceremony, they performed the dances of their homelands in Africa.

Many of the blacks who had escaped the white man's slavery and fled to Florida were of fierce tribes like the Fanti and Ashanti or the Dahomey, Yoruba, or Mandingo. Most of them were magnificent—tall and muscular and dark as the tannin-dyed Suwanee itself. Those chosen to dance here were the best in the settlements.

As the drums quickened the men leaped and whirled and stamped in unison. The women trembled and shuddered as though possessed. With their bodies, arms, and hands they wove sinuous patterns that held Osceola spellbound.

When their performance ended they filed past the Snake clan's shed where Osceola now sat with the other warriors. The pungency of the dancers' sweat brought a rush of memories into the quiet they left behind them. Their collective power began to tug Osceola back to the last time he had been among so many black people.

Osceola didn't want to go traveling in the past this night. The Green Corn festivities were still in full swing. He would have preferred to stay in the present, where he was a man, not a child. Where he was the hero of the hour. Where young women who hadn't noticed him before were glancing coquettishly his way. But he never resisted when dreams or memories overtook him. Dreams and memories offered wisdom. A man ignored them at his peril.

Fatigue, excitement, and the Black Drink made this vision particularly vivid. Osceola felt the spirit of Big Feet sitting beside him. Big Feet's presence was so strong, Osceola knew if he turned he would see the boy sitting there, looking as he had three years earlier, when he was twelve. Big Feet would be forever twelve.

When Osceola had last seen Big Feet, the boy had had gentle brown eyes, full lips, and a disorderly mass of soft black curls. He had been darker than his Mikasukee father and lighter than his African mother. When slavers stole his mother, he and his father and Osceola had gone to the Negro fort for help in recovering her. The fort was on the Apalachicola River, seventy-five miles from the Georgia border.

They had walked together into the turmoil there. In 1815, when the British troops left Spanish Florida, they had stocked the fort and turned it over to their black allies. In 1816 the blacks had need of it. Blue-jacket forces had invaded. The blacks knew if the Americans captured them—free men or Mikasukee property or runaways—they would send them north, into slavery.

The fortifications had looked able to withstand attack. High earthen breastworks and a V-shaped salient with side wings fronted the river where the Americans' ships were anchored.

The fort's four cannons and a howitzer kept the sailors ducking. A vast, grassy swamp behind the stockade made attack from the rear unlikely.

As Osceola fell deeper into the spell of his vision, his heartbeat quickened. Sweat glistened on his face. He and Big Feet were standing once more in the fort's magazine, trying unsuccessfully to cadge muskets from the men handing them out. Through the magazine's log walls they could hear the dull thud of the ships' cannons as they fired at the front breastwork.

Besides two thousand five hundred British Long Land Service muskets, the magazine held four hundred and fifty casks of powder. Hundreds of cannonballs were stacked in square wooden frames. With all this weaponry Osceola and Big Feet had been sure they would defeat the blue-jackets here and earn their war names.

Crowded around the magazine were the palmetto-thatched shelters of more than two hundred refugees—women and children from the black settlements along the Apalachicola. Their men stood on the ramparts.

Osceola had been on his way to those ramparts when someone grabbed his arm and hauled him into a niche between two water barrels. It was the first time he had ever seen his uncle's old friend, Wococoi Clark, sober. Wococoi was British. He had been trading with the Maskokee for thirty years, and he had no love for the Americans. He spoke an unpredictable melange of London gutter slang and Maskokee, but Osceola had always understood him well enough.

"Come with me!" When Wococoi tried to haul Osceola toward the low door in the rear wall, he dug in his heels.

"Listen to me, you feckless muttonhead." Wococoi ran a distracted hand through a tangle of cinnamon-colored hair that looked as if it had been struck by lightning. "The Yanks and the Creeks are thicker than fleas and twice as bloodthirsty. Old Mad Jackson has given orders to blow up this nest of rebellion."

"I'm staying with my friend."

"Bring your friend."

"I can't leave." Big Feet crossed his arms and planted his

feet firmly, as though to resist any attempts to drag him away. "When we kill all the blue-jackets I have to look for my mother. The slavers have probably taken her to Georgia."

Wococoi stooped to look directly into Osceola's face. "These niggers are mad as David's sow if they think this tinderbox will stop Jackson. Remember the Horseshoe, lad?"

"Yes."

"You all thought the wall there would save your red arses, didn't you?"

"Yes."

"Did it?"

"No."

"Then come with me."

"No." Osceola turned to leave when Wococoi struck him across the head with the butt of his musket. Osceola awoke slung over Wococoi's broad shoulder with his forehead knocking against the old trader's back. Each bump sent another bolt of pain to skewer his eyeballs.

He moaned, and Wococoi dumped him unceremoniously on the thin crescent beach of a hammock, a raised hump of dry land just big enough to support one cabbage palm and two stunted oaks. Wococoi's feet and legs were black and misshapen with the muck clinging to them.

"Getting closer." Wococoi stared across the grassy bog toward the back wall of the fort. He listened to the muffled *whump* of the cannons. "The curs are finding the range."

Osceola was gingerly getting to his feet when the first explosion knocked him down again. The ground trembled, and the bushy fronds of the cabbage palm shivered. Osceola rolled onto his back and stared in horror at the fort.

"The bloody bastards," breathed Wococoi.

The Americans on the ships had heated the cannonballs until they glowed, then deliberately lobbed them into the magazine. Osceola watched the ball of flame ignite the palisades, then mushroom upward. He saw the bodies soar up and outward, dark against the fire. The roar of exploding powder temporarily deafened him. When the screams reached him they were muted and unreal.

The first piece of charred flesh landed on his bare leg, and Osceola brushed it away as though it were a live ember. He had the horrifying thought it was part of Big Feet. Still half-reclined on his back, he scrambled, crablike, away from the inferno. He shuddered and whimpered far back in his throat.

He was still whimpering when someone bumped into him. Osceola returned abruptly to the crowded tiers of seating in the Snake clan's shed. The sweat felt chill on his body. Tears left warm tracks on his cheeks. He could still see Big Feet's face, and he realized he felt responsible, in some way, for his friend's death. He understood what it meant to be haunted by the unavenged spirit of a warrior killed in battle. He knew, suddenly, how his uncle felt.

CHAPTER 4

In the bow of the dugout, Heartless Snake's liver-colored mongrel stood with his forepaws on the prow and his tongue lolling. Heartless Snake, his head cradled in the crook of his right arm, lay asleep among the crudely tanned deer hides in the front of the canoe. His feet and scarred legs were bare. The calluses on his dirty soles looked like the pads on a wolf's paws.

He wore only a torn breechclout and a red bandanna tied loosely around his neck. His shade-dappled skin blended with the russet-colored deer hides. Bits of dried grass and leaves were caught in Heartless Snake's snarled scalplock. As usual he had neglected to shave his head. The black fuzz made it look smudged and dirty. His tattered alligator moccasins sat atop a huge gourd of bear oil. A lot of wear was required to reduce alligator hide to tatters.

The fish oil Heartless Snake had rubbed on his body to keep off mosquitoes was rancid. Osceola reflected on how much his friend needed a woman of his own to take care of him. No one would ever accuse Heartless Snake of being handsome or brilliant, but he was tenacious and loyal and strong. He was a clan brother, and he and Osceola had shared their boyhood in Talasee, in the north country.

The dugout was crammed with gourds of bear and fish oil. With silky otter pelts, egret plumes, and baskets of dried pumpkin and bear meat and *koontee* starch. A brace of gopher turtles was wedged on their backs between the baskets and gourds. Their stumpy legs waved in slow motion.

It was Heartless Snake's turn to pole the dugout, but Osceola let him sleep. He didn't want to talk to him and disturb the moment that had become, like so many in this sunburnished land, magical. The pole seemed an extension of Osceola's arms. He pushed, swinging slowly into it with his entire body. As the canoe slid forward he grasped the pole, hand over hand, until he reached the top. He crouched slightly, shoved, and walked his hands back down. He lifted the pole with a sudden upward pull, then planted the butt end firmly in the sandy river bottom and started over.

The three-hundred-pound cypress shell glided downstream as though weightless. Osceola kept it in the middle of the river to avoid the cottonmouth moccasins looped like thick black vines around overhanging branches. The cottonmouths' pupils were narrow, jade-green ellipses that glowed in the dim light.

Since dawn, Osceola and Heartless Snake had floated through this maze of streams and backwaters, cypress and bayheads, bogs and towering hardwood hammocks. The sun was high, but the dugout moved through a shadowy-green twilight. Over the wet, treeless prairies, sand ridges, and pine barrens to the east, the sky at midday glowed like hot brass. Here, the dense roof of leaves trapped shade and cool air.

Among the pale green cypress needles anhingas dreamily fanned their outstretched wings. A spindle-legged limpkin minced across the shifting surface of a raft of duckweed. Thousands of pink and yellow and white orchids filled the tree branches.

The line where the jungle met its reflection in the dark water was almost invisible. The tree trunks seemed to grow downward, leaving the dugout and its reflected mate not floating on water, but soaring on air, in the mirrored green canopy. When Osceola looked down he had the dizzying sensation of seeing the earth from a great height. A silent green world of trees and birds and animals existed below him. His passage rippled it but couldn't touch it.

As he passed the dark rim of a den in the river bank, he laid the pole along the gunwale. He cupped his hands around his mouth and gave the deep, hollow call of the bull alligator. Heartless Snake sat up with a grunt.

"Your turn." Osceola leveled the pole at him. The butt end stuck nine feet back over his shoulder and dripped mud and water. A line of droplets dimpled the surface behind the canoe. From the riverbanks several alligators responded to Osceola's call.

By midafternoon a dense stand of mangroves crowded out the other trees. Scattered among them were hardwood hammocks that sheltered small clusters of cabins, gardens, and a few fruit trees. Slender cypress dugouts crowded the river here. In each one, the man of the family stood in the back and poled. His wife sat bolt upright in the bow, and the children were strung between them. The only way to travel from one hammock to another was by water, and families visited constantly.

As Osceola and Heartless Snake neared the coast, amber-colored water flowed from the river in a fan-shaped stain that faded to sepia in the crystalline waters of the gulf. The river's frayed ends became entangled with thousands of deep green mangrove islands set in dazzling azure. A flock of egrets rose and expanded in slow motion, like a flower opening. Dolphins breached and dove lazily.

Heartless Snake's dog leaped out before the dugout beached and took up his post as guard. He would still be sitting there, snapping at mosquitoes, when Osceola and Heartless Snake returned.

Osceola and Heartless Snake folded their shawls diagonally, then into long strips. They wound them around their heads and tucked in the ends. They stowed their flints and small tobacco pouches in the folds of their turbans. They pulled on their moccasins, straightened their breechclouts, and slung their powder horns and bullet pouches across their chests. Osceola draped his best scarf over one shoulder. He carried his musket in one hand and fanned himself with a turkey wing as he walked.

Watermelon Town was a bustling place that thrived on trade and intrigue. It attracted refugee blacks, mestizo fisherfolk, Cuban traders, Mexican freebooters, and Indians of various tribes. Wreckers and smugglers and former men of marque anchored here. Masts of pirate schooners and blackbirders often blended with the live oaks and cabbage palms in the quiet bays.

Osceola and Heartless Snake made their way among the garden plots of the Spanish-Indian fisherfolk. They dodged the strings of curing mullet, drum, pompano, and grouper. They ducked under the seines strung between poles to dry. Heaps of discarded nets gave off a redolence of tar and mildew.

Muffled laughter and talk sifted through the thick, palm-thatched roofs of the open huts called *chikee*. The roofs swooped so low they showed only the ankles and feet of the people on the sleeping platforms. In the arbors and cooking *chikee*, hammocks dangled in narrow crescents from the eaves.

Osceola stepped to the side of the path to allow a huge, glowering man to pass. He was dressed in a breechclout. The wooden disks inserted into holes in his earlobes and upper lip warned Osceola and Heartless Snake that he was a Calusa, a descendant of the earliest inhabitants of the peninsula.

The Calusa had been almost wiped out by white men's diseases and their own fierce, intertribal warfare. Legends said they didn't take scalps. They took heads. This one looked capable of doing it with very little provocation.

Osceola turned to watch as the man stalked away. He thought about what a terrible fate it was to be the last, to walk the earth alone, after his nation's fire had burned out. To live among *tsilokogalgee*, people of a different speech.

Osceola stopped at a cluster of *chikee* that were in good repair and ringed a freshly swept yard. Garlands of dried manatee and fish hung from the smoke-blackened rafters of the cooking hut. A large kettle simmered on the star-shaped fire. A snake was painted in charcoal and bear fat on a corner post. The man who sat near the fire was the husband of a woman of the Snake clan. Osceola didn't know the man, but he knew he and Heartless Snake would be welcome here.

He and Heartless Snake squatted near the fire. Heartless Snake regarded the kettle with interest while Osceola offered their host some tobacco. "We are come," he said.

"You are," the man replied.

After the three had eaten their fill of fish stew and hominy, their host stared at the ground while he talked around his pipe. He was generous with his wife's food but miserly with words. He set each one out slowly, as though reluctant to part with them.

"New trader," he grunted.

"What happened to the old one?"

"Sun gave him fever. He cut his throat with an oyster shell. First cut his babies' throats. Messy."

"Does the new trader have a heavy thumb?" It was a turn of phrase Osceola remembered his great-grandfather using. The stranger understood immediately and grinned.

"No." He paused. "But crazy, too."

"Is he in the old trader's house?"

"Yes. Always in the hammock."

"How is life here, brother?" Osceola had an unquenchable thirst for information. His uncle had taught him to find out as much as he could about everything.

"One must walk far to find game now. I eat so much fish, I'm growing scales. My penis is shrinking to the size of a fish's." He puffed out his cheeks, bulged his eyes, pursed his lips into a circle, and opened and closed his mouth rapidly a few times. His transformation into a grouper was as brief as it was astonishing.

They left him brooding about the ill effects of his diet and walked toward the trader's ramshackle warehouse. It stood on the beach, near a hunchbacked wharf that looked as if it would surely succumb to the next high tide. The glittering white sand heated the soles of Osceola's feet through his moccasins.

Several small lighters, precariously overloaded, carried cargo from the schooner anchored beyond the bar. Sunlight flashed from the fretted gold of the gulf's chop. It glinted on the ship's coppered bottom and the chipped gilt paint that spelled "Flossie." A large crowd had gathered to watch sailors stack crates and barrels on the beach. They were preparing for an auction, which meant the schooner bobbing about so tranquilly was a privateer that had taken a prize.

A coffle of contraband slaves was being hustled out of sight. Now that the Americans were in charge of Florida, the smugglers would have to be more discreet. The trade certainly wouldn't stop, though. The slavers already had found the prominent American citizens of Pensacola to be a lucrative market. Even the fishermen returning from Cuba brought a dark human cargo back in their empty holds.

The store was a fifteen-foot-square hut thatched top and sides with cabbage palm fronds. It sat atop an ancient mound of oyster shells. From the dizzy height of thirty feet above sea level it boasted a commanding view of the gulf. A room of weathered driftwood clung to its side like one of the barnacles on the walls. The former trader and his family had slept there. Osceola wondered if he had murdered his children inside it.

A thatched bower, two of whose corner posts supported a frayed net hammock, stood forty paces from the store. Besides the hammock, the bower sheltered a few stools and two huge cypress stumps that served as tables. Flies buzzed around the dried oyster juice on them. The floor was of the same crushed shells that made up the mound.

The hammock sagged almost to the ground with the weight of the new trader. Its high sides hid his face. Osceola saw tufts of cinnamon-and-pepper-colored hair poking through the netting like deer hair stuffing coming out of a kickball's seams.

"Greetings, friend," he said.

The hammock rocked and bounced on its taut lines. The trader's arms and legs flailed above it as he fought to pull himself out of the deep trench of its middle. "Bloody contrivance. No wonder people of southern climes are so backward. No one ever built a civilization from a hammock!" One hairy hand clutched the side and pulled it down so the occupant could look over it.

"Greetings, old friend," Osceola amended.

Wococoi Clark stared at him.

"I'm Billy Powell, the grand-nephew of Peter McQueen." Osceola had not used the name of his long-gone stepfather or his uncle's English name in years. The words sounded strange in his ears. "This is my clan brother."

The name McQueen was magic. Wococoi's red-rimmed eyes widened. A grin parted his felted beard.

"Billy Powell, old sod!" Wococoi stared, gape-mouthed, at the slender young man whose smile had a shy, tender quality about it.

Osceola's narrow, aristocratic nose ended in slightly flaring, backswept nostrils that added an untamed dimension to his grace and charm. Dark, arched brows framed luminous brown eyes. He had a full, sensuous mouth. Silky black hair fell in loose curls from under his red turban. His bronzed body was lean and muscular. The awkward child had turned into an elegant warrior.

"God's blood, don't you cut a dash, though!" In his excitement, Wococoi almost fell out of the hammock. "I'm electrified. Simply electrified! It's been, what, five, six years since I carried your skinny red arse from that hell on the Apalachicola?"

Wococoi stood shakily and selected a bottle from the nearby shelf. He offered it to Osceola and Heartless Snake, who had hunkered and were steadying themselves with their muskets. Osceola made a small pass with his hand, declining the offer.

"This is mother's milk," Wococoi assured them. "I hide it in a common bottle among the gut rot."

Wococoi uncorked the bottle and took a long pull on it. He sat sideways in the hammock with his bare feet dangling. Filthy cotton drawers were rolled up just over the hairy bulge of his calf. "How is my dear old chum, your uncle?"

"He's well in body," Osceola said, which was the truth as far as it went.

"How's your sweet-natured brim of a grandmother? Is she still as skinny as a plucked heron?"

"She has a suitor. He says she looks like spicy jerked beef. He says she tastes like it, too."

Wococoi laughed so hard he almost fell out of the hammock. "It's devastated I am to hear it. I was meaning to propose to the jilt meself."

The years hadn't improved Wococoi's Maskokee. His grammar and pronunciation were execrable, and he still tossed in unintelligible words. But his hands and eyes were eloquent, and he knew the proper courtesies. He didn't use Osceola's childhood name, and with thick fingers he offered them tobacco.

As Wococoi leaned forward to strike a light with his flint, Osceola smelled the gin. The odor seemed to have permeated Wococoi's skin. He smelled like Watermelon Town's middens of overripe fruit pulp and rinds.

"The years have mistreated you, friend," Osceola said.

"Aye, that they have. I was in Pensacola when Old Mad Jackson and his lemon of a wife took possession from the Spaniards. How the old Spanish baggage wept when their colors came down and the stars and bars went up. But that was only the beginning of the trouble.

"A Boston schooner dumped its load of spoiled codfish in the shoal waters. Caused a terrible outbreak of yellow jack. The fever took my wife, Queen Ann. It took my precious squabs. Turned yellow as squash blossoms, they did. Vomited blood, rolled their beady little eyes, and transferred their souls to the Reaper." Wococoi snuffled and consoled himself with another swig.

"My heart grieves with you." Osceola remembered the way Wococoi's eyes used to glow when he spoke of his beautiful Maskokee wife and his unruly swarm of children.

"Kind of you, me colt, me chum, me bob cull. It was a horror," Wococoi went on. "Bodies stacked like cordwood in the streets. Nor a wagon to be had. All were hauling stiffs to the burning place. The stench of it!

"Jackson's regime brought hordes to Pensacola, mostly land sharks, swindlers, the whole canting crew. The Reaper called in accounts on most of them, and a small loss it was. But me wife, me babes . . ." He fell silent for several heartbeats.

"Even before the yellow jack, Pensacola was a bleak place," he finally resumed. "Old Mad Jackson's wench has no sense of humor. I can forgive anything but a lack of humor. She turned Pensacola into a cesspit of religion.

"With my muff and my squabs belly up, the grog houses boarded tight as a virgin's cunt, and the streets paved with dead, I absquatulated. Here you find me, a fence for that rabble." He waved the bottle at the sailors on the beach.

"They're men not tethered by too exacting a sense of moral obligation," Wococoi confided. "But I hold a candle to the devil and subsist."

Heartless Snake started to ask what all that meant, but Osceola gave the smallest of motions with his hand to tell him he would try to explain later. Wococoi would only compound the confusion.

"She's done it again!" Wococoi suddenly shouted. He clutched fistfuls of his snarled hair and yanked it in frustration. "That mawk, that muff, that coming wench will be the ruin of me!" All three men stared at the trio of plump young women walking by.

They held their right forearms demurely across their torsos to shield the area where their blouses stopped a few inches short of their skirts. The drawstrings of their long calico skirts were pulled so tightly, rolls of brown flesh hung over their waistbands. They each sported about twenty-five pounds of shiny new beads and tinkling necklaces of silver Cuban coins. They looked harmless enough, but Wococoi's eyes widened at the sight of them.

"What's the matter?" asked Osceola.

"It's me own fault, lad. I wearied of mounting a corporal and four, you know." He winked and made a stroking motion at his groin. "I craved someone to dance the blanket hornpipe with me." He vaulted from the hammock. While it bounced on its lines he waved the whiskey bottle and cavorted unsteadily, rotating his hips lasciviously.

"Buxom, she was." He nodded toward the woman in the middle. "Demure as an old whore at a christening. But she's like the persimmon—sweet, with a bitter aftertaste. She gives my goods away to every relative who comes to the door. Her relatives are like the mosquitoes at eventide. They're sucking me dry. I beg her to stop. She smiles like an angel. She swears she will stop, but she does not."

"You know our customs."

"Aye. You redbellies are the most generous folk on earth. But so *many* relatives." He shook his head wearily and took another drink.

"Speaking of presents, lads, you've come at a propitious time. Yon 'free trader' had captured a fat prize. Besides the usual goods, I'll have loaf sugar, pepper, cheeses, nankeens, silk for a fine new warrior's turban. But we must hurry, before my rib pitches it all to the whirlwind." He turned abruptly and set a weaving course for the beach. Osceola hurried to walk beside him.

"*Tasikaya.*" Wococoi looked at him fondly. Tears brimmed in his red-veined eyes. "You're a warrior now. You were like a nephew to me."

"Old friend, what of Jackson? Now that he claims he's *Miko Nope*, Great Chief of the peninsula, what will he do?"

"He will devour us all, lad," Wococoi said. "He will not leave even the hooves and stomach."

CHAPTER 5

"That's the nephew of Talasee *Tastanagee.*" With her chins, the woman pointed to the approaching dugout. The wattles on her upper arms quivered as she pounded a wet skirt on the limestone outcropping.

"The one with the frog's legs?" When Morning Dew glanced up from her own laundry, she saw Heartless Snake standing in the stern of the canoe.

"The other one," said a tall black woman.

"Heartless Honey Tongue," called someone from among the four or five dozen women standing in the river shallows.

The women were red and black, young and old. They came from Chukachattee and from the settlements around it. They were scrubbing their families' clothes for the annual festival of renewal. In the two years since Osceola had received his war title here he was mentioned frequently when the women gossiped over their corn mortars. Heartless Honey Tongue was just one of their names for him.

Osceola was reclining next to Heartless Snake's hound in the bow of the dugout. One of his long legs trailed in a most undignified way over the gunwale. Morning Dew's gaze met his for an instant before she looked down. The gossip had been true. The nephew of Talasee *Tastanagee* had the most compelling eyes she had ever seen.

Morning Dew's face grew hot. Her heartbeat quickened. She felt a tingling warmth in her groin. To hide her confusion, she twisted and wrung her uncle's dripping, voluminous red shirt as though she were trying to wrestle it into submission. She shook it to snap the wrinkles from it, dipped it in the river again, and whirled it to gather momentum. Then she slapped it across a half-submerged log.

All along the bend in the narrow river the other women were doing the same. As they worked they kept up more than the usual amount of laughter and banter. The cool water was working its magic, dispelling the summer's heat and conjuring up the child in everyone. Some of the women deliberately spun their wash hard enough to splatter Heartless Snake and Osceola. Others waded out farther to smack the surface of the water with the palms of their hands and drive a hard spray into the boat.

The wet, heavy fabric cracked against wood and stone like a cheerful gun battle. Rainbows flickered in the silver drops that arced around the women's heads as they spun the clothes. Their own wet skirts and ruffled blouses clung to their bodies.

"Heartless Snake has rubbed his member with the sap of *pukpukee holatee tihus thlakita,* flower blue penis makes big." One of the women pointed her wooden laundry paddle at Heartless Snake's midsection. The center of his breechclout pointed staunchly, conspicuously, outward.

Heartless Snake was mortified by the chorus of laughter and by his own roguish cock. He turned the dugout abruptly away from the women and toward the opposite shore. Dozens of beached boats, rocked by the swell from the women's activity, gently nudged each other there. The slope of the bank had been scoured of weeds and the black mud polished by the countless hulls dragged across it over the years.

Heartless Snake gave the pole a shove, sending the boat aground harder than he intended. As its prow wedged firmly in the mud, the dugout lurched and almost unbalanced him. To cover his clumsiness, he stowed the pole, grabbed the gunwale, and leaped jauntily out to push the canoe farther ashore. He was so distracted he forgot the stern was fifteen feet from the landing, and he sank to his waist in the water. The ends of his breechclout floated out fore and aft.

He was also so distracted he didn't notice Osceola wasn't laughing at him. Osceola, in fact, had pulled his leg into the boat and sat up straight. When they landed he climbed out with more than the usual care. He was embarrassed by Heartless Snake's ineptitude and ashamed of feeling that way about his friend. But feelings were flying too thick and fast for Osceola to dodge.

He was elated. He was euphoric. He was flustered. He was self-conscious and awkward and terrified that the woman whose eyes had just pinioned him was spoken for. In his agitated state, just the possibility that she might already be married started him planning an elopement.

Osceola had been poleaxed by passion. Stunned and aflame, he hesitated on the bank while Heartless Snake, with his musket held horizontally behind his thick neck and one wrist hanging over the stock and the other over the barrel, waded ashore. Heartless Snake called his dog, who was snuffling after fiddler crabs, and stomped off in search of a dry breechclout. Osceola followed. He didn't dare look back at the sprite who had bewitched him.

Young women often invented reasons to visit Osceola's mother's compound when he was there. They were drawn not so much by his good looks as by his quiet smile and his self-effacing charm. His honeyed tongue. He always had found it easy to joke with them. He was fond of most of them. On occasion he had slipped away with whichever one struck his fancy at the time. He relished the aroma of them and the warm pliancy of their bodies pressed against him in the dark.

But they always expected him to send his mother or grandmother to ask for them in marriage afterward. When he didn't, their adoring looks turned angry or sad or bewildered. Finally he had stopped making assignations. Now he understood his own detachment. He had never experienced anything like love.

Osceola found his uncle and Mad Dog sitting in the shade of a huge, moss-draped live oak near their camp. Mad Dog was shaking hard kernels of corn in a flat basket, and both men were betting on whether more white or painted sides would land uppermost.

Mad Dog had become Fighting in a Line's fourth husband. From the perpetual glint in Mad Dog's eye, Osceola figured he must be the object of considerable passion himself. Someone who didn't know Fighting in a Line might have been surprised at that, but Osceola wasn't. He hunkered to watch the betting and wait for an opening.

"I just won your uncle's best shawl, his pipe, his ceremonial shirt. I'm trying to get him to wager his wife." Mad Dog's method of cheering up his brother-in-law was to give him something more immediate to brood about than the battle of the Econfina. It seemed to be working. Mad New Town looked almost jovial.

"Uncle."

"Yes, nephew." Mad New Town continued staring at the corn in the basket. He suspected Mad Dog of cheating.

"I've found her."

"Who?"

"Her."

"What clan?" Mad Dog recognized the look in Osceola's eyes. He'd had that look himself not so long ago.

"I don't know."

"Don't fall into your own *sofkee* pot, nephew," Mad New Town said. "If she's a Snake, marriage is out of the question." Mad New Town felt a sudden sense of loss. The one he loved most would marry and move to his wife's village. Osceola would become a visitor in his mother's compound. He would beget children to carry the fire of another clan.

"Will you help me find out who she is? I've never seen her before. She must be Mikasukee."

"Describe her."

"The most beautiful woman ever born."

Mad Dog chuckled. "That should make identification simple."

*   *   *

Even though it would undoubtedly be destroyed by the end of the day, Osceola had put on his best breechclout. He had oiled his bare, muscular chest and arms and long, slender legs. His bangs fell in a glossy black fringe around his face. His shaved skull tingled. Mad Dog had given him water in which the root of black nightshade had been boiled.

"Rub it onto your head," Mad Dog had said. "Then walk through a crowd. You'll attract all the women, but you must choose only one or the medicine will turn back on you."

"I want only one, Grandfather."

I want only one. Osceola could see her among the women on the other side of the target pole. Mad Dog had found out she was of his own clan, the Panthers. Her name was Morning Dew. She was a Mikasukee, and she lived in Abihka's village. She was not promised, and her older sisters were already married.

Osceola had to concentrate to keep from grinning. He and his twelve teammates dug their toes into the loose sand. They crouched slightly, shifted their grips on their rackets, and stared at the deerskin ball in Mad Dog's hand.

The game between the unmarried men and women was always the best entertainment of the Green Corn ceremony. Hundreds of spectators rimmed the field. Children sat in rows on the broad branches of the surrounding oaks.

Osceola ignored the shouting and the frantic betting from the sidelines. He stared at the most beautiful woman ever born. She stared back.

She was small, but Mad Dog said she had seen sixteen seasons. She had tied her thick black hair into a hank that reached past her waist. The red ribbon holding it fluttered when she moved. A broad sash gathered in her old-fashioned doeskin dress. Her waist was tiny. Osceola imagined encircling it with his hands, and the thought sent warm shudders through him.

Unlike most of the young women, she had not plucked out her eyebrows. They arched like raven's wings over her straight nose and gave her a fierce, boyish look. As she flexed her knees into a slight crouch and waited for the toss, her eyes glittered.

Mad Dog leaned back and threw the ball up until it seemed

the sun would swallow it. The women shrieked, and both teams lunged forward. The women had declined the men's offer of two strong players to even the odds. Osceola could see why.

The maidens who stared at the ground and lowered their voices when a man walked by had turned into demons. They charged and feinted, blocked and wrestled and clawed for the ball. They were oblivious to everything but the bedraggled lump of leather and deer hair that appeared, then vanished under their feet.

The object of the game was to throw the ball against the pole. If it struck against the red line painted eight feet up, the player's team scored a point. If the ball hit the wooden mask grinning from the top of the pole, the team added five points. A hundred points won the game. The men used their ball-play rackets to catch and throw, and the women used their hands.

Once, the ball disappeared altogether. The game stopped while each team accused the other of cheating and the men began searching for it in the crowd. A player from the black settlement of Pumpkin Town pulled it from her blouse where it had nestled between her generous breasts. She whooped as she bounced it off the mask and scored five points.

Most of the women knew Osceola was the fastest and most skillful player, and as the afternoon wore on they began to crowd him. Heartless Snake stayed close, too. If asked, he would have said he was trying to block assassination attempts on his friend. But he wore a crumpled alligator grin every time he collided with a soft hip or chest or caught a glimpse of breast under the short hem of a blouse.

The sun was about to set when Osceola found himself face to face with his beloved. Her right cheek had a raw, abraded strip where she had slid in the dirt to recover the ball. Staring down into those radiant eyes, Osceola forgot he held in his racket the filthy, frayed shreds of deer hide and hair. When Morning Dew smiled up at him she caused an ache and a stir in his breechclout. Then she stamped on his instep.

Osceola dropped the ball. He felt the sting of her hair across his sweaty chest as she scooped it up and flung it. Osceola hopped on his uninjured foot and rubbed the other as he watched it. Trailing its raveling thong behind, it soared upward, slowed at the apex of its arc, then glanced off the mask.

The women, and those foolish enough to bet on them, trilled the victory cry. The last Osceola saw of his beloved was her back. The women lifted her onto their shoulders and carried her away.

"I'm in love," Heartless Snake confided as they walked through the taunts of the men who'd bet on them and lost.

Osceola drew in his breath sharply. Heartless Snake must be in love with the beautiful Mikasukee. Every man was in love with her. Every warrior was preparing to propose to her. Even now men were trying to maneuver her into meeting them somewhere alone. Osceola knew his fears were so unreasonable, he wondered if love was driving him mad.

Heartless Snake pulled something from his breechclout and held it out reverently. The remains of the deerskin ball were still warm from riding next to what he referred to as his turtle eggs.

"This has lain between her breasts," he sighed. "Between breasts as large, as soft, as doeskin pillows stuffed with down."

"Whose breasts?"

"My beloved's."

"The black woman from Pumpkin Town? The one big enough to hold *you* between her breasts?"

Heartless Snake just grinned and wandered off in search of her.

The long summer twilight turned to night, and still Osceola had not found Morning Dew. He stood at the edge of the square, empty now and waiting for tomorrow's ceremonies. The full moon had brushed its freshly sanded surface with pale silver that shimmered with power. Osceola stood at the corner of the ordinary warriors' shed and stared at the tranquil piece of ground.

Maybe it was no coincidence he had seen her now, at the annual time of renewal. This was a time for beginnings. It was a magic time. Maybe she was the Star Woman who, now and then, descended to earth in her Sky Canoe to play ball with the mortals. Whoever she was, Osceola knew his life had changed this day, as irrevocably as when he had received his war title.

Osceola walked slowly through the village toward the camps of the Mikasukee visitors. While the women worked at the few chores remaining to prepare for the festival, they spoke softly to each other. A mother sang her baby to sleep in its tiny canvas hammock. A horse whickered.

Osceola always thought of each town as having a life of its own, a pulse composed of the heartbeats of all who lived in it. Now the rhythmic beat of life steadied his own emotions. On the eve of the festival of renewal, the settlement seemed to catch its breath in anticipation, even as its pulse speeded up.

Osceola calmed down enough to feel sad. When he married the Mikasukee he would leave his uncle's town and go to live near his wife's family and clan. He would be a cordial stranger to his own sons. His wife's brothers would teach them, discipline them, and love them. He would have to wait for his four-year-old sister to grow up and bear sons before he would have a boy to train.

He ghosted slowly through Abihka's people's camp. The palmetto-thatched lean-tos, the star fires, and the horse pickets were scattered under the massive live oaks festooned with long silvery beards of moss. Masked by night, Osceola studied the faces around the cooking fires. Desire and anxiety played over him like hot sun and cold wind.

Morning Dew saw him immediately. She had been searching the night for signs of him. She murmured to her sisters that she had to relieve herself and was mortified by the possibility the nephew of Talasee *Tastanagee* might hear her say it. She gathered her long skirts, tugged down the hem of her blouse, and stepped into the darkness.

Osceola thought she moved like ripples through river grass. He made a wide circle around the fire and followed her. When she paused near the river he stopped several yards away. He had been rehearsing phrases in Hitchiti, the language of the Mikasukee.

"Someone lost his heart in the ball game this afternoon." Osceola's mouth felt as though it were lined with ashes. He had trouble catching his breath. "The face of his beloved is

radiant as the moon. The stars are reflected in her eyes. Her
hair is sunlight on a raven's wing. She must be the Star
Woman. She must have arrived in her Sky Canoe to play ball
here." Osceola had been practicing his speech. Now he wondered if what he said sounded as foolish to her as it did to
him.

"Someone is sorry she stepped so hard on the foot of the
warrior who has her heart." Morning Dew's voice was laughter and lark song and a panther's purr. Osceola felt as giddy
as when he was a child and his uncle would grab him under
the arms and swing him in wide, swooping circles.

"The ache in his foot is nothing compared to the one in his
heart when he's not with his beloved." Osceola moved closer.
While he was frantically trying to think of something else to
say, they both heard a loud rustling in the bushes. Morning
Dew vanished, leaving behind the scent of the orchids she
wore in her hair.

Heartless Snake blundered into the clearing. He had found
someone to share whiskey with him, and he had drunk a large
quantity of it.

"Someone told me they saw you come this way," he said,
and Osceola realized this tryst had never been secret to the
people of the Mikasukee encampment. It had just been discreetly ignored. He'd been foolish to think his own intrigue
would be unnoticed, when every other affair was known and
gossiped about.

Heartless Snake spoke very slowly. He swayed and braced
a hand against a tree trunk. "I need your help."

Osceola took a deep breath, as his uncle had taught him to
do when his temper threatened to rage out of control. His
friend had tried his patience often, but never to this extent.
"I'll help you tomorrow," he said.

"I need your help. I really need your help." Heartless Snake
was having difficulty mastering the intricacies of conversation.
"Why?"

"She's promised to another. We're going to run away."

Osceola sighed. Heartless Snake was indeed in trouble. Osceola waited while his friend retched loudly. Then he sat up-
wind of him on the riverbank.

All night the two of them talked about Heartless Snake's flight south to the limitless swamp called Pahay-okee, Grassy Water. If Heartless Snake and his woman could stay hidden there a year, they might be forgiven at the next Green Corn ceremony. If they were caught, they might die, or at least be disfigured.

CHAPTER 6

"I am come." Fighting in a Line's knees creaked as she slid down from her mare. The pony was only fifteen hands high, but Fighting in a Line still had a considerable drop to the ground.

While Peeping dismounted, Fighting in a Line disappeared into her winter cabin to change into her old clothes. She took so long Osceola was sure she had fallen asleep. When she finally returned to the cooking arbor she rummaged around in the food baskets. Behind her mother's back, Peeping smiled at Osceola to encourage him to be patient. She pushed the four big palm logs in toward each other and blew into the embers in the center.

"You men are worse than starveling hounds," Fighting in a Line grumbled. "The food baskets look like a swarm of grass-hoppers has camped here."

Patience is hard, Osceola thought. Sometimes his grand-mother required a great deal of patience. "Surely the Mika-sukee fed you before you left their town."

"Travel makes me hungry." Then Fighting in a Line knew she had teased her grandson as much as she dared.

Osceola's red-gold skin was marked with pale, spidery lines left by the teeth in Fighting in a Line's garfish jaw. The dis-ciplinary scratchings were from his childhood. The sharp teeth had drawn evil out, along with the tiny beads of blood strung on the parallel red lines. The scratchings were punishment for Cricket's temper.

When Cricket became Osceola he learned to control his fury. He usually looked distant and serene. His mouth often twitched into a half smile, as though he were here and somewhere else, too. His rages were no longer evident, but Fighting in a Line suspected that if provoked, they would be impressive. She decided not to risk it.

"Her family accepts you as a suitor," she said.

"How many others have asked to marry her?"

"None." Fighting in a Line found a thick orange slab of *koontee* bread in the bottom of her travel satchel. She sat on one of the logs radiating from the fire and munched on it as she talked.

"She's beautiful. Many men must have asked for her."

"Only a foolish Maskokee would ask for her," Fighting in a Line said. "The men of her own fire know her too well. She's strong-headed. She has a rattlesnake's tongue. Her younger sister thought she would grow old waiting for her to find a husband. She was happy as a heron in a puddle when I presented your mad request." Fighting in a Line squawked and flapped her elbows and stretched her neck in her conical collar of beads. She became a flock of herons feasting on fish in a drought pond.

Osceola was not amused. "Now what happens?"

"I told the mink's uncles they should give *you* a present to take her off their hands."

Osceola didn't reply. He had learned that ignoring his grandmother's teasing was the best way to discourage it.

"The woman's mother's brothers have agreed to let you send a gift of venison to her. If she accepts it, I shall have *istee seminole*, a wild runaway, for a granddaughter-in-law."

Fighting in a Line had had difficulty being polite to Mikasukee who weren't sure her grandson was good enough for their niece. She usually referred to Mikasukee as *seminole*, runaways, although to most the word meant people of a distant fire. It was the Maskokee word for those of the Creek federation who had gone to Florida generations earlier. Her main complaint against the Mikasukee was that they claimed to be better fighters than the Maskokee.

"You mustn't see her or talk to her until you kill a deer to present to her," she reminded Osceola. "They may be Mikasukee, but they honor the old ways."

Osceola wasted no time. That night he purified himself in the sweat lodge by the river and worked his hunting magic. He unrolled his doeskin medicine bundle and reverently laid out the small packets of herbs, roots, and dried cedar. He rested his fingertips lightly on his *sabia*, his three magic stones, and sensed the magic pulse up into his arms and spread through his body. He felt the stones tremble under his fingers.

He chanted over his most powerful hunting medicine, a waxy red granule from the horn of a great horned snake. The granule had been a gift from Abihka, and it was coveted by every warrior not fortunate enough to have one.

He awoke before dawn the next morning, happy that his dreams had been favorable. He dressed in his old cotton shirt and turban and breechclout. He tied a faded blue kerchief around his neck and knotted a piece of flint and a bit of punk into the ends of it. He put the strap of his medicine bundle over his head and settled it comfortably on his hip.

He rolled up a doe hide tanned with the head still on it. He left his blanket-wrapped fusil in the rafters and slung his bow and quiver across his shoulder. He would show his beloved's family that he too honored the old ways.

As he walked past the embers of his mother's cooking fire, huge leopard frogs that had passed the night in the warm ashes hopped into the palmettos. Dogs and pigs still slept in indiscriminate heaps under the platforms of the storage *chikees*. Roosters crowed and hens stretched and preened on the shaggy ridgepoles. Cattle lowed from the pens in the pasture.

Osceola's bobtailed, fiddle-hipped mare nipped him playfully as he saddled her. He rode out, softly chanting an ancient hunting song. As the sun rose above the horizon, he stopped at the river to bathe and greet the Breath Maker. His sense of urgency faded as he settled into a comfortable solitude. He always enjoyed time alone with his thoughts and with the faint humming of power from his medicine bundle.

For three days he traveled slowly southward until he reached the upper fringes of Pahay-okee, Grassy Water, the swamp white men were beginning to call The Everglades.

Pahay-okee was a shallow, slow-moving river of freshwater sixty miles wide and a hundred miles long. It was treeless except for the pines and cabbage palms and oaks on the high ground of the scattered hammocks.

The Maskokee had named it for the sawgrass that grew to the horizon. Now, in August, the sawgrass flowers tinted the watery expanse pink. Black rafts of grinning alligators floated among the glittering, silica-edged grasses. The water was bright indigo, a reflection of the sky overhead. Millions of birds darkened the sky and covered the trees on the hammocks. Herds of deer waded from island to island to graze.

Pahay-okee was the country of solitary hunters, of outlaws and of exiles. It was wild even by Osceola's standards; but those who returned from there said the hunting was beyond describing. This was the peak of the mating season, and the deer were on the move. Their traces were everywhere.

As he rode, Osceola passed hundreds of rut signs until he found one particular buck's scrapes. He left the mare on a long tether on a small hammock of pine trees, saw palmettos, wax myrtle, and poisonwood. Then he began trailing the buck, wading along the alligator trails from one hammock to another.

The going wasn't easy. The springy, porous muck was made of centuries' accumulation of decayed vegetation and a tangled mass of roots deeper than a man was tall. In places it was too soft to cross without sinking. Osceola had to cross over tussocks and logs, only to step into bog holes on the other side. The water was usually from knee to shoulder deep. The razor-toothed edges of the grass tore at him. Osceola wished he had a dugout for this hunt, but he slogged on.

He followed the line of battered trees on the hammocks until he came to a patch of torn-up earth among the pines and palmetto thickets. He hunkered at the edge of it and imagined the animal that had wreaked such havoc. The buck was ready for love. He was frantic for love. Osceola understood how he felt.

With his front hooves, the stag had pawed out a mule-sized basin in the sand, then urinated on it. He had hooked an antler over a branch and rubbed his forehead and eyes on it, leaving scent from the glands located there. He had rubbed the tattered velvet of his antlers against the pine saplings until he stripped the bark from them or broke them.

With his hooves he had churned up the ground around them. He'd torn off palmetto fronds and ripped up scrub oaks. He'd bitten off twigs. He'd left the area looking as though it had suffered a barrage of heavy artillery fire. Some of the trees he'd attacked were four to five inches around. This buck was big.

Osceola had yet to see him, but he could picture him clearly. He was a thick-necked eight-pointer that weighed almost as much as Osceola. He was enormous for this southern country. Wild-eyed. Sure of himself. Scarred from past battles. Rags of velvet fluttered like war banners from his towering rack. He was restless, on the move. He was patrolling his line of scrapes, looking for a mate.

Osceola squatted, scooped up a handful of the urine-soaked dirt, and sniffed it. The doe hadn't been here. Her scent wasn't mingled with the buck's. Osceola rose with the grace of the hunter who knew sudden movement would startle his prey. He faced the wind and tasted it. He unrolled the deerskin, put the head over his, and arranged the hide across his back. He nocked an arrow. Looking out through the deer's empty eye sockets, he settled down behind a deadfall to watch and wait.

As the sun set, its brassy light softened to a hazy sepia. Shadows crept outward from the trees and bushes. Alligators boomed their beguiling twilight songs. Raccoons began rattling through the palmettos in search of their favorite delicacies—hard, black palmetto berries and rattlesnake eggs. Both were in plentiful supply.

With his head held high, the buck stood shielded by the bushes. Osceola was motionless but for the steady rise and fall of his heart and lungs and the flow of blood through his veins. After several minutes the deer stepped into the clearing and snuffled the dirt of his scrape. With a single motion Osceola drew his bow, aimed, and fired. The shaft sank to the feathering between the buck's third and fourth ribs.

The deer snorted, leaped, and crashed away through the dense thicket. Osceola threw off his disguise and raced after

him. Barefoot, he chased him through the saw palmettos while
the serrated stalks slashed his arms and legs and chest. When
he finally knelt beside the fallen deer, Osceola was bloodier
than his prey.

"Forgive me, my brother," he murmured as he cut the animal's throat. The buck quivered and lay still. Osceola
chanted his hunting song as he cut a strip from the buck's
thigh and left it as a sacrifice.

Only then did he notice the swelling of his right foot and
the pain knifing up into his leg. The rattlesnake's two punc-
ture wounds were located in the skin stretched tightly across
the knobby bone just below his ankle. The area around them
had turned the color of a ripe grape.

Osceola unrolled his medicine pouch and opened the packet
of snake-button root. He chewed it as he gutted the warm
carcass. He swallowed some of the root and pressed the rest
of it onto the snakebite.

"O, spirit of the white fox, come," he chanted. "O, hater
of snakes, come. Snakes who have hurt this man, come.
Come, O white fox. Kill this snake."

Then he shouldered the hundred-and-thirty pound deer. He
walked quickly back to where his mare was tethered. Using
the full moon for light he rode all night and into the next day
without stopping. He did not want to present his beloved
with a deer that had spoiled. In spite of the nausea and dizziness that washed over him, he didn't worry about the snakebite. The rattler had been a small one, and Osceola's medicine
was potent. Besides, he was now fortified with the magic of
love.

Once, when exploring one of the hundreds of limestone caves
in the forests around Mad New Town's village, Osceola had
fallen through a hole and into a deep, underground cavity. It
was shaped like an inverted funnel, and it was filled with
water. Osceola had felt weightless and disoriented in the total
blackness, unable to tell which way was up and which was
down. He knew if he swam in the wrong direction, he would
reach the bottom of the pit instead of the surface.

He knew if he couldn't find the opening, he would die there,
trapped like a fly in one of Wococoi Clark's whiskey bottles.

But the release from the pull of gravity and from physical sensations had been magical. He had swung between panic and exhilaration. Finally, when his lungs had been about to burst, he'd stopped struggling. He'd gone limp and let his body rise to the surface.

He felt that same panic and exhilaration and disembodiment now as he held Morning Dew's soft warmth tight against him. His spirit flowed into the slender extension of himself that joined him to her. He felt the grip of her muscles, tightening and loosening around him as he moved inside her. He heard her moan far back in her throat and felt the caress of her fingertips on the base of his spine.

When the climax came, he rode its crest into pleasure beyond imagining. Then he lay, limp and spent and happy in the darkness. His pulse roared in his ears. He buried his face in the heavy, fragrant waves of her hair, soft as a mink's tail. He felt her breath brush his cheek.

"*Tahalyeh',*" he murmured. "My wife." The Hitchiti word sounded strange and lovely. "Our breaths are one. Our two lives will be a single life."

Osceola sang to himself as he cantered back to Mad New Town's village. Tradition dictated that he leave Morning Dew's cabin before dawn and avoid his in-laws for a month. He knew that when the month was over he and Morning Dew still would spend most of their days apart, he going about his affairs and she about hers. But the diamond-and-sable nights would be theirs. He smiled, caught up in the enchantment of love. He was happier than he had ever thought possible.

He found his family gathered around the morning kettle in the yard of Peeping's compound. Fighting in a Line was eager to see him. While Peeping served him *sofkee* and roasted turtle steaks, his grandmother unloaded her cargo of news.

"Your clan brother with his wretched, pig-chasing dog is gone." Heartless Snake's escapade was the choicest kind of gossip. Mad Dog and Mad New Town pretended to be absorbed in their first pipes of the morning, but they were listening attentively.

"He ran away with a black woman from Pumpkin Town." Fighting in a Line cackled with glee. "The woman's intended husband found moss stuffed under her blanket. They used watermelons to form her breasts. Her man is so angry he intends to kill them both.''

Fighting in a Line hadn't forgotten that Osceola had a wife now himself. But even her grandson's marriage wasn't as interesting as an elopement. She considered a wife a convenience for Osceola, rather like getting a new firelock or a horse.

"The pale-eyes have called a council." Mad New Town had news of his own. "Many of the warriors will go toward the sunrise, to the country of Emathla."

"Will you go, Uncle?"

"No. I'm too old for such foolishness."

Osceola glanced at Mad Dog and saw the flicker of pity in his eyes. Like Osceola, Mad Dog remembered the bold war leader Mad New Town once had been and still would be if he could shake off the shades of the Econfina dead. He had earned his war name by bravery reckless to the point of insanity. In the old days, when he announced a war party, men had flocked to follow him.

While the usual morning talk passed over Osceola's head, his elation faded. He remembered the flight from the north country, after the Red Sticks' defeat at the Horseshoe nine years ago. He remembered lying curled up, with eyes closed and hands clasped between his knees. His bare feet had been scarred and swollen from months of walking, of fleeing the hunting parties of blue-jackets and enemy Creeks.

His uncle had stood over him for a long time as he'd lain there, pretending sleep in the litter of the forest floor. Mad New Town had taken off the stained, blue wool U.S. Army jacket he'd worn since the battle of the Horseshoe. He had crouched and draped it over his nephew. As though it were covering him now, Osceola remembered its smell of pale-eyes sweat, of his uncle's essence, and of mildew.

Before he stood up, Mad New Town had run his palm tenderly over the furry stubble of the boy's skull. It was the only caress Osceola ever remembered receiving from his uncle. As Mad New Town walked away the leaves had rustled softly under his feet. *I love you,* the leaves had whispered.

CHAPTER 7

Alexander Arbuthnot and the prophet, Crazy Medicine, hung from a yardarm of Arbuthnot's trading schooner, *Chance*. Their bodies revolved slowly on the ropes, like live-oak catkins caught on lengths of spidersilk. Buzzards and crows fidgeted on the yard and on the corpses' shoulders and heads. They seemed unsure of how to eat this aerial carrion.

Osceola stood on the shore and called to Arbuthnot and Crazy Medicine, but they didn't answer. He tried to wade out to them, but the mud of the river bottom sucked his feet down and held them fast. He waved and shouted to scare the birds, but they didn't fly away. A crow clung to Arbuthnot's bushy white hair as he leaned down to peck at the old man's eyeballs.

Osceola stopped shouting when he realized he was in the territory of his enemies and was drawing attention to himself. He heard the beat of hooves and swiveled his torso to see Old Mad Jackson cantering his gaunt gray along the shoreline. The horse was the color of the beards of Spanish moss hanging from the live oaks. Old Mad Jackson wore a long tattered shroud of the same moss. It fluttered around him as he rode.

As Osceola tried desperately to free his feet from the mud and swim to safety, Jackson rode closer and closer. The flesh of his lank hands and face began to shrivel and melt away from the bones. Horrified, Osceola saw him transform into a skeleton. The ivory bones of his fingers gripped the reins. His hollow eye sockets glowed with a spectral light. He opened his mouth, but only a distant roaring, like a waterfall, issued from the gaping black hole.

Osceola grunted and sat up on his blankets. He gasped and panted and waited for his heart to stop thumping. Morning Dew had propped herself up on one elbow, with her cheek resting in the palm of her hand. She reached out her other hand and stroked his arm.

"I dared not wake you," she said.

As always, her touch soothed him. "You were right not to." He lay back among the sweaty, tousled blankets. "I have to ride my dreams into whatever country they take me."

"Old Mad Jackson again?"

"Yes." He rolled on his side so he could look at her, calm and sinuous and naked in the moonlight coming through the doorway.

They had this cabin to themselves, but still they lay so close their mouths almost touched, and they spoke in hushed tones. Voices carried in the stillness of the night. Besides, Osceola welcomed the warmth of her breath on his face and the tension of being so close without touching.

"I dreamed I saw Jackson kill my uncle's cousin, the Prophet, before the battle at the Econfina," he said. "I dreamed I saw him kill *istee skatsi*, the old Scottish trader."

"Did you know the Scotsman?"

"He sold me my first musket. He was an honorable man." He was a jolly man, a kind man, Osceola thought. He remembered Arbuthnot bending over the large book on the polished counter and explaining how he would mark Cricket's account in it. From then on, Cricket could consult the leaves to know how much he owed the trader. Having his own leaf in Arbuthnot's book wasn't as momentous as receiving his war name, but it was close. Only adults enjoyed the privilege of going into debt.

Alexander Arbuthnot's ledgers, with leather bindings nibbled by cockroaches and silverfish, had contained the lives, tallied in skins and honey, bear oil and beads, calico and knives, of hundreds of Arbuthnot's Indian customers. They recorded the daily ebb and flow of commerce, the lifeblood of that remote corner of the wilderness.

"He got weapons for us Red Sticks so we could fight the blue-jackets. He told our leaders when Jackson was planning to attack. But Jackson caught him. He caught the Prophet, too. He hung them like pumpkins ripening on the vine." Osceola nodded in the direction of the dead pine tree slowly taking form in the gray predawn light. Morning Dew had trained vines to grow out onto the bare, spiked branches so the pumpkins would be out of reach of the pigs.

"Do you think Old Mad Jackson will be at the big council in the east?" she asked.

"I don't know."

"The Americans want us to live in a small country so they can have the rest. They want to take our black people from us. Maybe your dream's a warning. Maybe it can tell you how to stop them."

"We can't resist the white men until we can agree among ourselves. Your people resent mine. The elders of the two Fires argue bitterly in council."

"Beloved," Morning Dew whispered. "A child is growing inside me. It will join your people with mine."

With the pale mantle of morning for light, Osceola traced his fingers along the blue filigree of veins on her taut brown breast. He stroked her stomach and the curve of her hip.

"Are you sure?"

"I'm sure."

The black bear was rummaging for crabs and turtle eggs along the narrow strip of shore. Now and then he stood on his hind legs and reached into the mangrove trees to claw down the cigar-shaped seedlings and eat them. He stared at the two dugouts as they glided by.

A young Mikasukee warrior named Koa'coochee, Wild Cat, poled the first one. He was the son of Emathla, the most powerful leader of the eastern Mikasukee. Wild Cat's friend, John Horse, and a thirteen-year-old white boy rode with him. The boy was John Joachim von Bulow. He was the son of Charles von Bulow, whose plantations were among the largest around Saint Augustine.

John Horse had been Wild Cat's friend from childhood. His pocked face hinted of Indian and Spanish blood, but his African ancestry predominated. He had bulging brown eyes and a broad slope of a nose that ended in swooping nostrils. Instead of bangs, dozens of thin black braids stuck out from under his turban.

Considering that each of his features was trying to dominate his lumpy face, John Horse should have been ugly, but he wasn't. He wore a stained white jacket with red lapels and a few tarnished gold buttons. It had belonged to John Horse's father, a soldier in the old Cuban colored militia.

Morning Dew, Osceola, and Alligator rode in the second canoe. Alligator was barely five feet tall. His childhood name had been Hatchling, and he looked like one. The sharp ridges of his brows and cheekbones and shaved skull resembled the hard facial plates of a baby alligator. He was of the Alligator clan.

Alligator was a Maskokee who had married a neighbor of Morning Dew's. The Alligator and the Snake clans were so closely allied that Osceola and Alligator considered themselves clan brothers. Lately they had been spending their evenings smoking together in the village square.

"I went fishing for bear once." Alligator grinned his toothy, raffish smile. Then he went on spitting pumpkin seeds at the striders skating on the surface of the water.

"Did you catch any?" Osceola asked.

"One almost caught me. It was the biggest bear I've ever seen. It was swimming like an otter. I started priming my piece, but before I could load, it was clambering into the dugout."

Alligator plucked a floating mangrove seedling from the water. The curved, slender pod was eight inches long. He held it up. "His claws were this big."

"What did you do?" asked Morning Dew.

"I decided I stunk like a horny panther anyway. It was time for a bath. I took my musket. I vacated the boat. The last I saw of it, it was gliding away with the bear still in it."

Osceola and Morning Dew laughed, then they went back to watching the scenery. The rivers of east Florida were at least as beautiful as those on the west coast. The two dugouts glided along a narrow waterway through the dense jungle. The sunlight spilling between the leaves seemed bright enough to ignite them.

Showers of white aster and spider lilies cascaded to the polished ebony surface of the water. Swarms of midges swam up the needles of sunlight. Sun glinted in the golden eyes of the giant orb weaver spiders. From deep in the forest an egret chuckled and flapped its wings with a noise like canvas snapping in the wind.

Morning Dew was reveling in the freedom of being away from the crowded camp. She was one of the few women who had gone with their men on the two-hundred-and-fifty-mile trek across the peninsula. Three hundred and fifty Mikasukee and Maskokee from the gulf coast were gathering in the east for a treaty council with the Americans.

Morning Dew rebelled against the name she and other women were given, *Tchuku lai'dshi*, Those Who Stay in the House. Before sneaking away that morning, she had dressed in one of Osceola's old hunting shirts. Even tucked up under her belt the shirt reached below her knees. She had hidden her long mane in a scarlet turban. With her knife she had cut short the hair around her face to form a boy's fringes and long side locks. Osceola tried not to look at her. Her fierce beauty caused his chest to tighten, his heart to pound, and his breechclout to stir. Osceola thought it fitting that Morning Dew belonged to the Panther clan. She moved with a cat's elegant grace.

"How much farther?" she called to the canoe ahead.

"Just a little," Wild Cat answered. Wild Cat and John Horse accepted Morning Dew as a boy. Osceola doubted they were fooled, though.

As he poled, Wild Cat whispered to John Horse. With his chin he pointed to a rattlesnake swimming with its head up and the tip of its tail erect. It was pursuing a shiny black knob of a nose that parted the water neatly as the rabbit attached to it swam toward shore.

John Horse reached out, caught the rattler behind the head, and hauled all six feet of it into the canoe. The boy grabbed the tail and hung on. While the snake thrashed John Horse held the head against the bottom of the canoe and hacked it off with his big knife. The boy coiled the body, but it was still writhing when Wild Cat shoved the dugout ashore on a small hammock of cabbage palms.

In the deep shade of the swamp, the island was a bright well of light. The azure dome of the sky was its cap. Framed by the surrounding trees, a pair of kites rose and dipped in a graceful quadrille. Their dance was mirrored in the blue spring near the hammock's center. The air was musty with the scent of cabbage palm blossoms.

Osceola began the tedious process of starting a fire while John von Bulow helped John Horse skin the snake. Morning Dew selected a fat young cabbage palm and studied it. If she cut too high, she would split the heart, too low and she would find only pithy wood. With eight strokes of her long Spanish blade she laid open the trunk. She reached in and pulled out the white heart. She sliced it into chunks and passed them around. Then she cut four more from other trees.

With his slender fish spear raised, Wild Cat stood poised like a heron over the spring. Wild Cat's mother was of the hereditary line of chiefs of the Alachua Maskokee, the earliest Creek settlers in Florida. His father, Emathla, was Mikasukee. Wild Cat represented the tangle of alliances among the Florida tribes.

Wild Cat was strikingly handsome. His eyes, under a thick fringe of lashes, were wide-set and intense. His main passions were love and war. He was slim and agile, and at seventeen he already had a large following of young men eager for war honors.

John Horse followed Wild Cat like a shadow and spoke about as much as one. Using straps around the trunks, he and Alligator ran up two of the cabbage palms. As they hacked at the limbs, the fan-shaped fronds fell with rustling crashes. To avoid the hair-fine splinters growing upward on the trunks, the two leaped off backward when they finished. Alligator landed in a somersault.

John von Bulow gathered dry, trough-shaped palm boots that burned easily, with little smoke. He stacked them next to the blackened circle of a fireplace. Then he used the heavy bone handle of his knife to knock oysters off the mangrove roots.

Others had camped here often. They had left the usual spoke-shaped fire of partially charred palm logs. They also had left a lean-to frame that Alligator and John Horse quickly rethatched for shade. They laid the excess fronds on the ground as seats and a table.

With her thumbnail Morning Dew separated the tightly

packed blades of palm shoots to make whisks. She and the others each ate roasted fish and oysters, frog legs and rattlesnake and palm hearts with one hand. With the other they maintained a rhythmic whir and slap of the whisks. The whisks divided the clouds of mosquitoes, but they didn't conquer them.

Morning Dew nodded toward Wild Cat and John Horse. "Where did you three first meet?" She was curious to know everything about her beloved Black Drink Singer. Osceola laughed.

"Those two almost cost me my first gun, before I ever fired it."

"You didn't have to help us," said Wild Cat. "We could have beaten them all."

"I met them six years ago, when I was a boy. Heartless Snake was with me," said Osceola. "We had spent all afternoon choosing our new guns in the back room of the Scotsman's store on Ochlockonee Bay." He smiled at the memory of walking from Alexander Arbuthnot's trading post, holding his shiny new firelock loosely in his right hand and swinging it jauntily.

"In the center of a mob stood your clan brother." Osceola waved his knife blade and rattlesnake meat at Wild Cat. "He was planning to fight a boy five years older, a hand taller than he."

"He called me a dog of a Mikasukee," said Wild Cat.

"Everyone thought he was mad." Osceola was unperturbed by Wild Cat's interruption. "He shoved the Red Stick so hard he almost fell down. They fought, of course. I handed my fusil to my grandmother when I stepped in to part them. It wouldn't do for a guest from the east, Emathla's son at that, to be treated roughly."

"The Maskokee hit him on the nose." Wild Cat grinned. "He flew into one of his famous rages."

"Heartless Snake jumped in. Then that one." Osceola nodded at John Horse. "Soon two tens of boys were pummeling each other."

"How did you almost lose your new fusil?"

"My grandmother wagered it. I could hear her above the noise of the fight."

"How did it end?"

"Neamathla stopped it." Osceola pictured his grand-mother, outraged when the contest was stopped and the bet-ting called off. She had risen to her full height, about that of a whooping crane on tiptoe. She had screamed insults at Nea-mathla, who towered over her, his massive shoulders strain-ing the scarlet British officer's coat. Peeping had laid a gentle hand on her mother's arm. It wasn't likely Fighting in a Line would attack Neamathla, but it wasn't impossible, either.

Wild Cat took out his pipe and offered it first to John von Bulow. John knew the strong tobacco would make him ill, but he puffed anyway. He would have kissed an alligator if Wild Cat had asked him to.

Next, Wild Cat passed the pipe to Morning Dew. He and John Horse and Alligator watched impassively as she sucked on it. When she exploded into a fit of coughing they laughed until they had to thump each other on the back.

While they were enjoying themselves, Morning Dew plucked a large land crab from the trunk of a palm. With legs waving the crab emerged from its borrowed shell, and Morn-ing Dew pressed it to Wild Cat's shoulder. It grabbed a hunk of skin in its claws and pinched hard.

Wild Cat tackled Morning Dew's bare legs and brought her down with a thud. Osceola, sure the roughhousing would harm Morning Dew's unborn child, launched himself at Wild Cat. John von Bulow leaped on Osceola's back. Morning Dew crawled from under the pileup. When she pulled off her di-sheveled turban her mass of black hair spilled down around her small face. Where the sunlight touched it, sparks seemed to be tangled in it. Osceola thought her loveliness would stop his heart.

"Who are you?" Wild Cat brushed himself off.

"I'm his woman."

"Do you always bring her with you?" Wild Cat pried open the last oyster. He tilted it in one hand, worked it loose with his knife, and let it slide into his mouth.

"I do as I please." Osceola knew Wild Cat was testing him. The boy was handsome and charming and generally good-natured, but he was also arrogant. Arrogance was only a fault when it threatened another's dignity, and Wild Cat pushed close to the limit at times. He retreated now, though. He was no fool. He only badgered those he thought he could intimidate.

"She's welcome, brother," he said. "If you consider her good enough to be with us, then she must be."

"She is." And she was. In the months since his union with Morning Dew, Osceola had learned why no one else had asked for her. Fighting in a Line was right. Most men would think her too willful, too bold, too singular. Osceola figured they were fools. He had found a precious stone that everyone else had passed over as a pebble.

"Who is he?" Morning Dew nodded toward John von Bulow.

"His father is a very rich pale-eyes," said Wild Cat. "He grows more cotton, more corn, more sugar, than all our towns combined. I call the boy Choontuh, Maggot, because he's small, he's white, he's blind to the knowledge a warrior must have. But he learns quickly for a pale-eyes."

John Joachim von Bulow, alias Maggot, listened intently, picking out the words he knew. He smiled at the compliment.

"We'll take him to his father's big house," Wild Cat went on. "His father will feed us. He'll give us presents."

Wild Cat handed the pipe back to Maggot, who was already looking sick from the effects of the tobacco. "Don't worry, little Maggot. When we drive the pale-eyes from our country, we'll let you stay."

CHAPTER 8

After an hour's travel the mangroves thinned. A forest of live oaks and cabbage palms, lofty magnolias and the umbrella-shaped canopies of the strangler fig indicated higher ground.

But the jungle close to the river had been leveled. All that was left of the massive oaks were ragged stumps, wide enough for two people to lie head to foot.

High mounds of moss-draped limbs, crushed bushes, and vines covered the churned earth. The ground was paved with shiny brown oak leaves and wood chips. The six-foot-high wheels of the log drags stood in abandoned pairs.

"What happened here?" asked Morning Dew.

"In winter, when the sap is down, the pale-eyes cut the oaks," Wild Cat said. "They use the arches, where the branches leave the trunks, to make ribs for their big canoes. They level the pine forests for poles to carry the great white wings of their ships."

"If a man walks a day, he'll still be in country scarred by their axes." John Horse scowled at the devastation. "The pale-eyes push at us from the north, from the east. They destroy our country. They steal our cattle. They steal our black people."

"When I was young, I visited the village of Bolek *miko* on the great Latchua savanna," said Wild Cat. "Thousands of head of cattle grazed on the green plain. We were rich then. Now we're poor as a picked carcass. We'll stay poor until we drive the pale-eyes back where they came from."

"Listen!" Morning Dew half stood and leaned toward the shore. The talk ceased. Everyone heard the usual noises—the strident *kark, kark, kark* of a rail, the rattle of a raccoon or a bear in the palmettos, an alligator's booming challenge.

Then, from the thick growth beyond the cleared area came the clank of metal and a woman's shout. Roseate spoonbills rose in a billowing pink cloud above the forest canopy. Osceola and Wild Cat poled their dugouts toward the bank.

A small black child burst from the underbrush and raced across the uneven ground. Her head had been shaved recently, leaving her torn cotton shift as the only clue to her sex. She couldn't have been more than nine years old.

When she saw the dugouts nosing in toward shore, she veered away. John Horse and Morning Dew jumped from the canoes and chased her. John Horse softly called words of reassurance in Ashanti, but they only spurred her on. He switched to Yoruba, then Fon, the language of the Dahomey.

She faltered when she heard *honton*, "friend," in Fon; but she didn't stop.

John Horse and Morning Dew cornered her against a downed oak damaged by white rot and left by the live-oakers. John Horse caught the child's foot as she scrambled up the fifteen-foot wall of vine-covered limbs. When she felt his hand close on her ankle, she grabbed a loose stick and began clubbing him in the face with it.

He was protecting his head when Morning Dew caught the club and pulled it from the girl's hand. Undaunted, the child attacked with her fingernails.

"She fights like a cornered mink." Morning Dew was panting with the exertion.

"She comes from a tribe of fighters." While John Horse tried to subdue her, Morning Dew pulled off her turban and shook out her hair. The girl suddenly stopped struggling and stared at her. For the first time, she looked frightened. Was this a shape changer turning from a boy into a beautiful woman? The child muttered a charm in her own tongue.

"What was the last word you said to her?" Morning Dew asked.

"*Honton*. Friend."

"*Honton*." Morning Dew placed her hand over her heart, then touched the child lightly on the wrist. "Friend," she said again in her low, musical voice. Reassured, the child threw her arms around Morning Dew and clung to her. She was crying, "*Non, Non,* Mother, Mother," when John Horse left them.

He retrieved his powder horn and shot pouch from the beached canoe. He loaded his rifle and raced after the others. The angry shouts and the clank of chains and shackles were easy to follow.

When the men came to the edge of the clearing, they fanned out and watched the coffle of blacks and the two white men driving them. The white men had a problem. John Horse signaled his friends to stay quiet and wait to see if they could solve it.

"Titus, you shitpot, stun 'er." Buckner peered from his long, matted hair and beard like a predator waiting in ambush.

"Stun 'er your own self. Ef you'd hired a couple extry men

like I tole you . . ." Titus was blond and handsome, with wide blue eyes innocent of intellect and integrity.

He knew he was at fault. The sight of the woman's swaying hips had started the usual furor raging in his pants. Lust was probably as much responsible for his dealing in slaves as greed was.

When they stopped to rest he had unshackled the woman to use her more comfortably. She had snatched the key and his knife quicker than the flick of a rattler's tongue. While Titus struggled to pull up his pantaloons and save his cock from being sliced like a blood sausage, the woman handed the key to her daughter. The child was gone before either man could gather his scant wits.

The girl's mother crouched. She was holding the men at bay to give her daughter time to get as far away as possible. Her hard muscles rippled under smooth, coffee-dark skin. She looked as though she would relish using the knife. The dozen men and women in the coffle watched intently, waiting for their own chance to escape. Suddenly they looked neither harmless nor defeated.

Titus and Buckner would have preferred to shoot the woman; but shooting her would have been like lighting their pipes with five hundred dollars' worth of Treasury notes. Since the African trade had been outlawed fourteen years before, demand for slaves far outstripped supply. The frayed line of Florida's coast, with its bays and inlets, islands and marshes, provided thousands of places for unloading illegal human cargo.

This woman had been schooled for two months at one of the best slave farms on the east coast. Seasoning, they called it in the trade. She supposedly had been broken to the whip and taught the rudiments of English and white ways. She was now worth twenty times what it had cost to transport her.

"Damnable, saucy bitch, I shall beat you yet a darker hue." Titus tried to hold her attention while Buckner edged closer.

With the speed and control of a skilled warrior, she lunged at Titus. She held the knife securely wedged in the palm of her hand and jabbed it at his face with quick, hard strokes. The knife's tip caught his eyeball.

He screamed and collapsed. With his knees drawn up and

his head tucked into his chest, he babbled in pain. Buckner started to load, but the snarling woman strode toward him as though he held a twig in his hand. He backed away while his shaking fingers tried to measure powder into the pan.

She looked quite capable of settling the score herself, which was why Wild Cat nocked an arrow and drove it through Buckner's back and into his left lung. He didn't want to lose an opportunity to kill an enemy, collect a scalp, and brag about it later.

With knife at the ready, the woman glared at Osceola, Alligator, Wild Cat, John Horse, and Maggot as they stepped from the bushes. Osceola held his bow up in salute. He waited while she decided if they were benefactors or just another set of foes.

"We're friends," John Horse said in halting Fon. "Your child is safe."

Wild Cat grabbed the greasy brown hair hanging from around Buckner's bald spot. Buckner moaned with a curious bubbling sound. His eyes pleaded for mercy. Wild Cat ignored him. Buckner was nothing more to him than a useless stalk attached to a trophy. Wild Cat wound the hair around one hand, yanked it taut, and sliced a large circle with his knife. He flayed off the long beard while he was at it, then he slit the man's throat. Maggot blanched and swayed, but he stood his ground.

Wild Cat held up the shabby scalp. "The top of this man's head looks like an overgrazed pasture." He was obviously disappointed in the trophy. He walked to the river to wash the bloody tokens before he tied them to his belt. "Brother," he called over his shoulder to John Horse. "Take the other one."

Titus had been curled up on the ground with his hand over his wounded eye. He tried to stand and stagger into the cover of the dense hammock growth, but John Horse caught him and threw him to the ground. He pulled Titus's hands behind his back and tied his wrists, leaving him facedown in the litter of the clearing. When Titus began screaming, John untied his bandanna and stuffed it into his mouth.

Unable to watch what was to come, Maggot searched the clearing until he found the big iron key the black child had dropped. He busied himself unlocking the manacles from the ankles and wrists of the thirteen blacks. He did it knowing his father would have bought this contraband himself.

"Take this trail until it forks." John Horse spoke to the blacks in Fon. "Then follow the narrower path until you come to a village of red people. Tell them John Horse sent you. They will shelter you."

John Horse had taken charge, and no one disputed his right to do it. Even Wild Cat stood back to see what his friend would do.

"Your child is safe," John Horse said again to the Dahomey woman. "She'll be here soon."

The other Africans left at a trot, and Maggot trailed after them. When the boy was out of sight around a curve, Osceola heard him retching. The Dahomey woman saw Morning Dew enter the clearing with the child by the hand, and she collapsed onto her knees. She held out her arms, and her daughter ran into their protective circle. The child was bruised and scratched from her headlong flight through the fallen live oaks, but Morning Dew had washed the blood off her.

Her scalp and her mother's had been shaved to discourage lice. The hair was growing back in tight curls all over their heads. Both still bore the scars of the middle passage from Africa, scars from the manacles and from the whip. The woman's eyes had a hunted look even her defiance couldn't hide.

"I'll skin the beast for you." John Horse squatted next to Titus and stared down at him. "His pale hide will make a mantle for you, Little Mother."

"Leave him for the carrion eaters." Osceola had always disliked torture. Maybe it was an aberration passed to him from his great-grandfather, James McQueen.

"This is a Moccasin Boy." John Horse didn't take his eyes from the white man. "The Moccasin Boys herd black people north to sell them." With the tip of his knife he slit Titus's nostril. "You erred this time, Moccasin Boy," he said. "You tried to rape a Little Mother, a Dahomey warrior woman."

Titus moaned. His cheek was pressed to the ground. Tears ran from one eye, and blood from the other soaked into the earth. John Horse poked the point of his skinning knife into the man's wrist, dimpling it. Titus realized he was about to be flayed. He tried to get away, inching along in the dirt. Osceola squatted next to John Horse so he could speak softly in his ear.

"Don't do this, brother." Osceola put a hand on John Horse's shoulder.

John Horse tried to shrug the hand off, but Osceola tightened his grip slightly. No one moved in the bright clearing while the two wills clashed.

"Do you know what his kind does?" John Horse said bitterly. "Do you know of the death ships that bring black people here?"

"I've heard the stories, brother." Osceola's voice was gentle and sad. It was irresistible. Power seemed to be flowing from his hand into John Horse's shoulder and arm, immobilizing them. "Kill him. Take his scalp," Osceola murmured. "Then we'll be on our way."

The two men stayed that way, frozen for a hundred or more heartbeats. Finally, as though shaking himself awake, John Horse shuddered. He grabbed Titus's hair and yanked his head back. With a single stroke he opened the man's throat.

While John Horse scalped the body, Osceola walked to the river and gave the high-pitched rubbing sound of a baby alligator in distress. For good measure he sounded the bull alligator's challenge. They all heard the splashes as the alligators slid off their basking places on the banks and into the water. Answering challenges reverberated through the trees.

"That will bring them here," Osceola said. "Help me throw the bodies into the water."

Joking about the vermin in the white men's clothes, Wild Cat and John Horse stripped the corpses. Alligator and Osceola carried Titus to the water, and Wild Cat and John Horse carried Buckner. They swung them several times by their hands and feet, then let them go. The bodies arced out over the water and fell.

Osceola could see the V-shaped ripples of the animals swimming toward them. With the Dahomey woman and her daughter between them, he and Morning Dew started back to the dugout. Alligator and Maggot followed. Wild Cat and John Horse stayed behind at the riverbank.

"We'll be along soon." Wild Cat grinned at them. "Aren't you going to watch?"

Osceola kept walking. He knew the alligators would get rid of the evidence. He didn't have to see them do it. They would clamp their powerful jaws down on the legs and arms. They would thrash until they crushed the limbs. Then they would twist and roll to tear them loose from the sockets. Pieces too large to swallow would be dragged back to the alligators' dens and allowed to rot until soft enough to be eaten.

The important thing was that the pale-eyes not know murder had been committed. They would use the act as an excuse for more harassment of the Maskokee and Mikasukee settlements.

CHAPTER 9

"The trouble with this particular tribe of red gentry," Governor William DuVal muttered from the corner of his mouth, "is that they do everything by committee."

"How is that, *monsieur*?" Achilles Murat pressed closer. The governor wasn't easy to hear over the drumming and whooping of the delegates, and Murat's English wasn't very good. He was not one of the commissioners appointed to negotiate this treaty. He had arrived with the members of Saint Augustine's elite, who watched the show from behind DuVal.

"Even in France you have perhaps heard of Indian chiefs?" asked DuVal.

"*Oui.*"

"Reason dictates that if you want to buy land from a tribe, you negotiate with the chief, correct?"

"*Oui.*" Murat was wary. For all his reputation as a soldier DuVal had a round, gnomish face and a penchant for telling entertaining lies.

"Seventy of those men are chiefs." DuVal nodded at the four hundred warriors marching across the clearing toward them. The measured rhythm of the bells strapped to their legs became more urgent as they began a shuffling stamp to the beat of the drum and their own chanting. Now and then they gave their shrill, warbling whoop. The two large white flags they carried stirred in the breeze.

"I thought only a few thousand Seminole inhabit Florida." Like everyone else, Murat had begun including all the Florida tribes under the name Seminole.

"They do. But every hamlet has a chief who considers himself king of all he surveys." With his arms still crossed in front of him, DuVal leaned back slightly so Murat could hear him; but he kept his eyes fixed straight ahead. The delegates were putting on quite a show, and he wanted to look attentive, if not impressed. The headmen still thought they were here at Moultrie Creek to negotiate. DuVal's job was to tell them they had no choices but those already made for them by the United States government.

"Each of those dusky potentates has a spokesman, called a sense-maker, and a cabinet of elders to advise him," DuVal went on. "Most of them also have former white men's slaves to act as advisers and interpreters." DuVal shook his head. "Their darkies are the thorn in the lion's paw. They're the reason for most of the Indian trouble in Florida."

"Our runaways aim for the Indian settlements." Reverend Moore was from Saint Augustine. He himself had lost two slaves to the Seminole, and he never passed up an opportunity to complain about it. "The savages must be moved away from our coastlines. Otherwise, their villages will be the resort of pirates and smugglers who excite disaffection and violate our laws."

"The two aborigines cavorting in front, in their birthday suits, are they chiefs, too?" Reverend Glenn reluctantly detached his attention from the procession advancing toward them. He and his festive party of parasoled ladies and gentlemen had arrived in a flotilla of small boats laden with picnic baskets. Reverend Glenn was having a wonderful time.

"I expect they're the current prophets," said DuVal. "Besides the sense-bearers and the darkie advisers, the lieutenants, the cabinets, and the war leaders, prophets throw in their two cents' worth."

"*Mon Dieu,* how do you resolve this?"

"The soldiers are here to impress them with our might, make them subservient to our wishes." DuVal raised his left index finger from where it lay against his right upper arm. The small gesture indicated the twenty-five men of the Fourth Artillery standing at attention in front of the platform. Their scarlet leggings, braid, and tall shakos and their polished brass buttons made them look more a part of the Seminole's ruffled and feathered delegation than the Americans'.

"We required the Seminole to select one chief to represent all of them." DuVal nodded at a hulking old man whose face looked as though it had been permanently forged into a ferocious glower. "They chose Neamathla. He's the only one these hardy individualists would allow to speak for them. He's a Mikasukee, the worst of the southern soreheads; but he can be bought."

"Bought?"

"You shall see." DuVal smiled almost sadly.

"You have sold us." Abihka spoke in a low voice, but he was so furious he could barely maintain his dignity. His jaw quivered with anger. "What was the price?"

Osceola, Wild Cat, John Horse, Alligator, and the other young warriors stood in a phalanx behind Abihka. A council had coalesced in the bubble of light around the older civil and war leaders' fire.

"Do you think I'm like a bat hanging in a dark cave?" Neamathla stared truculently around the circle of angry men. "Do you think I can't see what's going on around me? Ever since I was a small boy I've seen the white people steadily encroaching upon us, driving us from our homes, from our hunting grounds. I will tell you plainly, if I had the power, I would tonight cut the throat of every white man."

"But you have not the power, so you cut our throats instead." When Osceola stepped into the firelight, a rumble of disapproval rose around him for speaking loudly and ahead of the elders. He ignored it and returned Neamathla's stony glare.

"Old Snake Bone has become an old woman." Wild Cat moved to stand next to Osceola. He compounded his insult by using the name from Neamathla's childhood. "We young men still know how to fight. We won't leave our homes at the pale-eyes' command."

The headmen, those who had signed the treaty and those who had not, rose in a body. The bells on their hunting shirts jangled, and the plumes in their turbans bobbed accusingly. They stared at Osceola and Wild Cat until they stepped back into the crowd of ordinary warriors.

"They're young, they're headstrong, they're inexperienced." Wild Cat's father, Emathla, was mortified at his son's behavior. One never spoke out of turn in council.

Wild Cat stalked off in a rage. John Horse and a few men followed him. Osceola stayed. While fury rattled inside him, he listened stoically to the older men's deliberations.

A few hours before dawn's long, golden-pink rays poked through the leaves of the live oaks and lit the prairie beyond the hammock, the council finally ended. The weary leaders dispersed to take the bad news to the people who waited anxiously in the scattered encampments. Osceola moved like a shadow among the fires. Around each sat the hunched forms of those who couldn't sleep. Osceola envied those who could sleep, those who would have the peace of a few more hours before learning their fate.

An owl hooted. A soul must be passing. Maybe someone had wandered into the dream world and couldn't find his way back. Osceola shivered and rubbed the owl's foot he wore around his neck. Abihka had given it to him as protection from evil in public gatherings.

When he came to the lean-to at the edge of the sprawling

encampment, Osceola took off his turban and powder horn, his medicine pouch and his moccasins, and lay down. Morning Dew rolled over. She threw her arm across his chest and nuzzled the curve of his neck. He stroked the disarray of her hair.

"What did the *mikalgee*, the leaders, decide?" she asked.

"Neamathla convinced his followers to mark the leaves. He says we have to do as the white men command. He says we have to move to a reservation, a small country set aside for us by the white men."

"What will be the limits of this country?"

"An area nowhere closer than a day's march from the coasts." Osceola lay silent a long time and listened to the singing of the wolves as they returned from their night hunts.

"The pale-eyes intend to cut us off from trade so they can control us," he said finally. "We won't be able to buy guns or lead or powder from Wococoi, from the Spanish."

"What will you do?" Morning Dew asked softly.

It was a difficult question. While the Moultrie Creek talks had dragged on, Osceola had lain awake night after night thinking about the futility of opposing the soldiers. He had listened to Morning Dew's steady breathing and had stared up at the bright stars beyond the frayed edge of the lean-to. He had thought of the child growing in Morning Dew's womb and wondered how much more the pale-eyes would try to impose their will on his people.

Like Wild Cat, Osceola longed to take up his musket and declare war on the white men. He wanted to avenge the slain warriors whose yellowed bones littered the ground at the Horseshoe and the Econfina. Even more, he wanted to punish the white men for treating his people with disdain. And he longed to do it now. "Do not concentrate so hard on the ground under your feet," his grandmother had once said, "that you miss the trail ahead."

"A generation of warriors was lost at the battle of the Horseshoe," he said. "In six or eight more seasons a new crop of young men will be ready. They'll be the warriors who were small children at the Horseshoe, or who were born afterward. One day we'll be so many the white man's fist won't be able to contain us."

Osceola clenched his fingers tightly. "Then I shall make a fist of my own to smash them."

Osceola and Wild Cat, John Horse, Alligator, and Morning Dew stood in a line with the tips of their moccasins just above the curve of darker sand marking the advance of the tide. From under the lace cover of foam, waves made passes at the moccasins, then were drawn back into the ocean.

Behind the dunes lay the huge cotton plantation of Charles von Bulow, Maggot's father. Even here the occasional rumble of machinery penetrated the steady murmur of the surf. But the white and black men there were busy grinding cane into syrup. They were loading taut bales of cotton onto lighters for transport down the Halifax River to a waiting schooner. They had no time to stand at the ocean's edge and consider the unknown and the unknowable.

Except for the *toc* of axes and the grumble of von Bulow's engine house, the nearby bustle of the plantation was hardly noticeable. The schooner riding at anchor looked like a gull resting between flights.

"My father told me Neamathla won't have to move to the reservation." Wild Cat dug his toe into the damp sand and kicked a spray of it after the retreating wave.

"The pale-eyes allowed him to stay in Tallahassee, in Old Fields, where he lived before." John Horse stared out to sea, as though expecting justice to arrive from the horizon and avenge this betrayal. "His people will stay there, too."

" 'We're poor. We're needy.' " Wild Cat imitated Neamathla but added an uncharacteristic whine. " 'We rely on your justice, your humanity. We hope you will not send us south to a country where neither the hickory nut, the acorn, nor the persimmon grows. For I am old, I am poor, too poor to move from my village to the south.' "

"So that was his payment for signing," Osceola said.

"Maybe the white men worked magic to influence his mind." Morning Dew still found it difficult to believe Neamathla, a Mikasukee war leader, would give in to the pale-eyes.

"White men have learned to buy what can't be sold," Osceola said. "They buy land. They buy souls."

They all stood listening to the ocean talking to itself. Restless spirits seemed to move under the green skin of its waves. *To stand here is to stand at the edge of the spirit world.* This was the first time Osceola had seen the Atlantic Ocean.

"This water is powerful," he said aloud. "Maybe that's why the white men want to forbid us access to it."

"White men forbid me nothing," said Wild Cat. "I'm like my namesake, the Panther. I roam where I wish. I roam far."

The five of them turned to walk through the hard-packed sand. They crossed the dunes spiked with saw palmettos, Spanish bayonets, and withered grass. Sculptured by the prevailing winds, the stunted cedars and sea grapes leaned away from the ocean. They leaned, but they didn't fall.

CHAPTER 10

At Moultrie Creek in September of 1823, the United States' treaty commission bribed Neamathla into selling twenty-eight million acres for about three-quarters of a cent each. The government granted the Florida tribes four million acres in the swampy center of the peninsula. Surveyors moved in to lay out the reservation boundaries.

A year passed and a second began as the survey crews dragged their plummets and chains, their transits and tripods, through the cypress heads and sawgrass swamps. They meticulously measured pine barrens and sand hills. They hacked their way through the vine-laced jungles of the hardwood hammocks. Where the limestone bedrock was exposed, like the honeycombed bones of some massive, antediluvian beast, it shredded boot soles and then feet.

Cuts and insect bites became infected. The surveyors sweated, swore, and grew ill. They died or decamped and were replaced. Month by month the work progressed, inching across the shimmering landscape. Meanwhile the Seminole, buffeted by rumors and conflicting reports, waited.

Because they were expecting orders to move, many of them sold their cattle. They didn't lack for buyers. Unscrupulous men flocked to take advantage of their misfortune. They circulated alarming stories of forced emigration or imminent army attacks to induce the Seminole to sell their stock cheaply.

Many families didn't sow their fields. In the summer of 1824 torrential rains washed away the crops of those who had. By the spring of 1825 more and more white settlers were competing for the dwindling number of deer, bear, and turkey.

In 1825 the summer rains never came. The corn and bean and pumpkin plants withered, then turned brown. The *sofkee* kettles as well as the drying racks sat empty. To induce the Seminole to plant, the government cut back on the promised rations, but that didn't matter. Most people refused to collect food from the government anyway.

They feared that if they accepted the white men's gifts, they would be accused of accepting the hated treaty, too. In the children's thin faces their eyes seemed large and bright with the false glow of starvation. At a time when Osceola's woman and his tiny new daughter needed him most, Abihka asked him to go on a solitary mission.

Now he lay on his stomach to drink the only water available. What had once been a small pond was a muddy puddle scattered with the bones of fish. There would have been no moisture at all if the resident alligator hadn't dug through four feet of baked mud, allowing water to ooze up from the porous limestone underneath.

Osceola spread handfuls of dried grass across the pond's surface. As he waited for moisture to seep through, he breathed shallowly, avoiding the stench of decay that rose from the gray-green scum. The grass filtered out most of the insects in the water, but it still tasted like mud and old death.

By this time in a summer's afternoon Osceola should have felt cold, storm-scented gusts on his face. A towering, anvil-shaped thunderhead should have filled the western horizon and rumbled promises of rain. But the cloudless sky glittered like new brass, forged by the sun that flared over the parched land.

Usually Osceola was able to concentrate completely on whatever he was doing. Today he let thoughts of Morning Dew and the little one interfere with the task at hand. He wondered if Morning Dew's uncles were able to hunt enough game to share with them. He pictured Morning Dew hauling river water to her garden, where it disappeared into the baked earth with hardly a trace. He saw the flies and gnats rim the child's eyes as she rode in the sling on her mother's hip.

He had a terrible vision of Morning Dew's breasts shriveling, the milk in them drying up as everything else had. He saw his daughter, the only joyous addition to his life in the past year, crying from hunger. The vision constricted his chest until he could hardly breathe.

He had almost refused Abihka's request that he make this journey. As soon as Osceola had heard that Heartless Round Wolf was stealing cattle, he knew Abihka would ask him to track him. If Heartless Round Wolf wasn't stopped, the pale-eyes would make reprisals again. They would ride through the small, outlying Seminole settlements. They would put torches to the thatched roofs, stampede the few remaining cows and pigs, and steal any black people they could catch.

The drought had already heated tempers to the igniting point. The young warriors were eager for battle. More raids by white men could start a war the Seminole were still too weak to win. But Osceola knew hunting Heartless Round Wolf would mean leaving his family. He had avoided Abihka until he discussed the situation with Mad New Town.

"It's a hard decision, Uncle."

"A decision means you have choices, nephew." Mad New Town had spoken patiently, as though to the child, Cricket. "In matters like this a *tastanagee* has no choice, except whether to keep his position as a leader or lose it." His tone was ironic. He knew what it was to fall from a height. No one had ever openly accused him of dereliction at the Econfina, but for ten years Mad New Town had sensed something worse than people's contempt. He'd sensed their pity.

"Neamathla chose to sacrifice his people for his own advantage," he went on. "He chose disgrace. He's a leader no longer. His name is now a bitter taste on everyone's tongues."

Mad New Town had affirmed what Osceola already knew. He had agreed to hunt the man. Now he stood as motionless as one of the slender pines that rose from the scrub oak and palmetto growth around him. He listened to the stillness under the insects' urgent skirling. He calmed his own heart so he could feel any eddies in the flow of life, disturbances slight as a wind that stirred only the hairs on his arms.

Nothing felt out of place except the tangled strands of tracks in the hot white sand. They led out of the pine flats and across the bare, glaring sandhills to the distant hardwood hammock. The footprints had been laid down one precisely in front of the other, which meant they had been made by Seminole. Only one set was visible, but the tracks were deep. Osceola knew Heartless Round Wolf was accompanied by at least two other men. They were walking in the leader's footsteps to obscure their numbers.

Intertwined with the men's tracks were hoofprints. They belonged to the two cows stolen from the pens of the white trader Dexter. Wisps of pale smoke curled above the trees. Osceola sighed. He was too late. They had already slaughtered at least one of the cows and were smoking the meat.

Osceola no longer needed the tracks to find his quarry, but from habit he put his own feet into the prints. He enveloped himself in the aura of the men's desperation, their anger. As though by walking in their steps, he was also walking in their bodies.

He found them slicing strips from the carcass that dangled from the limb of a live oak. The small fire was hemmed in by the red rags of meat hanging on low wooden frames. The second cow stood nearby, bawling as though she knew her fate.

"I am come." Osceola recognized Heartless Round Wolf and two of his Wind clan brothers.

"You are." The three men hardly glanced away from their work. Like Osceola, they wore only breechclouts. The fact that all three were lean, of average height, and covered with blood made them look strangely identical.

"You're very considerate." Osceola hunkered instead of sitting. A man who hunkered didn't intend to stay long. "Or is the cow's owner paying you to smoke the meat for him?"

Heartless Round Wolf rinsed his hands in water from a small spring bubbling from a white limestone bowl. He brought some in a gourd for Osceola to drink. From the wrists up his arms were still bloody.

He squatted within arm's length so Osceola wouldn't have to stretch if he were inclined to share tobacco. Osceola took a pinch from his pouch, then held out the rest, the last of his own supply. The other two, drawn by the seductive aroma, joined them. Like everything else, tobacco was in short supply.

"The trader is a perverse man," Heartless Round Wolf said. "He gave my wife's cousin whiskey. While I was away on the hunt he took my last two cows. He said he'd bought them with the whiskey. But I didn't sell them. My wife didn't sell them."

"Are these the cows he took from you?" Osceola had heard many such stories in the past year.

"We couldn't find my cows. We took these." Heartless Round Wolf waved his pipe at the carcass and the lowing cow. "They're almost as skinny as mine."

"The white men will punish innocent people for your act. Women, children, will suffer."

The men stared at the ground. They knew about the reprisals. Everyone was drawn into them, either directly or indirectly. And because of anger or hunger or desire for war honors, warriors were unable or unwilling to break the cycle of vengeance.

A tense silence settled in. The men knew Abihka *Tastanagee Thloko* had sent Osceola to bring them before the town council. They knew they would be judged as perverse ones themselves. Their desperate women's eyes would still accuse them. Their children would still cry from hunger.

"Finish drying the meat of the cow you killed. Take it home. Give it to your families," Osceola said.

The men's expressions didn't change, but Osceola sensed the tension leaving them. He also felt the weight of this new problem being added to the considerable burden he already carried. "I'll return the other cow. I'll hold council with Hum-plee, the pale-eyes sense-maker."

Osceola decided that if he couldn't convince the new Indian agent, Gad Humphreys, to settle accounts with the larcenous trader, he would replace the cow himself, somehow. He knocked the dottle from his pipe. Then he stood and tucked the tobacco pouch back into the sun-faded folds of his turban. Without a word, he turned and walked away. If he hurried, he could be with his family by afternoon of the next day.

Morning Dew stood too quickly, and dizziness swept over her. The points of light dancing in front of her eyes became shards of pain behind them. She swallowed the bitter taste of the gorge in her mouth. The harsh stridulation of insects seemed to vibrate in her skull.

To steady herself she leaned against the trunk of a pine. Her hand came away blackened. A grass fire had roared through the pine flats a few months earlier. It had burned the bottom ten feet of bark and sapwood of each tree so only the charred heartwood remained. The fire had left the trees much slenderer below than above, giving them a peculiar, tottery silhouette.

Morning Dew wiped the hand on her bandana and laid it on her swollen womb as though to comfort the baby inside. The sun pulsed in a sky as faded as Morning Dew's clothes. She imagined the child could feel the heat. She brushed damp tendrils off her neck and tucked them into the knot of hair on top of her head. Then she pulled back the gauze mosquito netting over the small canvas hammock.

The gesture was just an excuse to stare down at her daughter, so trusting and vulnerable and serene in sleep. And so quiet. If she had been awake, Morning Dew would have known it without looking. The child was rarely quiet. From the depths of her hammock she usually carried on an endless, cheerful conversation with the world at large. And at fourteen months she had already developed the feisty charm that inspired her father to name her Tastanuhkuchee, Little Warrior.

Morning Dew looked longingly at the dome of cypress trees rising from the prairie beyond the pines. Cypress heads meant low ground and standing water. But the cypress needles were brown and brittle. The water had dried up. Morning Dew moved to the next low-growing clump of *koontee*. Scattered among the yellowed palmettos, her sisters and a score of other women and girls dug the *koontee*'s tough roots.

Dahomey Woman joined Morning Dew. She was dressed in the long skirt and short ruffled blouse of a Seminole. A large red kerchief was pulled tightly across her forehead, just above her thick, arching brows. The ends were twisted and wrapped in intricate folds around her head and tied at the nape of her neck. The bandanna's oval frame set off her full, bold features.

To be near Morning Dew and Osceola, Dahomey chose to live in Swamp Town, the black settlement near Abihka's village. She always brought them a portion of whatever she caught or harvested. Many a dawn, when Osceola and Morning Dew went to bathe, they found some small present at the cabin's stoop. They knew Dahomey or Mink had left it.

Using a wide, shallow gathering basket as a hat, Mink trailed her mother. The sun shining through the weave threw a grid of light onto her mahogany-brown face. Mink's long, thin legs covered large chunks of ground, but at times she didn't seem to know quite how to coordinate them. They gave her the look of an exotic bird, awkward on the ground, perhaps, but with promise of astonishing grace in flight.

Dahomey had braided Mink's hair into sinuous rows that followed the curves of her long, narrow skull and emphasized her handsome profile. With a quiet sigh Mink squatted next to her mother. She murmured an apology to the earth before she chopped into it with her digging stick. She wrestled the long taproot out of the ground. She cut off the leathery fronds, knocked the dirt off it with her stick, and dropped the root into her basket.

Morning Dew noticed how thin Mink's wrists were. Hunger is eating up our children from us, she thought. She found a strip of dried pumpkin in her pouch and handed it to Mink. Mink shied her fleeting half smile sideways at Morning Dew as she cut the pumpkin into three equal pieces and shared it with the two women.

Morning Dew dug gamely on around her large belly, while her eyes drooped with fatigue. For a while the only sound besides the shrill drone of the insects was the dry thump and creak of roots hitting the baskets.

"This heat reminds me of home." Dahomey had learned Mikasukee and a little Maskokee.

"Does the sun burn this hot in your country?" Morning Dew asked.

"The sun will cook your bones to *sofkee*."

"Do you want to go back to your country?"

Dahomey laughed, a low, husky riffle of sound. When Dahomey laughed Morning Dew found it difficult to believe she once had been an officer in a regiment of women warriors, or that she had endured the horrors of the middle passage. "I want to be there, but I don't want to go back."

"You don't want to ride in the white man's death ship?"

"No, I don't." With her stick Dahomey hacked savagely at the dirt around a *koontee* plant. "Those ships, they turn death into a friend. They make life your enemy." She threw the root into her basket with such force it bounced out. "But yes," she continued. "I want to be in my country again. My people say, 'One who does not speak his native tongue is lost.' "

Her voice faltered, and she concentrated on her digging. When she spoke again her voice was much softer. "I miss the music. Always there was music in my village." She began a haunting, mournful song in an incomprehensible tongue. It allowed the afternoon to slip away unnoticed.

By the time the baskets were full, the pines were sifting the sun's rays into low-slanting shafts. Morning Dew stood and stretched her cramped legs. She wiped her filthy, bloody fingers on a torn bandana and massaged the small of her back.

Mink played with Little Warrior while Morning Dew tied the hammock's ends and put it over her head. She settled the knot on her right shoulder and the center on her left hip. Mink put Little Warrior into it and helped Morning Dew lift the heavy basket onto her other hip. As they walked back to camp, Little Warrior clutched Morning Dew's calico ruffles and sang to herself.

While Mink gathered wood and Little Warrior collected twigs, Dahomey coaxed a reluctant flame from shreds of palmetto fiber. Morning Dew threw the last few handfuls of cornmeal into the small, soot-blackened pot of gritty water. They would make tomorrow's long march back to the village with no food and very little water. When Osceola and Alligator returned from their day's hunt, they sheepishly handed over two small rabbits and a squirrel to add to the kettles.

That night, in spite of the heat, they all sat around a spoke-shaped fire. To avoid the mosquitoes, they burned green wood and sat in the clouds of heavy smoke.

"This weather reminds me of how Rabbit fooled Alligator." Osceola leaned over and blew in Little Warrior's ear. She clapped one hand over it and giggled into the other.

"You've all heard of Old People Burner, haven't you?" Osceola asked.

"The white man's devil." The girls hugged their knees inside their long skirts and grinned in anticipation.

"One day, Alligator Warrior was sunning himself on the riverbank." While Osceola started the story, Alligator stretched out on one of the pine logs radiating from the fire. He pretended to bask in the heat.

"Alligator Warrior, did you ever see Old People Burner?" Osceola played Rabbit.

"No, Mad Rabbit. But I'm not afraid of him."

"If you'll crawl up the hill tomorrow, I'll introduce you to him. Don't be afraid if you see smoke. He lives in the Burning Place." Osceola gave the children a sly, mischievous look. He dangled his hands in front of his chest and wriggled his nose, then his ears. The children laughed.

"I'm willing," Alligator said.

"When you see birds flying overhead or hear deer running by, you must not be afraid."

"I'm never afraid," Alligator said.

"The next day, Alligator Warrior crawled far from the river. He lay in the tall grass just as Mad Rabbit had instructed him. Mad Rabbit lit a stick. He set the grass ablaze. Then he ran away to watch the fun."

"Oh, Mad Rabbit," Alligator called out. "What's that smell?"

" 'That's only Old People Burner starting out,' Mad Rabbit shouted. 'Just lie still.' "

"Oh, Mad Rabbit, what's that crackling noise? Why are flames sweeping the meadow?"

" 'That's Old People Burner's breath. You'll see him soon.' "

Alligator began to swing his head from side to side and make small grunts of distress. He lifted his hands as though the ground were hot. Osceola rolled over on his back, held his stomach, and kicked his feet with silent merriment. The children giggled and shrieked at the sight of two bold warriors transformed into a rabbit and an alligator.

"Mad Rabbit, the heat is burning my feet. My tail has caught fire." Alligator slid off the log. Using his knees and elbows, he belly-crawled into the night. His grunts of alarm floated back to them from the darkness. A bull alligator answered from the cypress dome silhouetted black against the star-bright sky.

"We'll do the Turkey Dance." Osceola couldn't bear to see the children's smiles fade. "The women will pretend to be men. The girls will pretend to be women." He and Alligator arranged the women in a line with the girls facing them.

"We'll begin." Alligator took the woman's part and faced Osceola. The girls tittered, but they began singing the Turkey Dance song.

Alligator and Osceola locked hands at chest height. Alligator stepped onto Osceola's feet so he was carried along when Osceola danced. Little Warrior stood on Morning Dew's feet. Everyone else laughed so hard that couples bumped into each other and fell down.

The singing and dancing went on a long time. When the women and children finally stretched out on their thin blankets and palmetto-frond beds under the lean-tos, they were exhausted. They soon fell asleep, despite their hunger and the oppressive heat.

Little Warrior slept between her parents. Osceola put his arm across her and laid his hand, palm down, on Morning Dew's stomach. She put hers over his as he caressed the taut bulge under the fragile cloth of her skirt. He knew the time was too early, but he was sure he felt the baby stir.

CHAPTER 11

The trail to Grandfather Squint's den was as familiar to Osceola as the path between Morning Dew's cabin and the council square in the center of town. It was also as well worn. For forty years Grandfather Squint had waddled along it, rather spryly for a creature that was over fifty years old, weighed six hundred pounds, and had legs twelve inches long.

In wetter times the alligator's trail was a thoroughfare for turtles and deer, raccoons, foxes, panthers, wolves, and bumbling opossums. It cut like a gash across the open savanna dotted with occasional clumps of busy-headed cabbage palms and squat dwarf cypress.

When Osceloa returned from the *koontee* expedition, he had asked Abihka's permission to hunt Grandfather Squint. Abihka was the leader of the Alligator clan here, and courtesy required Osceola to consult him before killing his brother. Osceola had found Abihka sitting in the square with some of the Beloved Men. Mad Dog, Old Squat, and Swamp Singer were there on one of their frequent visits.

"So you think you can kill Grandfather Squint," Abihka had said solemnly.

"I must, Uncle." Osceola didn't have to add that he must because his family was hungry. Everybody's family was hungry. The flour the women were laboriously extracting from the *koontee* roots would not last long.

"If you think you can kill Grandfather," Abihka had said, "you have my permission."

"Maybe you should take one of Old Mad Jackson's cannon with you." Mad Dog had squinted at Osceola through the tattered veil of tobacco smoke shrouding his seamed face. "Boom!" Mad Dog had exploded. Sparks from his pipe had added to the effect.

"The leeches in Grandfather Squint's mouth are big enough to eat you." Old Squat had leaned over to light Mad Dog's pipe with an ember held between a split palmetto rib.

"The meanest creature I ever hunted was an alligator with a head at each end," Swamp Singer had quavered.

"If he had a head at each end, how could he shit?" Old Squat had heard the story, but he'd forgotten. "Do you know, nephew?"

"No, Uncle." Osceola had patiently played the innocent. The uncles needed something to laugh about.

"An alligator with a head on each end *can't* shit." Swamp Singer had stared at his pipe as though it had bitten him. "That's why he's so mean."

Osceola had left the old men crackling and slapping their withered thighs. The sound of it had cheered him. Laughter had once been as common as smoke, but it was rare now. The sun had dried it up, as it had dried up everything else.

Next, Osceola had gone in search of Alligator. He had found him watching fire smolder in the cypress log he was hollowing for a canoe. Alligator had painted yellow stripes on his face in imitation of an alligator hatchling and had come along.

As he walked now beside Osceola, his short legs took two steps to each of his friend's. But Alligator never lagged behind anyone. Over his shoulder he carried a rusty shovel with a broken handle.

Osceola held his eighteen-foot alligator pole loosely balanced in his hand. The pole was made of a cypress sapling as thick as his wrist. Fitted over one end of the shaft was a large iron hook with a heavy point projecting from the top of it. As Osceola walked, the weight of the iron seemed to pull the pole forward and push it back, in time with his strides.

Grandfather Squint's road was a straight one. It was the shortest distance between his favorite fishing hole in the river and his den. The den was at the least accessible end of an almost inaccessible slough. Grandfather hadn't reach his impressive length by being careless.

Osceola and Alligator stopped where the trail had once

ended in the waters of the slough. The water was gone. They stared across the gray stretch of mud.

The site of the den was easy to see from a distance. A female alligator, Grandfather's mate, perhaps, had laid her eggs near it for years. The accumulation of plant debris used in her nests and the muck and trash from Grandfather's dredging had formed a curved mound. It was the highest ground in sight.

People called it Grandfather's Mountain. Willow, myrtle, and buttonbush grew there, above the surrounding sawgrass. Osceola and Alligator studied the lake of thick, evil-smelling mud between them and the tiny island of trees. They both knew the mud was chest deep.

"I'm glad no one else is here to see this." Alligator took off his moccasins and breechclout and began stuffing them into the pouch at his bony hip.

"The uncles can see us." Osceola was stripping, too. "They know about the mud. They're sitting in the council square right now, chuckling like rails at us."

He savored the sun's hot breath on his skin. It was better than a sweat lodge for flushing the bad humors from his pores. The sweat on his body gleamed. It highlighted the smooth, golden-brown curves of his muscles. Osceola looked as self-possessed naked as he did clothed.

Alligator glanced sideways at him, briefly envying the beauty of his friend's slender, muscular body. Envying also the ease with which Osceola did everything. Alligator could run as fast, play ball as skillfully, and hunt as well as Osceola, but he had to work much harder to do it. Alligator's body was too bony for his tastes. Maybe that was why he demanded so much from it.

Osceola balanced the alligator pole across his shoulders and hung his wrists over it. He knelt and splayed his ankles outward so they jutted as near to ninety-degree angles from his thighs as possible. If the muck was thick enough, the base formed by his outspread lower legs would hold him up.

Sliding one knee forward, then the other, he began a slow, ludicrous progress across the mud. He tried to avoid the decaying fish carcasses, but his legs and haunches were soon covered with gray slime. The sun quickly baked it to a brittle crust.

"Baldy doesn't like this one bit," Alligator called from behind him. "He's very particular about which warm, moist, odorous, sticky stuff he dips into." Alligator was small, but Baldy wasn't. The penis and testicles hung heavily between Alligator's bowed thighs like a drowsy animal. Osceola started to laugh and almost lost his balance.

"Did you hear what happened to Neamathla?" Alligator asked.

"No." If Alligator envied Osceola his body, Osceola envied his friend's ability to find out news before anyone else.

"The white people are building their capital, their main council fire, practically on his doorstep. They're calling it Tallahassee, after the people they drove out. Neamathla is surrounded by white people. The stink of them is in his nostrils daily.

"With the opportunity so close, Neamathla's young men have been stealing the pale-eyes' cattle." Alligator's voice took on a bitter tone. "The white *miko nope*, DuVal, grabbed Neamathla by the shirtfront. He threatened him in front of his young men. He deposed him, named Tukose Emathla *miko* in his place. Neamathla let DuVal escape with his life. Now not even his own people listen to him."

A large bubble of sulfurous gas rose to the surface behind Osceola. It exploded with a moist plop, releasing a foul stench. It scattered Osceola's and Alligator's gloomy contemplation of Neamathla.

"Baldy's in love," Alligator said casually. "He's pestering me to marry again."

"Tell Baldy this isn't the best time to take on another hungry mouth."

"He never listens to reason. Besides, when my woman has her monthly visitor, Baldy can't indulge himself."

"Who has captured his heart?"

"Hopping Bird."

Hopping Bird had no family to care for her, and she was of Alligator's wife's clan. Osceola suspected Alligator was offering to marry her because she and her two children would starve if no one took them in soon.

Osceola and Alligator crawled onto the mound above Grandfather Squint's den. With their knife blades, they scraped mud off themselves. The pond, the mound, the scattering of bones, the slick depression of scoured dirt where Grandfather sunned himself, made up his settlement. The sky was Grandfather's roof, and the sun was his hearth. His presence, like his musky smell, pervaded the earth and air here. The place was as homey, as familiar in its own way, as Morning Dew's cluster of cabins and storage *chikees*.

Osceola knew Grandfather Squint was probably asleep two feet below him. His tracks, long since set in the hardened mud of his personal highway, pointed there. Osceola felt comfortable, sitting on Grandfather Squint. I'll bring your bones back here, Grandfather, he promised. The sun can leach your spirit from them.

In wet weather the trees and bushes on his island provided nesting places for birds. Turtles laid their eggs in the female alligator's nest and trusted their hatchlings would escape to the water before the nest's guardian ate them. Rabbits, marsh rats, and raccoons lived here. They could smell the breath from death's jaws, perhaps, but Grandfather gave life as well as took it away.

A few weeks earlier the hole deepened by Grandfather at his den's entrance was one of the last places with water. It was an oasis in the swamp. It had attracted raccoons digging for burrowing crayfish and birds preying on the fish suffocating in the shrinking pond.

In turn, the raccoons and birds had brought *their* predators. For a while the area teemed with desperate animals fighting to survive. Grandfather had withdrawn from the noisy struggle. In his underground burrow, he could sleep through the dry time.

Osceola rose and measured eighteen paces behind a willow growing on the edge of the mound. Grandfather had dug under the willow's roots, using them to keep his tunnel from caving in. Osceola plunged the pointed end of the alligator pole repeatedly into the soil until it punched into Grandfather's passageway. The solid stench of decay rose and mushroomed outward. It was so powerful it had weight and boundaries.

Osceola probed until he felt the pole hit something that gave slightly. "He's here."

They heard a muffled grunt, and Grandfather moved, dragging the end of the pole a little. Alligator and Osceola took turns digging away the mud in front of the den's opening. The alligator's regular dredging had kept the area relatively clear, and the mud was only a few feet deep.

Osceola knelt on the firm sand underneath and began feeding the hook into the tunnel. To lengthen the pole's reach, he slid his arms into the opening. "He's moved farther back."

"He hasn't lived this long by being stupid." Alligator sat in the meager shade of the willow and dangled his legs over the edge of the embankment. He chewed a strip of leather to coax moisture into his dry mouth. He imagined soaking in cool, fresh water. His stomach rumbled loudly.

Osceola rested his cheek against a willow root jutting from the bank. Bracing himself, he pushed the hook hard into Grandfather's armored side. He felt the alligator writhe under its probe. He pushed harder. In spite of the sixteen feet of dark tunnel between them, he could sense Grandfather's anger.

When Grandfather snapped his jaws on the hook, the muffled ring of ivory on iron jarred the still air. The vibrations shuddered along the pole and into Osceola's hands, wrists, arms, and shoulders. He tugged and met with immovable resistance. Then the pole lashed back and forth, smashing Osceola's arms against the roots lining the sides of the tunnel.

Blood oozed from the scrapes and gashes the roots left and mixed with the mud. Grandfather was sure to smell the blood. The smell might lure him out and make this job easier. Or it might bring him out in a rush that could overwhelm Osceola.

"Grandfather is eating the hook," he panted.

"He's eaten the equipment of every hunter who's gone after him." Alligator chewed thoughtfully on his leather belt. "Sometimes he's eaten part of the hunter, too."

He wiped his palms on a clump of withered grass. Then he slid down from the embankment. He reached into the opening and grabbed the pole slightly ahead of where Osceola held it. The two men dug their heels into the ooze and heaved. Grandfather moved forward a fraction of an inch, and the pole whipped back and forth again. With one quick jerk Osceola and Alligator twisted the hook suddenly upward and pulled it back.

"He's caught." Osceola imagined the iron hook cutting into the roof of Grandfather's jaws, and he felt a twinge of pain on his own mouth. He tasted the cold metal.

Two hours later he and Alligator were in about the same position, but ten feet from the den's opening. They were coated from head to foot with mud. Although neither would admit it, they both thought their arms would wrench from their sockets before they saw Grandfather's homely face; but they had hauled him almost to the entrance. If the hook became dislodged now, he might chew his way up the shaft toward them. The pole had never looked so flimsy.

Grandfather's rumpled black snout emerged slantwise from the den. The shaft projected at an angle from the side of his jaw. Osceola stared into the mouth. From this close, the curved ranks of jagged yellow teeth seemed to extend like twin mountain ranges to the horizon. A fat black leech clung to the rim of skin under the ninth tooth, long as a tusk. As Grandfather rumbled into the glare of sunlight, the bright, vertical lens in his good eye narrowed until it almost disappeared.

When Osceola saw the ancient, rusty arrowhead still lodged in Grandfather's left eye socket, he let go of the pole. He took his knife from its sheath and edged to one side of the opening. Alligator maintained a steady pull and backed slowly into the deepening mud beyond the cleared area. Attached to the other end, Grandfather followed. He watched Alligator from his good eye.

When he cleared the den the huge, lumbering creature surged forward, knocking Alligator off balance. His massive, armored tail rose and slammed down to the left, then to the right, showering them all with mud. He inflated his body and loosed a tremendous throaty cough, somewhere between a hiss and a roar.

He raised his upper jaw, lifting the embedded hook with it. He closed it with such force he drove the thick point of the hook through the bony plate of his snout and snapped the sapling like a twig. He charged Alligator, who had fallen when the pole broke and was now scrambling to avoid him.

Osceola leaped for Grandfather's back, but Grandfather was moving fast. Osceola landed just above the base of his powerful tail. He felt the lash of it graze his ear, and he almost lost his grip on the twisting animal. He could barely hear Alligator's cry over the ringing in his head. He was horrified when he saw his friend's arm pass under him. Grandfather was trampling him.

Osceola put his knife in his teeth and hooked his arms around Grandfather's front legs. As he pulled himself forward he felt the thick bone plates of Grandfather's hide dragging against his bare skin. Desperately Osceola wrapped one arm around the alligator's neck. He rubbed his face on his arm, trying to wipe the mud from his eyes.

"I'm sorry I must kill you," he crooned into the large, crescent-shaped flap of skin that formed the alligator's ear. "We all must die. Today is your turn, not ours."

He could barely see when he raised his knife and drove it into a very small target, the ridge on Grandfather's skull, behind his eyes. The blow seemed forever taking effect, and Osceola feared he had missed.

Finally Grandfather gave one last quavering hiss, a sigh of anger or resignation or the forgiveness Osceola had requested. His gyrations slowed, and Osceola leaped off. Alligator lay on his back under Grandfather's broad tail. He was almost submerged, and the weight of the dead animal was pushing him deeper.

Osceola heaved the tail off. He lifted his friend's head and frantically clawed the mud away from his face. Alligator coughed and choked. He sputtered and spit and shook his head like a wet dog, spattering Osceola with slime.

Osceola tried to help him out of the mud but lost his balance and fell on top of him. The two of them lay there, side by side, spitting mud and laughing like lunatics. When they calmed enough to stand, they used Grandfather's bulk to haul themselves to their feet. They slogged to the embankment, retrieved the shovel, and dug away as much mud as they could. They and the corpse were all the same color gray.

Alligator stretched out on his back on top of Grandfather and lined his head up with the tip of the tail.

"Mark where my heels are," he said.

Osceola wiped the mud off and cut a groove in one of the armored plates. Alligator hitched along Grandfather's back and put his head against the mark. Osceola made another cut two lengths up, then a third three lengths. When Alligator put his head on the third mark, his legs draped over Grandfather's skull and between his bulging eyes. His feet stuck out past the end of the snout.

"Grandfather Squint is almost four Alligators long."

Osceola stared at the immense body, then at the expanse of mud over which they would have to carry the meat and hide. Already the tangerine-colored sun was sinking in the west. Osceola sharpened his knife on his whetstone and made the first cut under Grandfather's chin.

CHAPTER 12

Osceola and Alligator balanced the longest section of the broken cypress pole on their shoulders. They had put Grandfather Squint's hide-wrapped remains in a palmetto-fiber sling and hung it from the pole. The tenderest meat was in the tail, but they had taken everything edible. They had left the crows squabbling over the heap of remains.

The two men walked single file among the neat cabins and around the carefully swept yards of Abihka's town, but no one noticed them. No one noticed them because almost no one was there. The women's log pestles stood upright in the troughs of half-mashed *koontee* roots. The waste water from the *koontee* hadn't been carried away, and its putrid odor seemed to have soaked into everything. Abandoned brooms lay among the sweepings. Digging sticks had been left scattered about the desolate gardens. The dogs lay panting in the shade. They were too weak from hunger to bark.

Only an ancient grandmother dozed by a fire in the ninety-eight-degree heat. A boy guarding the *koontee* mash from marauding hogs turned to stare at them. Osceola couldn't blame him. Both he and Alligator were filthy, bruised, and bloodied. Where they had wiped the sweat from their eyes they had left dark smudges of mud. They looked like raccoons. Alligator made a hideous face at the boy, and he giggled.

From a cabin came the hesitant cry of a baby, just waking from a nap. The cry rose to a wail when the child realized she was alone and very hungry. Osceola detoured to where the old woman napped and gently shook her knob of a shoulder.

"Mother," he said, "comfort the little one."

The woman labored to her feet, swiveled stiffly until she located the crying, then tottered toward it.

"Mother," Alligator called after her, "where is everyone?" She didn't answer.

"They must be in the square." The silence in the deserted village made Osceola uneasy.

He glanced over the palings into the dusty gardens as he passed them. The bean and melon plants would crumble to dust in his fingers were he to pick them. Suddenly it seemed perfectly possible the people too had withered, shrunk, and crumbled to dust while he and Alligator were gone.

One of Grandfather Squint's flayed feet stuck from between the sling's meshes. A quarrelsome swarm of flies reeled around the lump of pale meat.

"Not much to show for all that trouble." Alligator was walking behind Osceola and could survey their spoils.

"Grandfather was mostly teeth, claws, hide, wiles." Osceola headed toward the square.

Like Alligator, Osceola was calculating how little of Grandfather would be left after he shared his half with his grandmother and mother and with Morning Dew's family. He also would take some meat to his hungriest clan brothers and their women and children. It didn't occur to him not to share the meat. "Whatever you become in life," Mad New Town once had said, "don't every be miserly. A miserly man is mean-spirited. He can never be a great leader."

That morning Grandfather had been the canny hero of the uncles' stories. He had been a mythical creature from long ago, when animals were god-sized and spoke in understandable languages. He had been three man-lengths of tough black armor. His mouth had been wide enough to contain one of the pots in which he would be cooked. Now he was a hunk of spoiling flesh that soon would render little more than a colorful film of grease on the stew.

As Osceola looked back at the flies clotting on the meat, he saw his own future there. Like every other man, he had craved rank and honor and the opportunity to be generous to those around him. He had imagined his woman and his children always laughing and well fed.

He had expected drought, floods, fires, and hurricanes, of course. But he hadn't expected nature to conspire with the pale-eyes to bring such ruin on his family and his people. He saw his ambitious dreams spoiling in the merciless heat, along with Grandfather Squint.

In a sudden rage he put his foot on the scarred haunch of a spindle-legged hog the size of a rum keg. He shoved him away from the *koontee* mash he was eating. The hog bucked and squealed and trundled off down the empty street.

With a start, Osceola realized whose hog it was. He threw his end of the pole and Grandfather Squint's bundled remains onto the high, pig-proof platform of Morning Dew's storage *chikee*. Alligator did the same. When Osceola broke into a trot, Alligator ran to keep up.

"Has war been declared?" he asked hopefully.

"War would be better." Osceola didn't slow down. "My grandmother is here."

"The one with a tongue like a gar tooth? The one your old woman doesn't get along with?"

"I have only one grandmother."

"Is she visiting?"

"She doesn't bring her pigs when she visits. She didn't tell me she was moving here."

Alligator grunted, then fell diplomatically silent. Osceola

was angry, and Alligator had learned to steer clear of his temper.

The crowd overflowed from between the long council sheds whose blank rear walls hid the drama in the square beyond. People craned to see over those in front. Children crawled between the adults' legs. As Osceola turned sideways to move through the crowd, he heard the women murmuring, "Most Ancient One has brought the mad trader, Heron's Nest."

A smaller crowd and their baggage occupied the center of the square. Peeping patiently held her six-year-old daughter by the hand. Fighting in a Line's seven slaves sat on the bundles of household goods. The family packhorse nibbled a loose end of fiber rope dangling from the heap. Osceola also recognized three Red Stick families who had followed Mad New Town from the north country years earlier. Mad Dog and Mad New Town himself had prudently vanished.

Fighting in a Line was shrewd, though. To assure herself a welcome she had brought Wococoi Clark with her. He led three of his remaining four pack mules. The fourth was almost obscured by Wococoi's young wife. She had doubled her weight since Osceola had met her on the gulf coast four years earlier. Her breasts, which Wococoi fondly referred to as "Cupid's kettledrums," were now of a size to smother him in his sleep if he wasn't careful.

Wococoi's treasures were piled high under canvas covers. With longing evident in their eyes, the women crowded the square and stared intently at Clark's canvas mountains. The children shoaled around his bandy legs until walking was an impossibility. Little Warrior rode on his shoulders. Her hands and forearms were buried in the wiry red explosion of his hair.

The late afternoon sun made Wococoi's hair look as though it were on fire. *Wococoi* meant Heron's Nest, and Heron's Nest was a good name for him. Osceola always expected to find a clutch of eggs incubating in the cavity formed by the bald spot on the crown of Wococoi's head.

"Be patient, kinchins. Uncle Wococoi has brought boodle enough for all." Wococoi was handing out chunks of sugar candy as fast as he could with one hand. He held his beloved gin bottle in the other.

"Billy Powell, me lad!" He waved the bottle over the plain of heads and the forest of outstretched hands. The children turned to stare at Osceola and Alligator.

"What brings you so far from the coast, old friend?" Osceola decided to settle one problem at a time. His grandmother could wait. And, hopefully, fret.

"Alas, lad, the blue-backs have built a fort on Tampa Bay. They confiscated my store. They said their nipping government would pay for my inventory. I decamped with all I could filch. I would rather give it to friends than see their nasty crabscratchers on it."

Osceola knew Wococoi's story was only partially true. Wococoi knew the Seminole were refusing to accept government rations. He knew they were starving. He was bringing life to his friends.

While Wococoi distributed dried fish and cornmeal, Fighting in a Line's chickens and pigs wandered around the square. Morning Dew watched everything like a bobcat preparing to pounce on a porcupine. Her arms were crossed on top of her swollen belly, and her mouth was set in the line that meant trouble.

Osceola knew what she was thinking. She did not want Fighting in a Line's camp near hers. In the past, after Fighting in a Line's visits, Morning Dew burned cedar to counteract any bad medicine her grandmother-in-law might have left. She stopped just short of putting dried thistle in the guest-cabin blankets to discourage the visits.

"You are come, Grandmother," Osceola said politely. He ignored the curious throng behind him.

"Grandson! My proud warrior!" Fighting in a Line opened her skinny arms wide, as though to welcome him inside them. "I heard you went to hunt Grandfather Squint. Grandfather has eaten many of my hogs. We've warred for years."

"I've told the sister of *Talasee Tastanagee* we're honored to have her," Abihka said diplomatically. This wasn't the sort of distraction he would have chosen. He knew how Morning Dew felt about her grandmother-in-law. He knew how Fighting in a Line felt about the Mikasukee.

"She will not raise her cabins near mine, old man." Morning Dew spoke in an undertone only Osceola could hear.

Already Fighting in a Line was directing her slaves to haul the household goods to Morning Dew's camp. Osceola stepped forward to intervene when, from the edge of the square, Dahomey caught his eye. There was urgency in her face. The woman standing beside her was Heartless Snake's black wife, Corn Grinder, whom Osceola hadn't seen in over two years. She had returned from exile, but she was alone.

"Billy Powell, lad," Wococoi called. "Shall I take my swag to your camp, then? We'll be staying a few days." He moved off toward Morning Dew's cabins, and the mob surged after him. Osceola waved to signify Wococoi was to make himself at home.

He caught his grandmother's hands, like chicken feet in chamois gloves, and squeezed them affectionately. "Wait here." Then he smiled at his mother, who went limp with relief. He picked up his sister and threw her into the air. She laughed when he caught her and hugged her.

"I'll raise my house near your woman's so we can talk at night as when you were young." Fighting in a Line beamed. Her scheme had worked.

"We must find the best-possible place for a woman of your status, Grandmother." Osceola knew Fighting in a Line wanted to listen to what was said in her daughter-in-law's household. Morning Dew knew it, too.

"This is not a thing to be done in haste." Osceola began considering various pretexts to locate his grandmother's compound at a distance from Morning Dew's. "Tonight we can feast on Grandfather Squint. You're welcome in my wife's house."

He heard Morning Dew blow out her breath in exasperation. He gave her a quick look that asked forbearance. He would placate her later. He hurried to where Corn Grinder stood with Dahomey and Dahomey's new husband, who was called Aury's Black.

"Your clan brother may be in trouble," Dahomey said.

"We've almost died of hunger." Corn Grinder kneaded her elbows nervously. "We've eaten the scrapings from green hides of those more fortunate in the hunt. We've eaten beetles, larvae, rotten meat. My husband became sad. He went away four days ago to steal cattle from the white men's settlements. Hunters say he was captured. Will you find him?"

Heartless Snake's wife was very great with child. She looked ten years older than the cheerful young woman Osceola remembered. Osceola wondered why troubles came in flocks, like crows, and stole whatever happiness people had been able to cultivate.

"I'll go right away."

"I'll go with you," said Alligator. "Maybe I can trade my share of Grandfather's hide for fish or corn."

"I'll go, too." Aury's Black shifted the rifle in its thick leather case on his back. He had come dressed to walk in the streets of the white men's town. A big-brimmed straw hat shaded his round face. He wore loose, navy duck trousers and a huge white cotton shirt. A cutlass was stuck into one side of his wide leather belt. From the other side protruded a gold-and-niello pistol, a miquelet made in Daghestan. How he came by it entailed several long stories.

"I know the coast where the white people cluster, like burs on the hem of your shirt," Aury's Black said. "I can translate for you."

Aury's Black was Ashanti, captured in war and shipped from the African port of Cormantine. Such slaves were called Coramantees. It was said that no man deserved a Coramantee unless he treated him as a friend rather than as a slave. Osceola and Morning Dew had rescued Dahomey, the woman Black had since taken to wife. Without saying so, either to them or to himself, he had pledged them tenacious loyalty.

CHAPTER 13

The newer structures in the village of Tampa huddled near Fort Brooke's palisades like chicks seeking shelter under a hen. The fort's walls were so new the peeled pine logs smelled strongly of resin. The palisades enclosed huge live-oak trees that shaded the house of an absent planter. Six months earlier the poor fellow had returned from a vacation in Pensacola to find his house and kitchens, storage sheds, barns, and slave quarters occupied by members of the Fourth Infantry.

Maybe when he finished cursing the army he cursed himself for choosing such a desirable location. His home stood on a point of land between the mouth of the Hillsborough River and the bay. Besides the shade of the oaks, a breeze from the gulf almost always found its way inland, no matter how hot the day. Jasmine perfumed the nights.

Schools of mullet, two or three miles long, passed over the flats for hours. Their splashing kept newcomers awake. The phosphorescence set off by their leaping created stunning fireworks. Mussel shells lay in iridescent windrows along the white sand beaches.

The mestizo fishing fleet still called twice a week at the planter's wharf, but now a grizzled mess sergeant met it. In stiff white apron and rolled shirt-sleeves, he chivied his orderlies and their barrows over the uneven planks. When the sergeant had selected the fish for the officers' mess, the rest was carted off to fertilize the officers' garden. Just beyond the wharf rode Major Brooke's double-banked barge, schooner-rigged and freshly coppered.

If the fort was all neatness and order, the recently built section of Tampa wasn't. The streets and vacant lots were of crushed shell, deep sand, and garbage. The untrammeled parts were covered with a sparse growth of brittle grass and sand spurs, spindly palmetto and scrub oak.

The older part of the village, Spanishtown Creek, was different. The Spanish and Minorcan and Cuban inhabitants had planted the trees of their homelands. Palm-thatched frame houses nestled in a tropical confusion of avocado and lime, orange, fig, papaya, banana, mango, and tamarind. The pungent odor of guava simmering into jelly floated out of Spanishtown Creek. The exotic smell aroused the hunger in Osceola.

Beyond the racks of drying fish, the shore was lined with beached smacks draped with tarred nets. The boats' brown sails hung from lanteen rigs like the drying wings of cormorants. Proprietary pelicans napped on the gunwales.

When Osceola, Alligator, and Aury's Black entered Tampa, the dregs of the settlement's social order sat around a long plank table. The table occupied most of the piazza of Count Odette Philippe's oyster shop and billiard hall. Philippe claimed to be related to King Louis XVI. He had been captured at the Battle of Trafalgar and exiled to the Bahamas. After his release he had drifted here, where he was in the process of prospering. Lumber for his proposed bowling alley lay stacked behind the oyster shop.

Private O'Reilly wiped the edge of his sweaty hand on his soiled blue trousers. Then he used it to slide the grains of corn off the square of cardboard and into a neat pile. The keno card was limp and frayed with use. Its red border had faded to a pale brown. The printed grid lines and numbers were almost illegible. O'Reilly handled it as delicately as a lace hankie, and delicacy was not O'Reilly's style.

"Sometimes I think I'm on the wrong side," he said.

"What do you mean?" Private Lewis kept a buzzard's eye on the banker, who was the owner of the cards. He was separating his percentage from the dimes and chits and pieces of doubloons in an upturned straw hat.

O'Reilly and Lewis sat with their kegs tilted so they could lean against the palm log wall. The seats along the wall always filled first. These were not men who liked to have their backs to the open.

"Look at them." With his chin O'Reilly pointed to Osceola

and Alligator. "Now there is a uniform a man might swagger in."

O'Reilly's oblique glance encompassed the fringe on their leggings and rifle cases and the brilliant colors and ruffles of their appliquéd hunting shirts. Osceola and Alligator had put on their finery. They wore silver gorgets, armbands, and bracelets, paisley shawls, beaded garters and belts, crimson sashes and hip pouches, and shell earrings. White egret plumes nodded regally in the elaborate turbans, whose fringed ends hung loose on the napes of their necks. The turbans gave them the disconcerting look of magi, camelless and strayed from their Eastern desert.

O'Reilly surveyed his own faded, stained, and rumpled uniform with distaste. "They have the air of satisfied men," he said. "I'll wager they're never bored or overworked or in want of the company of obliging women."

"They look to be dressed for a ladies' sodality." Private Lewis was far more interested in swapping his keno card for a luckier one. He studied the available cards as though the winning one would somehow notify him of the fact. "They's just Injuns," he added. "And tame ones at that."

"No, they ain't." At nineteen Private O'Reilly was already a shrewd judge of character. He would make sergeant some far-off day. "Those partic'lar boys is powder in the pan, waitin' for a spark."

"It's the niggers what gall me." Lewis spared Aury's Black a resentful glance. Black was six feet four inches tall. Even if he'd been humble, he would have stood out in a crowd. And he wasn't humble. "Look at that one. Struttin' like a rooster in deep shit."

A scuffle broke out when Juan Gomez pulled a dirk from his boot. He reached across the table, grabbed a fistful of his neighbor's shirtfront, and lifted him off the stump that served as a chair. Gomez raised the man's chin with the point of the knife until he was looking him in the eye. Gomez had very expressive eyes.

"*Cabrón.*" He spoke softly. "Have you no consideration? Do not sully the *caballero*'s cards." When he let go, the man dropped back onto the stump and growled threats, sotto voce, at the tabletop.

Dame Gossip said Gomez was a blackbirder, a slaver. That
he had sailed with Gasparilla, the pirate. Until recently he
had been hiding out on Panther Key. In his absence stories
circulated. They expanded ominously, like a summer thunderhead. In Tampa Gomez was the loose carronade on the
deck. So in spite of his mumbling, this man was more careful
with the oyster juice that coursed through the thick hair on
his forearms and dropped off his elbows.

A harried pair of sloe-eyed sisters delivered buckets of sweet
raccoon oysters and pitchers of warm beer from the dim interior of Count Philippe's establishment. The older woman
wore a large knife in the belt slung low on her ample hips.
She looked capable of using it. Even Don Juan Gomez confined his attentions to come-hither winks.

A tide of discarded oyster shells was rising slowly around
the men's feet. A pack of surly dogs prowled under the table.
Nearby, a flock of seagulls paced and fidgeted, complained
and chuckled. Osceola and Alligator and Black stopped at
the edge of the piazza's rough-cut cypress floor, raised a heady
six inches above the drifts of sand in the street.

They watched the game without comment. Even though
the men here wouldn't understand their words, the three were
silent out of habit. They wouldn't risk betraying their
thoughts with a gesture.

While he watched, Osceola took it all in—the game, the
players, the soldiers patrolling the streets, the mournful cries
of the gulls, the garble of English, Spanish, and French. He
smelled the men's sweat and marked how it differed from the
odors he was used to. The men also gave off the rank smell
of the vanilla they chewed and the mangrove punk they
burned in smudge pots to discourage mosquitoes. Osceola
enjoyed the fitful salt breeze stirring the curls around his face.
He relished new places, even places as disagreeable as this.

The banker shook the large gourd and drew out the first
wooden block. He studied it until the players began to threaten
his manhood and his mother's virtue. When he called the number on it, each searched his card for a match. If he found one,
he covered it with a kernel of corn. Then everyone sat back to
swig beer, eat oysters, belch, and wait for the next call.

In spite of their mission, Osceola, Alligator, and Black watched raptly. Alligator slipped Osceola a sidelong glance. He flicked his eyebrows almost imperceptibly and twirled the silver bracelet on his thin wrist. Alligator loved gaming even more than he loved women. Osceola twitched the muscles around his mouth. It was a signal that meant no. They had no time for gaming today.

The afternoon sun's rays crept across the table. The sisters dropped the rolled canvas hanging along the piazza's eaves. The mildewed shades blocked the view and broke the game's mesmerizing effect. As Osceola and his friends walked away, they heard Gomez.

"Who's the big nigger, you ask?" Gomez spoke loudly so Black would hear him. "He's one of Aury's Blacks, the most desperate, bloodthirsty set of savages ever to harry a coast-line."

Black didn't look back, but a small smile played across his ravaged face. He heard the salute in Gomez's voice. Over the ensuing silence came O'Reilly's shout.

"Keno!"

Osceola, Alligator, and Black passed Major Brooke's extensive turtle crawl near the fort's wharf. At the foot of the dock a group of Seminole women waited for the fishing fleet. After the mess sergeant made his selection and before the remainder was carted away as compost, the women could take what they wanted.

"Famine seems to have stopped at the shoreline." Alligator sniffed the aroma of fish chowder mingling with the simmering guava.

"The sea doesn't suffer drought, nor flood, nor pestilence." Black's eyes unfocused until he was looking toward the line where water met sky. Like the desire for a woman, yearning for the sea would pounce on him when he wasn't expecting it. He wanted to feel a deck tilt and surge under his feet. He longed to see balls of Saint Elmo's fire crackling at the ends of the yardarms, sending the power of magic rushing through the planks and beams of the ship. He wanted to move while standing still.

"Those are Chalo Emathla's people." Osceola stared at the

waiting women. "I thought Trout Leader was refusing the white man's food."

They found Major George Brooke chewing the end of a fat Cuban cigar that looked ridiculous poking from his boyish face. His wispy reddish-brown hair curled in a most unmilitary manner. He seemed to be trying to compensate for it by growing a set of muttonchop whiskers. Brooke's high collar reminded Osceola of his grandmother's conical pile of beads. For Major Brooke and for Fighting in a Line, turning their heads was not a carefree move.

The major was gesturing at the Seminole men standing among the rickety two-wheeled carts outside the sutler's store. The carts' white owners were in the store trading. The Seminole were a snag in the swirl of messengers, patrols, parades, visitors, farmers, and drifters.

"May I be of assistance, Major?" Aury's Black saluted elaborately, and the bells on his shirt tinkled. He spoke English with a French accent that gave him a cultured air. The effect was belied by the saber scar that cut a wedge-shaped trough across his broad, flattened nose and high cheekbone. His piratical look was heightened by the cutlass, the pistol, and the two gold rings in his left earlobe.

"Please." Brooke chose to ignore Black's appearance and his sardonic tone. The fort's official interpreter was ill with a fever, which he had been treating with liberal doses of whiskey. "Tell them the rations have not arrived. We expect them any day."

"The white men have tricked you again," Black told the Seminole amiably. "They have no food for you."

The men muttered among themselves. None of them met Osceola's or Alligator's eyes. Finally one spoke. "They promised us food. Our children are starving."

"Go home," Osceola said. "Hunt. Fish. Dig roots. Do what you must to survive."

"We *are* doing what we must to survive."

"Don't depend on the Americans' promises," Osceola said. "They do not tell the truth when a lie will serve them better. If you accept their food, you accept their treaty. You accept the treachery coiled in its pages like a rattlesnake in dry leaves.

Are you hens to squabble at their feet, waiting for a few grains
to fall from their hands?"

The men studied the ground. They had waited for days
already, but at least food was promised here, and their wives
could beg fish. Their children could forage in the fort's opu-
lent garbage dumps. In their village kettles were empty. Crops
were dead.

"Go." The shift from suggestion to command in Osceola's
voice was unmistakable. One by one the men slowly went to
find their women at the wharf.

"Thank you." Brooke was relieved. "They've been on the
begging lay for weeks. They're all supposed to be moving
inland, anyway. Though how they shall survive there I do
not know. They are in a deplorable state of depriva—" Brooke
stopped suddenly when he realized he was speaking to some
of those in a deplorable state of deprivation.

"We're looking for a friend." Black tactfully changed the
subject. "A Red Stick named Heartless Snake. He wears a
green turban with yellow plumes."

"I've not seen him. But we've been feeding five hundred or
more Indians a day here. I could easily have missed him. A
patrol did report complaints of two suspicious bucks lurking
in the vicinity of McGirth's lair. Although what would qualify
a man as suspicious among that gallow's fodder I can only
conjecture."

"Does McGirth sell whiskey?"

"We've not caught him at it." Major Brooke sounded defensive.

"Thank you for the information." Black turned to translate, and Brooke added an afterthought.

"Ask your master if he'll consider selling you. I could use
your services, and you would be well treated."

"Tell the American *tastanagee* I do not sell my black people." Osceola didn't mention that Black was not his to sell.
That would have made his freedom even more precarious.

But Brooke didn't pursue the matter. He had more important problems on his mind. As the three warriors left, he was
instructing the sergeant major to restrict the enlisted men to
only fourteen to a toothbrush.

CHAPTER 14

Heartless Snake had lost count of the days. He also had lost the feeling in his arms and shoulders. The white men had tied his wrists together, then thrown the rope over the ridgepole of the storage shed. They had hauled him up until he swung helplessly with his toes just grazing the ground. They had tossed his dog's corpse onto the sandy floor, and the carcass was beginning to smell.

The white men had come back once to roll away a barrel from the dozen of them in the shed. They had shoved Heartless Snake to set him swinging like a pendulum, measuring his own mortality. They had laughed at him and gone back to their dice game in front of the hovel that served as a store. Since then they had ignored him.

Numbness had started in Heartless Snake's fingers and spread through his chest, but it did not blunt the pain. The stiff hempen rope had worn away the flesh of his wrists and become saturated with blood. Flies formed jeweled clusters on them. His left shoulder had been dislocated in the fight with the white men. The agony from it reminded him he had not yet passed to the spirit world.

His companion hung in front of him and stared at him from sightless eyes. During the night, his spirit must have taken the form of an owl and fluttered away. Heartless Snake chanted a silent song for him.

Be patient. Heartless Snake talked himself away from the chasm of despair yawning in the tobacco-stained sand at his feet. *You'll join him soon.*

As he hung there hour after hour he had, of necessity, befouled himself. Heartless Snake imagined himself a chrysalis, hanging in the dark, dusty vault of the shed. He was an ugly caterpillar transforming into a spirit. He saw himself breaking loose from his mortal form and flying free in death.

In his less philosophical moments he berated his *sabia,* his magical stone. He had cared for it as instructed. He had stroked it and sung to it and fed it, but it had turned on him nonetheless.

Heartless Snake judged a second night was approaching, although it brought no relief from the suffocating heat in the shed. He had watched the brilliant strip of sunlight fade around the canvas that hung in the doorway. He could hear the night walkers—the mice and cockroaches—rustling in the thatch of the roof and walls. The mosquitoes grew more numerous. He tried to measure the passing of time by its effects on his body.

Blowflies had laid eggs in the grid of cuts made by the white men's whip on his back. Heartless Snake couldn't feel any movement of larvae there. The eggs hadn't hatched yet. *Brother Maggots, you'll be too late, but I wish you good health.*

Heartless Snake knew that by the time the maggots began their healing work of eating the putrefying flesh, he would be dead. Other forces were carrying him toward the spirit land. The major one was thirst.

Heartless Snake had passed the sleepy stage of dehydration, then the nausea. Dried vomit covered his chest and sunken stomach. Now he was dizzy. His head throbbed with pain. His tongue swelled until it was a lump of purple meat bulging from his bleeding lips. Heartless Snake wished he could lick the blood to allay his thirst, but that was impossible. His bloated tongue had become an immovable intruder in his mouth.

Just when he thought the worst had happened, the itching started. His skin felt as though cockroaches were crawling over every part of him. He was sure he would go mad. He writhed feebly. The pain seared through his shoulder, but the itching only grew worse.

Heartless Snake could endure the pain. He could die with dignity, even while strung up like a deer to bleed. He could ignore the evil-smelling husk his body had become. But he couldn't stand the itching. He tried to scream around the obstruction of his own tongue. If he could attract the white men's attention, maybe he could goad them into killing him.

When he thought he saw water cascading from the walls and flowing across the sand, he knew the end had come. He joyously, inaudibly, began his death song. In his halucinatory state he was angry at the gentle hands that groped at his waist. Their spidery touch only intensified the itching. The rope slackened, and more hands eased him to the ground. They untied his wrists, and Heartless Snake luxuriated in the feel of his arms, like deadwood, at his sides. He tried to scratch himself, but his fingers refused to move.

Osceola pulled the cork from his gourd canteen. He poured water into the palm of his hand, then trickled it onto Heartless Snake's flayed lips. He kept trickling it until Heartless Snake was able to swallow a bit. Heartless Snake thanked him profusely, although Osceola heard nothing but incoherent mumbling around the tongue.

Aury's Black moved to pick Heartless Snake up, but Osceola had already lifted him and, with Alligator's help, hoisted him across his shoulder. Osceola carried his friend effortlessly across the crowded floor of the shed and out through the hole they had made in the thatch of the rear wall.

"The pale-eyes owe us a life." Alligator shook his musket at McGirth's grog shop.

"We'll collect it later," Osceola said. "There are too many of them here."

Black paused in the opening. The body of Heartless Snake's dead companion seemed to be hovering over the barrels as though halted in its journey toward the spirit world. Black looked longingly at all the whiskey and sighed. He pulled a frond from the thatch and held it against the embers smoldering in the punk in his horn container. He blew lightly until the brittle frond caught. He waved it slowly until it was blazing, then lit the thatch with it.

By the time he caught up with Osceola and Alligator, the fire was roaring. They could hear the distant shouts of McGirth and his henchmen.

"I expected to see you with a keg of wes'kee on your shoulder." Osceola grinned at Black.

"That's tafia. Rotgut. If his customers are lucky, he only mixed it with pepper. With pond water. More likely he's cut it with turpentine." Black glanced over his shoulder at the fire, which had grown to a thundering blaze. "McGirth'll try to save his wares. That'll delay him."

"Do you know all the perverse white men?" Osceola asked.

"I know most of the old ones, but new ones are flooding in faster than I can make their acquaintance. Georgia has an abundance of them to export." But Black smiled to himself with grim amusement. Georgia's banditti were pale imitations of the monumental scoundrels he had known in his day.

Black had heard of Osceola's endurance, but he was still astonished that so much speed and strength could be compressed into such a slender, graceful frame. Osceola was burdened by Heartless Snake's weight, but Black barely managed to stay ahead of him.

Black and Alligator burned dried palmetto fronds as torches, lighting new ones from the old ones before the flames died. There was no dearth of palmetto fronds. After half an hour's travel Black extinguished his torch in the sand and signaled for Alligator to do the same. Osceola laid Heartless Snake gently in the bushes. He and the others waited until their eyes became accustomed to the dim light of the waning moon before they moved ahead.

A fire was blazing in the center of a clearing in the hardwood hammock. Its light illuminated the undersides of the oak canopy and gave a ghostly air to the dense shreds of Spanish moss hanging from the branches.

"Here's your chance to avenge the warrior's death," Black whispered. Osceola and Alligator might be wise in the ways of the wilderness, but they were woefully uneducated in the perfidy of white men.

"McGirth usually sends someone after red people who've bought whiskey from him." Black spoke so low his voice could almost be mistaken for the sigh of the wind. "The man waits until they get drunk enough to fall asleep. Then he slits their throats. He steals their weapons, their jewelry, even the whiskey they haven't drunk yet."

McGirth's man hadn't bothered to leave the trail. He was crouched with his back to Osceola and the others. His old half-stock contract rifle was balanced across his knees. Black sneaked close enough to grab his hair, yank his head back, and slit his throat. He took the scalp and threw the body across his shoulder. Then he picked up the dead man's rifle.

"I'll dispose of this in the swamp." He inclined his head toward the man's dangling legs and grinned, his even white teeth almost glowing in the darkness.

In the clearing no one had noticed them. A warrior sat morosely beside a pile of knives and muskets, bows, arrows, and hatchets. With his chin in his hands he watched his friends dance around the fire. He had been elected to stay sober, to guard the weapons and stop fights while his three friends drank.

"The pale-eyes will blame them for burning the cabin," Osceola said. "We have to take them with us." He walked into the fire's light and gave the shrill, drawn-out cry of the Black Drink. He startled the men into an unsteady silence.

The cry and the scalp at Black's belt confused them. Had war been declared? They tried to sort it out as they stumbled toward the stack of guns.

"Come." Osceola reached the weapons first and began picking them up. When their owners objected, Alligator advanced, musket leveled.

"You." He pointed it at the sober one. "Carry as many of those weapons as you can."

Osceola shouldered Heartless Snake again. With Osceola leading the caravan, Alligator following, and Black guarding the rear, they started the long night march to Abihka's village.

The shadowy forms of small children, like shiny-eyed cotton rats scuttling among the cornstalks, ran from cabin to cabin in Abihka's town. An older boy disappeared into the woods. He was headed for Swamp Town to take the news to Dahomey and Heartless Snake's wife.

Osceola carried Heartless Snake to Morning Dew's guest cabin. Fighting in a Line, by the light of a resin-filled stick of pine, was already awake and putting on her dozens of strands of beads. Mad Dog was performing his own morning ritual of blowing his nose in a series of loud honks.

To spare Heartless Snake's flayed back, Osceola laid him on his stomach on a pile of blankets. He sat next to him for several minutes, listening to his friend's ragged breathing. He chanted his most powerful medicine song.

If Heartless Snake lived to see the dawn, Abihka would work his medicine. And Dahomey and Heartless Snake's wife would be here soon to wash him and tend him and spread healing salves on his back. In Swamp Town, Dahomey was a powerful healer.

Osceola found Morning Dew kneeling by the banked fire, blowing it into life. Little Warrior sat sleepily on a fireplace log next to her. In the cabins around them he could hear people talking in low voices. He heard the rustle of mattresses of Spanish moss and the creak of palm log floors under bare feet.

"You are come, husband."

"I am." Osceola was equally polite. But when he sat wearily on the log next to his daughter, he felt the delicate caress of Morning Dew's fingers across his neck. Through the thin cloth of her blouse he felt the softness of her breast on his cheek as she leaned over his shoulder to serve him *koontee* bread and cold *sofkee*. The touch wasn't accidental.

Like moths, people began circling the two star-shaped fires, the women at one and the men at the other. The children sat in sleepy lines on the logs. They all spoke even more softly than usual, as though not quite awake or reluctant to disturb the stillness of the warm night.

Alligator's wife hurried into the fires' light. With one arm she held her son balanced on her hip. With her free hand she was adjusting the scarf she had thrown over her plump shoulders. She said nothing, but with the baby still on her hip, she began helping Morning Dew with the food.

The men arrived casually, as though they happened to be up at three in the morning and in the neighborhood. They joined Morning Dew's uncles and brothers-in-law. Mad Dog yawned cavernously and scratched his crotch. In his drowsiness, Old Squat misjudged the distance between his hollow-cheeked buttocks and the log. He sat harder than he intended, and Swamp Singer chuckled at his look of surprise and chagrin.

Even though the night was hot, Mad New Town had wrapped his cotton blanket tightly around him. The men greeted him politely, but he only grunted in reply. With his blanket hooding his face, he stared into the flames. Abihka, who sat next to him, looked as if he had been up for hours.

"That's a handsome rifle case," he said to Black. Abihka politely delayed asking his young warriors to report on their foray. He would talk of other matters until they had eaten and rested a bit.

"The case is yours to keep, beloved Uncle." Black untied the wrapped thongs and drew out his Hall's breech-loading flintlock. He handed the heavy bag to Abihka.

"It has no seam."

"No, beloved Uncle."

"What kind of rifle case has no seam?"

"One made from the pizzle of a whale."

Abihka, Mad Dog, Swamp Singer, and Old Squat stretched the bag out in front of them. It reached seven feet, from Abihka to Old Squat at the end of the line.

"What creature has such a pizzle?" asked Abihka. From the women's fire came stifled laughter, then silence. They didn't want to miss the answer.

"It's a creature larger than one of the clan sheds. It lives in the ocean, like a fish. I . . ." Black hesitated. "A sailor who hunted them gave it to me." He didn't mention the sailor had given it under duress, while his ship was being plundered.

"It's a wondrous thing," said Abihka.

Dahomey, Mink, Corn Grinder, and another black woman materialized from the darkness.

"Forgive the interruption, Uncles." Dahomey probably never would learn to be as discreet as a Seminole woman. When she wanted to speak to a man, she did. "We were told only Heartless Snake returned. Our sister wants to know if you saw her man, also. He left with Heartless Snake."

"He's gone to the spirit land." Even though Osceola had not led Heartless Snake and his friend on the trail to Mc-Girth's, he felt responsible. "He's been avenged." Osceola nodded to Black, who held up the bloody scalp.

The woman backed away from the fire and into the night

of which she seemed a part. Dahomey looked long and hungrily at Black before leaving to comfort her. From the depths of the hammock came the high, desperate wail of a woman's grief. Wolves joined in the keening.

"I am old," Abihka said. "When I walk, my knees creak like cypress trees in the wind. I shall journey to the spirit land soon."

No one believed that, of course. For years Abihka had threatened to die; but he still paced the youngest men.

"My eyes are becoming feeble, but I have young eyes that can travel while I warm my aching joints at my home fire. Three pairs of our people's best eyes have just returned. They saved the life of one man. They avenged the death of another. This evening we will celebrate their achievement." Abihka gave Osceola one of his penetrating looks that always made Osceola feel the old *tastanagee* was peering into his soul. "Tell us of your trip," he said.

Osceola would have liked to fall onto his bed and into Morning Dew's arms. He would have liked to hunt a dream. But, holding his sleeping daughter, he stood up. He left the description of Heartless Snake's trouble until last. He was pained to have to describe such a humiliating circumstance at all.

Into the fire-lit kitchen yard Osceola's words summoned shimmery scenes of Tampa Bay and its beaches sparkling in the sunlight. In creating his word pictures he left out nothing. His listeners smelled the fish and guava, the mangrove punk and sweat and oysters and the dogs under the table. They heard the waves and the seagulls and the clank of sabers as the soldiers patrolled.

"Chalo Emathla's people are begging at the pale-eyes' walled town." He told this part of the story reluctantly. Chalo Emathla was Morning Dew's uncle. "They're accepting the treaty food. The women, the children, pick through the white men's garbage like rats."

"What conclusions have you drawn, my son?" Abihka asked.

"We must move to the land set aside for us." Osceola expected the angry murmur that followed.

"Does he think we're geese?" Fighting in a Line said in a loud voice. "Does he think we change our homes with the seasons?"

"Why?" Abihka asked.

"The white men's villages are sprouting like toadstools after a heavy rain. Their whiskey, their treachery, are blights spreading along the coasts. If we move to the center of the peninsula, we'll be farther from them.

"I don't believe Sense-Maker Hum-plee when he says the soldiers will protect us from these men," he went on. "But we'll be closer together. We can protect each other better."

Silence followed. Osceola knew his proposal was repugnant to everyone. His voice hardened when he continued.

"We have to keep our warriors from the pale-eyes' settlements. We have to keep them from buying *ueho'mee,* whiskey. Whiskey will destroy our will to fight far more effectively than all of Old Mad Jackson's cannons. I tell you this: If we don't move, we're doomed. Our fires will die. Our children's laughter will be heard no more. Our moccasins will leave no tracks in the sand." Osceola sat down wearily.

He already had decided if the others didn't agree with him, he would pack his own family and go with the few he could convince. He would save as many as he could.

"The young men of two towns brawled while my nephew was away." Mad New Town's voice sounded harsh, stiff from lack of use. "Their minds were addled with whiskey. Bad blood now exists between them. I'll support my nephew's proposal. I'll convince the other members of the Snake clan. The time has come to move."

Dawn was only an hour away when the impromptu council ended and Osceola finally lay down beside Morning Dew. The baby in her womb had grown so large that he cupped his body against her back. She sighed and pressed against him. She stretched her legs along his. They fit together well.

"I've missed you, Old Woman," he murmured into her hair. He lay still for a few moments, breathing in unison with her. "Abihka has asked me to go with the pale-eyes who are determining the limits of our land."

"The ones with the poles, the balls of lead? The ones who think they can measure the earth like cloth?"

"Yes."

"We need you here."

"Abihka wants me to make sure the pale-eyes don't cheat us again."

"White men are unpredictable. You'll be in danger."

"The safest place for the fly is on the hand that would swat it." When he felt her against him and smelled the smoky perfume of her, his anger at the white men melted. It flowed into his love for her and was lost.

"I'll be scouting the whole region," he said. "I'll pick the most beautiful spot to build your new house. We'll raise our children there, far from the white men. We'll be happy."

CHAPTER 15

A driving rain kept Osceola company as he trotted into Abihka's village. A fickle wind pushed him from behind, then swirled around and blew its cold breath in his face. Water flowed down the steeply pitched roofs of the cabins and *chikees* and cascaded from the eaves. Osceola was soaked, but he didn't care. Neither did the children who ran naked in the downpour. They sailed leaf canoes on the unruly creek and splashed in the puddles.

"You are come, *Tastanagee*," they called cheerfully. As they watched him pass, they stood sturdy and brown and glistening. Their short, rain-soaked hair plastered to their heads made them look like so many otters. Osceola loved them all. They were assurance that his people would continue despite every adversity.

Many of the women and most of the girls stood in the rain, too. They laughed and turned their faces into it, tasting its coolness on their tongues. This was November, Falling Leaf month. The rain was too late to save the shriveled crops, but at least it brought moisture to the parched earth and relief from the relentless heat.

For the past two months Osceola had been guiding the white surveyors as they laid out the boundaries of the new reservation. In his absence the open, palm-thatched huts called *chikees* had been built in Abihka's town. Even in the storm men were at work under them, although now the younger ones all were resting at once. They were watching the wind mold the women's wet clothes to their bodies.

Each *chikee* sheltered one or two huge cypress logs being hollowed into canoes. After fires had smoldered on the logs, the shallow layer of charred wood was chopped out. More embers were spread in the cavity and the process repeated. It was slow, tedious work.

When the insides were ready a few old men skilled in such arts shaped the hulls into their graceful lines. The sides of the finished canoes would be about the thickness of a finger joint. Fire and iron and sinew would transform the massive logs into long, delicate shells with curved, overhanging prows. Osceola stopped to watch Mad Dog supervise a crew of teen-aged boys.

"You are come, grandson." Mad Dog ran his arthritic fingers along the gouges made by the axes. He had to speak louder than usual to be heard over the thrumming of the rain. "Not so deep, not so deep, boys. Take pride in what you do. A task easily done gives little satisfaction."

Mad Dog sighed. "The young ones are so impatient. They don't want to exert themselves. They forget the old ways. When I see them working carelessly, I grieve that we lost so many men at the Horseshoe. We old farters must do all the teaching. We're too few to do it properly." Mad Dog flexed his ropy shoulder muscles and coughed.

"The American sense-maker Hum-plee was here." As Mad Dog talked he kept an eagle's eye on the work. "He offered five to ten metal beads for each canoe we build, depending on size."

"Why, Grandfather?"

"Hum-plee may be white, but he isn't stupid." Mad Dog fumbled reflexively for the pipe in the folds of his turban. He realized the rising wind would never allow it to stay lit, and he put it back. "The Americans promised us transportation to the new country. Canoes are cheaper than horses, so he's paying us to build them. Now the young ones are crazy for metal beads. What can they do with them?"

Mad Dog had no word for money, so the words for metal beads served. They were appropriate. People drilled holes in the coins and wore them as jewelry.

"If we travel by canoe, we'll have to leave the cattle, the horses, the pigs." As Osceola spoke he measured the work, feeling the sides with his fingertips.

"Yes," Mad Dog said solemnly. "Cows are especially troublesome in canoes." To attract his apprentices' attention to an uneven section, he rapped the hull with his hatchet handle.

"Hum-plee says when we reach the new country, the pale-eyes will replace our stock. Speaking of that, did you measure all the land, grandson?" Mad Dog was obviously amused by the outlandish notion of measuring dirt and swamp. When he grinned up at Osceola his eyes narrowed and folded into the network of wrinkles around them. He became all nose and chin and lopsided yellow teeth.

"No, Grandfather." Osceola laughed at the memory of the surveyors. "But I had an agreeable time. I watched the white men flounder in the swamps. I listened to them curse the mosquitoes."

"Instead of asking cooperation from the elements, they curse them," Mad Dog said. "They curse the heat. They curse the cold. They curse the wet. They curse the dry. If I were a spirit, I wouldn't like to be so maligned."

"They mark the rivers, prairies, swamps, bays on a leaf as big as the floor of Grandmother's cabin." With his toe Osceola drew a rough map in the sand. He included the nearby Withlacoochee River, the creek that ran through the town and the local hammocks. "They insisted on being quite precise. They wouldn't vary their course the length of a finger, even though it led through morasses."

The surveyors' rituals of plummet and rod and chain, their marks on paper, gave Osceola the uneasy feeling their activity was magic.

"Did you find a good country where we can kindle our fire?"

"The best, Grandfather!" Osceola's smile was sunlight through darkling clouds. "The best!"

As he and Mad Dog ran toward Morning Dew's compound, the wind-driven rain stung them like cold needles. By now the increasing storm had sent most people inside.

Osceola burst happily into Morning Dew's big kitchen arbor and shook like a dog. Morning Dew and her mother, Pipe Smoke, were there. Pipe Smoke was telling a story to Little Warrior and a few of her small cousins. If the storm had become a nuisance, its curtain of rain also provided privacy. This homecoming didn't have to be as formal as most.

Osceola threw Little Warrior, screaming with laughter, into the air. Then he tossed the other girls in turn. He threw convention to the wind and hugged Morning Dew. His arms barely reached around her now that her time was close. Laughing, she held the *sofkee* ladle out so it wouldn't drip on him while he embraced her.

Mad Dog wiped the water from his skinny arms and his hard little burl of a stomach. A drop dangled from the promontory of his nose. He wrung out the ends of his breechclout and warmed his hands at the fire. He craved the warm aroma of tobacco smoke in his mouth, but the wind made that impossible. He helped himself to the watery *sofkee* instead.

"You are come, Old Man." Morning Dew handed Osceola a ladleful of *sofkee*. Even though the baby was due soon, she moved as gracefully as a flower bending in a gentle wind. A calm radiated outward from her. The drawstring of her flowered calico skirt rode up over the bulge of her belly, hitching the hem several inches from the *chikee*'s muddy floor.

The fire under the kettle fluttered and almost went out. The logs hissed as drops fell from new leaks in the roof. Wind was clawing at the thatch. More water splashed in from the rain pouring in a solid sheet from the low eaves. Pipe Smoke grunted as she crouched and spread her skirts to protect Grandfather Fire from the storm.

When Pipe Smoke squatted she looked like a billowy tent folding in on itself. Her soft, sprawling breasts lolled on her stomach, which in turn settled comfortably onto her broad thighs. From her position near the ground, she stared out. Because Pipe Smoke was a large woman, she had developed the habit of considering a situation carefully before doing anything that required effort. The habit had earned her a reputation as shrewd and imperturbable.

"Hutalee huyana, wind passing." She said it matter-of-factly.

As though to confirm her observation, Abihka's prize possession, a five-gallon copper whiskey measure, clattered by.

"It's too late in the season for hurricanes," Mad Dog said.

"Hutalee huyana!" Mink burst into the shelter as though ejected by the storm. To keep her wet skirt from tripping her, she had tied it high up on her long legs. "The river is rising fast."

Osceola held on to an overhead beam and leaned out to survey the situation. Fascinated by the storm, Little Warrior wrapped her arms around his leg and looked, too. The rain formed a shifting wall that hid Fighting in a Line's cluster of new cabins across the creek. She and Mad New Town's followers had begun another settlement there. They had built within sight but out of hearing of Morning Dew's compound, thus restoring relative tranquility to Osceola's household.

The wind had stripped the needles from the pine trees. The cabbage palms bent almost to the ground. Fronds and cypress bark shingles ripped loose from the roofs and whirled into the torrent. The blurred forms of people heading for higher ground slanted into the wind.

A dog blew along the ground in an eddy of clothing and cooking utensils. Her howls couldn't be heard over the wind. When Little Warrior started out into the storm to save her, Osceola scooped her up.

"Link arms." He had to shout to be heard over the screaming gale. He carried Little Warrior in one arm and hooked his other elbow through Morning Dew's. She in turn formed a chain with her oldest niece and Mink. Pipe Smoke hung, like an anchor, on the end. She wrapped her stout, unoccupied arm around Little Warrior's smallest cousin's waist. The child dangled at her grandmother's side like a saddlebag, but this was not a time for niceties. Mad Dog helped the last child onto Pipe Smoke's back, where she clung to her grandmother's neck.

"Hold on, Grandfather," Morning Dew called to Mad Dog.

"I must find Old Woman." Mad Dog lowered his head and pushed out into the storm toward the overflowing creek and Fighting in a Line's compound.

"Grandfather, come back!" Little Warrior screamed.

They all watched helplessly as the wind knocked the old man down and rolled him over. The jagged broken end of a flying branch narrowly missed his head. On hands and knees, Mad Dog crawled into the maelstrom and disappeared.

Leaning into the rain, Osceola, Morning Dew, and the others moved out of the shelter of the *chikee*. The roof followed them. Rain pelted them like cold gravel. Osceola oriented by counting his footsteps and searching for landmarks in a village that had become alien and malevolent. Trees were uprooted or broken or distorted by the wind. The familiar pattern of cabins and kitchen *chikees* was jumbled. Propelled by the wind, kettles and skillets, digging sticks, pestles, and branches became deadly missiles.

Little Warrior wrapped her arms around her father's neck and pressed her face into his chest. Osceola held Morning Dew as close as he could, to shield her from the debris spinning past. When he reached a tree or corner post he clung to it, to rest and check his bearings. The people strung out behind him stumbled constantly, dragging him back. The music of the hurricane resonated in his skull.

When he reached a big oak in the center of the hammock, Osceola helped the women and children up into the broad hollow where the tree's massive lower limbs branched. The women tore the ruffles off their skirts, then they tore the skirts. They knotted the strips together and began lashing the children to the limbs.

Morning Dew saw Osceola start back toward the village. Cramps began to knot just below her stomach. The baby was coming. "Come back, Old Man." She hung on to a branch and screamed into the wind.

"I have to find my family." Osceola cupped his hands around his mouth and shouted up at her.

"Please come back." Morning Dew hadn't cried since she was a child. She had never begged for anything; but she was crying and begging now. "Come back. Stay with me."

The rain washed the tears from her face. Osceola could

barely see her, much less hear her. Unaware that her time had come, he lifted a hand in farewell and leaned into the wind. Morning Dew slid down the rough wet wood until she was crouched with her back resting against it. Wide-eyed, Little Warrior reached out and touched her arm, to comfort herself and her mother.

The storm had arrived late, and the baby had arrived early. The cramping intensified. Morning Dew shivered with the cold. Mink crawled to her and put her arms around her. The limb they leaned against was as big around as a tobacco tierce, and still it vibrated.

Morning Dew lifted her face to the rain that penetrated the thrashing leaves of the oak's canopy. There would be no comfortable lying-in in the new baby house her uncles had built for her. Morning Dew closed her eyes and felt the child begin its slow journey toward a midday darkness, a hurricane, and a cradle of waterlogged leaves in the crotch of a tree.

Osceola pulled himself along, holding on to thrashing trees and shifting piles of wreckage. He had to wade the last hundred feet to the remains of his grandmother's compound. Water swirled around his knees as he struggled up the slight incline from the creek to the two-story structure that had been Fighting in a Line's pride.

She had directed her slaves to build it in the old style. It had a storehouse on the first floor and a cool, open room above where elders visited the taciturn Mad New Town. It reminded Fighting in a Line of Talasee in the north country and of her brother's exalted position there. It recalled a place and time buffed to a satiny glow by memory.

The building was the grandest in Abihka's town and in the outlying camps. If that annoyed Abihka, it hadn't stopped him and the other men from dropping by frequently. Through the long autumn afternoons the feathers in their turbans could be seen nodding up there as the men smoked and surveyed their domain.

Osceola assumed his family had sought shelter on higher ground but he found Fighting in a Line and Mad Dog frantically clawing at the ruins of the collapsed storehouse.

"Leave it, Grandmother." As he slogged toward them he waved them toward the hammock and the big oaks.

Then he saw Fighting in a Line's hands. They were red with blood that flowed faster than the rain could wash it away. She had torn her nails to the quick. Osceola saw the look on her face. He splashed through the water and grabbed the beam she and Mad Dog were struggling to lift.

"Who is it?"

"Your uncle." Mad Dog's hands were bloody, too.

Osceola saw Mad New Town's arm under the rubble. With Mad Dog and Fighting in a Line, he strained to lift the heavy pine beam. It took all his strength to raise it slowly and shove it out of the way. The smaller beams and log flooring that lay on top of it rattled off into the wind. A ragged splinter raked Osceola's arm, but he hardly noticed. The three of them tore at the logs and thatch as the water rose around their ankles.

When he had cleared enough, Osceola saw the two-foot-thick center beam that had supported the second floor. It lay across his uncle's chest and pinned him to the ground. Mad New Town's lips were blue, and one eye was swollen shut. A gash had laid open his head from his hairline to his chin. He struggled to breathe. The beam rested on another log, which kept it from crushing him but didn't allow him to move.

Osceola wedged a pole under the beam. He and his grandmother and stepgrandfather threw themselves across it to lever the beam up. The lever snapped with a loud crack that sprained one of Osceola's wrists and broke the other one.

The muddy water advanced until it lapped around Mad New Town's face. Fighting in a Line began to wail as she dug furiously at the slippery planks and barbed palmetto ribs. Osceola looked desperately around for help, but everyone had fled. Tears mingled unheeded with the rain on his face. He lifted his uncle's head, to raise it above the water, but he knew he was only delaying the inevitable. Mad New Town began to cough, then choke as water washed into his mouth.

"I can find help to move the beam," Osceola shouted over the storm. "We can dam the water."

"We cannot, beloved grandson," Mad Dog shouted.

"He can breathe through my pipe stem." Osceola fumbled for his pipe, but it was gone. He tried to breathe into Mad

New Town's mouth, but the water rose too fast. He choked and gagged.

"We can send him on his journey with our prayers." Mad Dog pulled gently at Osceola's shoulder. He rocked back on his heels. He placed a hand on Mad New Town's chest and began his death chant. It blended with Fighting in a Line's howls of grief and with the shrill of the wind. Fighting in a Line had found a saw palmetto rib and was using its sharp serrations to tear the skin on her arms and wrinkled chest.

"The heavens are bidding you farewell, Uncle." Osceola supported Man New Town's head as high as he could. "But they do not weep nearly so much as I will."

Mad New Town couldn't speak. He would have drowned that much sooner. He said his farewells silently. Now that he was leaving the mortal world, life returned to his eyes. They spoke more than he had in years.

They told Osceola that he welcomed death. That his spirit would be close if Osceola ever needed him. Slowly the flood rose until it covered Mad New Town's face. Kneeling in the muddy water, Osceola watched his beloved uncle leave on his long, lonely journey to the world of shades.

CHAPTER 16

The hurricane passed as abruptly as it had arrived. It left a stunned, suspended silence. People moved quietly into the stillness, as though afraid of arousing the elements again. They began to recover what they could of their homes.

Whenever Osceola passed the wreckage of Mad New Town's aerie and saw his uncle sitting in front of it, he felt a sudden, brief ache in his chest. Mad New Town seemed to be waiting for him to pass and share a pipe. Peeping, Fighting in a Line, and Mad New Town's widow had braided his scalplock and combed his bangs. They had arranged his turban and painted his cold, stiff face red. They had washed what they could find of his best clothes and had dressed him. They bent his legs into a sitting position and wrapped a sodden blanket around his shoulders. They propped him up among what they could find of his belongings.

For a day Mad New Town's corpse sat there, contemplating the uncertainties of this world and the possibilities of the next. Osceola kept him company for an hour or two, smoking and holding silent council. He told his uncle about the death of his son, stillborn into the wet leaves of the oak. He told about Morning Dew's grief and his own.

Even though our son is not the son of your sister, or your sister's daughter, care for him in the spirit land, Uncle. Osceola stood, feeling as old and weary as his uncle had looked in his last years. Then he went back to work.

People shoveled at the thick, evil-smelling mud the floodwaters had deposited over the village. Children scooped it up with wooden buckets or cabbage palm boots, conch shells, or the flat paddles their mothers used to wash clothes. The women and girls searched for unbroken utensils. They sorted through the heaps of soaked clothing and bedding. From the outlying settlements came the crack of gunfire and the clang of iron hatchet heads against kettles. The men were frightening off the spirits of the hurricane's victims.

Mink searched feverishly through the muddy jumble scattered among the remains of her mother's cabins. In spite of her hurry she was careful not to poke her hand into dark crevices. Snakes flooded out of their holes had sought refuge in the village. What had been a disaster for the humans had been windfall for Mink's pet king snake. A rattlesnake's tail dangled from his unhinged jaws, giving him the look of a two-tailed oddity. Mink reached out and stroked the king's cool, smooth scales. If a snake could purr, he would have.

Mink never had had many possessions. Now those few were destroyed or missing. As she dug through the smashed remnants she began to cry, but not for her loss. She cried because she could find nothing to leave as a present to accompany the spirit of Morning Dew's dead son.

"Come, daughter," Dahomey called softly. Black stopped clearing the debris and joined her.

"I have nothing to give the baby." Mink stood reluctantly and clambered over the fallen poles and thatch.

"Give him your good thoughts." Dahomey put an arm around her daughter's thin shoulders. She noticed that the top of Mink's mane, like a mass of finely crimped black wire, reached Dahomey's chin now, although most of the child's height was legs. "His soul is on the way to the ancestral world."

"He's so young to make the journey alone, among ghosts."

"Talasee *Tastanagee*'s uncle will watch over him," Dahomey said. "Besides, dying is not so different from sleeping. We all die a little each night. In dreams our souls fly out of our bodies. They experience the life beyond this one, just as Morning Dew's baby will."

"Help me pick up the pieces of this pot, girl," said Black. "It's dead. Its spirit's free to travel with the baby."

The three of them put the pottery shards into a bandana and knotted the corners to form a sack. Then they splashed through the mud-covered ruin of the landscape. Dark clouds veiled a sallow sun. What once had been a short, easy trip along the trail to Abihka's town was now fraught with obstacles. Splintered and uprooted trees, tangled in vines, lay across the path. Snakes slithered away as they approached.

At twilight the long procession of mourners wound through the center of Abihka's town, and people left their salvage work to join it. It would be dark when they returned, and many carried sticks of lighter pine to use as torches. As they fell in line with the others, the women began to sob and wail. Shared, their grief was more intense, yet easier to bear.

Mad New Town was given the place of honor at the head of the cortege. Abihka, Mad Dog, and the elders who had shared countless pipes with him now carried the board that held his body. Osceola walked beside him and held him in a sitting position.

Mad New Town's widow, Peeping, and Fighting in a Line followed. Their uncombed hair hung loose and tangled. Their clothing was torn and disheveled in mourning. Mad New

Town's wife had never reconciled herself to life in this new land, among people of a different fire. She had been even more reclusive than her husband. She had already announced she was returning to her family in the north country. Peeping and her daughter and some of Mad New Town's followers were going with her.

Surrounded by the women of her family and clan, Morning Dew walked behind Mad New Town's retinue. She carried her dead son wrapped in a blanket. Little Warrior rode on Mink's slender hip. Behind them walked the wailing mother of a drowned child and the two widows and three children of a warrior pierced by the sharp end of a wind-driven tree limb.

The three tombs, rectangular log boxes about three feet high, were all oriented from east to west. They looked peaceful under the protective arms of the huge live oak. The gray tatters of moss hung like shrouds from the branches. The men carried the bodies around the tombs three times while Abihka chanted under his breath. As they came to the beginning of each circle, they paused.

"Yah!" Abihka barked the word in a low tone. When he raised the pitch and cried, "Yo!" the mourners sang it with him. They sang, "He!" with him, then they lowered their voices and finished with "Wah."

Osceola and Mad Dog lifted Mad New Town from the board. Holding him aloft, they straddled the low walls of the log crypt. Inside his shirt-sleeve Mad New Town's arm was as thin and stiff as the rib of a palm frond. Osceola tried to lower his uncle into the hole dug in the center of the crypt and lined with cypress bark. The corpse's stiffened limbs made the task awkward. Osceola marveled that death could turn such a once agile man into a clumsy object.

When Mad New Town was sitting in the hole, Osceola gently brushed off the bits of bark that had fallen onto his head. He straightened his uncle's turban. Then he positioned a cane frame over the opening and piled clay on it.

He laid Mad New Town's Hall carbine with the tip-up breech inside the log crypt and on top of the grave. He added his uncle's gun pouch, his pick, his hammer, and his old Spanish dagger with the ebony handle and Damascus blade.

People passed him gifts of food and tobacco to lay next to the rifle, but they were careful not to touch him. They didn't want to risk being contaminated even by someone who had touched the grave's soil.

When Osceola finished, the men laid logs on top of the tomb. Mad New Town's clan brothers fired their fusils at each corner to send his spirit on its way. Others did the same for their dead relatives. When the noise faded, Abihka chanted his farewell. Then he blew through his medicine tube into a gourd of powdered ginseng and sprinkled it on his clothes. He used the powder to purify each person who had touched the dead.

Morning Dew carried her baby to the tree where she had borne him. Little Warrior followed solemnly. Morning Dew and Mink wedged the tiny body, blanket and all, high into a hollow in the trunk. Morning Dew pushed a small canvas hammock after the body. When others had left small gifts, Morning Dew, Dahomey, and Mink closed the opening with clay. To bury a child any other way would invite certain disaster. They had had more than enough disaster.

For the next four days Morning Dew, Mink, and Dahomey came to the tree each day at dawn to mourn. Several times each day Little Warrior helped her mother replenish the small fire at the baby's grave. Each day, as was the custom of their people, Mink and Dahomey added more bits of broken utensils to the expanding pattern in front of the oak.

Each day, after Fighting in a Line had grieved at her brother's grave she wandered, as if accidentally, by the oak. She knelt next to Morning Dew, bent over until her tangled hair touched the ground, and wept with her.

Osceola lounged gratefully in the dugout while Alligator poled. He would never complain about his broken wrist. He had wrapped it tightly with a leather band to brace it. But Alligator knew the wrist must hurt after days of pushing against the river's sluggish current. He had left his own canoes in the charge of his first wife's two young brothers and had insisted on taking over for a while. Now he rode with Osceola, Morning Dew, Mink, and Little Warrior ahead of the fleet that stretched for miles behind them.

Osceola watched the dark, enigmatic jungle glide by as the Oklawaha River wound deeper into the heart of the peninsula. He felt as light as one of the snowy egrets soaring past the towering magnolia and beech. Bottle-shaped cypress with their silver drapery of moss rose like columns from the black water. They supported the vaulting mosaic of greens and golds and blues overhead. The leafy corridor echoed with the plaintive calls of birds and the croaks of frogs and alligators. *Oklawaha* meant "Bad Water," but Osceola didn't consider it so.

"Imagine my problem," Alligator said. "Out of the goodness of my heart—"

"To satisfy Old Baldy," Osceola reminded him.

"Perhaps to humor Baldy a little, I took a second wife. Now they both entertain the Red Man the same time each month. I have extra mouths to feed. Still Baldy must languish. Still I must wander to the *sofkee* kettles of my clan brothers because *both* my women have withdrawn to their private hut to loaf for a week at a time. I can hear them giggling there." Alligator looked deeply aggrieved.

Morning Dew laughed so hard she almost tumbled off the sack of *koontee* roots and into the water. She laughed as much for the pleasure of laughing as at Alligator's predicament. It was the first laughter Osceola had heard from her since the death of their son. It was the sweetest music imaginable.

"Often when women live together their cycles occur in rhythm," she said when she'd calmed.

To make room for Alligator, Mink perched among the sacks of United States government seed corn piled in the center of the boat. She sat with her ankles crossed and her knees spread. Her king snake lay coiled in the hammock formed by her skirt stretched across her lean thighs. Little Warrior sat next to her and stroked the snake.

"Are we almost there?" The rich hues of the foliage and the golden flecks of sunlight were reflected in Mink's sea-green eyes.

"Yes." Osceola felt as though he were being carried toward peace and paradise. The previous weeks had been hectic. Abihka had depended heavily on him in preparing for this move. It was no simple matter to uproot hundreds of people.

Osceola had spent most of his time reassuring families. He had explained the route and suggested what to take and what to leave. He had settled disputes and problems and acquired tools and seed to replace what had been lost in the hurricane. He had made several trips to Fort Brooke for the supplies promised by agent Humphrey.

Wococoi Clark and his buxom bride had come to bid them good-bye. He had brought more gifts, this time from the spoils of a shipwreck whose barrels and crates had washed up after the hurricane. "I figure 'tis only fitting the storm should give you back something of what it took," he had said. And he had given Osceola a lovely Spanish miquelet-lock fowling piece that obviously had *not* washed ashore.

"You are more of us than of the pale-eyes." Fighting in a Line had tried to persuade Wococoi to come with them. "Your heart hears our hearts."

"I cannot leave the Big Water, not even for you, me wanton brim." The hour had been early, and Wococoi hadn't had time to drink enough to become bumptious. With a furry forearm he pretended to wipe the sweat from his eyes and erased the tears. "If I leave the sea, my soul will shrivel and die. I'll think on you every day, though."

He and his woman had stood on the riverbank and waved for hours while family after family collected stray puppies and piglets and children and settled themselves among the bundles of goods in the dugouts. They waved until the last of the hundred canoes were out of sight around a bend in the river. By now the two of them must have arrived at Charlotte Bay where the Caloosahatchee River emptied into the gulf. They must be starting a new life among the Spanish and Seminole fishermen of Captain Bunce's colony.

"Do you think Wococoi will fare well among the fisherfolk? I hear many perverse men live there." Morning Dew's question startled Osceola. As a rule not much surprised him, but Morning Dew did it regularly when she divined his thoughts.

"Wococoi knows how to spy the cloven foot." Without thinking about it, Osceola used one of Wococoi's favorite phrases.

"What does that mean?" asked Little Warrior.

"It means he can recognize a perverse man, even if he's in disguise."

When Alligator pushed the dugout into a smaller branch where the trees weren't as dense, sunlight splashed over them. After an hour the canoe skimmed onto a vast, sapphire-colored spring glinting with sparks of light. Little Warrior hung over the gunwale, hypnotized by the wonders below.

They floated over the center of the spring, over silent mountains and canyons and ornate sculptures in limestone. Fifty feet below them they could see every detail of the darting, iridescent fish and the crimson-and-purple shells. Shoals of silver shiners shifted and veered in unison, like tiny beams of light from a single source. They saw plumes of algae waving in the turbulence boiling up from underground. Facing into the strong current, stout, bewhiskered, blue-black channel cats hovered in the underwater forest.

"They say the grass is the hair of the beautiful daughter of Okihumpkee *miko*," Osceola murmured. "Her lover was a Yemasee, one of her people's enemies. They say she drowned herself here when her father killed him."

"I've heard of this place," Morning Dew whispered. "I've heard of this place all my life."

"Will we live here, Father?" Even Little Warrior was subdued by the magic of the spring.

"We'll live near here." Osceola leaned over so only Morning Dew could hear his voice, soft in her ear. "May this place bring as much peace to your soul as you do to mine."

CHAPTER 17

Morning Dew carried Little Warrior on her hip while with one hand she upended short sections of logs and split them into kindling with a hatchet. Little Warrior was almost three and perfectly capable of walking. That was the problem. Little Warrior had a talent for mischief.

She couldn't sit still long, either. She grew fractious, and Morning Dew let her slide to the ground. The child gathered the pieces of kindling and began building cabins with them. She chanted her own unending medicine song while she worked.

"My uncle visited last night." Osceola sat on one of the logs projecting from the fire and smoked the first pipe of the day with Mad Dog.

"What was the dream about?" Mad Dog asked.

"The Horseshoe."

"Uh." Mad Dog grunted. The Horseshoe was where many of his own dreams took him.

Osceola's dream hadn't begun at the Horseshoe, however, but on the trail south after the battle. Once again Mad New Town stood over the eleven-year-old child Cricket, who pretended to be asleep in the cold, damp leaves. Once again Mad New Town took off the stained, blue wool army jacket. Once again he crouched and draped it over the boy. He draped it over the boy. He draped it over the boy.

Over and over Osceola had sensed Mad New Town's presence bending closer, felt the scratchy wool drift around him. Felt its weight settle onto him. Over and over he smelled the mildew and white man's stale sweat mixed with his great-uncle's aroma in the cloth.

The scene had blurred and shifted suddenly, as it often did

in dreams. The dark cold forest became a green field, full of sunlight and flowers, birds and busy summer insects. Skulls were scattered like pale, smooth melons in the lush grass. This was the battlefield at the bend in the Talapoosa River called the Horseshoe.

Pieces of another blue army jacket had been matted into lumps by sun and rain. Cricket had covered a shivering boy with it months earlier as they lay among the hundreds of dead and dying men. The boy had been dying, too, with his vitals exposed by a bayonet and glistening in the light of the setting sun.

"I returned to the Horseshoe to bury a boy's bones," Osceola said. "I think he wasn't old enough to be an ordinary warrior."

"Was he a friend or a clan brother?"

"I didn't know his name, but I had promised to bury him. I peeled away the wool cloth of a blue jacket from his bones. I began stacking the arm bones, the leg bones, the ribs, like firewood in my arms. I counted all the finger bones, the toe bones, so that none were missing. I balanced the skull on top."

"Did you do that in this world or in the dream world?" Mad Dog and Morning Dew were both paying close attention. Mad New Town's spirit had delivered a message, and they had to decipher it.

"Both. Before we all came south, I returned to the Horseshoe. I buried the bones. But in the dream the bones kept multiplying. The stack reached past my eyes. I was stumbling over heaps of them. Their weight made my arms ache, but I knew I had to bury them all." Sitting by the fire with the morning sun warm on his chest, Osceola shivered, "Too many bones, Grandfather."

Mad Dog stared into the flames as he considered the dream. "What do you think it means?" he asked finally. It was always better if the dream hunter found his own answers.

"I think he was telling me to cooperate with the white men, to avoid war. I think the bones mean that fighting them now will mean death for us all."

"Then let us fight. Let us die." Morning Dew startled them. She was so angry she almost raised her voice. "Women from Mad Partridge's town left the reservation," she said. "They went to the coast to collect salt. White men caught them. On the trail back they drove the women so hard one of them delivered her baby early. The mother died. The child died. That's the story the women tell while they grind corn."

"Sense-Maker Hum-plee says the soldiers will protect us from perverse men," said Mad Dog mildly.

"The soldiers will protect us like the alligator protects the turtles who hatch in her nest," Morning Dew hissed.

"*Shta,* beloved. Calm yourself." Osceola caught Morning Dew's skirt and pulled her down beside him. Mad Dog rose and went off diplomatically to find his friends.

"Think of the peace we have here." Osceola found Morning Dew's hand on the log under her full skirt and covered it with his own. He could feel her hand still stubbornly gripping the hatchet.

In his heart he was as angry as she was, and he knew she knew it. When the time for war came Osceola would welcome it. The difficulty wasn't in fighting, but in waiting to fight. Mad New Town knew that. That was why his spirit sent the dream.

"There have always been perverse men. We can't let them ruin our lives."

"In the past we fought our enemies."

"Red men fight short wars," Osceola said patiently. "When they earn war honors, when they avenge their dead or the weather turns cold, they go home. White men's wars are long. They're ruinous. White men fight until they've destroyed their enemies, until they've extinguished the fire of an entire nation."

"How long must we suffer humiliation?"

"Until the new generation of warriors is old enough to replace those who died at the Horseshoe. Abihka asked me to go with him to the new soldier town. We'll hold council with Sense-Maker Hum-plee. He's an honest man. He'll punish the perverse ones."

Morning Dew sat for a long while without speaking.

"If he doesn't satisfy our requests, we'll send you on the warpath with your hatchet." Osceola squeezed Morning Dew's hand tighter around the hatchet handle.

Helpless to resist him, she smiled sadly. "Forgive me, beloved. I know it's harder for you than for me. I haven't your strength."

She stood, buried the hatchet blade in the log, and began to grind corn. The sound of her oak pestle blended with the others as the women established the morning rhythm. Puppies growled and children laughed. Fighting in a Line's pigs grunted as they rooted for acorns. The birds' clamor was almost deafening. Osceola sat still, welcoming the return of the usual tranquillity.

His new settlement was about fifteen miles south of the prairie called Latchua, the Great Bottomless Jug. For a hundred years Seminole cattle had grazed the prairie, although from time to time the hole in the limestone bedrock became plugged. Then the Great Bottomless Jug filled with water and turned into a lake.

It had drained again only recently. Once more cattle and deer and horses grazed it, although now they belonged to white settlers. The Great Bottomless Jug lay outside the boundaries of the reservation. Osceola's town was situated as close to it as possible, though, and only three miles from the beautiful crystal spring. This was rich country of rolling hills, savannas, pine forests, and hardwood hammocks.

The village wasn't big. It hardly covered as much area as the ceremonial ground of Mad Partridge's town five miles away. When Abihka's people reached the new country, eight families chose to follow Osceola and Morning Dew. They were mostly young families, headed by *tasikayalgee,* ordinary warriors.

They called Osceola *Talasee Tastanagee* now. He was twenty-four, but they considered him an elder, a man of vast experience and skill. Maybe I am getting old, he thought. I can see how easily impressed they are. I can see how the stories don't quite match the events they describe.

The small settlement had a vigorous, insouciant air about it. It differed from the older communities with their ancient rivalries and prejudices between Maskokee and Mikasukee. Like Osceola and Morning Dew, several of the couples were mixed, Red Stick and Mikasukee.

A year and a half ago they all had stood under the mammoth oaks, the laurels, and the bays and decided where they would build. They had raised their cabins, laboriously riving planks and lashing them to the frames with strips of oak. They had plastered the walls with mud and roofed them with cypress bark or cabbage palm thatch.

The ridgepoles were twelve feet high, and the roofs sloped steeply so the heavy summer rains would run off. To hold the thatch in place, they lashed short cypress saplings in pairs scissored over the ridgepoles.

As soon as the cabins were finished, the lizards, crickets, mice, and tree frogs moved into the thatch. Spiders began spinning their webs in the steep triangle under each ridgepole. The women stowed their tools and fishing poles in the rafters. They hung their everyday clothes on pegs and spread deer hides on the dirt floors between the palmetto frond beds. They suspended blankets from the rafters to suggest privacy.

In those early days Osceola delivered a bundle of sticks to each man, just as his great-uncle had done. The sticks represented the size and number of logs each household must deliver to the site of the village square. When all the materials were assembled, the men fitted the clan sheds together perfectly.

They leveled the playing field and brought baskets of clean river sand for its surface. At night they gathered in the square. Surrounded by the growing frames of the clan sheds, they danced and feasted, told stories and sang the old songs.

Abihka's town was an hours' brisk walk to the south. Between the two was the small black settlement where Dahomey and Mink and Aury's Black lived. Feet and hooves were already molding the trails to the springs and the other settlements into comfortable, shallow troughs just wide enough for a horse to pass.

When the grapevines and hemp, the wax myrtle bushes and tough palmettos, had been cleared and burned, the men found the old corn mounds of previous inhabitants. In honor of Osceola, they would have called the town Talasee anyway, but now the name Old Fields was doubly significant.

On calm, leisurely mornings like these, Osceola felt as though he had lived here forever. He crushed a wax myrtle leaf in his fingers and sniffed the fragrance. It reminded him of the early days, when the men's axes and hoes had released this incense. They had found fruit trees, too, ancient plum trees and the sweet-sour oranges planted by those long-dead residents.

Mink stepped over the low ridge of sand formed by Morning Dew's daily sweeping. On her head she carried a basket of corn from Dahomey's fields, a gift for Morning Dew. On her back bumped a large gourd. Before she went home she would fill it at the rock-lined spring near Morning Dew's camp. Everyone believed the spring had curative powers.

"I am come," Mink said.

"Just in time for a game, sister." Morning Dew bounced her leather ball off the back of Osceola's head. "Here's our goalpost."

Osceola grabbed for her ankle, but she feinted and dodged. Mink recovered the ball and threw it against Osceola's back. He whirled and chased her, giving Morning Dew a chance to score on him again. Little Warrior shrieked with laughter and got in everybody's way. The other children lined up with their toes against the yard's sand ridge and watched.

Mad Dog, Swamp Singer, and Old Squat paused to watch, too. Mad Dog soberly scratched his crotch and jiggled his rumpled scrotum into a more comfortable position under his long shirt, although how it could have felt confined in such a baggy breechclout was a mystery.

"What's that? What're they doing?" Old Squat had lost his front teeth, and his nose and chin were turning in toward each other, as though squaring off. He was rangy and wrinkled, all knobs and knuckles. He was becoming stoop-shouldered from addressing the frayed hem of his long shirt, which he held up in front of him. He'd been talking to his shirt a lot lately. Old Squat had begun to take dream trips while he was awake. Mad Dog caught Osceola's eye and gave a brief, despairing look. Then the three friends resumed their morning stroll.

"I saw your woman castrating her pigs yesterday, brother," said Swamp Singer. "Pinch. Zip. Then all the fun's gone from their lives. You'd best sleep lightly. She might decide to alter you." Swamp Singer chortled. With his hands clasping the front of his breechclout he gave a little hop.

The old men's walk ended as always in the town square. They spread their deerskins in the usual place under a magnolia whose immensity dwarfed them. The magnolia's enormous, waxy white blossoms perfumed the entire village. The old men ladled out the morning *sofkee*. They lit their pipes, then settled back to enjoy the day.

As the sun made its leisurely progress across the sky, people would stop to sit with them. They would ask their advice or their help in mediating disputes. Or they would just relate a bit of gossip or sit and smoke and not say anything at all.

The children came, too. They were encouraged by the fact that the old Panthers were not like the men who noticed nothing below their own belts. The children brought broken bows to be fixed or skinned shins to be treated. Sometimes they asked for a story or a charm for insect bites. And they always brought food or tobacco in payment.

While Morning Dew worked, Osceola melted lead in an iron skillet and poured it into his bullet mold. Tomorrow he would hunt. From Morning Dew's yard, through the open sides of the east clan bed, Osceola could see the old men entertaining their continual stream of visitors. He could hear Mink imitating the mockingbirds who guarded the spring.

Little Warrior was busy chasing the chickens around the yard when she stubbed her toe on a root and fell sprawling. Morning Dew picked her up and wiped away the tears. She sat next to Osceola and held Little Warrior on her lap so she could inspect the damaged toe. As she bent over, the wisps of hair that always came loose from her bun reminded Osceola of the glossy black down of an ibis chick. Like waves beating on a shore, love followed lust and was succeeded by an overwhelming tenderness.

As Osceola studied his woman and his daughter, the uneasiness caused by his dream of the Horseshoe faded. He marveled that the Breath Maker had created such beautiful creatures to share life with him. He realized he was far happier than he had thought he could be.

CHAPTER 18

Agent Gad Humphreys's temporary office was in a shed shingled with packing crate lumber. It was almost too small to contain Governor William DuVal and Agent Humphreys, much less six Seminole, the army interpreter, and Aury's Black, whose plumes brushed the ceiling. The Seminole stirred the hot, sluggish air with fans made of turkey wings. Sweat had stained large dark patches on the white men's clothes. Their biting odor made Osceola's nostrils twitch.

"All this could be averted if you people would move west, join the rest of the Creeks on the lands across the Mississippi." Governor DuVal paced restlessly. There was no trace of his gnomish good humor.

Aury's Black impassively translated DuVal's words sotto voce for Osceola, Alligator, Abihka, and Chalo Emathla. Chalo Emathla was the source of DuVal's irritation, but not the source of the problem. He was caught in the meshes of the slavers' usual schemes.

Chalo Emathla was almost sixty years old, but erect as a cypress. His full lips and protruding lower jaw gave him the look of a pugnacious grouper; but his small eyes were sad and gentle. The faded blue wool uniform jacket strained across his barrel chest. Dark blue stripes marked where the officer's braid had come off the tunic.

"We armed ourselves because we were warned the perverse ones were bringing savage dogs to track our black people," he said in a quiet voice. "The perverse ones told the white settlers we were preparing to go on the war trail when we only intended to defend ourselves. The settlers complained to your war leaders. The soldiers came. They took our guns. They left us helpless. The next day the perverse ones raided our settlements. They laughed while they took our black people away. Our black people are like our children. We weep for them."

"We'll try to get them back for you." DuVal charged from one side of the shed to the other, like a mouse in a cage. Osceola wondered if white men often held their councils while in motion.

"Agent Humphreys will fill out the forms to request indemnity from Congress, to pay you for your loss." DuVal didn't speak more slowly for the interpreters, only more loudly. He ignored the fact that Chalo Emathla didn't want money. He wanted his people back. While Black struggled to explain the concept of filling out forms, Governor DuVal turned his wrath on Gad Humphreys.

"This garrison is here to protect them from that scum."

"This garrison has all it can do to build shelter in time for winter." Humphreys gestured to the large penciled sketch nailed to the rough wall behind his desk. The drawing of the proposed Indian agency hung within a border of handbills advertising for runaway slaves. They were already yellowing and curling in the heat.

Gad Humphreys's plans for the agency were elaborate and ambitious, but the funding was not. With appropriations for window glass, bricks, lime, and floor planking refused, the men were improvising. Through the open doorway Osceola could hear the steady clamor of their axes and saws and froes.

"These people are helpless before the criminal element." William DuVal stalked his battered slouch hat hanging on a peg by the door.

"They don't even have a word for criminal, Billy. Of course they're helpless," said Humphreys.

DuVal whirled in a rage, while even Chalo Emathla looked on in somber amusement. DuVal ignored the fact that Black continued a running translation of his tirade.

"Don't tell *me* what they have words for. *I* have spent the last four months slogging up to my arse through this four-million-acre bog they call a reservation." To his credit, William DuVal had made the effort to inspect his charges' new land, and he had found it wanting. He had suffered from heat, mosquitoes, dysentery, fever, and guilt. "*I* have seen them starving while you skipped home to New York."

"The sickly season—"

"You left without notifying me! I was sending dispatches to President Adams—'Agent Humphreys had been difficult to contact in recent months.' You made me look the fool." DuVal jammed the floppy felt hat over his generous, jutting ears.

"And another thing," he said. "The president is not pleased with the way you always take the Indians' part. You're here to carry out your government's policy, not jig to the tune of red malcontents." When DuVal's conscience nagged him, he outshouted it.

Osceola pictured this portly little man facing down the fearsome Neamathla and his warriors in his own village. Mad, Osceola thought with amused admiration. He deserves to be named Mad Billy.

The air in the shed seemed to be sucked after DuVal in a vortex as he left. For several beats everyone was quiet. Then Chalo Emathla, his sense-maker, his second-in-command, and the army interpreter silently filed outside, into the glaring sunlight and the noise.

Gad Humphreys looked up from his search for the elusive indemnity forms. The bushy, graying whiskers growing from his ears to his jawline reminded Osceola of squirrel tails.

"May I help you?" As soon as Humphreys said it he regretted asking. Every Indian who came through the door had some infuriating or tragic problem to be solved.

"Maybe we can help you," Osceola said through Black.

"That would be a welcome change."

"My name is Asee Yaholoe, Black Drink Singer. This is Abihka *Tastanagee Thloko.*" He inclined his head toward Abihka. "Halpata . . ." Alligator nodded his plume. "Luhstee, Black."

Abihka had asked Osceola to be his sense-maker. Abihka liked to run things from an unobtrusive position in the background. He had no trouble being unobtrusive. He looked like a harmless, unkempt old man come to the sutler's to trade his salted fish. He resembled his wares, in looks and aroma. The soldiers treated him with a benign contempt and had taken to calling him Sam Jones, after the fisherman in a popular comic poem.

Just outside the office was the large basket of dried pompano and red snapper Abihka had brought. The fish were contraband. They had been caught by Abihka's nephews on a clandestine trip to the gulf coast. No one inquired too closely into the fact that these were saltwater fish.

"We bring you a small present." Osceola handed Humphreys a slender pipe, with an alligator carved on one side of the stem and a heron in flight on the other. It was wrapped in a narrow leather sack soft as satin. "Abihka Great Warrior says to tell you he wishes you success in your endeavors here."

"My heart thanks Abihka Great Warrior for his generosity." Gad Humphreys brightened. Here was a man who wasn't asking for anything. In fact, here were four men who looked quite capable of solving their own problems. "You're Osceola, the one they call Billy Powell? The surveyors tell wild tales about you. Is it true you kept up with their horses, at a trot, for days?"

"Yes." Osceola's people didn't hold modesty to be a virtue, but running all day was hardly worth bragging about. He went on with the business at hand. "Your messenger said three of our men crossed the line. They killed cattle."

"Yes. I thought it better if your Seminole light-horse police took care of your own . . . perverse ones."

"We brought them back. They say they killed the cows. They say their families were hungry."

"I envy you your job, Powell. Being a policeman is easy for you. Your perverse ones admit their wrongdoing."

"If they lie, their souls will wander homeless through eternity when they die." Osceola shrugged. "Don't your holy men give the same counsel?"

"They do, but few follow it."

"We'll take the strayed ones to their village. The elders will decide their punishment." Mad New Town had taught Osceola to proceed as though his own course of action were the obvious one. Mad New Town always said it saved hours of needless discussion.

Osceola knew the white men's councils never heeded a Seminole's words in his own defense. He knew of warriors who had died of despair in the dank cells of the old Spanish fort in Saint Augustine. He would not be responsible for condemning anyone to such cruel punishment just for being hungry.

Humphreys considered the proposal while Osceola waited as though the issue were settled. Humphreys was too relieved to quibble. He knew he was being maneuvered, but he'd always said he'd rather be shaved by a sharp razor than a dull one. He recognized that young Osceola was a very sharp razor indeed.

"Very well," he said. "As long as they realize the seriousness of the offense. Tell the men of the council that DuVal *miko* gives them permission to go to the western waters to fish. DuVal *miko* is a fierce warrior, but an honest man. He holds the welfare of your people in his heart."

"We were much better off before white men became concerned about our welfare," muttered Alligator.

"Halpata says he's grateful for the American civil chief's concern." Black took liberties with Alligator's words. His Seminole friends would never lie, but Black would. He maintained that white people were so unaccustomed to the truth that it only confused them.

"It has been a distinct pleasure to meet you." Humphreys stood and held out his meaty hand. Humphreys had been a colonel in the militia for thirteen years. He was a large, sturdy man going slowly soft. He still loomed over everyone but Black.

"He wants you to shake his fingers," Black said. "It's a white man's custom."

When Osceola took Humphreys's thick, sweaty hand in both of his slender ones, they barely contained it. He pumped the arm until it threatened to come loose at the shoulder. Alligator and Abihka solemnly did likewise. Black knew better than to offer his hand. When he had done it in the past, the look of distaste on white men's faces made him want to bypass their hands and go for their throats.

"Stop by the paymaster's office and give him this note." Humphreys handed Osceola a scrap of paper. "He'll give you three dollars for each man you brought in, same as if they were deserters." Then a thought occurred to him. "Powell, the army could use you to track deserters. The surveyors claim you can follow a fly through a hurricane at midnight."

"The measurers are not as precise with their words as they are with their weights, their chains." Osceola's guileless smile charmed Humphreys as completely as it did everyone else.

The agent repressed a sudden desire to clap an arm around Osceola's shoulders, to walk out with the four men. He wanted to spend the afternoon talking with them over fishing lines at the nearby paradise DuVal had named Silver Springs.

"Those stories are wrong," Alligator said. "Black Drink Singer can track a gnat through a hurricane at midnight." As he turned to go, he winked, a mannerism he'd picked up from Wococoi Clark. He and Osceola left Gad Humphreys feeling as though the temperature had dropped twenty degrees, God had revoked mosquitoes, and Congress had relented on the brick and lime and planking.

"What are deserters?" Osceola asked as he gestured to the three culprits squatting patiently in the meager shade cast by the shack. The three men fell in line as Osceola, Abihka, Alligator, and Black walked the hundred yards to the site of the fort.

"Deserters are warriors who choose not to fight. The blue-jacket war leader locks them up there." Black nodded toward the small guardhouse. It stood silent and isolated in the swarm of construction. The temperature inside must have been hot enough to melt lead.

"Do you mean they run away from battle?" asked Osceola.

"They have no battles. They just run away from here."

"I don't blame them." Alligator surveyed the gangs of glistening, shirtless men working in the heat while sergeants shouted at them. "They have no women here. I'd desert, too. Baldy would never tolerate this."

"How can they cage a man for deciding not to fight? To fight or not to fight is each man's decision." The more Osceola saw of white people, the less he understood them. That he couldn't learn their methods and motives by simple observation as he could other animals made him uneasy.

But he could appreciate their ingenuity. The seven men walked through the clutter and turmoil being slowly enclosed by a high palisade of split logs. Recent rains and the constant traffic of men and animals and dray vehicles had turned the site into a mud flat. One group of men shoveled the mud into heaps and mixed it with dried grass. Another group used the mixture to plaster the log chimneys rising at each end of the officers' quarters. It was a messy job.

The warriors stood at the edge of one of the sawyers' deep trenches. A huge squared pine log rested on transverse rollers across the length of it. They watched the sawyer walk the log as he guided the saw along the chalked line. In the pit, his partner pulled the long blade down for the cutting strokes that would turn the logs into boards.

"Maybe we should get one of those." Alligator studied the device closely.

"I think not." Abihka moved close to peer into the pit. "At first they seem a good idea. They save time. But they only save time to do more work. Like the white men, we would start building things larger than we need. We would build more than we need."

Osceola stopped to stare at the enlisted men's barracks rising on five-foot pilings. He admired the practicality of the design. It would avoid flooding and snakes and catch whatever breezes might happen by. He stored the idea away in the back of his mind.

Nearby, a construction detail spread a six-inch layer of lavender-and-pink coquina shells over the floor area of the officer's quarters. The shovels full of tiny shells in the dark mud made Osceola melancholy. He remembered drifts of them glittering on the shores of the gulf. He suddenly longed to hear the cry of a gull. To see porpoises cavorting.

"Black, what will they do with the shells?"

"They'll mix them with lime, with water, then crush them with heavy iron pestles. When the mixture dries it will make a hard, smooth surface."

The sound of axes and splitting mauls never stopped. Drivers cracked their whips and shouted to the oxen and mules pulling out stumps or hauling supplies. In the surrounding forest, trees crashed. The hammering of blacksmiths and nail makers and shingle rivers added to the din. Four men dropped a load of lumber. Osceola flinched as the boards fell with an echoing clatter behind him.

Osceola let the chopping and sawing, the pounding and shouting and swearing and braying, fill his head until it rang.

This was the music of white people, of their abilities and their affairs. It was cacophony now, but maybe someday it would arrange itself into a song, the pattern that would explain the singers.

"When we receive our pay, brothers," Osceola said, "let's give part of it to them." He indicated the three men walking behind them.

"Agreed," Alligator said. "But we'll go to the store with them. If they find the whiskey sellers, they'll become like Heartless Snake."

Osceola's expression didn't show his sorrow. Saving Heartless Snake from McGirth's thugs had burdened him with gratitude. The weight seemed more than he could bear with good grace. He was frequently drunk. He spent most of his time with his wife and child in the black settlement nearby, and he rarely visited Osceola.

Sometimes friendship, the knowledge of what was in a brother's heart, faded. The line between friendship and enmity became indistinct. Fire became smoke and gave no warmth. So it was with the love Osceola felt for Heartless Snake.

CHAPTER 19

For some inexplicable reason, one of the small ball-play fields on the outskirts of Mad Partridge's town was unoccupied. It lay at the end of a narrow path almost obliterated by the exuberant summer growth. The surrounding jungle was sending exploratory tendrils out onto the field. Weeds grew up through the hard-packed surface. The goalposts stood stark and forlorn looking at each end of the field.

Mad Partridge and his people had lived in the north central part of the peninsula for decades. His town had grown until an hour's time was required to walk from one edge of it to the other. Now it and the surrounding settlements were aswarm with visitors celebrating the Green Corn ceremony. Hundreds of young men were practicing for the games being played in the main fields of Mad Partridge's town. Mink and Morning Dew could hear their shouts in the distance. The ball-play rivalries were numerous and complex, and the commotion in the town made this field's desolate air astonishing.

Little Warrior and Mink chased a small king snake through the tall tangle of azalea bushes intertwined with yellow jessamine and out onto the field. Three-year-old Little Warrior wore only a breechclout. Thirteen-year-old Mink had tucked the hem of her long skirt into the drawstring waist. Her lean brown legs were crosshatched with paler scratches from the bushes. Laughing at the fervor of their pursuit, Morning Dew followed them.

Little Warrior circled the yellow-speckled snake, which had looped back on itself and followed her with its head.

"Speak kindly to it, child," Mink crooned. "It is *Da*, the creative force. To my people it represents life, motion."

The king snake struck at the frond Mink swished in front of it. Mink bent swiftly and caught it behind the jaws. She coiled it around her arm and held out a bandana-wrapped finger. The snake chewed on it a while, then submitted to being draped around Little Warrior's neck. He hung there peaceably while she stroked him.

Morning Dew and Mink eyed the field, then smiled conspiratorially at each other. They usually played the game with one goalpost, not two, but this was too good an opportunity to pass up. Little Warrior knew what the look meant. Her mother and Mink practiced ball play every chance they got. When they weren't bouncing balls or rocks on their insteps, they were throwing them against trees to improve their aim.

"I want to play, too." Little Warrior unwound the king snake and set it on the ground. It slithered away.

"You haven't trained with the owls or the snakes." As she talked Morning Dew tied a knot in her full skirt to hike it up out of the way.

"How do I do that?"

"Go to the ball field alone at dusk," Morning Dew said. "Call the owls by imitating them. When they discover you've tricked them, they'll attack you. If you can avoid their talons, you're ready to play."

Little Warrior looked dubious. Witches and ghosts took the form of owls. Owls were not the sorts of beings to irritate, especially not while alone at dusk. "What about the snakes?"

"Not just any snakes," Mink said. "Black racers. If you can outrun racers, you can play ball." Mink was yanking down the vines of sweet-smelling jessamine flowers growing halfway up the goalposts.

Both Morning Dew and Mink carried balls in the leather bags they wore at their waists. Like the balls the men used, these were made of turtle legs stuffed with Spanish moss, but they were only for practice. They hadn't been chanted over to permeate them with magic. They didn't contain inchworms to move them out of the way of opposing players.

Little Warrior stationed herself at the east posts and beat on sticks to call her mother's ball toward the goal. For an hour Morning Dew and Mink were the fiercest of enemies. They pushed and shoved and screamed with laughter as they fought for the ball. Neither of them noticed the blood. Little Warrior had to scream and run out onto the field to get their attention.

Mink looked down in horror. Thick, deep crimson blood ran in sluggish stripes down her brown inner thighs. They dripped from her knees, forming round stains in the sand.

"*Iboskee. Iboskee* has come." Mink tried to rub the blood off, but more flowed downward. She had faced hardship and terrible danger in her young life, but she almost panicked at the sight of her own menstrual blood.

She had reason to fear it. If the wind blew from her to a man, it might debilitate him for life. For a man to touch her might cause death. To break the taboos of a woman's monthly time was a crime equal to murder or adultery.

"Don't be afraid." Morning Dew remembered her own terror the first time she'd bled. With her thumb she wiped a stray tear from the corner of one of Mink's enormous slanted green eyes. "You're a woman now."

"Don't be afraid." Little Warrior caught Mink's hand and held it as though to protect her from the evil in the blood.

"We must hurry." Morning Dew put away her ball, unknotted her skirt, and shook out the creases. She hefted Little Warrior onto her hip so they all could move faster.

As she hurried along the path to their camp, she worried. This was the worst possible time. Mad Partridge's town, the nearby settlements, and the entire hammock for miles around teemed with people. To make matters worse, the whites were here, too, demanding an election of one man to speak for all the Seminole. The Maskokee and Mikasukee naturally didn't agree on who that man should be. Tempers were short.

Mink was young and inexperienced. She could easily blunder near someone and cause dreadful misery, for herself and for the other person. Women had been murdered by families that blamed them for the illness or death of a relative. Morning Dew knew she had to get Mink to safety. Quickly.

She and Dahomey spent the afternoon building a thatched lean-to away from everyone. That evening Mink sat there alone. She fed a few green sticks into the fire so the smoke would discourage the mosquitoes. She stared through the night toward the glow trembling in the distance. The overhanging oaks around the council square seemed to dance in the light of the flames. Billows of smoke from the huge fires draped a gauzy haze over the village.

No one there was lonely, Mink thought. They weren't despised and outcast. Mink sat cross-legged, with her elbows resting on her knees and her chin in her palms. The sound of drums and singing ebbed and flowed, carried in eddies on the wind. Under her breath, Mink chanted along with the singers. Her voice was full and husky and sweet, a gift from her mother.

Dahomey had spent most of the afternoon with Mink. She and Morning Dew had brought food and a long list of instructions. Mink must not eat salt. She must not comb her hair. She must bathe far downstream from the usual place. She must avoid the gardens, or she would wither the crops. She must cook and eat from special pots. She certainly must never cook for men when she has having her monthly flow.

"Why did the flux have to arrive now?" Mink had asked more than once. "I'll miss the celebration of the Green Corn."

Dahomey had laughed. "Child," she said. "The flux always arrives at the worst time, like when your man's been gone.

You want to welcome him back between your blankets the best way you know how. *That's* when the flux comes."

After the women left Mink tried to imagine sharing her bed with a man. She remembered the nights she lay stiff and alert, listening to the sounds from the other side of the calico curtain. She well knew the aural pattern of love—the murmurs and sighs and stifled laughter. She knew that the rustle and creak and slap of flesh on flesh became more urgent as the night deepened.

The performance always ended in a startled gasp from Aury's Black and a languorous moan from Dahomey. The gasp seemed particularly absurd, coming as it did from a man of Black's size and ferocity.

Mink knew the mechanics of love, too. She had seen birds and animals discharge their procreational duties. And often while she ground corn she had listened to Morning Dew and her sisters discuss the subject over their own mortars and pestles.

The carefree flow of their talk riffled around her head like a bubbling brook around a boulder. The women's soft, demure voices and the lilting trill of the Mikasukee language disguised the graphic intimacies they described with such relish. If a man approached, they switched without pause into their usual gossip. And they laughed good-naturedly behind his back as he walked away.

Mink was brooding about the entire preposterous arrangement between male and female when she saw the torch. It dipped and yawed like a drunken firefly along the twisting path. The path itself was part of the webwork of trails connecting the settlements and family camps around Mad Partridge's town. As the torch came nearer, Mink heard Fighting in a Line singing her usual innumerable variation of three notes.

The torch's flicker glanced off parts of Fighting in a Line, now a shoulder, now a hand, now the tangled spikes of her hair. When she poked her head into the lean-to, the torchlight flowed into the deep creases around her eyes. The impressive massif of her nose threw a triangular shadow across the right side of her face. It blackened her mouth and nostrils and eye sockets, turning her face into a skull. The skull was smiling.

"I am come." She flicked her palmetto whisk just often enough to brush away the mosquitoes, without wasting effort on extra strokes. She extinguished the flaring stick of lighter pine by plunging it into the sand. Then she rummaged around in her sack and pulled out four ears of corn, still warm from the roasting. "Eat, Night Daughter." She used her pet name for Mink.

For a while the only sounds were the crackle of the flames and the moist crunch of the corn. Then Fighting in a Line produced two Seville oranges, roasted in their rinds. She put a small tortoise shell of honey between herself and Mink so they could dip the tart fruit into it.

"You'll miss the dancing, Grandmother," Mink said wistfully.

"I've seen dancing." Fighting in a Line peeled one of the oranges, releasing its tangy scent into the air. She split it with her long thumbnails and gave half to Mink. "Dancing is for young people," she said. "All the flirting, eyelashes fluttering like hummingbird wings. The noise makes my head buzz like a wasp nest. This is a good dance, though. Like the old days, except for the anger."

Fighting in a Line fell silent. She had felt the tension in Mad Partridge's town. It wasn't the usual aura of magic and excitement that always accompanied the Green Corn ceremony. The air vibrated with antagonism like a summer morning vibrated with cicadas.

Governor DuVal wanted his candidate elected Great King instead of Mikanopee, who by lineage was the rightful leader of the southern Maskokee. Mikanopee's followers, mostly the large, influential Alachua bands, were squared off against the Mikasukee and Talasee, who supported DuVal's choice, Mole Leader. And to be honest, tall, handsome Mole Leader looked like a chief. Mikanopee didn't.

"Have they chosen the Great King?" Mink asked.

"No. Tomorrow the men of the council will announce the decision."

When she finished the orange Fighting in a Line wiped her fingers on her skirt. She pulled five strands of blue pony beads from the small pouch hanging among the amulets and bags of protective herbs on her bony chest. She arranged the beads around Mink's long neck and knotted them into graduated tiers.

"You have an anhinga's neck, Night Daughter," she said.

"But these are your prettiest necklaces." Mink rubbed the cool, glossy curves of the beads.

"I'm mourning my brother. I don't need them."

"Grandmother . . ." Mink stopped, at a loss as to how to continue.

Fighting in a Line knew what was on Mink's mind. It was on the mind of every young woman at the time of her first flux. "I can't tell you about men," she said. "No one can." She hiked up her skirt to expose a knee, swollen with arthritis. Her scarred, gnarled brown feet and legs looked weathered to the tough heartwood.

"When I was young my legs were the prettiest in Talasee. I could wrap them around a man's arse. I could ride him all night. I've been on some spirited moonlight rides." She chuckled softly at the memories. "When I was young I thought someday I would be wise. I would understand men. But I don't. They're like young bears. We can capture them." She leered slyly at Mink. "We can half tame them. We can share our cabins with them, but we can't understand them. Don't try. You'll only be unhappy."

It wasn't the talk Mink expected from Fighting in a Line, even though she knew the old woman rarely said the expected.

"What story do you want to hear?" With a flick of her palmetto whisk, Fighting in a Line dismissed the subject of men.

"Tell me what your name means," Mink said.

" 'Fighting in a Line' is an old name. My mother's mother gave it to me. It commemorates our people's first meeting with the red-jacket soldiers."

Fighting in a Line began describing the time, seventy-five years earlier, when the squad of British soldiers quick-stepped into Talasee. They had come to recruit Maskokee warriors for their war against the French. Fighting in a Line marched stiffly up and down in front of the lean-to. She played the part of the British colonel drilling his soldiers in the town square to bedazzle the amused savages. Mink laughed at her antics.

"Our people weren't impressed with such a foolish way of fighting," Fighting in a Line concluded. "But they liked the soldiers' red jackets. They made a fire with the British. The men smoked with them. They became their allies. My mother's father looked handsome in his crimson coat."

Fighting in a Line grew pensive. "Maybe their way of fighting in lines was bad magic," she said. "The blue-jackets hid in the trees, like panthers. They fought as we do. They beat the red-jackets. Now the blue-jackets tell us where we must live. They tell us what we must eat. They tell us who we must have as Great King."

Fighting in a Line thought of the men assigned to drive away the dogs and pigs that skulked around the square, looking for charred bear ribs left after a feast. Like dog whippers, they drive us, she thought.

CHAPTER 20

The huge alligator rose above the surface as though he were being inflated with air, which in fact he was. He raised his long blunt snout up at a sharp angle and slapped the water with his tail. It cracked like a whip. His throat puffed outward. His body contracted in powerful, spasmodic jerks.

As the black armor of his skin vibrated, hundreds of finger-sized jets of water rose like geysers along his sides. They danced and glittered in the sunlight, sending wavelets outward in graceful, concentric arcs. The alligator bellowed and was answered by challenges from miles around. His booming call rippled the water. It set Little Warrior's diaphragm to vibrating and stirred the wispy hairs on the back of her neck as she crouched in the grass.

"A sign, Father?"

"Yes." Osceola smiled. "Definitely a sign."

On expeditions with her father, Little Warrior had learned to recognize signs. Even though they took an infinite variety of forms, they each stopped her in the midst of whatever she was doing. They spoke to her in a language beyond words. They were flashes of visible magic.

They assured her she was as much a part of the forest's magic as the tawny panthers rippling through the trees. As free in her own heart as the great blue heron gliding low overhead, silent except for a faint creaking of feathers. They were winks that included her in the Breath Maker's grand joke.

The alligator finished his performance and went back to enlarging his den. When he backed out of the hole in the embankment, mud and roots roiled up, pushed out by his webbed feet. He waved his tail back and forth in the water, dispersing the mud before he disappeared inside again. The willow on the bank shivered as he tugged at its roots from underneath, biting them off to clear them out of his way.

"Was the alligator you hit as big as this one?"

"No. It was as long as your uncle Alligator is tall. But when we played that game your uncle was much smaller." Osceola knew Little Warrior knew that. She had heard the story many times, but she was asking for it again. Of the hundreds of tales that made up Talasee's lore, Little Warrior preferred those of the adventures and mischief of her own parents' childhood.

"The alligator was asleep on top of her nest. Your uncle went first because he's brother to the alligator, but Heartless Snake protested. 'You'll get your strike in, then wake her,' he said. Alligator grinned that raffish smile of his."

"What did Uncle Alligator look like when he was small?"

"Like the hatchlings that were his namesake. As he ran toward the mound where the alligator snoozed, Heartless Snake gave the distress call."

Little Warrior pressed her lips together and sucked them inward, producing the high-pitched squeaks of a baby alligator. The alligator in the nearby pond stopped his work and boomed again. Osceola and Little Warrior pushed the dugout into the channel the alligator had cleared through the reeds. Little Warrior scrambled over the baskets of dried fish she and her father were bringing from the coast and sat in the bow of the canoe.

"Alligator had to do some fancy dodging." Osceola continued the story as he poled. "He tagged the tip of her lashing tail. Then he climbed a cable of vines up into the crotch of an oak. While the alligator was hissing at Alligator, Heartless Snake touched her tail, then ran away."

"Then it was your turn." With other people around, Little Warrior wouldn't have interrupted. But when she was alone with her father she could participate in the story she had memorized. "Did you run fast?"

"I walked toward her. 'Hadjo!' Alligator shouted down at me. 'Crazy!' I slapped her on the tip of her jaw. She almost bit my hand off. While I ran from her Alligator climbed down and began pelting her with mud to blind her."

"What did Uncle Heartless Snake do?"

"He thought of his stomach, as always. He gathered as many eggs from the nest as he could carry. But we went on throwing mud at the alligator. We chased her into the water. She swam away. We were covered with mud. We caught Heartless Snake, pinned his arms, dragged him into the mud, too. The eggs smashed all over him."

"Then what?" This was her favorite part.

"We didn't wash or get dressed. Alligator plastered more mud onto his head. He stuck palmetto fronds into it. We ran through the town. The girls giggled. They hid their faces." To illustrate, Osceola held a hand in front of his eyes but peeked through the fingers at Little Warrior.

Little Warrior laughed, as she always did, at the picture of her father running naked through the town. "Did Grandmother punish you?"

"No. I was too big for her to scratch." Osceola remembered Fighting in a Line struggling not to laugh as she scolded him for scandalizing the young women.

Osceola poled them out of the glare of the wet prairie and into the dimly lit labyrinth of water oaks and bays, pond apples and the enormous, bottle-shaped cypress trees. The gray draperies of Spanish moss hung all the way to the black surface of the water. Thousands of conical gray knees, large and small, rose above the water around the bulbous bases of the cypresses.

Now and then a thick water moccasin slithered off one and cruised away, trailing long, undulating folds of water. A stench rose from the eggs and fledglings that had fallen from the nests in the guano-whitened branches of the cypress trees. Tangles of rattlesnakes, smelling like overripe melons, feasted on the carrion. Pendant masses of orchids added their fragrance to the pungency.

Osceola watched Little Warrior lean out over the prow of the boat and, like a puppy, sniff the still air. She breathed in the mystery of the dark cypress maze along with its smells. After years spent passing through the swamps, Osceola had learned to survive in them and even to appreciate their beautiful menace. But Little Warrior had been raised near them. She was at ease here.

When confined to her mother's neatly swept yard, she was as restless as an egret captured and tied to a post so its feathers could be collected. Her boundless curiosity and enthusiasm got her in trouble. Her stocky arms and legs were covered with the marks of her mother's and grandmother's scratchings. But here the propriety that tethered her spirit was loosed, and she almost quivered with excitement.

"Will we camp at Some Whiskey There?" she asked.

"Maybe." Osceola himself was happily anticipating a swim in the spring. If the cypresses' dark magic had a sinister air about it, the spring was sunlight and birdsong and pure, sparkling color.

The swamp gradually opened, allowing more light to penetrate the pale green canopy of the cypress. The water became clearer and faster moving. Slate-colored herons stepped daintily in the shallows. In the branches overhead cormorants faced the sun and spread their wings to dry. While Osceola hid the dugout downstream, in the undergrowth that spilled out over the river, Little Warrior ran to the edge of the pool.

The clear, azure eye of the spring, a hundred feet across, stared up at the summer sky. Throngs of mullet and silverfish seemed suspended among the clouds reflected on its surface. The bleached bones of alligators and manatees blended with the brilliant white shell rock covering the bottom and steep banks of the spring.

Ueho'mee Sassa, Some whiskey There, had always been a favorite camping place for the People of the Peninsula. The spring had gotten its name from the Spanish and English who had unloaded Bahamian rum there. Old hearths blackened the ground. Half a century earlier someone had planted a few orange and peach trees at the edge of the grassy slope along the sandy rim of the spring. Now the spring was beyond the reservation limits, and white men camped there.

Their blankets and pots, musty grain sacks, empty whiskey bottles, food tins, and animal bones littered the clearing. A tottering arbor of palmetto fronds sheltered a stacked cord of peeled oak, three oaken barrels, and a turnip-shaped copper pot big enough to cook Little Warrior. Copper tubing ran from the cooker to the nearby spring-fed creek, where it coiled on the bottom like a shiny snake. The other end led out of the creek and downhill to a smaller barrel. A low fire burned under the cooker.

"Daughter," Osceola called softly.

When she came up beside him he pulled her into the cover of the vines and azalea bushes. The two of them crouched, studying the intricate pattern of boot prints in the damp sand of the clearing. Osceola felt the hot tide of rage rising in him.

"Go to the canoe," he whispered. "Stay there."

Looking back over her shoulder, Little Warrior walked quickly down the familiar tunnel made by deer moving through the thicket. She didn't want to go; but though she might occasionally be disobedient in camp, she had only disobeyed her father in the forest once. He had vanished and had stayed hidden until she had grown thoroughly lost and frightened. She had never disobeyed him again.

Osceola ghosted around the perimeter of the clearing to the first barrel. He lifted the heavy lid and looked inside. Bubbles of carbonic gas had formed a thick, foaming cap on top of the fermenting corn. The gas kept the mash rolling and released strong, sweet-sour odor.

Osceola knew he had to move fast. The moonshiners had to be nearby. White men never left their distilleries unguarded. Even if there were no other perverse men to steal the whiskey, bears were especially fond of the mash.

Osceola took the lids off the other two barrels. One by one he put his shoulder to them and tipped them over. The thick yellow liquid flowed out onto the ground. The copper cooker presented more of a problem. If he tried to destroy it with his hatchet, the noise would alert the moonshiners. He could either pour water on the hot metal, causing it to cave in, or he could blow it up. Blowing it up appealed to him more.

He fed logs into the fire and fanned them with his breech-clout. He took mud from the pile near the cooker and plastered an extra-thick layer of it over the hardened mud seal already in place around the lid. When he could sense the steam building dangerously inside, he walked backward across the clearing.

As he went he paused to reach down and brush his palm lightly over each footprint, erasing them from the sand. As he crossed a grassy patch he pulled and twisted each bent blade, so that it spiraled back into place. His uncle had long ago taught him that to pass through the world without leaving a mark was to be invisible.

When he came to the deer run he unstrapped his musket from his back. He got on his hands and knees and held the piece in front of him as he backed into the tunnel in the underbrush. He lay on his stomach and watched the clearing. He didn't have to wait long.

The moonshiner was whistling to himself, pulling up his baggy homespun pantaloons, buttoning his fly, and reattaching his cord braces as he ambled into the clearing. When he saw the overturned barrels and the golden flow of mash, he fired his rifle at the sun.

"Git your arse back here, Billy," he shouted. "We got bears."

He reloaded and, with his rifle primed and at half cock, scanned the bushes for the creature that had dumped over the barrels. As he neared the deer run Osceola tightened his grip on his hatchet. He came so close Osceola could see only the frayed hems of his mud-stained pantaloons and the cracks in the dried leather of his boots just beyond the opening of the run.

"What bears?" The man's partner emerged from the other side of the clearing.

"Look for yerself." The moonshiner was directly over and in front of Osceola. His voice boomed in Osceola's ears.

As he turned and walked toward the arbor, Osceola's view of the pantaloon hems extended up to baggy knees, then on to include a solid set of buttocks and the dirty cord braces. The two moonshiners converged on the still just as the trapped steam built up enough pressure to blow out the sides of the cooker. It showered them with boiling liquid and mash.

As Osceola crawled along the run to the point where Little Warrior and the canoe waited, the men's screams of pain and rage were music. His anger danced to it and changed to laughter.

CHAPTER 21

The mangy gray pyramid of blanket twitched. It slid in a rocking motion a few feet across Dahomey's kitchen yard, then stopped. A peculiar whistling emanated from inside its tentlike folds. Mink squatted in the dust and watched the blanket rotate three times in place, then whistle again, like a deer that scented the hunter.

Dahomey and a score of curious neighbors stood silently behind Mink. The black women wore bright bandanas wound around their heads and tied in elaborate knots at the napes of their necks. They held their arms crossed where their ruffled blouses stopped short of their waistbands. Their naked children chittered nervously to each other and peered from behind the cover of their long skirts.

A large kettle of cold *sofkee* water could have come to a rolling boil before the blanket stopped whistling and twitching and casting about the yard. The children stopped twittering and waited, wide-eyed, for the prophet to emerge into the expectant silence. She took her time. The success of prophecy lay largely in the suspense.

While Mink waited she laid down a broad palmetto frond. On it she spread out her gift of food from the old country—boiled yams and corn dumplings dipped in fish sauce, with tomatoes and fiery chilis from her garden. She added a mirror and two strands of beads while Dahomey looked on disapprovingly.

The gray blanket's contents claimed that while in Saint Augustine she had ascended to heaven in a sky ship twice as high as a cabin and red and round as the setting sun. Dahomey doubted it; but then Dahomey had never been to Saint Augustine. She had never seen Rich and Row's Mammoth Pavilion Circus arrive on the Charleston steam packet like a Noah's ark, with exotic animals, clowns, calliope, and a hot-air balloon eighteen feet tall and fifty-two feet around. It was unlikely the prophet had actually ridden in the balloon, but she had created a stir in the village with her high-flying claims and her divinations.

The children jumped back when the blanket's torn edge suddenly flew up to reveal a thin young woman. She was sixteen, but her wizened face looked much older. She wore only a wide piece of white cotton cloth wrapped around her spindle hips. Sweat had transformed her sunken, knobby chest to ebony with a high polish.

She blinked into the slanting beam of late afternoon sunlight. Her bulging eyes, one yellow and one green, reminded Mink of a fiddler crab. A woolly fell of hair stuck out in fat, dusty spikes all over her narrow head. Her nose looked as if someone had put a thumb in the middle of it and pressed very hard. Her skewed left eye gave her a deranged air.

"Saint Erzulie has ridden me," the prophet hissed. "She has spoken."

Dahomey scowled. This whistling, posturing newcomer was a fraud. Dahomey was a priestess of *vodu*, and the *vodu* she practiced did not have saints. Still scowling, she rubbed several dry fish scales in her hand until they squeaked. She was pleased by the alarm she saw dip and skim across the young woman's face. If the blanket prophet had no real magic herself, she certainly recognized it when she heard it.

Mink ignored her mother's devilment. Mink was to accept *Talasee Tastanagee* into her bed tonight, and she was determined to know every possible augury. Even if it meant defying her formidable mother.

Mink and Morning Dew had discussed the alliance as they pounded the daily ration of corn, their pestles beating out a rhythm in the same massive, oaken mortar. Seven days ago Morning Dew had served up her decision along with Osceola's morning *sofkee*.

Morning Dew's fire was the meeting place for warriors who traveled as much as three days to speak with *Talasee Tastanagee*. They stayed in her guest house. They ate from her kettles. Morning Dew needed help. She wanted to share her man and her responsibilities with Mink, the slave child who had grown to become her dark sister.

"What does Saint Erzulie say?" Mink asked.

"You will have happiness in your marriage," the prophet answered.

Mink smiled and reached for the beads and mirror to offer in payment.

"Then you will suffer great evil." The prophet's mismatched eyes widened in dread of their own inner vision. "There will be betrayal. Death."

"Who will be betrayed?" Mink was upset. This wasn't like her mother's prediction.

"Evil. Betrayal. Death."

"Begone from my house, woman." Dahomey had had enough. "Scat!" She lifted her hand and rattled the fish scales. The fact that their voice was so whispery, like a scorpion in the night thatch, made them more ominous. Dahomey's own low-pitched, husky voice was as ominous as the fish scales. "Look carefully to your shadow soul," she whispered. "Someone might drive a spike into it."

"Evil! Betrayal! Death!" The prophet snatched up Mink's presents. But as she scuttled away she glanced nervously back at the vulnerable, long, late afternoon shadow trailing behind her.

Dahomey balanced her wooden bucket of water on her head and continued her interrupted journey from the spring. Until recently the spring had been haunted by the spirit of a jug, but Dahomey finally had managed to exorcise it. She filled the water gourd hanging from the rafters of the cabin where she and Mink and Black slept. If no water was nearby during the night, a thirsty soul might wander off in search of it while its body slept. It might drink from foul puddles or drown in a spring. A thirsty soul was in imminent peril.

"That one's a fool, bouncing about under her filthy blanket. She whistles like a horse with the roars." Dahomey moved from her compound to the small bridal hut Black had built for Mink. "She's a fool who intends to live well off bigger fools."

"What you do think she meant?" Mink followed her mother so closely she almost bumped into her when Dahomey turned abruptly.

"She means nothing," Dahomey said firmly. "She knows nothing. No spirit speaks through her." She only knows I'm her rival here. She must get at me however she can, Dahomey thought. "Remember this, daughter. If the Breath Maker gives you sickness, he also gives you medicine. He gives you strength to overcome whatever adversity he sends."

"What did her *sabia* mean about my marriage to *Talasee Tastanagee?*"

"Marriage? Child, we could walk from here to Saint Augustine talking about marriage, but we would not finish." Dahomey was patient with Mink's confusing the African spirit, *vodu*, with the Seminole one, *sabia*. She also understood Mink's insistence on taking the blanket shaker seriously.

For a woman marriage was the hunt. It was her livelihood, her means of survival. She sensed the visible and invisible links between people as the hunter sniffed the air to detect the faintest trace of quarry.

"You're descended from a valiant line of warrior women." Dahomey's husky accent always thickened and slowed when she talked about the old country. "Your great-great-grandmother marched at the head of a regiment of women. She fought the Oyo Yoruba when the capital city was sacked. You have the strength to survive trouble or to die with grace. Neither life nor death can hold any threat for you. Now go. Get you ready for your man."

"*Abayi, nana',*" Mink murmured in the old tongue. "Thank you, Mother."

A black string of birds unreeled toward the rim of the world. Trees sighed under the wind's caress. The dying sun decked the sky in a blaze of color for Mink's wedding night.

Darkness had fallen when Osceola dismounted in front of the small cabin and looped his gray gelding's reins around a bush. The rising moon was misshapen, not quite full. It hung, splotchy and opalescent, like one of Dahomey's fish scales. It frosted the roofs and trees and idle mortars and pestles with platinum.

"Woman," he called softly.

"I am here." Mink knelt with her haunches resting on her calves. Dahomey had plaited ribbons into the thick braid that lay like a club to Mink's waist and ended in a tight curl. The braid barely contained her wiry black mane. Already tendrils were escaping and coiling into tight whorls around her face and neck.

When Osceola loosened Mink's hair it sprang outward into a gossamer thicket. Moonlight spilling through the doorway sparkled like fireflies caught in its meshes.

Osceola reached out and gently turned Mink's face so the moon shone on it. Mink's upper lip formed a voluptuous triangle under her strong, broad nose and flared nostrils. Her full mouth was taut and glossy, dark and sweet as a ripe plum. Her large eyes were always startled innocence. Their luminescence was moonlight on sea shallows. From her green eyes stared the Portuguese adventurer who had loved Mink's great-grandmother.

Her skin had the color and sheen of mink. The continuous slope of her long skull, forehead, nose, and chin merged with the gracefully curving stalk of her neck. As Osceola pushed aside her hair with his cheek and nuzzled her ear, her head fell back, exposing her throat. With his lips Osceola brushed the tender skin in the cavity at the base of it. He felt her muscles vibrate there when she moaned.

For seven years Mink had been a helpful presence in Morning Dew's household. For seven years she had loved Osceola silently from her place on the other side of the evening fire.

That she would lie with him as a lover almost panicked her. Osceola could hear the thumping of her heart.

She presented her love like a bouquet of flowers, common and unique. A simple, unfathomable miracle. In the tender, insistent pressure of their bodies, the twining of their arms, in the soft, moist warmth of their skin and the stir of their breaths, the made an unspoken pact.

Osceola lay with Mink's long legs wrapped like grapevines around his. His cheek rested in the hollow below her shoulder. The taut, ripe swell of her dark breast, as it rose and fell, brushed his face. Her lissome fingers traced the ridge of his vertebrae and stroked the shallow valley at the base of his spine. Osceola's entire being contracted into the point under her fingertips.

They heard the crickets in the thatch overhead, then a wolf howling and dogs barking in reply. They heard a baby cry and someone cough and the night song of a mockingbird. But the sounds were muted, as though they issued from a cave.

They heard the grunting of a hog outside the door. He was probably looking for his favorite delicacy, the deer brains women wrapped in Spanish moss to use later in tanning hides.

"Shoo!" Without moving her one hand from Osceola's sleek spine, Mink reached for a small three-legged stool. Black had carved it from a solid piece of pine, and it had a good heft to it. She lofted it and hit the snout that had appeared in the doorway. The pig squealed in reproach and left. Mink and Osceola laughed softly together before drifting off to sleep and light-hearted dreams.

To find one loving companion was the Breath Maker's greatest gift after life itself. Osceola had found two. He was a very fortunate man.

When Osceola returned to Talasee, Morning Dew was already directing her uncles in building a cabin for Mink. Mink's home would always be in her mother's compound, but she spent most of her days with Morning Dew. When her turn came to sleep with Osceola she discreetly draped her pet king snake around her neck and returned to Swamp Town. Osceola followed.

The new arrangement ran into the stream of life with hardly a ripple. Perhaps the only difference was that Morning Dew and Mink radiated an aura of unity that bordered on exclusivity. Now and then, as they pounded corn in tandem, one on each side of the oak mortar, they smiled in a way that could only be described as conspiratorial.

Osceola had heard about this from Alligator and the others. Mothers of wives and pairs of wives were standard topics in the men's evening talks. Not all households with two women were as harmonious as they appeared to outsiders. Now Osceola found that what Alligator said was true. If sharing a man didn't drive two women apart, it made them inseparable. Osceola wondered if his women ever discussed his blanket prowess, but he never asked.

CHAPTER 22

"I'm a charmer," Little Warrior chanted. "I can charm my enemies at a distance."

She whooped as she shot again at the blue-jacket soldiers hiding in the palmetto thicket. Her weapon of choice was a musket Osceola had carved for her from a pine branch. She carried it loosely in one hand and tilted it to keep the imaginary priming powder away from the imaginary touchhole.

With her wooden war hatchet poised over her head, she stalked into the palmettos in search of survivors. Her high, piercing war cry spiraled up from the fronds. In the sling on Morning Dew's back Little Warrior's baby sister began to cry.

"*Shta*, be quiet," Morning Dew called after her oldest child. "Or Old Mad Jackson will get you."

"I'll kill Old Mad Jackson," came Little Warrior's disembodied voice.

"Look out for rattlesnakes," Mink added.

Rattlesnakes in the palmettos were a certainty, but Old Mad Jackson wasn't. He had become a bogey man, a toothy demon to frighten disobedient children. When he was elected president in 1828 the elders had become alarmed, too. But he had issued no threats to his old enemies. The former Red Sticks and their Mikasukee allies assumed he would treat them as the Creeks treated the tribes they vanquished in battle. He would demand tribute and consider them part of his own nation, free to go about their lives.

Life did flow on in Talasee Old Fields as though Jackson had never invaded Florida fourteen years earlier. As if a rowdy, private army of Georgians hadn't driven out the Maskokee from this area five years before that. As if the Yemasee hadn't swooped down over a century ago to capture Timacuans for the insatiable American slave market.

As Morning Dew worked the sandy soil of the hammock, her heavy hoe turned up another arrowhead. This was the ancient type, hand-chipped from trade flint. Morning Dew turned it over in her fingers and imagined the hands that had shaped it. As usual, it set her to wondering about the women who first built up these corn mounds generations ago. On days like this, when the air was hot and dusty and vibrant with cicadas, she could almost hear the spirit-women singing.

In Talasee, the herds of horses and tough little Spanish cattle increased. They cropped the grass and the lower leaves of the hammock's trees to a uniform height, giving the village a manicured appearance in the midst of the riotous jungle growth. The ancient, overgrown network of trails between the settlements had become neat tunnels in the dense greenery. As the young families grew, more children laughed and shouted though the village streets and played in the branches of the oaks. More men brought their nephews to Osceola for special training.

Fighting in a Line's pigs rooted in the hammock's depths. Deer passed like russet ghosts through the undergrowth and deadfalls, all woven together with grapevines and the thorny, snarled loops of greenbriar. At night wolves howled from the darkness.

A lame panther claimed this hammock as his hunting

ground. He was a good omen. The Panther clan predominated here. The people of Talasee called him Uncle and considered him a member of the *pawalgee*, the elders.

Talasee's rhythm was slowest in winter. Tranquil dawns were measured in the steady drip of dew from the eaves. Morning Dew woke then to find the cabins becalmed on a lake of ground fog. Winter was when she saw her own life force, her breath. When mist rose like breath from the river nearby.

In spring the musty odor of cabbage palm blossoms thickened the air. Squirrels, addled with passion, almost blundered into the stew pots. Male egrets grew long, wispy trains of white plumes. Pairs of sandhill cranes danced in gangly courtship out on the wet prairies.

Summer tasted of roasted sweet corn and orange-blossom-flavored honey. Each afternoon in summer, winds swept the clouds into ornate heaps a mile high on the horizon. They turned brown and slate and purple as though bruised. Rain fell in a clamorous rush that cooled the air and washed it clean of dust. The dampness charged Morning Dew's and Mink's hair into feathery black clouds around their faces. Mildew formed green patches on the leather pouches.

In fall the leaves of the swamp maples flamed carnelian and gold. Tiny cypress needles fell with a continual whispery rattle. Among the tousled fronds of the cabbage palms, sprays of berries sagged and bobbed under their burden of migrating robins.

In fall rafts of ducks floated on the ponds. When alligators breached them with sideways slashes of their gaping jaws, the ducks exploded in a blur of wings and hysterical quacking. At night the flocks rose in a fiery shower of phosphorescence.

Each fall Osceola and his family loaded the dugout for a trip to their hunting camp. Dahomey and Black followed in a second canoe. They traveled down the Oklawaha, then along the narrow waterways through the mashy savannas above the upper Withlacoochee.

The camp was another site Osceola had found while guiding the surveyors. He knew it was a place white men would not likely visit again. The inundated prairie was too shallow for their boats and too deep to camp or take measurements.

They had pronounced it a worthless, wretched wasteland. They said the Breath Maker had created grass and forgotten to put land under it.

As Osceola poled, the grass stretched level and tawny around him. The flat expanse was interrupted only by clumps of arched cabbage palms or oaks, indicating higher ground. The sun's forge burnished the grass, the water, and the trees to brass, pewter, and verdigris. The world shimmered with tremulous, metallic color.

Anhingas and egrets, silvery cranes, bright pink spoonbills, and herons the color of tarnished steel flashed by the thousands across the landscape. A red-shouldered hawk gave its peremptory cry, then dipped its wing as though in salute.

The island that sheltered the hunting camp was on the verge of the vast marsh called the Cove of the Withlacoochee. The hammock's wall of vegetation looked impenetrable, but Osceola guided the dugout toward a pair of cabbage palms marking the landing site. The two families emptied the canoes and piled their equipment on the small beach. They shouldered their loads and followed the narrow trail through the ferns and palmettos, the rattan vines, scrub laurel, myrtle, and hardwoods.

The vegetation was so dense they couldn't see the camp until they were almost in the center of it. Besides the three small sleeping huts, Osceola and Black had built the usual kitchen arbors. Osceola had added another *chikee* with a raised platform to store their household goods away from snakes and wild pigs and high water. Little Warrior had taken to sleeping there so she could look out at the stars.

The clearing held a garden surrounded by a low palisade of palm logs, a dead pine hung with pumpkins, a few orange, cocoa, plum, and pawpaw trees, three corn mortars, and two *koontee* troughs. A cow horn hung from a thong. It was used to signal camps on nearby hammocks.

There were also frames for drying hides and venison and fish and a half-finished dugout. Beyond the clearing was a midden of terrapin shells and deer and fish bones. Drinking water came from a nearby seep.

Mink swept away the abandoned cobwebs in the rafters so the spiders would have room to spin new webs. In the kitchen arbor she hung up a bag of corn, a few bottles for water, and several basketware sieves. A few pots and skillets already hung in a cluster on the corner posts.

Little Warrior cut armfuls of palmetto fronds for her bed among the clutter in the *chikee*. She piled them overlapping like snake scales, several inches high on the platform. She bounced up and down to reduce the springiness and laid her blankets over them. Then she made a precarious pile of boxes and climbed on them to string the patched mosquito net from the rafters.

Dahomey cut a handful of brush to sweep debris from the yard. When she finished that, she gathered firewood. Morning Dew hung a canvas hammock for the baby, whom Little Warrior had named Crying Bird after the limpkins whose mournful wails also kept her awake nights. Then she chivied half-burned logs into spokes for a fire. She began the tedious chore of striking a spark into a small pile of gunpowder and punk. Black sat on the unfinished canoe and inspected the fishing lines.

Little Warrior took Osceola's hand and pulled him away before her mothers could require work of her. When she came to a nearby meadow she crawled through the coarse grass. Osceola followed, smiling at the dirty, callused soles of her feet.

If Little Warrior had been a boy, Morning Dew's uncles would have schooled and disciplined him. But they would hardly bother with a girl-child. Osceola was glad of that. At age eight this particular girl-child was already a fine tracker.

Little Warrior was looking for the family of owls that lived in the meadow. She found them ringing the entrance to their underground burrow. The adults were not much bigger than the length of Osceola's hand. Their six tiny offspring were miniatures of their parents.

Little Warrior cupped her palms around her mouth and imitated the owl's mild coo-coo, coo-coo. The female and the young ones disappeared into the hole. The male stayed behind, a handful of fluff ready to defend his den. The droll effect of his spindly legs and bulging, slightly crossed yellow eyes was heightened by his incessant bobbing.

When Osceola gave a challenge cry, the owl held his wings

away from his body to make himself look bigger. Hooting indignantly, he advanced on his rival. Little Warrior cooed to soothe him before continuing the inspection tour.

Osceola always walked the hammock when he arrived. Little Warrior always went with him, taking huge strides so she could walk in his footprints. He didn't take smaller steps, and he didn't slow down. To learn to survive, this child must always be pushed farther than she thought she could go. But she never complained, no matter how grueling the pace. And she seemed to absorb knowledge through her skin along with the sunlight.

"Is this a dog or your brother, the panther?" They crouched over a set of large round prints in the damp sand by the water.

"My brother."

"How do you know?"

"A panther's tracks are bigger than a dog's, but they're shallower." With the tips of her fingers, Little Warrior traced the indentation. "A panther places his rear paws in the tracks of the front ones. His prints show claw marks only when he leaps." She studied the prints leading along the shore. "A dog veers here, there, when he hunts. A panther follows a straight course."

"How many times will a panther return to feed on a kill?"

"Sometimes twice. But almost never three times."

"Are these recent prints?"

"Maybe three days old."

They went on to the low end of the island and stopped at the wood stork rookery in the old cypress there. Then they checked the alligator nest. In the mud around it they found shell fragments and a scribble of small claw marks leading to the water. The babies had hatched.

Osceola stood suddenly. He grabbed Little Warrior and gave ferocious alligator grunts while he nibbled her back and sides. She screamed with laughter and hauled on his scalplock braids to make him stop. It was a signal that their inspection was done. It was a reward for her performance.

When they returned to camp the sun had almost set. Clouds of mosquitoes shrilled in their ears. Shafts of light sliced low diagonals through the dense smoke in the clearing.

Black had caught a three-foot garfish from among the dozens that hovered, stacked like cordwood, in the lee of a submerged log. Now the gar leered from the coals at the center of the fire. The heat had pulled the skin away from its long narrow jaws and exposed rows of needlelike teeth. Dahomey was baking it in its hide, and its enameled scales glowed with iridescence.

A plucked egret carcass, its reedy black legs primly aligned, roasted on a spit. The fat dripping from it sizzled on the coals. Besides the usual kettle of *sofkee*, disks of pumpkin bread wrapped in corn husks were baking in the ashes.

They all quickly adjusted to the routine of the hunting camp. Each morning Osceola and Black left in the dugout to track deer through an inundated country without cover. The clearing became crowded with racks of drying deer meat. The three large frames had deer hides stretched on them. Otter and raccoon hides hung drying in clumps of smaller palm rib frames.

Every night they sat around the fire, talking and telling stories. When bedtime came they shook the tiny, translucent green frogs from their blankets. They called their last conversations back and forth among the *chikee* and the shelters. Then they listened to the swamp's night sounds echoing across the emptiness of the prairie.

One evening, when they had finished a meal of venison and honey and pumpkin, they sat as usual around the fire. Mink was telling them the tale of why mosquitoes buzz in people's ears. The story was a complicated one from her homeland. It involved dancing and drumming and sound effects, some provided by the mosquitoes themselves.

When Mink finished, Abihka cleared his throat from beyond the fire's light. "I am come." His scrawny, bowed legs looked like a wishbone in leggings. His gear rattled and clanked around him. He lowered himself onto one of the radiating logs and accepted the tobacco Osceola offered him.

"I come from the coast." He hawked and spit into the night before he lit his pipe. "I stopped at Ueho'mee Sassa, Some Whiskey There. The white men are still making stupid water. They repaired the pot you broke." Abihka didn't mention that he'd bought a bottle of stupid water from the white men.

Abihka strongly disapproved of whiskey, but only when other people drank it.

"Did you bring the leaves, Uncle?" Osceola asked politely. Whenever Abihka went to the coast he gathered leaves for the ceremony of the Black Drink.

"I did." Abihka found a green coconut in one of his pouches and opened it with his hatchet. He produced a dented pewter spoon, and each person in turn scooped out some of the sweet coconut meat, soft as custard.

Abihka finally came to the cause of his detour to this isolated camp. "The Americans held council with the *mikalgee* of the largest towns. Old Mad Jackson's sense-maker asked us to move west, to kindle our fire across the wide river."

"Did you see Old Mad Jackson?" asked Osceola.

"No. Only his sense-maker. Only his lieutenants. Only the *Tastanagee Thloko* of the blue-jackets."

"Did you mark the leaves?"

"Yes, but we agreed to nothing except to send leaders to inspect the western country. The Americans want us to share the land there with your enemies, the northern Maskokee. That's impossible. When they come back we'll all hold council. Even if the country there is a paradise, we'll vote to stay here."

"They want *you* to go across the Mississippi," said Black. "But they shall keep us here, to labor in their fields."

"We'll send out the messengers of war if they try to drive us out," said Osceola. "Or steal our black people. We'll hold council with Sense-Maker Hum-plee about it."

"Hum-plee has been replaced by a fool of a man," Abihka said. "His name is Fay-kahn. He's gone west with Jumper, Chalo Emathla, Mad Wolf, Mad Partridge, Blue King, Mole Leader, Black Dirt." Abihka was supposed to have gone west also, hence his sudden trip to the gulf coast. Abihka nurtured a fervent distrust of white men and their proposals. He especially disliked Old Mad Jackson's new Indian agent, John Phagan.

"Fay-kahn looks like a dog having a troublesome shit," Abihka said. "He shouts at us as if we were children. He doesn't listen. He doesn't laugh. I don't like him. I don't trust him."

Little Warrior grabbed a double fistful of Mink's skirt and held on, as though the white men were about to arrive and abduct her. "Will we have to go to another country? Will the white men take Black Mother?"

"They'll never make us move west," Osceola said. "They'll never take your mother. I promise."

"We shouldn't have let the white men spread their blankets in our country." The smoke from Abihka's pipe curled, mingled, and disappeared into the smoke from the fire. "They're like the strangler tree. It starts small, just a weak tendril on the trunk of the sturdy oak. It grows more tendrils, sends down roots from the oak's branches. The roots thicken, enclose the oak. Finally the oak dies. It rots until only the strangler tree is left to flourish in the forest."

"If war comes, Uncle," said Osceola, "we'll cut the white men out at the root. We'll watch them wither, then die."

CHAPTER 23

Osceola stood straight and relaxed. He wore only a breechclout. In front of him, the Irishman crouched slightly. His sunburned face, neck, and hands were the color of raw beefsteak. The rest of him resembled old, boiled oatmeal. His thick arms dangled past where most men's would have ended. The cording of muscles made them look like two ship's hawsers weighted at the ends with huge, knotted fists.

His sparse, reddish-gray hair gathered like lint around the perimeter of his bare pate. But it didn't end at the nape of his neck. It covered his shoulders, bare chest, and back in a kinky, grizzled red mat. The temperature was unseasonably warm for March, but not what Osceola considered hot. Still, sweat accumulated like heavy dew on the Irishman's hair.

His filthy summer uniform trousers clung so low on his meager hips that they exposed his nether cleft and the sallow

valley under his huge belly. Even hunched over he topped
Osceola by three inches and outweighed him by at least fifty
pounds.

He danced a lumbering circle within the crude ring traced
in the sand. Osceola turned slowly in place to face him as he
moved. A throng of men surrounded the arena outside Fort
King's front gate. Some of those in back stood on crates to
give them a view over the others' heads. The only woman in
the crowd was Fighting in a Line. She had used her sharp
elbows to clear a path to the front, and she was screeching
wagers.

Like most wrestling matches, this one had no rules. The
spectators figured if they were lucky, they might see an eye
gouged out or at least some blood spilled. When the soldiers
saw the size of the Seminole's champion, most of them bet
heavily on the Irishman.

Fort King had been closed for almost two years. These men
were newcomers, members of the Fourth Infantry, sent to
rebuild it. They had been doing carpentry and earning extra
wages, fifteen cents a man, a day, to augment their five dollars a month army pay. To them Osceola was just another
tame Indian, more slightly built and effeminate looking than
most. Certainly he was no match for their man.

"Get the sun to your back, Irish."

"I'll warrant the Injun's life for a gingercake."

When the Seminole realized the blue-jackets were backing
the soldier, they could barely contain their glee. The betting
became more frenzied as the warriors stripped off bracelets
and gorgets, armbands and their gaudy appliquéd shirts. They
piled everything they could gather, including a few trade fusils, into heaps on blankets.

Elders of the village councils stood solemn guard over the
loot. The precious sixteen-gauge muskets with the brass drag-
ons on the lock plates would have alerted more seasoned soldiers. A Seminole wouldn't part with his weapon unless he
was absolutely sure of getting it back.

When the shower of goods finally stopped falling on the
blankets, Irish and Osceola advanced and gripped arms, testing each other. They stood, rigid and ummoving, while their
muscles bulged. Irish looked vaguely surprised when he

couldn't budge Osceola. A glimmer of alarm lit the darkness between his ears.

Strength was the least of Osceola's assets. He only resorted to it when agility and cunning failed. He saw that the soldier's feet were set too wide for a solid base, and he took a step backward, as though retreating. When the big man surged forward to press his advantage, Osceola ducked and pushed off with his back foot. In one fluid motion he drove his head into the Irishman's stomach, hooked an arm under his knee, and heaved upward.

Irish lost his balance and fell with a thud. Gasping for air, he wrapped his arms around Osceola's ankles, dug his heels into the sand, and threw his shoulder at Osceola's knees.

"The hairy one has as much chance as a fish with an otter after it." Heartless Snake was disgusted.

"At least a fish can swim." Black was in rare good humor at the prospect of Osceola humiliating a white man. He looked particularly resplendent in full Seminole war dress and his usual pirate's arsenal. He carried his firelock in defiance of the new territorial law forbidding weapons to blacks. So far no one had been suicidal enough to try to take it away from him.

"The fat one can't wrestle his way out of his blankets in the morning." Alligator was already bored. He was wondering where he could find a good dice game to stake his winnings from this match.

Osceola and Irish were slippery with sweat, and the soldier's solid bulk didn't provide many handholds. The two grappled in the sand. They yanked hair and ears. They gouged and kicked and flailed. Irish hooked a forefinger into Osceola's left nostril and pulled sideways until he tore the skin and cartilage. At the sight of blood pouring into Osceola's eyes, the crowd pressed closer. The soldiers roared encouragement.

Osceola wrenched his head away and bit down on the fleshy pad at the base of Irish's thumb. Irish howled in pain. Osceola rolled away and wiped the blood from his eyes. Irish, wheezing and panting, staggered to his feet. With blood dripping off his fingers he shrieked and lunged. He flung his arms around air.

Osceola directed the full force of his body through his elbow and into Irish's kidney. The soldier collapsed with a grunt, like a stunned shoat, and Osceola pinned him. The soldiers hissed and hooted and stamped. While the Irishman limped away everyone turned to the noisy business of settling the bets.

"Black, find someone else to wrestle *Talasee Tastanagee.*" Fighting in a Line tugged impatiently at Black's belt. She couldn't reach much higher without standing on tiptoe. "My grandson can beat any of them."

Black disengaged her fingers gently. "They all know that, Grandmother. They're not likely to bet against him today." He granted her a smile like sunlight through storm clouds. "But pale-eyes have short memories. Give them a day or two to forget."

"You should have played him longer." Alligator handed Osceola his clothes.

"It was like trying to hold on to a sack of warm lard." Osceola wiped his face and shoulders with his largest bandana. He held another kerchief against his bleeding nose while Alligator helped him into his long shirt.

Carrying his belt, pouches, sashes, turban scarf, jewelry, powder horn, and musket, Osceola headed toward the river to bathe. Alligator and Black went to find a dice game. Heartless Snake began his usual search for a whiskey seller. Fighting in a Line left to cadge tobacco from the hapless pale-eyes *Tastanagee Thloko.*

After a cold hard winter and months of work, the soldiers had finally finished rebuilding the fort. Now they were celebrating. White settlers from the Alachua savanna to the north had ridden their gaunt ponies here to join the fun. Their two-wheeled mule carts had been loaded with work-worn women and towheaded progeny. There were a lot of towheaded progeny. The settlers and Seminole had set aside rancor today to join in shooting matches, knife-throwing contests, and ball play.

One soldier wasn't having a good time. Osceola found him behind the officers' quarters, out of sight of the celebration. He wore only a breechclout. He lay on his stomach, straddling a log laid across two supports. His arms were tied under the log, and his fettered ankles were hooked over it, leaving him helpless in the fierce glare of the sun and the swarming insects.

He had been there since morning roll. His lips were cracked and bleeding. His bare back, arms, legs, and face were covered with mosquito bites and so badly burned he looked flayed. Osceola had seen the punishment often, just as he had seen soldiers caged in the tiny guardhouse.

In the years before the fort closed, Osceola had tracked deserters. Some of them had been hard cases, but many were little more than homesick boys. Some of them had never traveled beyond the next valley of their mountain homes in Georgia, Tennessee, and the Carolinas. Their low-topped army bootees were the first shoes they had ever worn. They were particularly confounded by the shoelaces.

They had stood all the loneliness they could in this forsaken outpost. Then they had shed the painful shoes, walked off into the towering forest, and headed north. Many of them talked disconsolately to Osceola on the way back to the fort. He heard their life stories. He heard about their sweethearts, their mothers, their dogs. He heard their diffident plans for the back acres of the family farm. He didn't understand much of what they said, just as he didn't understand why men should be punished for going home.

For Osceola, tracking deserters was a job. It brought extra income for his family. It presented him with the challenge of hunting the canniest of animals. But tracking men was like tracking deer. Even though Osceola was the hunter, his sympathy was with the quarry.

The physical pain of the white men's punishments didn't bother Osceola. Men should be tested, but the testing should be voluntary. The deliberate humilation of this made Osceola angry.

He filled a cedar bucket at the nearby spring and brought it back. The soldier's face was pressed against the log's surface. His eyes were closed. His cheeks were covered with a sparse blond fuzz.

Osceola soaked his kerchief in the water and held it to the boy's lips. The soldier moaned. Osceola squeezed the cloth so moisture trickled into his mouth. He could feel the heat radiating from the burned skin. He trickled more water across

the boy's back and legs, but even the fall of drops was agony.
The soldier moaned again and writhed. Osceola draped the
damp kerchief over the soldier's head, to protect it from the
heat.

He regretted leaving his special medicine on Talasee, especially the salve that would ease the boy's suffering and the
burning pain of Osceola's torn nostril. He could only chant
a curing song and trust it to have some effect. In any case the
sun would die soon and the boy would be set free. The white
Tastanagee Thloko usually sentenced a troublemaker to one
day of this, and most survived it. The culprit would hobble
about for a week, unable to bend his knees or sleep at night.
Under his stiff, badly fitting linen uniform, the skin would
itch, blister, then peel off in moist, fragile sheets.

By the time Osceola had bathed and dressed, the sun had
set. He walked through the gate and skirted the festivities on
the parade ground. He sat on the banquette that ran the length
of the palisade. He drew his legs up and crossed his ankles.
He took his tobacco from the folds of his turban and slowly
packed his pipe. He struck sparks with his flint against his
knife blade and sucked on the stem until he managed to light
the pipe.

He sat motionless, except for the occasional sucking of his
cheeks and the deliberate scan of his eyes behind his bangs.
He felt comfortable here, in this town of warriors. Today the
parade ground was doubling as a dance floor, and it reminded
Osceola of Talasee's ceremonial square. The pale-eyes warriors had a system of rank that Osceola could understand.
The men who lived here followed a warrior's code. Their
actions may have seemed foolish at times, but Osceola never
doubted their courage.

In the center of the parade ground, a slave played a reel on
his fiddle. Men who didn't have female partners paired off
with each other. One of the settlers, at the fag end of a long
spree, was dancing by himself. His capacious overalls bounced
on the ends of their braces.

"Do you speak English?" The lieutenant had approached
so quietly Osceola hadn't noticed him. He held nine-year-old
Little Warrior by the hand.

"Mebbe li'l bit." In all Osceola's dealings with surveyors,

agents, traders, deserters, and soldiers, he had never let on he understood any of what they said. His admission now surprised him. The lieutenant's gentle eyes were responsible. They were the clear, intense blue of a very hot flame.

Osceola was also distracted by Little Warrior. She was wearing a pair of linen drawers that transformed her into a familiar-looking stranger. The drawstring waist of the baggy white underwear was pulled up around her chest. The hems reached past her scuffed knees. They were held in place with a gentleman's black satin muffling cravat wrapped twice around her middle.

"I didn't know if it would be proper for me to go to your bivouac to find her mother. . . ." The lieutenant stopped, unsure how to explain that he was too shy to walk through a Seminole encampment occupied largely by women.

"What happened?" Osceola asked Little Warrior in Mikasukee.

"I fought." She climbed onto the banquette and inspected her father's injured nose. A bruise was spreading from it across his cheek. "You fought, too?"

"Yes."

Little Warrior patted the splintery wood beside her. The lieutenant preferred to stand, but he couldn't refuse her request. His experience with children was limited, but this one had the wisest eyes he had ever encountered in one so young. She had woven an artless spell and caught him in it.

The lieutenant sat gingerly, leaving plenty of room between himself and Little Warrior and her father. He was only twenty years old and very new here. He couldn't begin to predict how this befeathered primitive would react to the news. Osceola's expression was unreadable as he waited for Little Warrior to tell him more.

"There were four of them," she said. "Pale-eyes boys. This big." She held her hand over her head.

"She wasn't at fault." The lieutenant had noticed the rows of spidery scars on Little Warrior's arms and legs. Maybe Seminole tortured their children as a form of discipline. He had heard the usual soldiers' stories about Indian cruelty.

"Four large ragamuffins were throwing stones at her." He pantomimed to make his meaning clearer. "They called her names, I'm afraid. Some of these people are totally without the benefits of a moral or academic education. Please take that into account."

My God, what if he decides to take revenge? A sudden vision of the party erupting into warfare flashed through the lieutenant's mind.

"I bit the nose of one of them." In general, Little Warrior was satisfied with her performance. "I think I broke another's finger. He cried like baby sister."

"She inflicted considerable damage before they threw her into a barrel of manatee lard, there by the cookhouse." The lieutenant decided honesty was the best policy. It was the only one he knew, anyway. "The sun had softened it, and she was a mess when I pulled her out. I took her to the laundress for a bath, but this was all I had for her to wear. I left her little, uh, apron for the laundress to boil."

Actually Little Warrior was small for her age, and the lieutenant had been surprised to discover she was a girl. He had wrapped his tunic around her for the short trip to his tent. While he had hunted for something for her to wear, she had chattered away to him in Mikasukee and investigated everything in his quarters.

Now he braced himself to defend her against her father's wrath. But Osceola grinned, gave her one of Wococoi Clark's winks, and hugged her to him. She sat next to him and pulled his arm over her shoulder. She soon forgot about the humiliation of the manatee lard and stared at the dancers.

The lieutenant nodded toward the farmer, still capering inside his baggy coveralls. "Doesn't he just look like two cats courting in a quilt, though?"

Osceola widened his smile to include the lieutenant.

"My name is Goode," said the lieutenant. "Lieutenant John Goode. West Point. Class of thirty-two," he added automatically. He held out his hand.

"I'm Powell." Osceola shook John's fingers hard enough to bounce the gold fringe on his right epaulet.

"Well, your young one's a handful, Mr. Powell, for being no more than yard-sized. You must be proud of her."

Osceola only smiled in response. Night had fallen, and the soldiers lit bonfires atop wooden platforms spread with sand.

Their wavery light gleamed off Lieutenant Goode's hair, the color of new corn syrup.

"You won me a fair amount of money this afternoon," John Goode said.

"Why did you bet for me?" Osceola aided his halting English with gestures.

"We have a saying, 'The bigger they are, the harder they fall.' "

Osceola nodded thoughtfully, appreciating that concept.

"You reminded me of little David facing Goliath. Have you heard that story?"

"No."

Lieutenant Goode slid closer. He drew up his shiny army shoes, carefully blacked with soot and grease. He leaned against the palisade. He had had just enough brandy to dissolve some of the West Point starch from his spine.

"This is how it goes," he said.

CHAPTER 24

"Uncle! Uncle!" Little Warrior hiked up her long skirt and ran alongside John Goode's big roan gelding. He leaned down, lifted her into the air, and set her in front of him. Her skirt rode up on her thighs, and her bare legs dangled just behind the gelding's shoulders. She took the reins and clucked and kicked with her heels, although by now the roan knew the way to Morning Dew's compound. He also knew Little Warrior would bring him armloads of juicy grass and a few ears of sweet corn when he arrived there.

The people of Talasee were so used to seeing Goode that they hardly acknowledged his passing. Which was not to say they didn't notice him. From behind their long bangs, many of the unmarried women watched him ride by. One in particular held her heavy oaken pestle above the dried *koontee* roots an extra beat, breaking the rhythm set by her sisters. John didn't hear the quiet laughter and teasing that rippled in his wake.

He pulled an amber bar of lye soap from his tunic, reached around in front of Little Warrior, and held it up so she could see it. *"Nakita?"* he asked. "What is it?"

"Suhkos'kuh." Little Warrior was used to this game. In his passion to learn Maskokee and Mikasukee, John played it so often that Morning Dew had named him Nakita.

"In English, what is it?" The deal was he taught her English in exchange for her help with Maskokee and Mikasukee.

"Soap."

"Did you bring presents?" Little Warrior rubbed the soap speculatively. Then she sniffed it, licked it, and made a face.

"Momes, echustee, it might be so, daughter."

John tethered his horse in the small pasture and left him to Little Warrior's care. He brought the saddlebags back to the kitchen arbor and set them across one of the logs of the star fire.

With her legs tucked under her, Morning Dew sat on a deer hide near the fire. She was weaving split cane, dyed black and orange and red, into a mat for her cabin floor. The long strips waved and shivered and whispered as though Morning Dew were weaving life into their intricate patterns. "You are come, Nakita." She smiled at him.

"I am." John watched Osceola finish stripping the bark from a cypress pole.

"Push the log in, brother," he said. While John eased the big pine trunk toward the center of the fire, Osceola did the same for the other three. When the ends caught and the fire began to burn hotter, he laid the butt of the cypress pole at the edge of it.

John took the ladle from among the utensils hanging on the kitchen arbor's corner post. He dipped it into the kettle and sipped the tart *sofkee* from it. Then he pointed it at the pole. "For hunting alligators?"

"An alligator pole is longer." Osceola answered all Nakita's questions patiently; but he was often amazed at how little his friend knew. "This one will push the dugout. The fire hardens the end so it won't split in the water."

"Nakita, show us what you brought." Little Warrior and two-year-old Crying Bird stood expectantly next to the saddlebags. Little Warrior was dressed in a long skirt and short blouse like her mothers. In fact, the outfit had been made from one of Morning Dew's old dresses. Crying Bird wore a few strands of beads and a coat of dust. John held one of the bags open so the children could look inside. Little Warrior pulled out two frilled smocks of bright red calico, one small and one larger.

"Two dresses for me!" She clutched them to her chest and smiled mischievously at John. "Thank you, Nakita."

Crying Bird began to wail as though she were being tortured. Morning Dew didn't say anything. She only reached for the pouch that held her garfish jaw with the pointed teeth still in place. Little Warrior gave Crying Bird her dress, and the child stopped sobbing abruptly.

John left Mink wetting a piece of sacking and washing Crying Bird so she could try on her dress. Little Warrior took hers to the cabin to change into it. They would wear them the rest of the evening, be admired all around, then put them away for special occasions.

John shouldered his saddlebags and went to the guest cabin. Like most, it was divided into two rooms. He found Old Squat sitting on his blankets in his half. He was mending his moccasins in a rectangle of light from the open doorway. As he worked Old Squat coughed occasionally and spat into his bandana. Now and then he picked up the edge of his hunting shirt and conversed intently with it. A wrinkled smudge of dirt at the hem indicated where his fingers usually clutched it.

Old Squat had arrived at the cooking fire one night with all his personal belongings in two large bundles. He had announced he was in his home. "You are, Grandfather," Morning Dew had answered. Old Squat was of her clan and welcome to stay as long as he wanted. He appeared to want to stay a long time. Whenever John stayed in the guest cabin, he went to sleep to the serenade of Old Squat's wheezing and coughing and mumbling.

"May you be well, Grandfather." John gave a small bow as he handed Old Squat a cigar. Old Squat inclined his head in thanks, like a monarch accepting tribute. He rose and tucked the cigar into the thatch over his bed. Then he went back to his moccasins and his conversation with his shirt.

John walked across the worn cane mats to the pile of fresh Spanish moss in the corner. Folded neatly on top of it was a new pair of leather leggings dyed with red mangrove bark. He picked them up and laid out his bedroll. He didn't bother to make sure the moss had been scorched to kill chiggers. Morning Dew always took care of that.

He untied the knot in the mosquito netting and dropped it over his bed so it would be in place when the mosquitoes attacked at dusk. He took off his boots and his white summer uniform. He reached for the leather pouch stored in the dusty cypress rafters and pulled out the pair of moccasins and the knee-length hunting shirt Mink had made for him.

He put his jacket in the pouch and replaced it in the rafters among the other bags and tools, sacks of seed corn and gray-brown *koontee* roots tied in bundles. He lined up his army shoes at the foot of the bed and hung his saddlebags on a peg. Everything had its place in Morning Dew's cabins, and he was careful not to disturb the order. A woman's attentive presence here, so far from his own mother's home, filled him with a wistful longing, as intense as it was brief.

Walking gingerly, he returned to the fire. This was the first time he'd worn leggings. The long hunting shirt covered him thoroughly, but the unaccustomed draft astern made him uneasy.

A kettle of venison and pumpkin stewed in bear oil had been set out on a low platform in the kitchen arbor. Mink had pounded turtle steaks to tenderize them, and now they broiled on heated stones. Nakita took one of the pale slices and for seasoning dipped it into a small gourd holding a salty paste of wood ash. He washed it down with *sofkee*. The rest of the family helped themselves when they were hungry.

Shadows, like shreds of night, extended through the village. Clouds of birds clattered back to their rookeries. Little Warrior piled green pine branches on the fire so the smoke would hold the mosquitoes at bay. Thwarted, they whined outside the thick clouds while the family gathered for evening talk.

Tonight they were joined by Mad Dog, Old Squat, Swamp Singer, Dahomey, Fighting in a Line, Black, and Alligator. They had come to sample Nakita's wares. For he was a peddler of sorts, and the commodity he carried was beyond price. He brought news, stories, even songs. He brought novelty to the village routine.

With Black translating, Alligator didn't waste any time before continuing his study of white people.

"Nakita, do your women drop children in farrows like pigs?" It seemed a sensible question to Alligator. How else could white people multiply in such alarming numbers? "Or do they lay eggs, like alligators?"

John Goode could adapt to every aspect of Seminole life but their candor. His face turned bright crimson.

"Are you sick, Uncle?" Little Warrior regarded him anxiously.

"No, niece." He turned to Alligator, although everyone was listening intently. "Our women bear one child at a time. Sometimes two. They carry them nine months." He was grateful that at least Alligator had left off asking him detailed questions about his anatomy.

"How many women do you have?"

John's blush deepened. "None."

"None!" Alligator was astonished. "Do you prefer men, like the Chickasaws do?"

"No. I'm hunting a wife."

"I hope you're better at hunting women than you are at hunting deer," Alligator said.

John smiled sheepishly. This was definitely the time to change the subject. He held up a piece of vellum, folded in half. "I received a letter."

The reading of John's letters from home were always followed by lengthy discussions, punctuated by Old Squat's demure snores. John had to recount the life story of each person mentioned and acknowledge that yes, it was a sad thing his kin had no clan to comfort and protect them.

As the stars and moon progressed overhead, the quiet talk, the barking of dogs, and the medicine chants from the other women's compounds diminished, then stilled. One by one Morning Dew's guests stood without ceremony and walked off toward their own beds to hunt dreams. Morning Dew carried the sleeping Crying Bird into her cabin, and Little Warrior followed.

Mink scattered ashes around the yard's perimeter. A witch was rumored to be in the area, and witches didn't like to cross ashes; but Mink was taking no chances. As extra protection she stuck another owl feather between the logs over the doorway of each cabin.

Mad Dog knocked the dottle from his pipe and grinned over at John, who was about to retire himself. John was stalling to see with which wife Osceola chose to spend the night. He was dismayed by the practice of two women sharing one man, but he was tantalized by it, too. Even though the arrangement seemed to work quite well here, he often lay awake considering the implications.

When Mad Dog stood and beckoned, John looked at Osceola.

"He wants you to follow him," Osceola said.

"Why?"

"Because you're lonely."

John knew he wouldn't get a better explanation; Osceola preferred teaching in riddles. He followed Mad Dog through the village, past the clusters of dark cabins and banked fires and across the empty ceremonial ground. Mad Dog stopped at one of the community storehouses and opened the door. He took John's arm in a grip as strong as a smith's pincers and pushed him inside.

"What am I to do here?" John asked from the blackness.

"*Huhte'tuhs.* Wait a while."

Mad Dog closed the door and was gone. Feeling foolish, John stood in the gloom. He breathed shallowly. The air was thick with the caustic odor of hides treated with turpentine to keep away worms and moths and rats. He didn't know if it was effective with worms and moths, but he could hear the rats.

Stripes of moonlight came through the chinks between the logs of the walls. As his eyes adjusted, John could make out baskets of corn and dried fish and gourds of beeswax. Then he saw the black, bloated shapes of bodies, withered limbs splayed grotesquely outward, hanging upside down from the rafters. Was this a joke or something far more sinister? Had they only pretended to like him? Where they about to kill him?

He reached out and felt the cool, stiff bristles on one of the hanging bodies. Either this was a deer hide or a very hairy corpse. He remembered then that Morning Dew poured clarified bear oil into deer carcasses and hung them for storage; but it took his heart a while to stop thudding.

He had almost decided this was another of Alligator and Mad Dog's pranks when he heard a creak of leather hinges. A ribbon of pale gray widened as the door opened and a shadow slipped inside.

"Who is it?" John whispered.

"Third Sister. Of the Panther clan." She moved so close he could smell the smoky perfume of her hair, which was about nose level.

When he tried gently to push her away, his fingers pressed into the soft, round breasts under her thin cotton blouse. He jerked his hands back as if they'd been scorched. He had never lain with a woman. He had never intended to lay with one until the act was sanctified by marriage. He felt with a sudden, clear certainty that his mother and father, starched and saintly and horrified, were standing behind him.

"Go away." John's parade-ground voice turned hoarse and undependable. What words he knew of Mikasukee had deserted him, leaving him stranded in a dark wilderness of sexual ambiguities. "There's been a mistake. Please go away."

Third Sister couldn't understand him, of course. She laid out the blanket she had brought and began undressing. John couldn't see her face in the shadows; but the moon shining through the half-opened door brushed the curves of her bare shoulders and her heavy breasts with light. John had difficulty breathing. Organizing his feet to retreat from the storehouse was out of the question.

Third Sister said something else, soft and pleading. When John didn't move she reached for his hands and held them against her breasts. He could feel her nipples taut against his palms. He could feel her heart beating under the smooth skin. She moved his hands downward, across her rounded belly and hips. He had to lean forward, burying his face in her fragrant hair.

He licked his dry lips and whimpered as his hands came to rest on the firm, cushioned mound between her sturdy thighs. Third Sister moaned and pressed his palms hard against her.

With one hand Third Sister kept John imprisoned between her thighs. He felt awkward in the stooped position, but he ached with longing. With her other hand she untied his belt. His breechclout and new leggings dropped around his ankles, and she reached up under his shirt.

When her fingers closed around him, ecstasy ambushed him. With a cry of exultation, remorse, and astonishment, he exploded; and unlike his army musket, he kept on firing. He covered himself and Third Sister with a warm, slippery stream. It dripped through her fingers onto his shirt and his new leggings.

Third Sister giggled and rubbed it across his flat belly and trim haunches. Now it was his turn to catch her hands.

"Forgive me," he stammered. "I must go." He fumbled for his breechclout, belt, and leggings. His fingers shook, and his face burned as he struggled to dress. Third Sister murmured to him and pushed his hands away. There in the dimness, she dressed him, arranging his shirt with care. John was too distraught to notice that the care was proprietary.

She stood, silent and naked and unmoving, as he rushed out into the warm night. As he hurried back to Morning Dew's compound, waves of revulsion at his shameful performance washed over him. The worst was, he didn't even know who she was, so he couldn't avoid her.

He couldn't come back here. He couldn't face the laughter in each woman's eyes. He couldn't wonder which one she was. And whom she had told.

But as he lay, still trembling, under his blanket, he couldn't get Third Sister out of his mind. He raised his hands to his face and smelled her. Her spirit, like the musky perfume of her, was on his skin. In his heart. In his bones. Part of him wanted never to blunder into her again. Part of him knew he would die slowly, from the inside out, if he didn't.

CHAPTER 25

John Goode did return to Talasee, of course. For John, love was an abiding itch in a place he couldn't scratch. Only the mysterious siren, a soft, smoky, voluptuous presence outlined in moonlight, could relieve the torment. His first time back, however, he arrived after dark and took a circuitous route to Morning Dew's cabins. He drew Osceola aside and explained his predicament, leaving out the part about the hair trigger on his ardor.

"I don't know who she is," he confessed. "I don't even know what she looks like."

"Her name is Third Sister." Osceola remembered how he felt when he didn't know Morning Dew's name or clan. "She's of my women's clan." He paused. John sensed he was holding something back.

"May I see her again?" He was suddenly frantic at the thought that he couldn't.

"Certainly."

"What if she doesn't want to see me?"

"She'll tell you."

"Help me, brother."

"I will." And Osceola did. But he didn't tell John that his woman had two older sisters who would have to find husbands before she could wed.

Mad Dog had proposed introducing John to Third Sister to dispel his loneliness while he lived here, far from his home fire. She would alleviate the urges that interfered with a man's more important activities. No one expected John to marry her, except perhaps Third Sister herself.

John and Third Sister began to meet in a tiny green glade, dappled with sunlight and scented with spider orchids. It had been used by Talasee's lovers for years. The passions that had filled it so often had made it an enchanted place.

John had fallen in love with Third Sister's voice and touch and smell before he ever saw her. So even in the uncompromising light of day he thought her beautiful. He was probably the only one who did. Her eyes were a bit too close together, her nose too flat, her mouth too wide. She was short and broad. Her generous breasts and hips were obviously meant for someone several inches taller. But Mad Dog had been wise to select her over her older sisters.

Third Sister was like a river pebble, drab and ordinary until polished by a swiftly running stream. The turbulence of her passion for John transformed her. She shone with a rainbow of sensual color and light. She loved John with a purity, intensity, and ingenuity that left him breathless. And though they didn't speak each other's language, they communicated in ways that had little to do with words.

Each time John made the five-mile journey from Fort King, he brought her presents of silk romal scarves and beads, bracelets, and calicoes. But she hid them in the bottom of her leather clothing bag in a far corner of the rafters; and she only wore them for him. John took a while realizing that her people disapproved of him as much as his would disapprove of her if they had known about her.

Their affair was discreet enough for the politest of parlor society. John's mother's Anglican ladies couldn't have carried on with more decorum. John even convinced himself only Mad Dog and Osceola knew of the affair. He was wrong, of course. Everyone in Talasee knew about it.

Fighting in a Line had misgivings about Mad Dog's meddling. She liked Nakita well enough, but she liked Third Sister, too. Fighting in a Line could see ahead as clearly as she could see behind. At best, tears would flow when this was over; at worst, blood.

One night when the family gathered, Fighting in a Line broke abruptly into the adults' discussion of weather and crops and cattle.

"Do you remember Me-le?" she asked.

"Yes, Grandmother." Osceola immediately knew what was coming.

"This story happened a long time ago." Fighting in a Line's arthritic fingers struggled with her pipe, and Little Warrior hurried to light it for her. Then she retreated back to the other side of the fire and sat down again with four of her female cousins.

"This story happened when Old Mad Jackson followed us Red Sticks south. When your father was not much older than you." Fighting in a Line looked at Little Warrior. "My brother led a war party out. They came back with a blue-jacket. They captured him while he was dozing over a fishing line." Fighting in a Line smiled at the memory of poor Duncan McKrimmon.

Private McKrimmon had gone jugging for cats in the middle of a war, in the middle of a few hundred square miles of the enemy's territory. He had baited five hooks with salt pork and fastened them to sinkers made from musket balls. He had set out his line of corked earthenware jugs as floaters and tied a hawk bell to it to alert him of a strike. Then he'd unbuttoned the tight collar of his wool tunic, stretched his legs out in front of him, and leaned back against a cabbage palm.

The warm sun and the slow pirouette of the cork float to the measured pulse of the swamp soon put him to sleep. He awoke to the sharp rap of the flat of a hatchet blade against the sole of his shoe. That was how he came to be tied, naked, to the tall scalp pole in the village of Crazy Medicine, Fighting in a Line's cousin.

"At first, I was happy see him there," Fighting in a Line said. "The blue-jackets had burned our towns. They killed our people. Stole our cattle. They drove us from our homes. I sang as the men danced around the pole where the blue-jacket was tied. We women laughed when he wet himself.

"Some of the women heated their knife blades at the fires to lay them against his pale skin. Some stirred the clay in the bowl."

"What was the clay for, Grandmother?" Little Warrior asked.

"To plaster on his head, so when we tested him with fire his hair wouldn't burn. We planned to take his scalp before he died. His hair was like corn silk. It would have made an unusual trophy to hang on the pole."

With rapt faces, the girls hung on every word. All they knew of war were the boasts of the old men at dances. This was not like the stories they usually heard. They were repelled and fascinated. "Did you burn the blue-jacket, Grandmother?"

"No one burned him. A foolish girl saved him."

"Did she love him?" Now all the cousins had questions.

"Maybe so. Her name was Me-le. She was the daughter of my cousin, Crazy Medicine."

"Where is she now?"

"I can't tell the end of the story first, can I?"

"Was she beautiful?"

"She was very beautiful. All the boys were crazy for her."

"What did she do?"

"She stood in front of the blue-jacket. She knocked the bowl of clay from the women's hands." Fighting in a Line's eyes grew misty as she thought of Me-le standing slender and stubborn in the frenzy of the celebration. Her new doeskin dress was spattered with the red clay. "Feelings were so high, the people might have decided to tie her to the pole with the blue-jacket. Her father was angry with her. Everyone was angry."

" 'He's too young to die.' " Fighting in a Line took the parts of Me-le and her father.

" 'We all must die. We're not consulted as to how or when.' "

" 'The Spanish will pay handsomely for him. They'd be pleased to give this man to Old Mad Jackson as a present, to appease him.' "

" 'I don't care about appeasing Old Mad Jackson.' "

"Then my brother stepped in." Fighting in a Line took Mad New Town's role, too. " 'A dead blue-jacket is useless. Alive, he can bring us powder, lead, muskets.' " Fighting in a Line laughed. "Powder, lead, muskets. Those were the things the warriors craved. My brother knew how to get what he wanted."

"If he didn't want the blue-jacket to die, why didn't *he* stop the people?"

"He was a war leader. Sometimes a man can be a good leader only by following. He knew his men needed to see this man suffer. He knew the soldier was a whetstone on which his men would have honed their fervor for war."

"What happened to Me-le?" Little Warrior didn't want her grandmother to stray too far from the important part of the story.

Fighting in a Line stared into the fire so long, Little Warrior was afraid she'd gone to sleep. "The boy Me-le saved showed the other blue-jackets where to capture her father. Crazy Medicine was a great leader. He was a prophet among the Red Sticks. Old Mad Jackson tied a rope around his neck. He hung him up like a deer carcass."

"Did he die?" Death by hanging was an unknown concept to the children.

"Yes."

"What happened to Me-le?"

"She, her mothers, her sisters, surrendered to Old Mad Jackson. He sent them away, to light their fire in a far country. He sent them to the country where now he wants to send us. No one has seen or heard of Me-le since."

"What happened to the blue-jacket?"

"He asked Me-le to marry him. He said he loved her."

"She didn't marry the man who betrayed her!" Little Warrior was so outraged she half rose off her seat on the log.

"No. Me-le refused to marry him."

Fighting in a Line drew no moral from her story. She sat back and retired to her own memories, while on the far side of the fire, the girls quietly discussed Me-le's fate.

Fighting in a Line had left out the part of the story that showed her own weakness. She had been old even then. She couldn't use a young woman's infatuation as an excuse, as Me-le could. Fighting in a Line was ashamed of the fact that she had tried to save the blue-jacket, too.

She had been shrieking a particularly inventive taunt at him when he'd raised his head and stared at her. The Florida sun had bleached his eyebrows white, giving him a look of startled innocence. He had seemed puzzled that so much hatred should be directed at him when he felt none himself. His guileless eyes had pleaded with her to help him.

His pale blue eyes and bushy white eyebrows had reminded Fighting in a Line of her father. Old James McQueen would not have approved of this. *Savages!* She could hear him say it in the brogue he never lost, even after living ninety years with the Creeks. In the end, one dead man had won out over several hundred living ones.

In her memory, Fighting in a Line watched herself weave through the dancers and the women taunting the blue-jacket from the sidelines. She had found Neamathla, the most influential leader in that part of the country.

"Old Snake Bone . . ." He was so tall she had had to lay her head back onto her shoulders to see his face. "Stop them. He's only a boy. Give him to me as a slave. I promise to make his life miserable."

"I'll not be happy until the heat of the fire splits his skin. Until the fat boils inside him." Neamathla's eyes had glittered in the fire's light. "The blue-jackets burned my village. They killed four of my warriors. They killed one of my women. Because of them my people are homeless. They're shoeless."

Old Snake Bone, she thought. When you signed the pale-eyes' talking leaves, you thought you could bargain with white people. Instead they humiliated you in front of your warriors. Where are you now, Old Snake Bone? Where is poor Me-le?

"I am come." John Goode's voice startled Fighting in a Line from her reverie. He appeared, pale as a spirit creature, from the darkness. "I come from Tampa. I have much to tell you."

Osceola had tried to teach Nakita to hold council with dignity and to control his facial expressions. But the anger was evident in his eyes now. "Your leaders have just landed there, returned from the west. They've betrayed you all!"

CHAPTER 26

Now that they all knew war was likely, Osceola felt a warm peace suffuse him from the marrow of his bones outward. He had been right. The waiting was over. If they didn't make medicine and set out on the war trail tomorrow, at least they would begin preparing. The young men would have the chance to earn war honors. Their women would have reason to be proud of them again.

Osceola had no illusions that the struggle would be an easy one. He wasn't even sure his people could win against the guns and numbers of blue-jacket soldiers. But after years of humbly acquiescing to the white men's demands, he was ready to fight, no matter what the cost.

He glanced at Wild Cat, who sat in the Panther clan's section of the long shed across the square. Wild Cat raised one eyebrow in greeting. Neither of them would likely say anything in this council. Even though he was the son of an important Mikasukee leader, Wild Cat was even younger than Osceola. And the people of Talasee were few in number. Osceola was a minor war leader at best.

He was as stony-faced as the other men in the clan sheds. But this council would seem calm only to an outsider. Behind the stoic expressions raged fury and shame, old suspicions and hatreds. Nakita's news was bad indeed.

The white men claimed that the seven leaders who went west had liked the territory set aside for them and the northern Creeks. The white men said that in signing the treaty in Oklahoma, the Maskokee and Mikasukee leaders had agreed to move *all* their people west. They said the chiefs had agreed to unite with the hated Creeks there.

Within a few days Abihka had become head of the faction adamantly opposed to moving. This council was taking place in his town. He had sent his fastest runners out with bundles of sticks to deliver to the leaders of the other towns. Each stick represented a day and was taken from the bundle at sunset and broken. When none were left, the men arrived for the council.

Now each leader who had signed the Oklahoma treaty stood in turn to defend his actions. They spoke at great length, but the core of their talks was simple. They denied touching the pen with which Phagan signed their names, or they claimed they had been tricked or coerced into signing.

"Fay-kahn threatened us." Because the white men had backed Mole Leader when he'd deposed Mikanopee five years earlier, he was particularly defensive. "He said we would be stranded, that we would have to find our own way back from the western lands unless we signed. I'm getting old. I wish my bones to be buried here. I asked the white leaders why they plague us so about going over the Mississippi. We hurt nothing on this land."

"The western lands are overrun with wild tribes who war constantly," added Mad Partridge. "We would never agree to move there."

"Fay-kahn is a passionate man. He quarreled with us all the time." Chalo Emathla, Trout Leader, always looked as though he considered life a series of trials to be borne with fortitude. His small black eyes peered out at a world that wasn't what he wanted or expected. Now he looked even sadder than usual.

He was approaching sixty years, but he had always held himself absolutely erect. Since his return he had acquired a slight stoop, like an old bow that no longer straightened when the string was loosened. His heavy jaw and chin sagged. "I signed thinking the treaty would not bind us unless the entire nation agreed to it."

"The white men tricked us." Jumper was Mikanopee's brother-in-law and sense-maker. Mikanopee had found an excuse not to make the arduous journey west, and Jumper had gone in his stead. As it turned out, Mikanopee had been shrewd. But then indolence was always hard to distinguish from wile in Mikanopee.

Jumper was about forty years old. He was long and lean, at least six feet tall. He had a narrow face, high forehead, and murky eyes. His eyes were like tar pools that absorbed light and reflected back no emotions. He spoke in a high, singsong voice; and as always, he spoke well.

"I tell you this, brothers," he said. "The white men lied to us. The first treaty said we would move if the entire Seminole nation agreed to it. The treaty we signed in the west said, *'If this delegation be satisfied,'* we would move, but no one told us that. I ask you, how could this have happened?"

Everyone turned to look at the slender black man sitting in Mikanopee's bulky shadow. When Jumper sat, he rose slowly.

His name was Abraham. He was Mikanopee's former slave

and the son of slaves. He had grown up in the household of a Pensacola doctor before Mikanopee bought him. Mikanopee had freed him seven years before, in gratitude for the services he had rendered. His large, wedge-shaped head narrowed to a pointed chin. His eyes were slits under the bulging overhang of his eyelids.

Abraham still served his king with the loyalty of a courtier, and he carried himself like one. He walked slightly bent forward, as though about to give a refined bow. Under his flowered turban a few strands of silver entwined in the tight black curls. In spite of the fact that his right eye drifted toward his large hooked nose, his polished manner gave him an air of breeding and dignity. His knowledge of Spanish, English, and Maskokee made him Mikanopee's most trusted adviser.

He had interpreted most of the meetings between the whites and Seminole in the past ten years. He had made the journey to Oklahoma. While there he had interpreted the treaty that now threatened to rob the Seminole of their homeland. He was on trial here, and he knew it.

"Some men say I lied. They say I betrayed you. They say I accepted two hundred of the white men's metal beads to mislead the Seminole, who have been my friends, my protectors." Abraham knew council protocol. First he would give the arguments against him. Then he would refute them.

"I tell you this, I have no reason to lie to you, my red brothers. Every good thing I have—my freedom, my family, my position, my home—is a gift of my king's generosity. I would not betray you, knowing I must live among you, at your sufferance. Aside from that, two hundred metal beads are not enough to receive in exchange for a life in chains.

"We all know the white men intend to send the red people west. We all know they intend to keep the black people here. They will buy us, sell us, whip us like cattle. No white man enters the territory but that he begins speculating in black flesh. I ask you, noble warriors, would you sell yourself into slavery for two hundred metal beads? Would you sell your wives, your children?" Abraham waited for them to consider that before he went on.

"This is what happened in the western lands. Fay-kahn read

the talking leaves to me in English. I interpreted them to our leaders in their own tongues. Because I cannot read, I did not know Fay-kahn told me the wrong words to say. He substituted 'should they be satisfied,' meaning the entire Seminole nation for 'should this delegation be satisfied.' He tricked us all.

"Some of you might ask why he would do that. I'll tell you. Fay-kahn is a perverse man. The American king, Old Mad Jackson, will pay metal beads to the ones who supply wagons or food to you on the trip west. I think Fay-kahn plans to get some of those beads. I think he plans to get even more from buying your property, your cattle, your black people, cheaply, then selling them dear to the other whites."

The discussion continued through the day and into the night. When the full moon hung directly overhead, many of the men slept in their places on the mats of the clan shed platforms. Abihka picked his way among them until he found Osceola and Alligator, resting on their elbows and talking quietly. He put a hand on Osceola's shoulder.

"Come with me." He led him to his own fire and shared tobacco with him. His fine, white hair looked like moonlight flowing down from his bony skull. "You will speak for me," he said.

"You honor me, Uncle."

"Our thoughts are the same on this question. You have a persuasive way with men's hearts. Here's what I want you to say." Abihka and Osceola talked in low voices until the first cock crowed and the others joined in.

Shortly after dawn, the council continued. After another day of debate, Osceola rose and walked to the center of the square. His high voice carried easily to the rear platforms of the clan sheds.

"Great Warrior Abihka has appointed me his sense-maker." The old men listened politely, but Osceola knew they were annoyed that Abihka had chosen one so young to speak for him.

"This is what he has asked me to say. The old leaders who counsel us to give in to the white men's demands are tired. Their thoughts are muddled. They're old women." He ignored the faint rustle of men shifting in their seats, the closest to an audible protest he would get from the old leaders. He had expected it. He had insulted them deeply.

"Once they were brave young warriors whose hatchets cried for the blood of their enemies. When the war standard was raised, they mounted their ponies. They fell in line behind it. They fought without fear. Now they're like the sun going down. The light of courage in them is dim. Soon it will be too dim to guide us on the war trail.

"Abihka says this: Any man who signs away our land or agrees to move west must be killed. We will not leave our country. If the old men will not fight, the young ones will.

"Tell your women to dry all the meat they can. Set aside all the corn you can spare, for we have hungry times ahead. War is more than killing. War is surviving.

"Tell your men to buy weapons, powder, lead. Buy the new guns, the ones with spirals etched into their barrels. They shoot more accurately. Tell the white men we need the rifles for the hunt. We must lull their suspicions while we plant. While we harvest our crops. While we prepare for war."

As Osceola walked back to his seat, he felt the tension in the air as surely as he felt the morning breeze riffling the long fringe of hair around his face. When he reached the Snake clan's shed he scanned the three tiers of faces, trying to read the effect of his speech. He saw Abihka's mouth twitch approval. Over Abihka's shoulder he saw his uncle sitting in his usual place in the far left corner of the third tier. Mad New Town's plumes bobbed as he smiled and nodded. Osceola blinked, and the ghost was gone.

"The pale-eyes complain of mosquitoes so big they can dress them out. They claim they can tan their hides," Alligator called out. "Tell the Americans we need the rifles to shoot mosquitoes."

The laughter that followed was bitter, but at least it eased the anger.

The council's decision wasn't unanimous. Many of the older men still advised appeasement while the young warriors talked only of war. While the leaders filed out of the clan sheds, Osceola tallied those Abihka could count on to fight.

A predatory stare replaced his mild expression. His jaw

tightened, and his mouth set into a tense line. His dark eyes narrowed as he studied the men who were still undecided about moving west.

"Selecting your war party, brother?" Now that war was in the air, Wild Cat was jovial.

"No, brother. I'm wondering which leaders we'll have to kill."

Fighting in a Line was using her demure, this-is-how-one-talks-to-white-people voice. Fighting in a Line looked at the floor. She spoke so softly, Erastus Rogers's black interpreter had to strain to hear her. But she didn't fool Rogers. His sour look shifted to pained distaste whenever he saw her dodging the foot-and-horse traffic in front of the store. He always assigned a clerk to wait exclusively on her. Then he made himself very busy until she was gone.

Fighting in a Line laid her bundle of egret plumes on the counter before she began her inspection of the sutler's store. Mink lifted the bundle of alligator hides off her head and set them on the plank floor. Little Warrior put down the four gopher turtles she carried in two nets, one brace in each hand. Little Warrior's face was puffy and her eyes almost swollen shut. She had been collecting the nests of paper hornets to use as wadding for her father's musket.

Morning Dew carried Crying Bird on her hip so the child wouldn't break anything. The three women walked slowly along the crude shelves lining the log walls. They paused in the corner where Rogers kept the goods for the Indian trade. They stared at the bolts of bright calicoes, the strings of beads heaped in tin cups, and the boxes of colored handkerchiefs and gaudy tinsel trim. They knew they wouldn't be taking any of them home.

Little Warrior only slowed down slightly as she went by the dusty cones of brown sugar. She stood in the doorway to Roger's back room and stared in at the long wooden crates stacked there. She knew each one held six rifles individually wrapped in chamois.

Giving up sugar and beads, silk thread and steel trade needles, didn't bother Little Warrior much. What she really wanted was a shiny new rifle. She turned to find Mink staring at her from across the room. Little Warrior knew what the look meant. Mink wanted a rifle, too. But a grown woman showing interest in the sutler's stock of weapons would have been suspicious.

"What do you want?" Rogers didn't like children near the guns. "Your gophers are worth fifty cents."

Little Warrior reached up and laid a hand on the small boxes on the counter.

"Flints? What would you do with flints?"

"Give them to my father for a present," Little Warrior murmured politely.

"James, give this youngster flints."

Little Warrior and her mothers and grandmother could only buy necessities. Everything extra they brought in to trade went to buy powder and lead and seed corn. That didn't stop Fighting in a Line from indulging in her favorite form of entertainment.

While the patient clerk trailed behind her, she opened every drawer and box. She peered into every keg. She examined every item in the Fort King sutler's store, including the limited supply of men's nether garments. Then she wrapped her meager purchases in a red bandanna and tied the four corners. She marched out regally, leaving Rogers and his clerks to shake their heads over the shambles she left behind.

CHAPTER 27

"Making war is such a manly exercise." Abihka puffed contentedly on his pipe. "I like to see the young men becoming proficient in it again." In spite of the pale-eyes' harassment, both official and unofficial, Abihka had never looked happier. A thin-lipped smile split his seamed face like a crack in old leather.

While Abihka smoked in the shade, Jumper, Alligator,

Black, and John Horse sat nearby, around a bed of glowing coals. They waited for chunks of lead to melt in three old skillets. While they worked they watched Osceola instruct the boys and ordinary warriors of Talasee.

Wild Cat lay stretched out on his stomach among the orchids and resurrection ferns carpeting a broad oak limb. His cheek rested on the backs of his interlaced fingers. One leg was bent up at the knee, and the foot rocked gently back and forth. He wore only a breechclout. At a glance he resembled a tawny panther, with eyes half-closed and tail twitching lazily.

The young men Osceola was teaching ranged in age from ten to twenty. Some of them were still too young to wear turbans over the shaved crowns of their heads. Black was especially interested in Osceola's teaching methods. Black had been training the men of Swamp Town.

Four huts with thatched sides rimmed this clearing deep in the tangle of the hammock. Three of them sheltered crates of lead and fifty-pound kegs of powder wrapped tightly in waterproof canvas. Osceola had insisted on the canvas, even though they'd had to pay twenty cents a barrel extra for it. The stores of ammunition increased slowly because men needed powder and lead to hunt.

The fourth hut looked as ordinary as the other three, but it wasn't. Abihka tutored boys there, infusing the shabby building with power. Abihka and his war knowledge were much in demand these days. So many uncles brought their nephews to learn a warrior's charms and medicine that Abihka had asked Osceola to help him teach them. Like the hut, the clearing had become permeated with the magic connected with death. Besides the fact that the boys trained there, Abihka had hidden his most powerful war medicine in the hollow of a tree nearby.

The clearing hardly seemed a place devoted to death. The shade of the graceful oaks cooled the August heat. Birds noisily conducted their affairs in the green depths of the surrounding jungle. The hammock hummed with life.

"Each of you who has a gun join with someone who has none." Osceola's instructions were emphasized by the crack of the bullet molds' cutters as the men trimmed the newly made lead balls. Each snap was followed by a dull clink as the ball dropped into a leather pouch.

Osceola's students didn't notice the drone of the men's conversation any more than they noticed the buzz of bees in the flowers around them. Even those who already knew how to shoot kept their black eyes fixed on Osceola's face. They obeyed him so quickly they seemed to anticipate his words.

Osceola was obviously on good terms with a strong source of magic. He could outrun, outshoot, and outwrestle everyone who challenged him. If the boys could detect what made him special, maybe they could coax from the spirits similar power for themselves. So they studied him constantly.

Many of the old leaders conferred with Osceola, too. He was the man Abihka Great Warrior had named his sensemaker. He was familiar with the white men and the strange, cacophonous rituals of their walled towns. He understood the messages of the drums that rattled against Fort King's high log palisades. He could hum the sprightly songs of the fifers' tunes. The white soldiers trusted him. They confided in him.

"Before you shoot you'll learn to clean your weapons." Osceola knew that wasn't what the boys wanted to hear, but it was more important than target practice. Many of the warriors allowed their pieces to become hopelessly fouled. "You must clear the touchhole after every three shots. A quill serves well for that."

He held each weapon up so sunlight entered the touchhole and shone into the barrel. In many of the rifles the spiral grooves needed rerifling. The flints were chipped or the notches in the tumblers worn or the lock parts badly aligned. He stored the problems away in his mind. Later he would speak to each boy about his particular gun.

Osceola's own rifled smoothbore had seen hard service. A tautly sewn leather patch held the barrel to the cracked stock just above the lock mechanism. The scales of the writhing brass dragon on the side plate had worn smooth. The scarred maple stock was buffed to a fine polish by the oils of his hands. The steel ramrod had long ago broken and been replaced by one of hickory tipped with horn. The caliber had been enlarged by repeated borings of the rifled barrel, until he'd had to double-patch it. But it was better suited to killing man-sized prey than his lovely Spanish fowling piece.

The boys and young men had a motley collection of guns, most of which had belonged to their fathers or grandfathers. Some of the weapons had been sawed off where balls had lodged in the barrels and the exploding powder had ripped them open. Most were the ancient fusils, cheaply made for the Indian trade. But their short length made them easy to carry. The barrels' small bore meant more balls could be cast from a pound of precious lead.

Osceola knelt on one knee so the boys could see over his shoulder. He set a half-ounce lead ball in the palm of his left hand. He poured fine-grained priming powder from his horn until a conical pile of it barely hid the ball. He held it up.

"If you have no charger, this is how you measure the powder for each shot." He held up his own ivory powder charger between the thumb and slender middle finger of his right hand. It was one of Grandfather Squint's hollow, four-inch-long incisors with a wooden plug fitted into the opening at the base. The boys silently estimated the size of the alligator that had trailed behind it.

Osceola poured some of the powder back into his horn. He held out the rest to the best shot in the group. "Load with this," he said. "Don't fill the pan full, or powder will leak into the touchhole. It will misfire. Go to the far side of the firing ground."

While the young man pricked the touchhole, rammed the charge and the patched ball into place, and poured priming powder into the pan, Osceola paced to the opposite edge of the clearing.

"Shoot me in the chest," he said.

The boys moved away from the one with the gun and fanned out so they could see clearly. Their faces were neutral, but their eyes flickered from Osceola to the musket and back. The men under the tree stopped their work and stared. The warrior raised his musket, sighted, then hesitated.

"Shoot me," Osceola said patiently.

He fired just as Little Warrior trotted down the trail and into the clearing. The report reverberated among the trees and silenced the birds. Smoke rose and hovered over the musket. The ball hit Osceola's chest with a thin smacking sound, then dropped to the ground. It rolled a short distance and lodged in a spiky tuft of grass.

Little Warrior didn't see the ball fall away. She didn't know why the ordinary warrior was shooting her father. She didn't stop to ask why Osceola's friends didn't help him.

She rushed into the clearing and launched herself, like a thirty-two-pound ball from a cannon, at the backs of the warrior's knees. She sent him sprawling and swarmed over him. She bit him so hard on the shoulder that she drew blood. He laughed at her as he threw his arms up to shield his face. She continued hammering at him with her fists.

When Alligator and Wild Cat pulled her off, she kicked and squirmed and punched Alligator in the center of his lofty nose. He rolled on the ground in mock agony. He clutched his bleeding nose and howled in pain while his friends laughed.

"I'm not hurt, daughter." Osceola crouched and showed her the pale purple bruise beginning to bloom in the center of his chest. "I was showing them why they should have a charger for their powder measures. If they pour in too little, the ball has no power. Tell them what happens if they pour in too much."

Little Warrior still looked as if she'd as soon kill someone as not, but she folded down the top two knuckles of her right index finger and held it up, palm inward. The hand looked as though it were missing that finger. The men laughed harder. Those whose own guns hadn't exploded from too much powder had seen it happen to others.

With his spare bandana, Osceola started to wipe the dirt off her face. Little Warrior pushed his hand away. She was angry. First her mother had insisted she help in camp instead of learning to shoot with the boys. Then Wild Cat had seen her humiliated when she tried to defend her father. And Little Warrior was quite taken with her uncle Wild Cat.

"When did Nakita arrive?" Osceola asked.

"A few minutes ago. How do you know he's here?"

"You always wear your new red dress when he visits."

"Mother's playing the moccasin game with him to keep him

from looking for you. She's telling him the story of how the moccasin-game player wagered away all the water in the world."

Silently the boys vanished into the jungle around them. Within seconds the clearing was empty except for Little Warrior and the older men. Not a leaf stirred. Not a twig snapped. Soon the birds and insects began their rabblement. Osceola picked up his musket and handed it to Little Warrior. She usually carried it for him, but now she lagged behind him, hoping Wild Cat would catch up. She was disappointed.

"It is wise to allow this blue-jacket to visit?" Wild Cat asked when Osceola and Little Warrior were out of sight.

"Osceola keeps constant company with him," said Alligator. "They're as close as nates rubbing in a breechclout."

"Nakita is valuable." Black stretched and yawned and scratched the trench of a scar across his flattened nose and cheek. "He tells us news we couldn't learn otherwise. But he suspects nothing of our plans. He watches the women boil cows' hooves for oil to keep our guns from rusting. He sees the quantities of meat drying, the sacks of pounded corn growing higher in our storehouses. I think we could fly the red war flag from the post where the white one now hangs. He wouldn't mark it."

"He's like the leech that lives in the alligator's mouth." Abihka stood up and rubbed his naked rump, spare as a pine knot. "He sees only the morsels of food between the teeth. He doesn't notice the fierce animal that surrounds them."

They covered the fire. Then they collected the molds and skillets and balls and sauntered down the trail. They reconvened around Morning Dew's fire.

John sat grinning as his friends observed the amenities. He thought he would burst before they finished eating, lighting their pipes, and making small talk.

"Fay-kahn is gone," he said. "Old Mad Jackson dismissed him. Fay-kahn's been altering vouchers for the merchants who supply your rations, your treaty goods. He's been collecting the difference from the government. He even robbed Abraham of the money due him for his services as interpreter."

"Who'll replace him?" asked Osceola.

"I don't know. But he has to be better than Fay-kahn."

"What of the treaty that says we must move?" asked Abihka.

"I don't know. Maybe the new sense-maker will be more reasonable." With all his heart, John wished it would be so. His eyes sparkled with pleasure at being able to bring his friends good news after so much bad. He also had brought two bottles of fine brandy to share in celebration.

After a few drinks Osceola felt as though sea foam prickled and popped in his veins and surf murmured in his ears.

"Dehm fah-yan chit." Now and then Alligator liked to show off the English he was learning at Fort King.

"It is indeed damn fine shit." John did not have much capacity for alcohol. He was too far gone to notice Jumper's hand twitch reflexively on the bone handle of his scalping knife when John reached for his powder horn.

"My friends," John said, "I'm going to show you how to tell if whiskey's good or not."

He shook a small amount of powder into Morning Dew's sand-scoured iron skillet. Then he sprinkled brandy over it. He lit the brandy with a splinter of lighter pine. The men watched, fascinated, while the alcohol burned. The last of it fired the powder, which exploded in a small flash. *"This* is firewater. If the whiskey's been watered down, it will dampen the powder so it won't burn."

John took another sip, then held the bottle up. The fire's light shone diffuse and amber through the brown glass, like a spirit trapped inside. "This is far better than what they sell in those damnable doggeries." The wave of his arm included all the taverns that ringed the northern end of the reservation. It included the watered-down, peppered-up whiskey desperate Seminole bought there.

Osceola stared into the fire as though he could see the future in its ceaseless dance. Nakita's *ueho'mee*, bitter water, was working its capricious sorcery in his head. The fire swelled until he could see nothing else. It formed a flame sprite with burning hair. She swayed and beckoned to him.

He understood, suddenly, why Heartless Snake sought whiskey so single-mindedly. Whiskey enabled a man to dream while he was awake. It opened the mind's hidden spring to the other world, always so tauntingly near. It sucked him into the whirlpool of that opening. Its power made Osceola wary. It was far more dangerous than *sabia*, his medicine spirit, because whiskey worked from inside a man. It could turn him not only against others, but against himself.

CHAPTER 28

Wiley Thompson, the new Indian agent, was fifty-two years old. He arrived at Fort King the first of December in 1833, during one of Florida's chill winter drizzles. He had served with General Andrew Jackson in the Creek war and had spent seven years as a major general in the Georgia militia. He was six feet tall and powerfully built. He carried himself with a military bearing that appealed to the Seminole.

Thompson was an honest man and a capable administrator. He was so amiable and fair that Abihka was faced with an unexpected dilemma. War no longer seemed imminent, and the young men were restless. They rattled their rifles and sang their battle songs. They wandered off at night to commune diligently with their guardian spirits. But no enemy appeared.

None of them understood the quirks of the United States Congress, nor the time it took Americans to ratify a treaty. It seemed as though the white men had forgotten the unreasonable demands of the papers signed in Oklahoma. During the year of 1834 the Seminole continued to visit Fort King and Thompson's two-story office and home just down the hill from the main gate.

Abihka brought in his baskets of dried pompano and still answered to the nickname Sam Jones, the fisherman. Morning Dew and Mink traded at the sutler's store across from the agency building. In the afternoons they watched the officers' wives play battledore on a corner of the parade ground.

Fighting in a Line and Mad Dog cultivated the fort's new commander, Brevet Brigadier General Duncan Clinch. Fighting in a Line exchanged barbecued alligator ribs, which Clinch relished, and turtle eggs, which he detested, for tobacco. Mad Dog offered extensive pleasantries and bawdy stories, to which Clinch nodded politely and uncomprehendingly.

Even though she was usually carrying Crying Bird on her hip, the fort was Little Warrior's playground. She cajoled the guards into taking her up to the cupola above the gate so she could enjoy a bird's view of the bustle below. She charmed them into letting her ride the dray horses with Crying Bird clinging to her waist. Best of all, now and then she rang the huge cowbell that called work details in from the surrounding forest.

Osceola became friendly with Agent Wiley Thompson. Someday he and Thompson might have to draw a bead on each other, but that was no reason not to be friends now. On this particular day in September of 1834, Osceola and his friends sat under the moss-draped oak that shaded the agency office. Thompson was shuffling a limp deck of cards and dealing them onto the top of a battered gun crate. The crate was stacked on a second one to raise it to camp chair level.

With his knees flung wide, Thompson sat precariously on the forward edge of the camp chair's canvas sling. Osceola, Alligator, and Lieutenant John Goode sat on upturned boxes. Alligator and Osceola were teamed against Goode and Thompson in a meditative game of whist. John served as interpreter. His Mikasukee had improved remarkably in the past year.

Osceola and Alligator would have preferred to play craps, which was much more exciting. But Wiley Thompson had explained it was an enlisted man's game. He would indulge in it on occasion, but not on this occasion. The dice, made from a pair of flattened musket balls, lay discreetly under Thompson's straw hat. They were hidden because General Clinch lounged nearby.

Clinch was not a tall man, but he weighed two hundred and fifty pounds. His bulk was exerting considerable strain on the canvas and wood of his camp chair. Even though the blacksmith had reinforced the frame with iron bands, the chair groaned piteously whenever Clinch shifted position.

"The blue-jacket *Tastanagee Tloko* looks like a manatee in a soup bowl." As he arranged his cards Alligator murmured it in Mikasukee and never hinted at a smile. If John Goode knew Alligator wasn't discussing his hand, he didn't let on.

"I'll wager my silver bracelet the chair gives way before the *Tastanagee*'s buttons do." Osceola solemnly rearranged his cards while he spoke.

Alligator surreptitiously assessed the general's blue wool tunic. The odds were close. Under the strain of holding in Clinch's stomach, the tunic formed a series of ellipses between the buttons down the front. "I accept the wager," Alligator muttered.

Osceola sat at ease with his elbows resting on his thighs. His new blue flowered hunting shirt was open at the throat. It hung in graceful folds on his lean, brown body. Over his own cards Thompson studied Osceola, as though trying to guess what kind of hand he held. The truth was, Osceola's eyes captivated him. The day before, he had described him in a letter home. "Eagle eyes," he had written. "Chiseled, sensuous mouth with a wild, sweet expression. A beguiling smile. A bold hunter."

"What does Osceola mean?" he asked.

"Black Drink Singer. For the cry we give at the Black Drink ceremony." Osceola was used to being asked that. White men seemed perpetually curious about Indian names. "Why are you called Sly?"

"Wiley." Thompson chewed on the ends of his bushy gray mustache and stared down at his cards. "My name's Wiley."

"Doesn't sly mean the same as wily?"

"It does. But Wiley is an old family name."

"Was Crane *Tastanagee* named that because he looks like one?" asked Alligator. Crane was tall and thin and gawky. His stiff hair stood up like a gray-brown crest of disheveled plumage. His Adam's apple looked like an egg caught in his throat.

"No," Colonel Crane called from the rocker on the porch that wrapped around three sides of the agency. "Just coincidence. My first name, Ichabod, means 'Ah, for the good old days.' "

"And is it coincidence," croaked Clinch over the edge of his Saint Augustine *Herald*, "that the hero of that Crayon fellow's ghost story shares his name with you?"

"I suppose so. It's a common name where I come from."

In spite of what white men said, Osceola knew that if names weren't given to commemorate deeds or appearances, the deeds and appearances developed to suit the names. His friend John Goode proved that.

The game resumed. General Clinch adjusted his spectacles on the blunt crest of his nose and returned to his newspaper.

" 'The abominable vice leaves its victims with a body full of disease, and a mind in ruins,' " he read aloud. " 'An advanced state of degeneracy is signaled by livid, shriveled countenance; ulcerous, toothless gums and a dwarfish, crooked body.' " Clinch looked up in triumph. Science had validated his worst suspicions about masturbation. "Colonel Crane, remind me to have this article read to the men."

"Yes, sir."

Duncan Clinch was a kindly man. He liked many of the Seminole who visited Fort King. He especially liked Osceola and Alligator. He was enchanted by Little Warrior, who called him *Pucha Chobee*, Large Grandfather. He even liked Osceola's grandmother, who had the color and grain of a tough palmetto root and always looked as though she were about to disappear down the inverted funnel of her beads.

For all his congeniality, Wiley Thompson firmly supported President Andrew Jackson's removal policies; but Duncan Clinch was heartily sorry about them. An article in the *Herald* saddened him. The afternoon was too pleasant to mar by reading it aloud. It reported the sessions of the Legislative Council of Florida. It said in part:

The portion of the Territory hitherto occupied by the Seminole Indians is about to invite a numerous population.

As far as the men in the territorital capital of Tallahassee were concerned, Andrew Jackson's removal policy would soon be an accomplished fact.

The dense, curled strands of the Spanish moss glinted silver in the sunlight. The leaves were as green and thick as ever in the glade. But the blooms of the ghost orchids no longer dangled from the oaks' branches like large white frogs. John knew autumn had arrived. He could feel the chill in the damp air. Last winter they had met in an abandoned cabin Third Sister had found almost overgrown by vines and bushes. This winter a trysting place wouldn't be necessary. John wouldn't be there.

"I have to go away." He had been rehearsing this speech in Mikasukee ever since he'd received the orders.

"For how long?" Third Sister's smile faded. She stared past his shoulder, waiting to hear the news she had dreaded from the first. He was leaving, and he wasn't coming back.

John stroked her hair and wiped away the tear that brimmed over and ran down her cheek. He lifted her chin and kissed her full mouth. "Six months. I'll return at the end of March, the Little Spring month."

"Where are you going?"

"*Tastanagee Thloko* wants me to go to the gulf, to stay at the soldier town there."

"Whom will you war against?"

"No one. The soldier town's been empty a year or more. The walls, the lodges, are in disrepair. My leader asks me to direct the rebuilding of it."

"If your leader asks it of you, you must go." Third Sister let no more tears disgrace her. Her man was a warrior. She was a Panther. She would be worthy of him, even if he wasn't going on the war trail.

"I'll wait for you," she said. "I'll ask Abihka to work medicine for you. When you build the new war town, be sure to kill the green wood so no harm comes to you when you enter the buildings. Do you remember how?"

"Yes."

John unwrapped the rose-colored calico from around the bulky package he had brought.

Third Sister took the long handle and inspected the square tin pan on the end of it. "Is it for cooking?"

"It will keep you warm this winter while I'm gone." John opened the lid. "Put live coals in here. Then latch it like this. Wrap it in sacking. Put it in your bed. When you get under the blankets they'll be warm. As warm as if I had just rolled over."

Third Sister accepted the gift without comment. She would have liked to say that a tin pan would not keep her warm the way Nakita did. But a warrior's woman said nothing to make her man regret his duty. She folded the calico neatly and put it inside the pan.

Then she unwrapped the duffel blanketing from around her gift to him. She had made him a fringed leather case for his army-issue smoothbore muzzle loader. She had tanned the leather with extra care to make it supple. She had dyed it red with mangrove bark and smoked it to make it waterproof. But she hadn't intended it as a good-bye present.

"Thank you, beloved," John said.

Third Sister sat on the blankets she had spread on the ground and smiled up at him as she lay back. He wasn't going on the war trail. They could love each other before he left.

John knelt and raised her to her knees so she faced him. He held both her small hands in his and risked making her uncomfortable by looking into her eyes.

"Third Sister," he said, "daughter of Running, woman of the Panthers, will you marry me?"

"I can't." Third Sister lowered her eyes. "My older sisters aren't married yet. My uncles would never permit it." Third Sister didn't tell him that her uncles would never permit her to marry him no matter if her sisters found husbands or not.

"We won't tell your uncles. When I return I'll persuade them to let me have you. Until then, with the One Who Lives Above as our witness, we'll pledge our troth."

For months in his Spartan quarters, John had tossed on his lumpy mattress stuffed with Spanish moss. Finally he had decided what to do, and he had slept peacefully ever since. He had taken a week to choose and translate into Mikasukee the words from his small, leather-bound prayer book. Still holding her hands gently in his, he recited them.

"Dearly Beloved, we gather here in the sight of the One Who Lives Above to join this man with this woman. Holy matrimony is an honorable state, not to be entered into lightly, but reverently. If any man can show just cause why we may not join, let him now speak or else hereafter forever hold his peace."

For several slow beats of their hearts, John and Third Sister knelt silently with their arms around each other. They waited, as though expecting to hear the voices of the scores of friends and kin, not to mention the army, who would certainly object to their union. Then John continued.

"I take you, Third Sister, to my wedded wife, to have, to hold, from this day on. I will cherish you forever, in plentiful times, in hungry times, in times of peace, in times of war, in sickness, in health. *Chee' noh a cho-le.* I love you. I will love you until death parts us."

John took a white linen handkerchief from inside his shirt. He opened it out carefully and held it on the palm of his hand so Third Sister could see the narrow, shiny yellow band. John had painstakingly fashioned the ring from a discarded brass trigger guard. He had buffed it until it glowed softly. It would have to do until he could buy her one of gold.

He slid it onto her fourth finger.

"With this ring, I wed you." John put his arms around Third Sister and held her tight against him. "In times of peace, in times of war," he murmured, "I will cherish you."

CHAPTER 29

Osceola's and Mink's breath hung trapped in moist clouds around their heads. A crystal wind, a wind with edges, scraped at the exposed skin of their faces. They had insulated their moccasins with grass and wrapped them in strips of tattered blanketing, but their feet were numb and heavy as lead.

Mink wore two blouses and three skirts. She had wrapped a feed sack around her shoulders and pinned it in place. Over that she clutched a worn blanket, the folds of which hooded her face. The wind fluttered the blanket's hem.

Osceola held his arms folded across his chest. He was trying to keep the wind from penetrating his cotton hunting shirt, whose ruffled hem hung well below his blue wool army uniform jacket. His leather leggings felt clammy against his legs. Mink had swaddled his hands in rags of sacking so that only the red, raw fingers showed.

With a sigh, Osceola readjusted the strap across his chest and shifted his new rifle on his back. He and Mink continued the search. They found the first three cows in a heap with a yearling underneath. They must have huddled together for warmth through the long brutal night.

The small Seminole cattle were the tough, irascible descendents of stock brought over by the Spaniards two centuries before. In better times they waded hip deep in the swamps, searching for the sweet grass that grew there. They patiently endured plagues of bloated, purple ticks, swarms of mosquitoes, and the attacks of panthers and red wolves.

They were inured to most hardships, including the kiln of the Florida summer. But in February 1835, when the temperature dropped to seven degrees and stayed there, their heads drooped until their lower lips brushed the ground. Their front legs folded in a genuflection to death. With his moccasin, Osceola nudged a rigid leg jutting from the tangle. The cow's eyes, glossy and lifeless as agate, stared upward in silent rebuke.

A gust of wind moaned through the hammock, shivering the brittle leaves. Osceola shivered, too. Like the Spanish cattle, bred for warm climes, he was no longer accustomed to winter's harsh breath. He thought of Morning Dew and Little Warrior and Crying Bird, huddled around the fire in Talasee.

They had had to break through a thick crust of ice to bathe that morning. Little Warrior had been fascinated by the hard water. She had broken it with her bare feet and walked stolidly into the river. Crying Bird had balked. Her arms akimbo and the rosy, crumpled bud of her mouth brought back Osceola's own childhood with a rush. He remembered shivering on a frozen riverbank, trapped between Fighting in a Line's sharp, turkey bone scratcher and the flat blades of ice skimming the top of the water.

That had been when he was very young. By the time he was six or seven he and his friends competed to see who could stay submerged the longest among the mats of ice. He usually was the last to stagger out on legs like sticks of kindling. His lips and fingernails would be gun-metal blue. His skin tingled, and until he encountered the transports of sex, many years later, he had never felt more alive.

This cold was different. Its dampness penetrated to the marrow, and Osceola's people weren't prepared for it. Few had built insulated dugouts for winter sleeping as they had in the north country. Their cabins were carelessly chinked, their clothes were of cotton.

Osceola rubbed the blackened leaf of a Seville orange tree between his fingers. The tree's branches sagged with fruit that was an even brighter yellow than usual. The frantic blush of color presaged its death. In a week the oranges would lie in heaps under the trees. The sharp scent of their rotting would taint the wind.

The trees had been struck to their roots. Time would pass. The sun would warm the air. But these trees wouldn't send up fresh shoots from the bases of the trunks. Their brittle branches would scratch at the sky until fire consumed them or they too rotted away.

No more would Osceola and his family camp in the grove, spread their blankets, and pile the oranges on them. No more would they roast and eat the tart fruit. Nor would they sweeten the juice with honey and sell pottery jugs of it to Fort King's officers for twenty-five cents a gallon.

With stiff fingers Mink peeled an orange. She handed half to Osceola. Already the fruit tasted faintly rotten.

While she ate, Mink looked up, following the cow's mournful gaze. The quilted, ash-gray clouds hung low. They looked like hillocks of earth in a plowed field. They seemed about to fall and smother her.

"We can smoke some of the meat," Osceola said. "But with

so many animals dead, most of it will rot before we can get to it."

Mink pulled her blanket tighter around her. She imagined skeletal Death stalking Talasee's streets. Dahomey said Death's eye sockets were empty, but it had ears. Death was blind but not deaf. She imagined Death listening to them now.

Mink rarely wasted time on regrets or despair. She had faced too many times of privation for that. But she dreaded the children's hungry cries and the guilty looks of their desperate mothers and fathers.

Osceola worried that the medicine in his people's sacred bundles may have become malevolent, in spite of Abihka's attention to the proper rituals. Only the deliberate interference of the spirits could explain the events of the past months.

"My *sabia* has failed me," Osceola said.

"Some say Old Mad Jackson is the source of all our troubles." Mink wiped the juice away before it froze around her mouth. "Some say Jackson is Old People Burner, the Devil. They say he caused the rains to stay away last summer. They say he caused the crops to wither."

"I would rather endure nature's acts than Jackson's. At least when the spirits send disaster they make no pretense of doing it for our benefit. Jackson talks of acting in the best interests of his red children, but he lies. He's impelled by greed, by power. I can understand one man doing harm to another. I cannot understand him claiming to do it out of love."

As they walked, Osceola and Mink found the bodies of deer in the small pastures, along with the frozen remains of the cattle. The hunting would not be good this spring. The howling of the wolves would have an insistent, hungry ring.

Spring was a cruel season anyway, when a cloak of leaves and flowers covered the skeleton of famine. In springtime the supply of corn and beans, dried meat and pumpkin, dwindled. Spring was when only dust and chaff remained in the bottom of the baskets. The herds were to have provided food until the new crops could be planted and gathered. Now it appeared that the Seminole would have to eat the food they had hoarded for wartime.

Mink stood silently to one side when Osceola stopped to speak quiet words of sympathy and encouragement to the owners of the dead cattle. Most of them were standing motionless, as though they too were frozen, and looking down at the corpses.

"What of the tally sticks, *Tastanagee?*" The man's round face was pitted with the pox's shallow craters. His slightly bulging eyes were shadowed by worry. He and Osceola were searching for a missing calf in the vine-shrouded deadfalls around the pasture. They could hear the calf's feeble bawl, shattering the icy silence of the hammock. Mink lowed in answer to keep it calling.

"When will we receive the pale-eyes' food?" the man asked.

"The towns' civil leaders make no bundles of tally sticks for food, brother." Osceola had explained this over and over; but he knew desperation clouded the man's memory. This warrior had children and relatives to feed. If he was desperate and afraid, it was for their sakes. "We survived before without the white man's scant rations. We'll survive now."

"It will be as you say, *Tastanagee.*"

If only it could be as I say. Osceola was a patient teacher for the children of Talasee. As a leader should, he gave away food and gifts bought with money the army paid him to track deserters. His advice was frequently sought and invariably good. Now he would pay the price of being *tastanagee*.

He knew that in the months to come, supplies in the communal granaries would run out. Distraught mothers and fathers would hesitantly approach his family's fire. They would take a long time coming to the reason for their visit. In voices so low Osceola would have to strain to hear them, they would make their requests for food. He wondered if he would be able to help them all. He wondered what his own family would eat.

After the calf and its dead mother had been found, Osceola and Mink continued down the trail. The path was a winding tunnel barely wide enough for them to pass through the dense growth and deadfalls of the hammock. Mink put her feet down so quietly, Osceola might as well have been alone. While he walked he indulged in bitter thoughts about Wiley Thompson, who, as it turned out, was living up to his name.

Osceola didn't care that Thompson had flown into a rage during talks last October. He had faced Thompson's rages

before and had remained on good terms in spite of them. He
didn't care that Thompson had cut off the government's
promised rations and annuities. He wished the Americans
never had started providing the food and goods that were
making his people dependent on them.

To wish that white people were other than their natures
dictated was useless. It was like wishing dogs wouldn't bite
the fingers that offered them meat. Osceola had always considered white people one more of nature's blights with which
red people had to contend. Now, for the first time, Osceola
wished they had never sailed across the wide water on their
winged ships. As he used the barrel of his new rifle to push
aside the loops of vines, he amended that slightly.

Spirits, he thought. Why didn't you keep the pale-eyes on
the other side of the water? Why didn't you send only their
knives, their fine steel hatchets, their guns? Especially their
guns.

Osceola shifted his new rifle in his hand. The delicate curls
of the brass trigger guard fitted precisely into the curves of
his fingers and warmed to his touch. It hung so light and well-
balanced that it seemed to have a life of its own. It was as
sleek and graceful as an anhinga, diving with wings folded
and serpentine neck outstretched.

It was almost as long as Osceola was tall. Its walnut stock
was incised with scrollwork and stopped just short of the end
of the barrel. Its unknown maker had darkened the wood
with soot and oiled it to a velvety luster. The ornate figure
of a bird decorated the brass patchbox plate. An eight-pointed
brass star was inlaid on the cheekpiece. Osceola had removed
the worn brass dragon from his old fusil and screwed it onto
the new one. Abihka had worked his medicine to give it
power.

Wiley Thompson had given Osceola the rifle after he'd dis-
suaded three drunken warriors from scalping the agent with
a pewter spoon. The men very likely would have killed
Thompson if Osceola hadn't rescued him. Thompson knew
it.

In spite of Thompson's flowery presentation speech, Osceola suspected the agent had meant the rifle as a bribe. Osceola
suspected Wiley thought to buy, if not his heart, at least his

tongue, and his influence with the older leaders. If the rifle had been a bribe, Thompson must have been disappointed indeed.

Osceola smiled to himself as he remembered the look on Thompson's face when his carefully planned council in October went awry. Thompson hadn't called the meeting to discuss whether or not the Seminole would move west. He called it to ask what form of transport they preferred, how they intended to dispose of their property, and if they wanted their annuities paid in goods or specie.

His well-made plans ran afoul on a reef on stubborn Seminole pride. Mole Leader had died, an inconvenience for the pale-eyes. Now Mikanopee was back in power. Mikanopee was malleable enough, but his advisers weren't. He was being influenced by Abihka, Jumper, and the rest of the resisters of Old Mad Jackson's removal plan.

"Your laws will be set aside." Thompson had spoken far too loudly for the small room. The four walls had amplified his words until they made Osceola's head ache. "Your chiefs will cease to be chiefs. Claims for your debts and for your Negroes will be set against you by bad white men." Thompson had plowed relentlessly on.

"Your condition will be hopelessness and wretchedness. I tell you for the last time, you must go. If you're not willing, you will be forced to go. No more annuities will be paid to you here."

Osceola saw the indecision flicker across Mikanopee's heavy face. He leaned over and whispered into Mikanopee's small ear, "Do not let him threaten you."

Thompson lost his temper completely. He wagged a caloused finger at Osceola. "What is that man saying?" he roared.

Osceola stood slowly while Abraham translated the question. Osceola knew his refusal to recognize English would infuriate Thompson even more, but he enjoyed goading the man. It was small enough revenge for Thompson's arrogance, for his betrayal of Osceola's friendship and trust, offered so freely, without conditions. When Thompson lost control of himself, Osceola gained control of him.

He planted the butt of his new rifle, Thompson's gift, firmly on the polished coquina floor. He held it by the barrel and slanted it slightly away from him, like a staff of authority. Thompson couldn't have missed the irony in the gesture.

"I say I do not care if no more annuities are ever paid." Osceola paused. As Abihka's sense-maker, he often had spoken in council with the Seminole leaders, but he was not a civil leader. He was not yet *Tastanagee Thloko*, Great War Leader. He had never raised his voice in official talks with the pale-eyes.

As he faced Thompson he heard the skirl of a hawk, a rush of wind, and his uncle's war cry. He felt as though he had hurled himself along a narrow trail, only to find it ended at a sheer precipice.

He slowly raised his free arm until his clenched fist was poised above his head. As the fist rose it drew everyone's attention after it. A tingling sensation traveled down Osceola's powerful arm and spread through his body.

"I consider a question," Osceola said calmly. "Then I make my decision. I speak my thoughts in council, then I do what I say I will do. So it is with my people. They have discussed this matter. They have decided to stay in the land where their ancestors are buried. Where the blood of their birthing splashed on the thirsty ground. They have charged their leaders with voicing that decision. Their leaders cannot do otherwise. Nothing more remains to be said."

Sometimes Osceola sank into the ground two curved, parallel rows of stakes twenty feet long. He put a piece of rotted meat at the end. An alligator would crawl between the stakes to reach the bait, only to find that when he tried to back out his tail became caught between the stakes. He was trapped. So Mikanopee was caught by Osceola's words. He was right. A leader must vote his people's decision.

"If the wind rattles, let the flowers be crushed," Osceola went on. "The sturdy oak lifts its branches to the sky. Straight, unbroken, it survives the storm."

As Osceola sat down, the silence around him was profound. Osceola had made more than an elaborate declaration of war. He had wrested leadership from those who hesitated to exercise it. If Thompson was oblivious to the portent of

Osceola's speech, Mikanopee wasn't. He rose heavily and stared around him unhappily.

"I do not intend to move," he mumbled.

Osceola had won. For the time being.

CHAPTER 30

As John Goode stood at the edge of the agency's porch, an attack of desire breached his sturdy West Point defenses. He suddenly smelled the smoky perfume of Third Sister's hair. The longing for her was so strong he felt dizzy.

Since returning from Tampa he had seen her several times, but that only made him miss her more. In his mind John had been writing letters home, telling of his decision to marry Third Sister properly. He had few illusions. His family wouldn't be pleased.

John tried to trace the smoky odor that had started his heart to pounding. He couldn't smell much except the garbage in the nearby ravine and the manure from the agency corrals. He felt a bit foolish, standing still and snuffling like a coon hound, but he wanted to be Nakita just a little longer.

When he was Nakita, his feet moved more lightly. Awareness hung patiently in the center of his being, like a spider on her web. He was alert to the slightest variations of sound and smell. When he was Nakita the wind spoke to him. Nakita was swift and skillful and touched by magic. He was loved by a shy, passionate woman.

John Goode, for all his military rank, was ordinary. And John wasn't Nakita here. He was a lieutenant in the United States Army. A private had delivered a message ordering him to report to the agency office.

John had another reason for hesitating before crossing the shady gallery and opening the door. Richard Keith Call, a prominent Tallahassee lawyer, was inside. The cloying smell of Call's cologne drifted through the open window. Call was a friend of President Jackson and an influential man in territorial politics. John Goode disliked him, but then many people disliked Call. To Wiley Thompson's credit, he certainly disliked him.

"Don't you realize, sir, that the Negroes are the main obstacle to the removal plan?" Thompson pointed to Richard Call's folded letter lying on the cluttered desk. The stiff paper was resisting the creases and opening slowly, like a rectangular blossom.

The letter was signed by some very important citizens of Tallahassee. It asked Thompson to give Call permission to buy blacks from the Seminole. The request had President Jackson's approval.

"The Seminoles fear that if they agree to move, unscrupulous whites will take their Negroes from them."

"If the niggers are sold legally, they can't be stolen," Call said. "The major obstacle to removal will itself be removed."

Now that Richard Call had seen some of the Seminole's blacks, he was in a fever to buy as many as he could for himself. He pronounced them magnificent specimens, large and healthy and muscular. They would bring premium prices farther north. Call was nothing if not acquisitive.

"I demand you honor this request." Call waved the letter, like a gauntlet, in Thompson's face.

"I'll tell you the consequences of *legal* requests like your friends'." Wiley Thompson kept his temper fairly in check. Antagonizing one of Andrew Jackson's cronies would only make bad matters worse.

"I've just returned from a trip to New Orleans with Blount, one of the chiefs agreeable to removal. He and his people lived near Tallahassee. Perhaps you know him." Thompson went from irony to sarcasm. One of the villains in this story had signed Call's letter.

"White claimants and their attorneys gathered like sharks at the dock. I turned them away. I accompanied Blount and his people all the way to New Orleans. I landed them below the city to avoid those scurfy dogs of the legal profession. But some of them still took Blount to court. They charged him

for two thousand dollars in debts and for leaving with mort-
gaged slaves. Blount paid with his annuity money, and I returned to Florida. But the attorneys invented *more* charges."

"The gentlemen only wanted what was owed them." Call
smoothed his pomaded hair for the fifth time since John
Goode had entered the room. John found himself keeping
count. He couldn't decide which of the venal sins Call best
represented—pride, vanity, greed, or arrogance.

Color began to rise in Thompson's face, and his voice took
on a strained quality. "The vultures in frock coats had not
yet picked the corpse clean. Blount and twenty of his followers were thrown in jail. And there they sit."

"Well, that is Louisiana." Either Richard Call didn't get the
point, or he chose to ignore it.

"Of course the Indians here heard of it before I did."
Thompson's outrage was tainted with self-interest. "Do you
realize how much more difficult that makes my job?"

"The jeremiad of some illiterate savage jailed in New Orleans does not concern me. My esteemed colleagues wish to
buy slaves from your Seminoles. And I will have satisfaction."

Call straightened the velvet collar on his tobacco-brown
cutaway. The swallow-tailed coat pinched his waist to an
extent that was stylish but highly improbable.

"Remember, General Thompson, the president does not
appreciate his officials coddling these natives." Call gingerly
arranged his black silk tophat so as to cause the least possible
disarrangement of his hair. He stomped from the room.

Lieutenant Colonel Alexander Campbell Wilder Fanning
absentmindedly rubbed the stump of his left arm inside the
pinned-up sleeve of his blue tunic. After Osceola's threats at
the tumultuous October council, Thompson became alarmed
and asked for reinforcements. He got this tiny, fiery, one-
armed man and four companies of artillery and infantry.

"Apparently the stories of Mr. Call are correct," Fanning
said. "He appears to be deficient in judgment and gentlemanly
candor. And I do believe he was wearing a corset."

"Padding in the seat of his trousers, too," said Colonel
Crane dryly. "A regular berdache, he is."

"Still . . ." Fanning shrugged. "I would imagine Call's right
about one thing. I hear these Indians are thieves."

"With all due respect, sir . . ." Lieutenant Goode couldn't keep silent any longer. "You would imagine incorrectly."

"I called Lieutenant Goode in, Colonel, because he's our resident expert on Osceola and Sam Jones and their malcontents." Thompson fell wearily onto a chair and waved the others to do likewise. He had a nagging ache in his stomach. It felt like hunger, but it wasn't.

"Excuse the lieutenant's lack of discipline," Thompson went on. "Perhaps some of the savages' ways are rubbing off on him." Since October Thompson had been condescending about John's friendship with Osceola. He acted as though John had adopted a clever camp mongrel for a pet. In fact, he behaved vaguely like a jilted lover.

"I've never seen a lock in a Seminole village," John said. "Can you say the same for a white man's town?"

"The poor devils have nothing worth stealing, wouldn't you say, Ichabod?" Thompson chuckled as he offered Goode and Fanning and Crane fat Havanas from a tortoiseshell case.

"They're starving, Colonel Fanning." Ichabod Crane trimmed a cigar, lit it with a flaring lucifer, took a few hard sucks to get it going, then held it out to Fanning. "The summer drought and the freezing winter were fortunate for Jackson's policies. Famine is a persuasive ally for us. The Seminoles have been subsisting on kooty roots and what some misguided philanthropes have been smuggling to them."

John knew Colonel Crane was referring to him. John would have shared with his friends and with Third Sister anyway. But he took seriously the marriage ceremony's words "and with all my worldly goods I thee endow."

"I can assure you, Colonel Fanning, there is no foundation to rumors about difficulties with the Indians." Thompson seemed to have forgotten that his request for reinforcements had started some of the rumors. He blew cigar smoke like a steam packet heading up the Oklawaha.

"The Seminole of the present day is a different being from the former, warlike sons of the forest," Thompson said. "I anticipate no real trouble in the removal of this pitiful remnant of the tribe, if only Call and his ilk will leave us to our jobs. We're being invaded by swarms of slave hunters as it is."

Perhaps some of the savage ways *are* rubbing off on me. John drew the cigar smoke into his lungs and closed his eyes, as though savoring it. Osceola was right. White men were blind. He had to admit he had been blind himself. Only since his return from Tampa had he realized that the kind, gentle people who treated him so hospitably were preparing for war.

He remembered his last visit to Talasee and the change he sensed there. Everyone had been as hospitable as when he'd first come to the village. That was a bad sign. Someone had stayed with him the entire time, chatting, offering food, smoking with him. John knew that was how the Seminole treated those they didn't trust. Friends could roam freely while everyone went about his daily chores. Only Third Sister had behaved as though nothing had changed. He had told her his plans of taking her north with him when his duty here ended.

He had tried to convince Osceola of the folly of resisting the United States Army. He described the northern factories and fields and the teeming cities that could send regiment after regiment to Florida if necessary. As always, Osceola had listened with absolute attention and courtesy.

"Your words are wise, my brother," he had said. "But they're like good medicine that still doesn't cure the illness. We will not leave our country. We've tried to live here in peace. The white men give us no choice but to fight them. Even a stone burns when the fire is hot enough."

John felt a terrible, oppressive weight of helplessness. He couldn't tell Wiley Thompson what he had learned about the Seminole's preparations, yet he knew he was betraying his commission and his country.

For an instant John Goode saw the men in the room as Osceola and Third Sister saw them. They were as narrowly bound by their own rigid thinking as by their high collars. Osceola didn't even consider them perverse men, only foolish ones. The worst epithet a Seminole could hurl at another man was "*Istee toko*, person, not. You are nobody." It seemed very appropriate.

Richard Keith Call looked nervously over the edge of the council platform. The saw palmettos and scrub oak looked far below him. Then he glanced at Colonel Clinch, who overflowed the bench nearby, and wondered if the scaffolding would suffice. A hastily built platform had collapsed in March of 1835, a month before. The treaty commissioners and the Seminole leaders had tumbled ten feet in a knot of bodies and splintered boards.

Even the padding in Call's trousers hadn't saved him from injury. The fort's surgeon had applied antiphlogistics and leeches, but the bruises on the lower half of Call's buttocks only recently had faded to a pale violet. Call wasn't popular at Fort King. A scurrilous rumor circulated that the Tallahassee lawyer's pallid fundament looked like the full moon rising in a livid sunset sky.

Call shifted to ease his aching hindquarters on the oak bench and returned his attention to Agent Thompson. After days of discussion, Thompson was still trying to wring cooperation from the Seminole leaders. Call fumed. He was furious because President Jackson had refused his repeated requests for command of the army in Florida. Call was certain he could resolve this farce if only he had the authority instead of that croaking walrus Clinch.

Pine branches shaded the new platform, but everyone was sweating in heat that was intense for April. Given the heat, the humidity, and the fact that for two years white officials had been badgering the Seminole to leave their homes, tempers were understandably short. Call wasn't the only one angry.

"Abraham, tell Bowlegs that if he breaks his word with us, I shall be obliged to call upon the white warriors to force him." Wiley Thompson had already exhausted bribery, cajolery, and his own version of reason. Threats were all he had left. He glared at the turbaned civil and war leaders sitting on benches on the other side of the platform.

Thompson knew Bolek couldn't be bullied as easily as Mikanopee. But Mikanopee was absent, as he often was when trouble loomed. He had sent Bolek and Jumper, his sensemaker, in his stead. As Mikanopee's nephew, young Bolek was of the hereditary line of Maskokee kings.

"Do not talk to me of war." Bolek held his arms out wide when he spoke. He had a large nose and mouth in a square, mournful face that belied his wry wit. "Am I a child that I should fear war? No! When I buried the hatchet I put it deep with a stone over it. But I remember where I left it. I can dig it up again to protect my people. I'll be sorry to injure the white man's warriors, but I will fight for my country."

"Will they attack?" Mink whispered to Morning Dew.

"I don't know," Morning Dew said. Ordinarily neither Morning Dew nor Mink would even consider such a thing. The white flag of peace flew here. Men in council were always safe from attack. But the leaders had suffered too much humiliation already. Thompson might reach the limit of their tolerance. The warriors had their rifles and muskets. They outnumbered the white soldiers two to one.

Morning Dew, Mink, and the other women waited in the live-oak grove, under a gray canopy of moss and broad, furrowed oak limbs. Babies napped on their mothers' hips or on cloths spread on the dry oak leaves covering the ground. Older children drew in the sand or played silent games of roll the bullet. The men who weren't taking part in the talks stood apart from the women and children.

About fifteen hundred Seminole listened under the trees. Many of them had come in the hope the agent would relent and distribute food and annuities. Everyone felt the cramping grip of hunger, and in most of the towns the situation was desperate.

Morning Dew and Mink stood almost motionless through the afternoon. They moved only to shield Crying Bird and Little Warrior with their skirts when a brief thunderstorm passed over. When the late afternoon breezes had dried the women's clothes and stirred the dusty hems of their long skirts, Wiley Thompson called on the leaders to sign this latest removal agreement. Twice he had to ask, "Who will sign?"

Abihka, Alligator, Bolek, and Jumper said, "No." Eight other leaders filed to the table and touched the quill pen. Osceola sat with his arms folded. His eyes narrowed to slits. His mouth tightened into a pale line. Mink's heart thumped with the fear that he would do something rash and the hope that he would.

"Where is Mikanopee?" Thompson shouted.

"Sick," said Alligator in English.

"I don't believe it. He has a shuffling disposition to shun

his responsibility." Thompson turned on Jumper. "You're his sense-maker. Tell us if Mikanopee intends to honor the treaty."

"He will not." Jumper crossed his arms defiantly. The people under the trees stirred slightly, as though ruffled by the wind that signals a hurricane.

Thompson picked up the quill and dipped it in the ink pot. It sprayed ink as he drew a large X across one of the papers. From the distance of Mink's position, the table looked frail and clumsy and long-legged, the paper easily torn and burned. How could such fragile objects cause so much sorrow?

"I have struck five names from the rolls of chiefs," Thompson shouted. "Mikanopee, Jumper, Abihka, Bolek, and Alligator no longer represent the Seminole people."

Abihka leaped to his feet with a shriek that was echoed by the others. For one man to depose hereditary and elected leaders was unthinkable.

As Abihka stomped across the platform he shouted the closest to imprecations the Mikasukee language provided. Clinch labored to his feet and shouted back. His trousers strained across his stomach and heavy thighs and gathered at his crotch, pulling the inner seams above the tops of his shoes.

"I will expel the Seminoles from Florida by force!" Good-natured General Clinch finally lost his temper. "I have warriors enough to do it."

Only Abihka's short stature and the colonel's prominent belly prevented the two from reviling each other nose to nose. Oblivious to the pandemonium around them, they went on assailing each other's characters, lineages, and military and sexual prowess.

When Abihka calmed enough to stamp back to his bench, the floor planks vibrated under his moccasins. The soldiers had come to attention with a conspicuous rattling of sabers, bayonets, and muskets. Through it all, Morning Dew, Mink, and Little Warrior watched Osceola. He sat motionless while eight lesser leaders added their names to the hated paper.

"Osceola," Thompson called. Osceola didn't seem to hear him. "Powell!"

Little Warrior had picked up a piece of oak and held it like a club. Crying Bird gripped a fistful of her mother's skirt. Her shaggy black hair almost obscured her face. The neckline of her faded dress had slipped down over one brown shoulder. The small weight of her arm on the shirt pulled at Morning Dew's heart, too.

"Daughter," she whispered to Little Warrior, "if they fight, take your sister. Run, hide in the swamp."

"Powell, will you sign?" Wiley Thompson shouted.

Osceola shook himself slightly, as though waking from a dream. He crossed slowly to the table and stared down at the paper. The black fringe of his hair curled around his face and shielded it from sight. He looked so fine in his new red hunting shirt and blue-and-white-trimmed leggings. Morning Dew's chest ached with the intensity of her love.

With one smooth motion Osceola drew his hunting knife and drove the blade into the table. The speed and force and sound of it, the blunt finality of it, spoke more eloquently than all the speeches.

Benches toppled as the Seminole surged to their feet and shouted approval. The warriors in the grove took up the war cry. It echoed through the trees. The soldiers closed in on the platform, but Osceola stood straight and motionless in the tumult.

Morning Dew asked the spirits not to let the blue-jackets kill her man. Mink's dark, delicate face was calm and lovely and implacable. She drew her skinning knife. Morning Dew pried Crying Bird's fingers from her skirt. She knotted up her hem so she could attack the soldiers unimpeded. Little Warrior was screaming the war cry when Morning Dew took her hand and put Crying Bird's small one in it. Then she drew her own knife.

While Thompson, Clinch, Call, and the other white men looked on, stunned, Osceola yanked his blade from the table and sheathed it. He walked slowly down the steps, between the silent corridor of soldiers. He crossed the trampled ground to where Morning Dew and Mink stood.

He handed Morning Dew his rifle. He picked up Crying Bird. He held Little Warrior's hand as he walked toward the horse pasture. Little Warrior carried the oak club with one hand at her side like a gun. Morning Dew shouldered the rifle. Mink followed as though to protect the family's flank.

CHAPTER 31

Just before dawn a naked black child raced into Tallahassee. He scattered sleepy chickens as he ran to Morning Dew and Mink's cluster of cabins. He was caked with mud and blood from the scratches and abrasions that covered his body. Leaves and twigs and dry grass were tangled in his hair, which was clumped into tiny nubs, like cloves in a pomander apple. He was gasping for breath and staggering with exhaustion.

He crouched in the dust next to the cowhide hanging in Mink's doorway. He took deep breaths until his chest stopped heaving. Then he chirped softly, like a cardinal. He listened. He warbled like a mockingbird. His Ashanti grandparents had taught him to wake a person gently so the soul would have time to return to the body. He didn't want to condemn Mink's soul to an eternity of wandering. His news would cause her sorrow enough.

When his birdcalls brought no response, he called quietly, "Little Mother." He waited, panting, in the dust while a pair of hounds growled perfunctorily from the darkness under the storage *chikee*.

"What is it?" Mink had draped a piece of sheeting around her. She peered between the lintel and the uneven edge of the cowhide door. Her hair stood out in a galvanized nimbus around her face. Osceola looked over her bare shoulder.

"Creeks," the child said. "They've taken your mother."

Before Mink could connect the words with the fact that something terrible had happened, Crying Bird, naked, left Morning Dew's cabin at a run to spread the news.

"They raided Swamp Town?" Morning Dew dressed while she questioned the tiny messenger.

"Corn Woman's camp. They took everyone they could catch, but I hid in the swamp, under a hollow log. They passed over me." To show how close they passed, the boy swept the palm of his hand over his hair, scattering some of the debris lodged there.

"Corn Woman's camp?" The unlikeliness of it confused Mink. Dahomey didn't live in Corn Woman's camp. This child must be mistaken.

"The pox was among us. The elders asked your mother to intercede with the gods. To convince them to cure the sick ones."

"Did you tell her man?" Osceola took his rifle from the rafters and leaned it against the lintel.

"Her husband went in search of her. But he's alone. The Creeks are well armed."

"What of Heartless Snake's woman?"

"They took her. They took her sons."

Mink took down Osceola's blanket-wrapped fusil, which he had given her when he'd received his new rifle. She checked the powder horn and bullet pouch.

Little Warrior led the tiny messenger to the fire. She began blowing on the embers to heat water in the *sofkee* kettle.

"What happened to your family?" she asked.

"All gone." The child snuffled, crossed his arms on his bloody knees, and buried his head in them. He was asleep before the water boiled.

Osceola put on his best breechclout of navy-blue stroud. He pulled up his blue-and-white woolen leggings with brass buttons sewn up the outer seams.

"You're not dressing for the trail." Mink paced around the cabin while Morning Dew stood in the doorway.

"I have to go to the pale-eyes sense-maker's lodge." He shrugged into his new red hunting shirt with blue-and-orange ruffles across the chest and shoulders and around the armholes.

"We have no time." Mink was almost frantic.

"The sense-maker has protected us from slavers before. He's returned some of those who've been stolen. He can help us. In any case, I have to ask his permission to track the Creeks, or the soldiers will stop me."

Morning Dew stuffed dried venison and parched corn into a small leather sack and put it into his pouch. Osceola put the long strap over his head and settled the bag on his hip. He reached for his powder horn and bullet box.

Osceola held Mink by her arms. "As soon as I speak to the sense-maker, I'll go to Corn Woman's town. I'll track your mother. Wait for me here."

Mink looked at the ground. Tears left glistening tracks on her cheeks. Osceola shook her gently.

"Wait here."

"I will." Her answer was almost inaudible.

"I'll find your mother." He held her tightly, and briefly, against him. "I'll find her, beloved."

"Old man," Morning Dew said, "if the white soldiers see your gun, they might take it from you."

Osceola paused, then put the rifle back in the rafters. After he had driven his knife into the table a little over a month before, Thompson had forbade the sale of powder, lead, or weapons to the Seminole. Supplies of ammunition had dwindled to almost nothing as men hunted to feed their families. Some people, especially those agreeable to removal, were grumbling that the young hothead Asee Yahola was causing them all a great deal of trouble.

Osceola knew Heartless Snake had been in Talasee the night before, and he made a quick search for him. Heartless Snake would want to help get his woman and sons back. When he couldn't find him Osceola went to the river to see if Heartless Snake's dugout was gone. But it was there, its bow wedged into the thick mud with the others. Three empty brown bottles lay near it. Osceola heard his friend's voice, unencumbered by a body, coming from the canoe.

Heartless Snake was lying on his back in the muddy bilge of his dugout. He was drumming time with his fingers on his bare chest and humming his endless medicine song through his nose. He was traveling in the waking-dream-country of the white man's bitter water. He wouldn't return for a while.

Osceola lost patience with his old friend. He put his hand on the prow, braced himself, and shoved. His feet sank in the mud, but the canoe began to inch backward into the water. When it broke free of the shore, Osceola gave it a hard push. It moved out into the middle of the stream. Caught by the slow current, it drifted away, still chanting.

Osceola sighed and walked to the pasture. He caught his skittish, bobtailed gray gelding and started at a lope up the five-mile trail to Fort King. When he reached the agency he leaped from the gray before it stopped. He ignored the big hitching ring sunk into the oak beside the office. He tied the reins around one of the tall posts supporting the raised piazza.

The frame building that housed Thompson and his office stood on five-foot pilings. The agency hogs snoozed in the shade under it. The cicadas were just beginning their shrill chorus as the cool morning air heated up.

Osceola took the steps two at a time. From the piazza he beckoned to Thompson's interpreter, Sanchez. Sanchez was a tall, lathy man of an indeterminate breed. He possessed the bushy hair of an African, a Caucasian's narrow nose, an Indian's cheekbones, and a Spaniard's name. He was sitting on an ancient wooden chair with the back leaning against the side of the agency store. Sanchez was always there, as though his weight and the chair were necessary to hold up the wall.

In the office, Wiley Thompson sorted through the stacks of reports and requisitions on his desk. In spite of April's disastrous council and the defiant knife slit in the table, he planned to begin moving the Seminole from their lands in January. This was only the first of June, but it was not too early to begin preparations.

To add to everyone's troubles, General Clinch's wife had died recently of scarlet fever. She had left Fort King's commander with eight motherless children. Clinch was understandably distracted. Added to his grief was the freeze that had ruined the orange crop on his plantation twenty miles to the northwest. As a result Clinch's second-in-command, Colonel Fanning, often visited Thompson's office to discuss the garrison's problems and needs.

This morning Fanning lounged on a ladder-back chair. His low-topped black boots were propped on the back of the chair's mate. He and Thompson looked up when Osceola blocked the faint breeze and strong sunlight coming through the open door. Sanchez was close behind him.

"Creek slave hunters raided. They stole our black people. They stole my wife's mother." Osceola didn't waste time with pleasantries. As far as he was concerned, most white people didn't recognize courtesy when they encountered it.

"I must have powder, lead," Osceola said. "I must have a talking paper giving me permission to track them outside the line you've place around us."

If Thompson and Clinch considered the Seminole weak and utterly dependent, the settlers around the reservation were less sanguine. A letter of introduction from Thompson was little-enough protection against white farmers who were swinging wildly in the winds of fear and violence. They were shooting at anyone with dark eyes and high cheekbones.

"I can give you neither lead nor letter, Powell." Thompson relished saying it. With his knife and his theatrics, this arrogant quarter-breed had defeated Thompson's plans at the treaty talks. He had set Mikanopee and most of the Seminole firmly against removal, just when Thompson was beginning to make headway. Thwarting Osceola was little-enough payment for his insolence.

"Am I a black man? Am I a slave?" Osceola put the heels of his hands on the desk. He leaned forward until his face was close to Thompson's. It was an uncharacteristic stance for an Indian.

"My skin is dark," Osceola hissed. "But I am not black. You cannot place me under the same laws as slaves. You cannot refuse me powder."

Colonel Fanning swung his feet in a wide arc and quietly set his bootees on the floor. Thompson slid his chair back a fraction of an inch. No Seminole had ever looked him in the eye before.

Lieutenant Goode had explained that avoiding another's eyes was the Indians' notion of courtesy, but they always had seemed shifty and subservient to Thompson. Maybe that was part of the reason he treated them like children.

Now Thompson was unnerved by the naked fury in Osceola's stare. In thirty-five years of military and government service, he had never faced such compelling power in a pair of eyes, with the possible exception of Andrew Jackson's. For a few long instants those fierce, dark eyes held him prisoner. They entered his mind and read his thoughts. They played havoc with his resolve. Thompson had to shake his head to break their control.

"You have thrown more embarrassments in my way than any other." Thompson stood and leaned across his desk. "You have incited your people to resist Father Jackson's removal policy, which he has proposed for your own good. I shall not provide you with ammunition or permission to roam and foment sedition."

Osceola heard a rushing in his ears, like a storm of wind approaching through trees. He felt rage, a clawed, fanged creature, rising inside him. He made no effort to control it. He was through pawning his pride to buy his people more time to plant, to prepare for war.

"The white men shall not make me a slave." He spoke quickly. He didn't care whether Sanchez could keep up or not. "They will not bind me with the laws that govern slaves."

As Sanchez translated he backed toward the door. The Americans might entertain the fiction that the Seminole were weak and demoralized, but Sanchez knew better. He wanted to slip a few extra words into his translation. He wanted to warn Thompson not to antagonize a rattler, coiled and prepared to strike. But he wasn't used to speaking his own words. He didn't know how much English Osceola understood. Besides, events were moving too fast for him, and he knew Thompson wouldn't listen anyway.

"I will make the white men red with blood." Osceola was exultant in his fury. "Their corpses will blacken in the sun. The buzzard will strip the flesh from them. The wolf will gnaw their bones." He drew his famous knife, worn thin with use and honed to a razor's edge. He held the point of it an inch from Thompson's purple face. "We will destroy you!"

The fingers of Fanning's only hand crept toward the old box-lock pistol stuck in his belt. It was unloaded, of course, but it had a spring bayonet released by a sliding trigger guard. It was a useful weapon for a one-handed man. Fanning's fingertips brushed the pistol's slab walnut butt. He dared not draw it for fear of provoking Osceola into murdering the agent. He no longer doubted Osceola was capable of murder.

Before anyone could react, Osceola sheathed his knife. He

whirled on the soft soles of his moccasins and stalked from the office.

"Colonel, put that man in irons." Thompson's hands trembled with anger. He felt a stab of pain in his gut. The stomach troubles that had plagued him for the past two years attacked with a vengeance.

If Fanning had doubts about the wisdom of Thompson's order, he didn't waste time arguing. He shouted through the window at the four enlisted men posted nearby. Their duty usually consisted of restraining drunken Indians, but few Seminole came here since Thompson banned the sale of weapons. The soldiers caught Osceola as he was mounting.

He felt their fingers close around his ankles and legs. That they would lay hands on him, as though he were a disobedient child, drove him into a frenzy. He pulled his left leg free, swung it over the gray's back, and leaped into them. In the second before he was surrounded, Osceola saw Fanning, Thompson, and Sanchez watching him from the piazza above. He saw Erastus Rogers and the customers lined up outside the sutler's store. They too were staring at him.

He heard the shouts of sentries as they called for help. He remembered, briefly, that John Goode was away, and he was grateful his friend wasn't there to see this. Then his vision narrowed to the men around him. He saw the eagles on their brass buttons and the rough weave of their linen uniforms and the stains on their white cross belts. He heard their harsh breathing and the grunts when one of his fists or elbows or heels found a target.

Soon the soldiers' summer uniforms were filthy. Osceola's turban was knocked off and trampled into the dirt. His new shirt tore. When two more soldiers joined the fray, they managed to drag him down. Two men threw themselves across his chest while a third pinioned his feet. Two more knelt on his arms while the last one shackled his wrists. They swore creatively as Osceola bucked and heaved under them.

He tried to kick out, but a chain brought him up short with a jolt. He felt the weight of thick iron bands cutting through his leggings and into his ankles. With his manacled arms drawn behind him and over a hoe handle, the six soldiers still had all they could do to get him on his feet.

When Osceola twisted free, the men holding the hoe jerked it upward, wrenching his arms in their sockets. Ignoring the pain, he turned and looked up at the piazza where Thompson stood. Thompson's legs were crossed at the ankles. He leaned forward with his elbows on the railing to ease his ulcer.

"I shall remember this hour." As Osceola shouted he rattled the chain connecting the manacles around his wrists. "The agent has his day. I shall have mine!"

The soldiers dragged him up the hill and into the tiny cell in the center of the fort's parade ground. A crowd gathered outside. Inside, the six men barely had room to secure him. When they finished, his wrists and ankles were locked into thick iron bands. From each band a heavy chain stretched to an iron ring bolted into a corner of the log wall.

When the soldiers left, the ponderous, iron-plated door crashed closed behind them. The sound of it echoed in Osceola's head. The heavy iron bolt shot home. The door shut out most of the sun's light but none of its heat. Air and light could enter only through narrow slits, one in each wall up under the eaves. Rats scuttled across the termite-riddled beams overhead. Flies buzzed around a dead rat in the corner.

CHAPTER 32

Osceola heaved at each chain in turn, but they were well forged. The huge eyebolts were sunk a foot into the oak logs of the wall. They were unyielding. He tried to pull his hands through the manacles until the burred metal edges scraped away enough skin to draw blood.

He threw back his head and howled as though he could turn from flesh to pure spirit and escape with the sound. Men looked up from their work as his rage echoed through the fort.

Private Wilson was shucking a small mountain of sweet corn outside the kitchens. A leather strap fit around his fingers and held the husking peg in place. He stopped his work to listen.

In the three years since Osceola had found the boy tied to the punishment log, Private Wilson had changed. The Florida sun sapped some men and invigorated others. Wilson was one of the latter. His hair and eyebrows had bleached the color of raw cotton. Hardened muscles rippled under his darkly tanned skin.

Private Wilson had adapted better to the climate than to the army. He had spent considerable time behind the same walls that now held Osceola. But even Wilson tried to stay out of trouble in the summer months. He knew that as the sun climbed higher, the temperature inside the guardhouse would soar. Men had died of the heat in there.

All day as Wilson worked he listened to Osceola scream and rattle his chains. He tried not to think about the man who could produce sounds like that. They were not even remotely human. As the afternoon shadows lengthened, the screams grew hoarse and shorter. They sounded like a panther. Finally they stopped. The silence was more disturbing than the noise.

While the garrison slept and guards paced around the building, Osceola sat in darkness so complete he couldn't see his own hands. He emptied his mind of thought, his body of sensations, most of which consisted of pain and thirst. His skin became the thinnest of membranes, barely separating the darkness outside him from that inside. He was no longer in the dark; he *was* the dark. He was invisible. He was night itself, hunting the dream that would show him the trail out of this prison.

Pain and exhaustion, heat and thirst and hunger, became his friends. They brought him visions. Spirits sang to him. Shifting shapes and colors and darting lights danced for him. He understood the conversations of the rats as they crept close to lick the blood-soaked sand, like cats lapping cream.

Around midnight, a pale beam of moonlight shone through the slit in the eastern wall. A pair of fireflies entered as though riding it. One of them hovered in front of Osceola. It grew

and shimmered and changed shape before finally condensing
into the form of Mad New Town. He sat cross-legged just
beyond Osceola's chains. He glowed with the ghostly luminescence of fireflies crushed in children's hands. Through him,
Osceola could see the faint outline of the door. The second
firefly became the light in Mad New Town's ghost pipe.

"You are come, Uncle."

"I am, nephew." Mad New Town's face was indistinct, but
his voice was unmistakable. "Your temper has gotten you
into a fix."

"I'm ashamed you've found me like this."

"If you weren't here, you wouldn't need me. I wouldn't
come. If I were you, two things would be on my mind. Escape. Revenge. What plan have you for getting out?"

"I can overpower the guards when they come." Osceola
paused. "If they come. If they unchain me."

Mad New Town didn't answer, which meant he didn't think
the plan was a good one.

"I could trick them like Grandmother tricked Old Mad
Jackson years ago." Osceola said it reluctantly. This plan
didn't appeal to him. It entailed choking on his pride. It involved deception and a loss of honor. "I could pretend to do
what they want."

"What do they want?"

"They want me to mark a talking paper. They want me to
agree to give up our land, to be driven out like dogs."

"Mark the paper. Mark a hundred papers if that will set
you free. You can't fight them here."

"How can I say one thing, then do another?"

"Are the men who put you here honorable?"

Osceola laughed so loudly and bitterly that the guards outside looked up from their dice. "No, they're not honorable."

"What must a hunter do to be successful?" Mad New Town
continued his questioning, just as he had when Osceola was
a child.

"He must think like his quarry."

"What must a warrior do to be successful?"

"He must think like his enemy."

"He must think like his enemy." Mad New Town's voice
deepened and thickened and rolled, as though he were talking

underwater. He wavered, contorted, and contracted until he became a firefly again. Then he was gone.

Osceola heard the sentinel challenge the third relief of the guard. The magic hour of midnight had passed. He was left with the squeaking of the rats and a shrill, steady whirring, like crickets, inside his own skull. He sat motionless except to shake off the bolder rats, until the cocks began to crow and the cooks rattled their pots.

The morning gun sounded at the first drum of reveille. Osceola heard the shouts of the sergeants. Horses neighed in the stable, and drums rolled for assembly. He heard the creak of hardwood rollers and gears as the bony old army mule, Harmon, his mournful eyes blinkered, began his work. All day he would push the heavy shaft in endless circles, crushing tons of sugar cane.

After the clatter of tin plates and forks and mugs had died from the mess building, sunlight began to shine in a widening shaft through the eastern wall slit. The angle of the light steepened as the sun rose higher. It disappeared when the eave cut it off. When the steady *thock* of the officers' wives battledore paddles set up a steady beat, Osceola heard the metal bolt sliding in its iron sleeve.

Private Wilson was dressed in white canvas fatigue coveralls. He came in with a shovel and four buckets. One bucket was empty, two were full of sand, and the last contained drinking water. He whistled cheerfully as he shoveled the bloody, urine-soaked dirt into the empty bucket, then spread clean sand on the ground. He looked furtively toward the glare of the open doorway.

He unwrapped a bandana that held greasy chunks of fried bacon and crumbled corn bread. "I asked for this detail," he said. "Figured I could smuggle you some tucker."

"I'm not hungry." Osceola spoke gently. He recognized Wilson from the punishment log years ago. He remembered putting his damp bandana over the boy's head to ease his suffering.

"Eat. You'll need your strength." Wilson hunkered and fed Osceola. Then he offered a ladle full of cool spring water. He almost recoiled at the sight of Osceola's wrists. The iron bands had chewed through skin and muscle and scraped on the bone.

"My heart thanks you, friend." Osceola's chains rattled as he tried to bring his hand up in the sign for thanks.

" 'Twern't no more'n you done for me."

"Tell the agent I will mark his paper."

"Will do." Wilson saluted and left.

Outside, the battledore game went on to the song of women's laughter. Around the small log building the bustle of a normal day continued, oblivious to the terrible consequences of one man's shackles. Not long after Private Wilson left, Wiley Thompson and Sanchez came in. Two guards stood with rifles at the ready just outside the door.

"What have you to say today, Powell?" Thompson stood with legs astraddle and arms folded.

"I will mark your paper." Osceola was careful to sound cooperative, but reluctantly so. He did not lie. He would sign the paper. But there were ways of deceiving without lying. Once Osceola made the decision to be deceptive, he carried it out with the same skill and thoroughness as everything else.

"That's not good enough. I don't trust you."

"What must I do to convince you?"

"Send for the rest of your band. Send for those who haven't signed." Thompson had given this a great deal of thought. "When they come here to guarantee your good intentions and to sign the treaty, you may go."

"I'll give a runner a message to take to Talasee."

"Fine. Food and water will be brought to you shortly. And straw to sleep on." Thompson was disappointed that Osceola wasn't putting up more of a fight to make this victory sweeter. But he looked satisfied enough as he walked out and slammed the door. At last he had tamed this troublemaker. All it took was a firm hand.

About midafternoon, when the sun had driven most of the garrison into the shade, Chalo Emathla, Trout Leader, pushed the door open with his shoulder. The iron plating was too hot to touch. The old man's knees creaked when he lowered himself slowly to the ground and crossed his ankles.

Dark purple, crescent-shaped pouches sagged under his

mournful eyes. The hair that hung limply from under his paisley turban was thin and gray. Worry had etched deep creases in his leathery skin since he'd signed the infamous treaty in Oklahoma. His shoulders were inclined to droop, but he made a special effort to sit erect. He was dignified, but the dignity was a sorrowful sort.

Osceola had known Trout Leader in the first Talasee, in the half-remembered north land of long ago. When Osceola was a small child Trout Leader had been one of the dashing young ordinary warriors he so admired. Now he was selling the land the Seminole had bought with their blood.

"It grieves me to see this, my nephew." Trout Leader wiped his high, bulging forehead with one of the three handkerchiefs tied around his neck. His protruding jawline was becoming more pronounced with age. It made him look obstinate.

"It grieves me to be here, Uncle." With the hand the guard had freed, Osceola accepted the pipe Trout Leader offered him. He filled his lungs with smoke and savored the lightness and lucidity it brought.

"My wife washed this for you." Trout Leader held out the flowered silk shawl Osceola used for a turban. His wife had not only washed it, she had laid it out so it would dry without wrinkles, then she had folded it neatly. Osceola tucked it into his shirt. It was soon as soaked with sweat as the shirt was.

"I sent word to Abihka." Trout Leader panted a little in the heat. "He will come in to mark the paper. I sent another runner to inform your family."

"Thank you, Uncle."

"You can follow on the messenger's heels if you wish. I told the agent I would stay here as hostage, to guarantee your return with your people. I told him I would guarantee your mark on the paper. You're free to go." Trout Leader made a deprecating motion with his hand when Osceola started to protest.

Trout Leader knew Osceola had no intention of honoring the treaty, and Osceola knew he knew it. But to cage a war leader was an affront to everyone. Besides, Trout Leader was fond of Osceola. That he and the fierce young *tastanagee* were enemies caused him no little anguish.

"I'm proud my people have produced a warrior as fine as

you," he said. "It's unthinkable that you be chained here. I, on the other hand, am an old man. Those of us who marked the papers are threatened with death. I don't stray far from the protection of the white man's walls anyway. It will make little difference if I camp in the agent's yard. I'm a hostage already."

"I'll stay until my people come for me."

"You'll do what you must." Trout Leader knew Osceola didn't want to be in debt to a man he might have to kill. He knocked his pipe on the log wall, then tucked it into his turban. He rose to go but stopped with his hand on the door. "These are sad times, my nephew."

"They are, Uncle."

Little Warrior led Old Squat back to Morning Dew's yard. He wandered to other compounds often, and Little Warrior's job was to retrieve him. She would find him talking to the amused residents as though they were his dead wife and child, lost at the Horseshoe twenty years ago.

Old Squat's mind may have been capricious about many things, but it was constant on the subject of roll the bullet. Little Warrior was his most frequent adversary. She found it easier to entertain him than to search for him.

With the dirty, callused heel of her foot, she dug a long, shallow path that ended in an oval depression. She gouged out five deeper holes in a line inside the oval. Each hole counted for different points when a stone or a musket ball was rolled down the trough and sunk in it.

While Little Warrior smoothed the trough and the holes, Old Squat conferred loudly with the ragged hem of his breechclout and massaged the shiny ginger-beer glassie Nakita had given him. When he hunkered to shoot, his scrawny legs framed his small, slack belly and his dangling breechclout. As he sighted, he darted his head from side to side, like a mating crane.

"What have you to wager, Sunflower?" he asked.

Little Warrior was used to Old Squat confusing her with his long-dead son.

"I wager my sister, Uncle."

"You can't do that!" Outraged, Crying Bird started to climb

backward down the log steps from the platform of the storage *chikee*. "I'll tell Mother!"

"He still might be under there." Little Warrior smiled mischievously.

Crying Bird hastily regained the platform and lay on her belly with her naked haunches in the air. She hung her head cautiously over the edge, and her strings of beads dangled in her mouth. She surveyed the weeds and shadows under the platform. "You're a liar," she said. "He's not." But she began to cry anyway.

"Stop teasing her, child." Fighting in a Line strode across the yard with Mad Dog close behind her. They were both unusually subdued. "Ignore her, little one. Old Mad Jackson isn't under the *chikee*." Fighting in a Line lifted the child and set her on the ground. She turned to Little Warrior. "Where are your mothers?"

"At the river." Little Warrior sensed something was wrong. "What is it?"

"The blue-jackets are holding your father captive." Fighting in a Line wasn't one to hide unpleasant truths from children. "Go get your mothers. Quickly."

Little Warrior wasted no time on questions or tears. She turned and ran. Her bare feet knew every dip and turn of the trail to the river. She and the others had trod this path so often they had worn it down until it fit as comfortably as an old moccasin.

Mad Dog crouched next to Old Squat and put a hand on his shoulder. "Come, brother," he said gently. "We must dress for a journey."

Silver-haired Abihka led the column of seventy-nine men, women, and children into the agency yard the next day. He rode with Talasee's twenty-one warriors, who were dressed in their best shirts and leggings, their jewelry and plumes. All the men were mounted, although Abihka had had to loan several animals to make this brave show. Some families had eaten their horses to live through the spring.

Behind the warriors and boys Morning Dew rode at the head of the women and girls, most of whom were on foot. Crying Bird sat in front of Morning Dew. Little Warrior rode a spotted pony. Mink rode a dark bay borrowed from Fighting in a Line's herd. Perched like a magpie on her big mare's back, Fighting in a Line rode beside Mink.

The people of Talasee filled the agency yard. Young and old, they waited silently while Abihka and Alligator conferred with Wiley Thompson. Morning Dew, Mink, and Little Warrior watched impassively as Osceola and his escort of soldiers walked down the hill from the fort. After the darkness of the cell, Osceola squinted in the bright sunlight.

Someone had bandaged his wrists and ankles, but blood seeped through the linen. His left eye was swollen and bruised from his fight with the soldiers two days before. He looked thinner than when he'd left Talasee. The beautiful red shirt Mink had made him was ripped and filthy. His woolen leggings hung in shreds about his ankles where the iron shackles had torn them.

Osceola, Alligator, and Abihka touched the pen with which Thompson signed their names. They listened, without expression, to his speech. Then they mounted. Osceola and his family rode side by side toward the trail to Talasee. Abihka, Alligator, and the others followed. Osceola turned his gray at the treeline and pulled away from the procession.

He stood in the stirrups and faced the neat, oak-shaded buildings of the agency. He took a deep breath and gave his high, quavering war cry. The eerie call rang for a long time.

It carried through the fort on the hill and to the wood details in the forest beyond. The hair on the napes of the men's necks stirred, and their skin prickled at the sound of it. A coon hound howled in response. All activity stopped. Silence accompanied Osceola as he reined his gray around and rode out of sight.

"As you well know, General Thompson, we have just heard the Seminole war cry." As Fanning watched Osceola go he rubbed the sleeve-wrapped stump of his arm. "I respectfully suggest that your former prisoner hasn't learned any damned lesson at all."

"Well, he's a bold devil and an insolent one." Thompson shook his head at Osceola's audacity. His own skin had crawled at the eldritch cry. Even after it stopped Thompson still heard it ringing in his head.

He knew he'd been gulled. But he also knew, though he wouldn't admit it even to himself, that he'd made a serious error when he'd imprisoned Osceola. The man fairly radiated menace, which was as close as Thompson could come to defining Osceola's magic. The agent was relieved to have him out of the guardhouse and away from the fort.

CHAPTER 33

Tendrils of sweat-soaked hair stuck to Little Warrior's face and neck. She had tied up her long skirt, and her feet and legs were gray with dust. She was covered with insect bites and scratches from the underbrush she'd been helping to clear. Now she stood in front of the burrowing owls's hole in the meadow near her family's hunting camp. She nocked an arrow and drew the string of her bow back until it almost touched her chin.

"If you harm them, I'll shoot you." Like her mother, Little Warrior was small but strong. She meant what she said.

Fighting in a Line glared balefully at her great-granddaughter, but her anger was mostly feigned. She loved this charming, willful child. She was secretly pleased with her mettle. And she was grateful for the chance to rest.

The palmetto thicket she and the other women were clearing baked in the July sun. It lay under a musty cloud of hot dust. Cicadas and mosquitoes shrilled incessantly. The air pulsed with sound as well as with heat. Sunlight on the water surrounding the hammock flashed as though reflected from a silvered mirror. The sun hung like a flare over the half-submerged sawgrass growing to the horizon in all directions. Sooty clouds were stacking up for the midafternoon thunderstorm. Now and then people looked at them longingly.

With long Spanish blades Osceola and the other men hacked at the tough, fibrous palmetto roots as thick as his thigh. The palmettos' roots and trunks crept along horizontally aboveground. Over the years they had woven into a tight, intransigent mass. The serrated edges of the fronds' ribs took their toll on clothes and flesh. From somewhere in the depths of the thicket sounded a dry, whirring rattle.

So far the work had flushed six large rattlesnakes, but everyone stood back and let them slither away. No one wanted to risk killing a rattler. Its spirit would incite living snakes to take revenge. The hammock harbored plenty of living snakes.

The women were clearing away vines and smaller bushes and piling them up. Most of them wore scarves over their mouths to filter out the dust raised by the machetes and hoes and axes. Perspiration plastered their ruffled blouses and skirts to their bodies and soaked the bandanas tied around their heads.

Burning the fields would have been easier, but smoke could be seen for miles in this flat, treeless country. It was a signal even white men could recognize. Smoke would betray this camp and others like it, hidden among the thousands of hammocks scattered in the Cove of the Withlacoochee. The hammocks were isolated but still within striking distance of the military road between Fort Brooke and Fort King. The Seminole built few fires during the day.

Morning Dew's two sisters and their husbands and children were moving here. Fighting in a Line, Mad Dog, and Alligator and his wives and children were setting up their clusters of shelters, too. They were all building the open, palm-thatched *chikees*. *Chikees* required much less wood, and the trees on this hammock were necessary for cover. Their platforms raised the household goods above possible flooding on this low-lying island. They also afforded a view in every direction. Enemies would find it more difficult to sneak up on *chikees*.

This was a large hardwood hammock, a hump of rich, black muck rising from the wet prairie around it. Live oaks and gumbo limbo grew on it, as well as hackberry, willow, magnolia, sweetbay, fiddlewood, and orange trees. It could sustain this many people, but they would have to cultivate the meadow where the burrowing owls lived. To do that, they would have to get past Little Warrior and her bow.

"A willful, insolent child is asking for a nibble from my gar tooth." In exasperation, Fighting in a Line sucked her cheeks into the hollows left by missing teeth.

Fighting in a Line forced her bony shoulders as far back as she could. She was trying to ease the points of pain on each side of the ridge of her spine. They were always there now, two fiery circles the size of the big silver disks the white men coveted.

"Children have no respect these days." Fighting in a Line crossed her gnarled hands on the end of her cypress digging stick and leaned on it. The brass bracelets on her wrists clattered. The high, conical stack of beads around her neck forced her to stretch it forward like a heron surveying a shallow pool. "You should be ashamed to treat your great-grandmother so rudely."

"The owls are my relatives," Little Warrior said. "I promised them protection."

"They can find another place to build a home."

"This is their home. If we drive them away, we'll be as bad as the pale-eyes." Little Warrior's lips trembled, but her hand was steady on the bow.

"We'll leave space around them." Fighting in a Line suddenly understood why this was so important to her.

While she held Little Warrior's attention, Morning Dew reached over her daughter's shoulders and wrested the bow from her.

"Never point an arrow at someone unless you intend to kill. The elders will speak badly of you in council for this shameful behavior." Morning Dew took a firm grip on Little Warrior's ear and hauled her away.

Once they were out of sight of the others, Little Warrior began to sob. Morning Dew let go of her ear and took her hand instead. They walked to the swampy end of the hammock and sat by the small spring near the big cypress.

The flat canopy of cypress needles sheltered a rookery of ramshackled wood stork nests. The large nests always looked as if they had almost weathered a hurricane. The rookery was cacophonous with squeaks and chuckles and the clatter of the young storks's beaks.

When the adults set up an alarm, they startled a few of the younger fledglings. The birds lost their balance and dangled precariously upside down, flapping their black-tipped wings frantically. Morning Dew figured the maladroit ironheads would cheer Little Warrior.

The rookery's furor faded to the usual din. Morning Dew and Little Warrior lay in the grass by the spring-fed pond and watched the wood storks fish. Five of them, with their wings wrapped around them, stood quietly among the reeds at the pond's edge. They were spindle-shanked and hunch-shouldered. With their wrinkled bald heads, they looked like old men conferring solemnly against the gray of the gathering storm. Lightning flickered, and thunder growled in the distance.

"Have you told the owls we have to grow our food here because Talasee might be attacked?" Morning Dew asked.

"I haven't seen them. I think they left the burrow."

"We'll look for them after the rain. You can explain to them how great our need is. You must understand, too. When war comes, life will be hard for us. We have to work together. We're Mikasukee. The Mikasukee are warriors. We fight the enemy. We don't fight among ourselves."

"Yes, Mother." But Little Warrior wasn't so sure of that. The removal and antiremoval leaders were quarreling bitterly. Children of the two factions had taken to calling each other names and throwing rocks whenever their elders came together for councils.

"You'll apologize to your great-grandmother."

"Yes, Mother."

Morning Dew stood up. She hiked up her skirt and waded into the water. She returned carrying a disgruntled snapping turtle by the carapace.

"Is it fat?" She held it out so Little Warrior could feel the turtle's leg at the shell. The firm flesh filled the opening between the carapace and plastron.

"Yes," she said.

Morning Dew laid the turtle upside down on an old square of cloth she always had with her to carry back any food she might find. She brought the ends up around the turtle and tied them to form a sack. The legs stuck through the openings at the four sides and churned the air slowly.

Morning Dew pointed with her chin to some drooping

spikes of white flowers growing in the boggy seep from the spring.

"Collect lizard tail for poultices. Everyone'll be sore after working so hard all day."

Little Warrior was still picking when thunder crashed, and large drops made cold, soft explosions on their heads and shoulders. They laughed as they ran back to camp through the pelting rain.

"I like tall women," Mad Dog said. "When I make love with a tall woman I like to bury my face between her breasts."

Swamp Singer cackled in agreement.

"You can't remember making love to a tall woman," Alligator said. "You haven't done it in thirty years."

"I can't remember what I did this morning." Mad Dog corrected Alligator with great dignity. "But I remember clearly what I did thirty years ago. I remember smooth young breasts, firm as if molded of warm wax. I remember the brown nubbins on the end of each, just made for tweaking." With his tobacco-stained fingers, Mad Dog gave two little twists in the air in front of him.

Swamp Singer stared into the fire as though trying to remember those breasts. His palsied hands never ceased shaking now, and he sat very close to the flames. Even in July he felt a chill when the sun died.

The camp was full of visitors, and the celebration would go on all night. The hammock's small landing was crowded. Boats were rafted three deep. A slimy algae had been allowed to grow on them so they made less noise moving through the water.

Tomorrow the young men would play ball. The older men would meet under the arbor Osceola and the others had built. Tomorrow they would discuss strategies for war; but tonight everyone gathered to catch up on gossip, tell stories, and dance. Tonight they could forget the white men who had forced them to hide in this bewilderment of sawgrass and water and solitary islands.

The women and children spent much of their time here now. While their men hunted and scouted along the military road, they dried fish and cultivated the gardens. They wove baskets of swamp cane and palmetto stalks to store the food. Their lives were lonely these days. They craved the company of friends and relatives they hadn't seen for weeks. The mood at this gathering was almost giddy.

From the distance beyond the fire's light came the teasing rhythm of brass hawk bells and tortoiseshell rattles sewn onto leather and tied around the women's legs. The delicate whir and chime of a woman's stride when wearing rattles and the hard-edged jangle of her footfall always sent a ripple of excitement through Osceola.

The bells and rattles created a sensual stir in him, maybe because they rode in the secret darkness under the women's skirts. When the dance started, the drumming and singing would quicken, the rhythm become more insistent, more passionate. Maybe it was no coincidence that Mad Dog reminisced about women's breasts as he listened to the dancers line up.

Fighting in a Line led the women into the fire's light and began the winding spiral of the snake dance. Osceola and Alligator, Wild Cat, and John Horse leaned forward, watching her intently. Alligator had mixed dried hemp leaves with the tobacco for her clay pipe. She probably tasted the hemp, but she didn't care. She was so tiny it affected her almost immediately. She smoked several bowls of it before the dance. Now, even burdened with the bulky rows of rattles on her legs, she added a sway and a hop to the basic shuffle step. She was grinning like a baked gar.

Wild Cat wore an orange silk hunting shirt. He glittered with silver—armbands, gorgets, bracelets, and earrings. His blue satin turban was bound by a silver band. His haughty beauty had speeded the heartbeats among the young women. Most of the evening he hadn't been able to turn without bumping into Little Warrior. Little Warrior knew she could never marry Wild Cat. He was a clan brother. But her heart chose to ignore the fact.

"Your grandmother reminds me of my young friend, Maggot," Wild Cat said.

"The white boy who lives on the coast?"

"He's a man now. His father died. Maggot owns that huge plantation."

"I remember it," said Osceola.

"When Maggot was a boy he used to feed wine-soaked palm berries to his rooster. The rooster would get drunk. He would swagger around the yard, looking for love. Once he tried to mount a wild turkey."

"Do you visit him often?" asked Alligator.

"No." Wild Cat was silent a few moments, thinking of the child who had idolized him and the man he had become. And the war that would make them enemies. "Maggot drinks a lot of bitter water himself."

The men chuckled as Fighting in a Line began the chicken dance in midsong, to the confusion of the singers and the other dancers. When she hopped about, flapping her arms and cackling, Alligator leaped up to join her. He turned the chicken dance into the crazy dance. Osceola picked Crying Bird up and joined him, dancing with the child in his arms.

As they danced, they beckoned to the others. No one needed much persuasion. One by one, then in twos and threes, they moved onto the dance ground, until almost everyone was leaping and gyrating. Wild Cat and John Horse took over the drums so the musicians could frolic.

The smallest children hopped and stamped among their elders' feet. They danced until everyone was too tired or laughing too hard to go on. They staggered off the dance square and collapsed, still laughing, onto the logs and deerskins and palmettos spread on the ground.

Only Mink sat quiet and apart. Dahomey had not been found. Aury's Black had not come back. Mink knew only Black's love for Dahomey had kept him so long away from his second great passion, the sea. If he found Dahomey, he would bring her here. If not, Mink knew she would never see Black's ferocious, ugly, loving face again.

When Osceola returned from his imprisonment at Fort King, runners from many of the nations' leaders were waiting for him. He had traveled to council after council. The initial preparations for war had gone on for weeks. Whenever he could, Osceola returned to Talasee, to his own fire and Mink's silence. One night, as she lay remote and grieving, he raised himself on his elbows and stared down into her face. The trails of her tears glistened in the moonlight. He wiped them away with the palm of his hand.

"The women, the children, are in danger," he said.

"I know."

"We have to move them to safety. I can't leave them to go search for your mother."

"I know."

"I can only promise you revenge."

"Revenge won't sing my children to sleep in years to come."

"I know, my love."

"She had such a sweet voice."

Osceola lowered his head onto her breasts, gathered her into his arms, and wept with her.

CHAPTER 34

"Is it yellow jack?" John Goode tried to conceal his anxiety. Yellow fever had been bad this summer. Like everyone else, he feared another outbreak.

"I don't think so. The lad's complaining of a stomachache. It appears he ate too many green pumpkins. It's a wonder anyone's healthy in this bedlam." Army surgeon Jacob Motte settled back on his heels and surveyed the squalor around him.

"It's a wonder anyone eats, what with a biscuit selling for three dollars." John hunkered in the dust beside the doctor.

The seven-year-old boy lay on a filthy burlap sack in the shelter of a discarded army tent half. His five younger brothers and sisters shared the small patch of shade. The family's meager possessions were piled around the canvas flap to provide a little privacy.

The noise in the camp was irritating. The stench was worse. Even though the sky was gray and thunder rumbled, it only made the heat oppressively humid. Motte had not expected July heat in mid-September.

"Osceola taught me a cure for stomachache." Goode spoke in a low voice. War hadn't been declared, but Osceola's name was not popular here. John knew the recent attacks on isolated farms were the work of young men eager to earn war honors. He knew neither Abihka nor Osceola nor the other leaders could control them. But among whites Osceola was the best known of the Seminole. They blamed him for every outrage.

"Did he now?" Jacob perked up. He had just arrived and was eager to hear about the mysterious Seminole. He envied them. They roamed the woods freely, while the terrified settlers holed up in cess pits like this one.

"You kill an alligator . . ."

"How large an alligator?" This might be a jest, but Jacob was willing to play along. A jest would be welcome about now.

"Not large." John was in earnest. "The length of your arm from elbow to fingertip. You heat the reptile's belly by the fire and lay it against the patient's stomach."

"A primitive disciple of Aesculapius, then, your Osceola? I should like to meet him someday."

"You'd like him. And he'd like you."

"Suh, one of my young-'uns is varsal sick." A small, raw-boned woman tugged at Jacob's sleeve. Her lank hair hadn't been washed in weeks. Dirt formed black crescents under her broken nails. She had the haggard, disheveled look of a hen very low on the pecking order. "Come see to'm, please, suh."

Jacob and John followed her rail-thin back and shanks through the maze of palmetto lean-tos, canvas awnings, and tents. A few hundred settlers had loaded chairs and spinning wheels, tables, hominy mills, and cradles into their crude, pine-box wagons. They had fled their scattered farms on the Alachua savannah. They were camping inside the palisade around the main buildings of General Clinch's plantation, Auld Lang Syne.

The ones who had arrived first built their shelters backed up against the fresh pine logs of the wall. The others camped wherever they could find a few feet of space. No one wanted to camp outside the palisade.

A Mikasukee war party had recently avenged the murder of one of their own by whites. The warriors had dropped from the overhanging branches of an oak onto a courier. The idea of death falling from above like rain or oak catkins was particularly disturbing. Settlers who hadn't actually seen the mutilated remains of the courier had heard vivid descriptions.

The men of the Third Artillery tried to organize the camp and enforce sanitary measures, but the task was hopeless. Garbage piled up faster than fatigue details could load and haul it away. Even getting wagons through the camp was difficult. Chickens, dogs, cats, pigs, cows, and horses roamed freely.

Children played and fought and cried. The younger ones wore no clothes, and many were covered with scabies. Hookworm from the feces on the ground burrowed tunnels under the skin. The settlers called the resulting bloody crusts "creeping eruption."

Maybe the constant sun and the hard life were what caused the children to look eerily alike, as though they were all members of the same family. They were as thin and brown as dried live-oak leaves. Their uncombed hair looked like wheat straw. Their large, watery-blue eyes stared from pinched faces. Their smocks and trousers of homespun or feed sacks had faded to the same dusty shade.

"It appears the people of Alachua county plant corn, hoe potatoes, and beget ugly little white-headed responsibilities," Jacob muttered to John.

"Don't you like children?"

"They're like calomel. Bearable in small doses."

The woman stopped at a large tobacco tierce. The barrel was lying on its side and partially buried in the sand to keep it from rolling. A small boy sat listlessly in the opening.

"What's your name, son?" For all his hard words, Jacob's hands were gentle as he pushed back the mat of cream-colored hair and stared into the boy's dull eyes.

"Nimrod, suh."

"A mighty hunter, are you?"

"The Good Book says 'a mighty one in the earth and a mighty hunter before the Lord,' suh. Book of Genesis, chapter ten, verse nine."

"And a mightly fine-looking lad you are," Jacob lied gallantly.

"It's the climate, " John whispered in his ear. "The warm climate breeds indolence in the parents, and the children suffer."

"It's this fire in the sky what's causing all our troubles." Nimrod's mother was close to hysteria. "It's the Lord's judgment on us."

"Madam, Halley's comet passes overhead every seventy-six years, regular as a tick in the infinite clock of the universe. It's no cause for alarm." Jacob could see the woman didn't believe him.

The territory had been plagued by fierce storms this year. The freeze last winter ruined many farmers. The Seminole were raising hell and all its demons. No wonder the camp was rife with talk of the comet heralding Judgment Day.

Jacob opened his battered brown leather bag whose creases had worn to a yellowish tan. He took out a pair of slender forceps.

"Open wide, son." He stuck the forceps down the child's throat and pulled out a mass of worms. John Goode gagged at the sight of them.

"Hookworm." Jacob held the writhing tangle up so everyone could see it. "Madam, 'tis nothing in the heavens that has caused your boy's problem, but something very much of the earth." Shit, as a matter of fact.

He picked out two or three of the biggest worms and pushed them into a small vial. He corked it and stuck it into his jacket. He dropped the rest into the dirt and smashed them with the toe of his bootee.

"Come by the big house this evening, madam," he said. "I'll give you some spirits of turpentine for the boy and a dressing of ointment. And you should get him shod. The parasites enter through the soles of the feet."

"Ain't got nothin' to trade fer shoes, suh, even if there was any to be had."

"I know." Jacob shook his head as he closed his bag.

John and Jacob walked toward Clinch's two-story frame house where the officers were quartered. The enlisted men were living in Clinch's slave cabins, and they weren't happy about it. The tiny, windowless huts were alive with lice, fleas, and chinches, bedbugs and mosquitoes. In spite of the heat, the men slept in their clothes and their hats. They pulled down the fur earflaps in their tall leather forage caps to mute the whine of the mosquitoes.

"The poor whites down here are called sandlappers," John said. "The name comes from the children eating dirt when they have worms."

"Lieutenant, I've seen more exotic maladies in my short time here than I would in a lifetime of practice in the North. In a way, it's grotesquely fascinating."

They found General Clinch sitting on a rocker on the farmhouse piazza. He was napping over his two-week-old copy of the *New York Sun*. A lassitude had settled over the teeming refugee camp in the muggy midday heat. For a couple of hours Clinch would have some relief from his troubles. He lurched awake when he heard John's and Jacob's shoes on the steps.

"You've looked better, General," Jacob said cheerfully. He and John unfolded camp chairs and sat down.

"I've felt better, thank you, Doctor." General Clinch always sounded as though he were about to clear his throat.

"I hear you sat up all night with that ailing soldier," Jacob chided him gently. "That's my job. I don't try to run this madhouse. You mustn't try to cure my patients."

"The boy was delirious. And so young. We lose so many of them, Jacob. Wait until you spend a summer here. Yellow jack, typhus, bilious fever, malaria, dropsy. And dysentery. Dysentery from drinking turbid water. The water gets so bad here it would spoil whiskey. Dysentery is a far more dangerous enemy than Lieutenant Goode's friend Osceola."

"I've never encountered Osceola, but I have some acquaintance with dysentery. A good cleaning of the surgery would help."

"With so many sick, it's hard to keep up." Clinch sounded weary indeed. He winced when he heard another tree crash in the forest nearby. At this rate his plantation would be stripped soon. "I'll put a detail on it this afternoon. While I was away last month, brine leaked from a barrel of salt pork. Three men died, though how they could have eaten any of it, I'll never know. The stench was overpowering. It set off an outbreak of yellow jack."

"I'll do what I can to help, sir." Jacob took out the vial and a pocket lens. He laid the hookworms out on the railing and studied them.

"You remind me of a surgeon I knew in Pensacola," Clinch croaked. "A remarkable man. Once a soldier died on the table. To our astonishment, the surgeon cut the patient's head off. 'This man has an ocular disease that interests me,' he said, cool as a melon. 'Since I hadn't time to study it while he lived, I shall do so at my leisure.' And he wrapped it in his handkerchief."

"How hideous," said John.

"There's more." Clinch chuckled. "The surgeon was called away just as he was approaching his house. He stowed the handkerchief and its grisly contents in one of his chicken coops. When he returned home in the dark hours of the morning, his horse reared and almost threw him. By the light of the torch, he found the severed head lying on the ground.

"He eventually reconstructed the events of the evening. It seems one of the rascally local darkies was in the habit of stealing chickens. He had reached into the coop and found the neat package. Having the childlike nature of his kind, his curiosity overcame him. He stopped to open his prize, to see what valuable he had purloined. One can only imagine the effect of finding a human head staring up at him in the moon's wan light."

The men were still laughing when Nimrod's mother toiled up the slope. She carried a rooster and a hen by their legs.

"Fer the doctor," she said. "Y'all can't live on 'thanky kindly.' You need hog and hominy."

Jacob was forced to take them or have them dropped, flapping, in his lap. The woman turned and fled down the hill.

"What shall I do with Hog and Hominy?" Jacob held them up.

"Eat them or feed them," said John.

A gust of wind blew Clinch's paper off his lap and sent it

fluttering over the side, as though trying to take flight. The three men heard shouts from the camp as clothes and shelters twisted and flapped and became airborne. Clinch looked up at the clouds tumbling overhead. Tongues of lightning flicked constantly at the eastern horizon.

"I think there's a hurricane brewing." Clinch lunged out of his rocker with surprising agility. Jacob and his two squawking birds followed as large, cold drops began to fall. John Goode paused a long moment, smelling the heavy odor of wet dust. He surveyed the trees to the south and west, the direction of the Cove of the Withlacoochee, Osceola's trackless sanctuary.

In July John had returned from temporary duty in Saint Augustine. As soon as he'd heard about Osceola's imprisonment he had saddled and galloped to Talasee. He had found it almost deserted.

A few old people worked the gardens or glanced up from the cooking fires. Weeds and vines had begun to reclaim the kitchen yards that once had been so carefully swept. Some of the cypress-bark shingles had blown off the cabin where Third Sister, her older sister, her grandmother, and her little brother had slept.

Morning Dew's compound was empty, too. The cabins that once had been suffused with the spirit of those who lived in them were only logs and bark and stiff oaken lashing. They were soulless and forlorn.

John found Osceola and Mink at the small log council house. Osceola was collecting the ceremonial bowls and pipes while Mink packed dance costumes into covered baskets.

"I am come," John said.

"You are." Osceola grasped him by the hand and arm, then hugged him. John was appalled at the ugly, half-healed scars Thompson's manacles had left on his friend's wrists.

"Where is everyone? Where's Third Sister?" John asked.

"Gone, brother."

"Gone, where?"

"Gone. You must go, too. Your life's in danger here."

"Where is she?" John felt the panic rising in him. "I have to see her."

"You can't. She's gone to the spirit world."

"She was with child." John was dazed. He heard his heart thumping. He heard blood rushing in his temples.

"Women of her own clan killed her, so there would be no retaliations, no clan blood feud. They feared she might betray us."

"Retaliations?" John feared he would faint.

"The women killed her for sleeping with an enemy."

"She died bravely, " Mink said.

"Son of a bitch . . ."

"Nakita . . ." Osceola came toward him, hand outstretched, tears in his eyes. "I was away. I didn't know. I would have stopped them."

"Murdering sons of bitches!"

John had mounted and ridden, pell-mell, through the village. In the two months since then, he had performed his military duties flawlessly. He saluted, he conversed, he even smiled. But inside he felt hollow. Inside, a constant cold wind blew. Whenever he tried to think of Third Sister, whenever he wondered how she had died and how he could have saved her, the internal wind rose to a shriek. Sometimes, when speaking with his comrades, he thought they surely must see the storm raging in his eyes.

While the trees bowed and flailed in the rising wind, John wondered where Osceola and his people were. He knew now why Osceola had never taken him to his hunting camp in the Withlacoochee swamp. He worried that the storm would destroy whatever shelter they had been able to build there. He wondered what Osceola was doing. What he was thinking.

Time at last had brought John a little peace. He had stopped hating Osceola, and now he missed him terribly. He wondered if someday he would find his friend in his gun sights. He wondered if he would be able to kill him.

CHAPTER 35

For three days Little Warrior prowled the perimeter of the sacred square. Each night she sneaked out of the *chikee* where she and her sister and mother slept. Alert to witches in owls' bodies and other maleficent night beings, she padded through the quiet camp. She hid in the shadows near the long, thatched cabin where her father and seventy warriors were fasting and purifying themselves for the war trail.

During the day, Little Warrior could hear her father's high, clear singing or Abihka's nasal chant. Or she caught the low murmur of the warriors' voices. But halfway between midnight and dawn, silence fell. Then she approached dangerously close to watch and listen.

Women weren't allowed on the square in times like these. In the morning the women would bring their men's weapons and rations of parched cornmeal for the trip. They would leave them a hundred paces from the square rather than defile it with their presence.

Little Warrior knew if she disturbed the rituals, she would call down her father's wrath. She knew the council of elders would reprimand her, and her mother would scratch her. Far worse than that, she might offend the spirits and destroy her father's magic. She might endanger his life and the lives of his followers. But the mystery and the power of the place drew her irresistibly.

Little Warrior had always been welcome among her father's friends. They treated her as a pet. But as she grew older she realized she was excluded from the most important part of her father's life. She had tried to persuade him to teach her a warrior's knowledge.

"You've taught me hunter's magic. Why can't I learn about war, too?" She had followed him around the camp as he talked with the men about this raid. Several times he had almost tripped over her. She had kept at him with such dogged persistence that he almost lost patience with her.

"Women don't go to war." Osceola continued methodically pouring lead into the bullet mold, letting it cool, then dumping the finished ball into a basket. "Women don't learn warriors' magic."

"The war may come to us women, Father," Little Warrior said. "Will you leave us unprotected?"

When he turned to stare at her, Little Warrior was alarmed at how sad he looked.

"I'm sorry." She often irritated her father, but to think she had made him unhappy shamed her. Sudden tears burned high inside her nose and welled up in her eyes. "I won't speak of it again," she said.

"You're right, daughter." He laid the bullet mold aside. "The war may come to you. I can't leave you unprotected."

He selected a slender stick of peeled oak from those seasoning near the fire. While she watched, he wrapped a strip of bark along it, then scorched the exposed wood. When he took off the bark the arrow was marked with a handsome, black spiral stripe. He sharpened the point and hardened it in the fire. He had selected the best hawk feathers for its fletching.

"This is a snake arrow." He handed it to Little Warrior. "When I leave on the war trail, hunt with it. You must kill an animal within four days."

"If I don't, a snake will bite me, isn't that so?" Little Warrior knew about snake arrows. Boys received them as talismans.

"That's so." Osceola smiled at her. "If you kill an animal in four days, the arrow will be your hunting charm. When I return, I'll teach you some of the cures for wounds, some of the songs to keep you safe in battle."

Little Warrior knew this was a distraction, something to keep her from underfoot while he prepared for his first raid. He also had given her a charge to keep her occupied while he was away. The arrow was hardly consolation for the tragedy of being a girl. But it was her father's promise that he would continue to teach her, even though everyone in the war faction was conferring with him and he was rarely home. Little Warrior carried the arrow everywhere with her, even here, to the sacred square, at night.

The moonlight gave the council arbor and the rows of empty log benches a spectral shimmer, as though the warriors had left but their spirits lingered, waiting. Little Warrior stood for an hour or more, trying to absorb the power through her skin. Then she walked back to her family's small *chikee*.

She lay awake, listening to the quiet breathing of her sister next to her and her mothers on the other side of the canvas curtain. As she lay there she wished for an omen. She waited for a dream or a sign to reassure her that her father would return safely, victoriously, from his first raid.

She didn't doubt his magic. It was pure and strong. But even though he had chosen his men with care, some of them were young. Many had never been to war before. One of them might lean against a tree on the trail. Or eat something besides the meager portions handed out by Alligator, Osceola's second in command. Osceola himself might have a dream that would cancel the raid.

Also, the council had just given Osceola the rank of *Tastanagee Thloko*, Great Warrior. Those who envied his sudden prestige were spreading rumors. They said the man who chained him still lived. They said until Osceola took revenge on Wiley Thompson, his magic was tainted. This raid would prove them wrong. When Little Warrior thought of Wiley Thompson she trembled with rage. She wished with all her heart she could kill him herself.

Little Warrior drifted toward sleep, then away, like a wave lapping at the shore. When the sign came she wasn't sure if she was awake or dreaming. The panther stood on his hind feet, put his front paws on the low sleeping platform, and stared at Little Warrior. She looked into his big yellow eyes while her flesh tingled as though ants crawled on it.

After what seemed hours, the big cat dropped down and disappeared. At the first light of dawn Little Warrior scrambled to the edge of the platform and looked over. If the panther had been a dream, its spirit had left a very real sign.

There in the sand were the huge, round, unmistakable prints. Little Warrior knew her father's expedition would be a success.

She lay on her stomach and hung over the edge of the platform. She traced the outline of the print with the tips of her fingers. "Thank you, Brother Panther," she murmured.

The wooden scalp hoops kept up a soft, arrythmic clicking as the breeze blew them against the top of the thirty-foot-tall pole. The willow hoops and the insides of the scalps themselves had been painted red. They looked as thought they were still dripping blood. Seven hundred warriors, their faces painted red and black, sat shoulder to shoulder on palm logs laid in ranks around the square. Osceola was part of the reason they were there.

He and his war party had just returned from the Alachua savanna. Osceola knew his people couldn't fight a war without supplies, so he'd arranged for the United States Army to provide them. He'd ambushed a wagon train. He and his men had taken scalps and a dozen horses loaded with weapons, ammunition, and food.

They had won the first battle of their war. Now Osceola was distributing the plunder. News of the victory had spread like a winter grass fire through the Seminole's scattered camps. Everyone gathered to hear about it and to learn the leaders' plan for the rest of the war.

To the west of the council square, a huge orange sun sank below the grass-fringed rim of the Withlacoochee swamp. Small brown bats plummeted from their perches in the Spanish moss of the cypresses and darted after mosquitoes. The dome of the sky was edged in red and gold, orange and lavender, changing to cobalt blue overhead.

The sunset was a fitting backdrop for Abihka's performance. He had become the most influential prophet of the war faction. He was *Imisee*, the One Carrying the Battle Charm for Them. The magic he worked was formidable, fearsome. Abihka's magic was worth traveling days to experience, as Wild Cat and his men had done.

Tall ostrich plumes nodded in Abihka's flowered turban. His ruffled shirt was dyed with the sunset's colors. He stood alone in the center of the ground laboriously cleared by eager young initiates.

The men sitting around the square watched Abihka silently. He had come to the culmination of his sorcery. He scooped a handful of white cornmeal from the basket at his feet and threw it into the air. It scattered upward and outward. The men sucked in their breaths as the meal transformed into a flock of Great White Egrets.

They flew with their long necks folded back so their heads rested between their shoulders. Their black legs and feet trailed behind them. They flapped their wings slowly, as though tired from their day's fishing. The hundreds of white birds coalesced into a cloud that exploded outward, then contracted again. As the egrets flew away, they slowly dwindled to the size of cornmeal.

Osceola was closer in spirit to Abihka than anyone. Abihka confided in him. He knew the old sorcerer's tricks. He knew Abihka had waited for the Black Drink's powers of illusion to take effect on the warriors. He had timed his throwing of the cornmeal to coincide with the egrets' daily flight back to their rookery. But no matter.

Osceola plainly saw the meal quicken and fly away. It didn't matter how Abihka accomplished it. He had the ability to mix this-reality with other-reality. He could make people see what wasn't visible. What wasn't possible.

With his plumes waving, Abihka danced out of the fire's light. When his quavering song faded, Osceola stood and walked to the center of the bare ground. The December wind was cold, but Osceola could smell excitement and impatience in the sweat of the men sitting around the square. He could feel their power growing, hardening, like a spear point annealed in the flames of Abihka's magic. As the shadows lengthened, the red-and-black paint on their faces became more grotesque.

These were the best. The fighters. These were the ones determined to resist removal. They were waiting to hear about the assault on the white soldiers. These were men who had feared they would grow old without the chance to earn rank and honor. Now they could tell their future grandchildren about these battles.

"We've spent two years watching the blue-jackets' war towns," Osceola said. "Our scouts have learned their drum signals, their routines, the number of their men. They've counted the big guns. They've seen where the powder, the lead, are stored. The black people who are their slaves tell us their movements, their plans.

"We've learned about discipline. To beat the white men we must change the way we've always fought. We must obey our leaders. We must put aside the quest for individual glory in favor of the common good.

"The white men think we're old women." He waited for the whisper of outrage to fade. "They think we lack the strength of purpose to fight in unity. We'll prove them wrong.

"From each of our towns we've received a bundle of sticks. They represent the men who'll join in the struggle. We have three times as many warriors as the blue-jackets. We know the country. They don't. They're like fish in the trees.

"We'll strike the white people in three places at once, so they can't go to each other's aid. Emathla, with his son, Wild Cat, will lead the raid in the east. Jumper, with Alligator, will lead the one in the west. I need only a small group to strike the middle, at Fort King. When you decide which war party you want to join, the leaders will give you detailed instructions.

"We're strong. We'll fight to our last breaths to defend our homes. Our hatchets, our rifles, thirst for the enemy's blood. Soon they'll drink their fill."

Osceola threw back his head and howled his war cry at the rising ghost moon. Seven hundred warriors joined him. Distant wolves took up the cry. The hair on Osceola's neck stirred. Elation expanded in him, made him light, strong, invincible. He was intoxicated with the prospect of war and a very personal vengeance.

CHAPTER 36

When Joseph Hernandez organized the plantation owners of the East Coast to protect their families and property, they dubbed themselves the Mosquito Roarers. They were John von Bulow's neighbors, but when they rode down the tunnel of live oaks to his house, they didn't anticipate a cordial welcome. John, whom Wild Cat called Maggot, had few friends around New Smyrna. His drunken sprees and wild behavior were too much even for their raffish society. They weren't, however, expecting heavy artillery.

Next to John, his little Spanish fieldpiece hunched between the big wooden wheels of its carriage like a faithful hound. The four-pounder sat back on the long wooden shaft of its trail. The raised muzzle of its barrel seemed to be sniffing the foe. The foe's odor was hard to miss.

Five of John's slaves, pressed into service as gunners, waited nervously nearby. Against the damp December chill they wore blankets and burlap sacks pinned around their shoulders. They held their artillery tools—the long-handled ladle and sponge, the handspike, worm, and rammer—at shoulder arms. This was not how they had intended to spend Christmas.

The house slaves peered from behind the dusty curtains of the front windows. Two of John's older children, the color of coffee with cream, had hidden themselves in the high crotch of an oak. Round-eyed as flying squirrels, they stared down at the standoff.

John held up the long rod with the slow match. He made a great show of sucking on his cigar and lighting the cord with it. It sputtered a little as he waved it near the cannon's vent hole. Some of the men jerked their mounts to one side.

John had been drinking, and he was unpredictable, not to mention clumsy. He might light the cannon by mistake.

"Don't be foolish, von Bulow." General Hernandez sat calmly on his horse, directly in the line of fire. "We must use your house to quarter our troops. Many of them are suffering yellow jack and the flux. We're defending Bulowville, too, damn it."

"Damn yourself and your macaroni rabble and the dirty hound that sired you." John's hand wavered dangerously close to the vent hole again. The children in the trees put their hands over their ears. "Wild Cat is my friend." John shouted loudly enough for Wild Cat to hear. John suspected he was in the neighborhood. "You'll only draw the hostiles down on us. My coloreds and I can protect ourselves."

"You're too drunk to protect the pot you piss in."

"War with you is like shearing hogs. . . ." John shook the match at them like a schoolmaster's ferule. "A great cry and little wool."

"Put the match aside, boy, or my *escopet* will leave you nothing to hang your ears on." Douglas Dummet stood on the broad piazza behind John. His bell-mouthed musket was aimed down at John's head.

"You wouldn't shoot, you ass-headed son of a bitch."

Dummet's smile was roguish. Under the matted black beard his tobacco-stained teeth flashed amber. "I would. With pleasure."

"*¡Carajo!* The pommelion's missing on this old belcher." Hernandez walked his horse closer to study the cannon and take the match from John's grasp. "The piece is useless. A pity. Get busy, boys. The cotton houses are over there."

"What do you intend?" John asked.

"We'll use the bales to build a breastwork around the house." Hernandez gestured with the match.

"Might as well bolt the door with a boiled carrot," John said bitterly. "Cotton won't stop Wild Cat."

John was right. Two days after the Mosquito Roarers decamped, with the able bearing the ill on litters, Wild Cat came to Bulowville. He knew the Mosquito Roarers had been there, and he assumed his young friend had betrayed him. He set fire to the plantation's forty-six slave cabins, the sugar mill, the cotton sheds, the docks, and the stables. He rescued the wine in John's well-stocked cellar, but when he burned the house the hundreds of books in the library went with it.

Wild Cat and his men burned five plantations on Christmas Day alone. For three hundred and fifty miles, from Saint Augustine to the Florida Keys, he destroyed houses and crops and spirited away slaves. About three hundred blacks joined the Seminole cause, some voluntarily, some not. Vines grew over the blackened rubble. Only the massive limestone chimneys remained. They reared up from the tangled growth like towering headstones for a once bustling society that was dead.

An icy drizzle beat a tattoo on the flat, overlapping fronds over Osceola's head. An icier wind rattled them. Osceola lay on his stomach in the dense palmetto thicket near the agency store. He had put a quill into the touchhole of his rifle to shield it from the rain. He trusted it to fire when the time came.

The sun had been up three hours, although it was hidden behind dark clouds. Osceola had lain here since the previous afternoon. His war party was scattered throughout the thicket, but he could see only the few nearest to him. The palmettos seemed to have swallowed the rest.

Like most of his men, Osceola wore nothing but the criss-crossing straps of his powder horn, bullet pouch, and the roll of leather that held his sacred medicine. They had bathed with Abihka's medicine, which made them invisible. Clothes, however, could be seen. His lean brown body blended with the palmetto trunks. A diamondback rattler, flooded from its burrow, had coiled itself for a few hours against the warmth of Osceola's side. He had conversed silently and amiably with it, then bade it farewell when it left.

In the twenty-four hours he'd been observing the fort, Osceola had counted forty-six soldiers, only fifteen more than his war party. He didn't see his friend, John Goode. He was glad of that. This would be easier than he'd planned. He had more difficulty controlling his elation than ignoring the cramps in his legs. If his bitterness didn't warm him, at least it made him oblivious to the elements. *We cherish our hatreds as much as we cherish our loves.*

As he lay there, Osceola spared a few bitter thoughts for Trout Leader, and how love could turn to hatred. Trout Leader had known he was under a death sentence. Stoically he had continued preparing to move himself, his family, and his one hundred followers west. Osceola had found him on the trail from Fort King.

"Greetings, nephew," Trout Leader said.

"In the name of the National Council, Uncle, I ask you not to forsake our land." For months Osceola had dreaded this.

"So they sent you, Cricket."

"I was glad to come. You've betrayed us. You deserve to die."

"I love my people. I cannot see them slaughtered. My soul could not endure it. I must take them away."

Osceola leveled his rifle.

"Consider what you're about to do, *Tastanagee*." Abraham reached across his horse and pushed the barrel skyward. Osceola glared at him, and he returned the stare calmly. Osceola knew Mikanopee had sent Abraham along to avoid bloodshed if possible. "Killing him will set brother against brother, as in the old days," Abraham said.

"*Talasee Tastanagee* must do his duty, just as I must do mine." Trout Leader sat up taller in his saddle, to present a better target. He took his feet from the stirrups so they wouldn't impede his fall. He watched Osceola raise his rifle again and fire.

The old man toppled from his horse. While his daughters wailed their grief, Osceola dismounted. He cut the leather wallet from Trout Leader's belt and poured the silver coins into his hand. They were the government's pay for the sale of Trout Leader's cattle. Osceola spat on the shiny metal disks and threw them into the air. They glinted in the sunlight as they fell across Trout Leaders's corpse.

For three weeks the body lay by the trail, until a detail from Fort King ventured out to bury it only a few days ago. Not even Trout Leader's family dared touch him. Until the soldiers came, the coins remained undisturbed, except for a few coins the crows managed to carry off.

Trout Leader's execution had panicked his people and the whites, too. It had emptied the countryside. Now most of

Fort King's garrison was at Clinch's plantation to the north
to protect the settlers there. That was why so few men were
here now.

A large raccoon rustled loudly nearby. The sutler, Erastus
Rogers, and his assistants were working ten yards away. Osceola waited for them to notice the noise. As the raccoon
waddled away, none of the white men spared a glance at the
thicket. The soldiers at work strengthening the pickets ignored it, too.

In their time at Fort King they had heard thousands of raccoons searching for berries and bird eggs in the thickets.
Newcomers often lay awake nights, listening to the raccoons
and skunks. From the volume of noise they made, it was easy
to imagine a platoon of bears or ravening hordes of savages
approaching. With time, the soldiers learned to sleep through
it.

They had even learned to find comfort in it. The acres of
rattling fronds were a warning device and a barrier. They
were the thorny resort of scorpions and bears and rattlesnakes. If a raccoon couldn't move through them without
making a racket, surely a man couldn't. Surely thirty men
couldn't.

Osceola let his breath out slowly as the white men went on
hauling and swearing and dropping things in the mud. Rogers
and his two assistants were loading the store's inventory onto
a wagon. They had carried one load up the hill to the safety
of the fort and were getting ready to take another.

The rain finally stopped, and the sun shone tentatively
through the clouds. Invisible around him, his men waited for
his signal to attack. If he chose to wait through the long,
frigid night and all the next day to give the signal, so be it.
As for Osceola, he had waited almost seven months to kill
Wiley Thompson. He was willing to wait a few hours more.

About two o'clock in the afternoon, Rogers and his men
drove the wagon up the hill and through the fort's gates.
When they returned, they went inside the sutler's house to
eat. At three-thirty Wiley Thompson and a companion
strolled through the gates.

Osceola watched them light their cigars and savor them.
They passed the sutler's house and came so close that Osceola

could smell the smoke of Thompson's Havana. He moved his head slightly to keep them in sight through the latticework of fronds. He propped himself on his elbows, slowly raised his rifle, and sighted.

When Osceola fired the other men did, too. Thompson threw up his hands. A look of astonishment crossed his face as he was knocked backward by the impact of fourteen balls. The shots reverberated against the fort's pickets and cracked the winter stillness. They were still echoing when the sentries began to swing the heavy gates closed. Thompson's friend was also dead before he hit the ground.

Osceola screamed his war cry as he burst from the palmettos and stood over Thompson's body. He raised his knife over his head and drove it down with all his strength. It pulled the heavy wool coat and shirt inward when it sank into Thompson's heart. Crimson spurted, them spread slowly to meet the stains from the other wounds.

"You should have killed me when you shackled me," Osceola hissed. "Now, when your soul passes on the wind, it will recoil from my path." But Osceola was disappointed that Thompson had died so quickly. Abihka said revenge was sweeter than a woman's love. He was wrong. Revenge was necessary. The anticipation of it nourished a man through adversity; but the consummation of it was a sorry, disappointing business. Osceola felt suddenly tired.

As he knelt over the body he could hear shots and muffled shouts from inside the sutler's house. He grabbed the agent's steel-gray hair and yanked it taut. With quick, deft strokes he carved a neat circle in the scalp. With a jerk of his wrist he tore the skin away. He stepped over the corpse without a backward glance. He tied Thompson's blood-soaked hair to his shoulder strap, next to his knife sheath, and ran to join his men in the house.

Rogers and three others lay near the table. Blood pooled in their plates. One man's skull had been crushed with a hatchet. His brains had spattered across the wall. The chairs had overturned as the men tried to escape. Their legs were tangled in the rungs. The muscles of their faces had gone slack when their scalps were taken. They looked as though they'd aged a lifetime in a few seconds.

The warriors were ransacking the store in the other room. They were looking for powder or lead or weapons, but Rogers had cleared everything out.

"We have more fighting to do," Osceola shouted. Now that he had settled his blood debt with Thompson, he was in a hurry. Most of the men in the war party had no horses, so Osceola had come on foot, too. Now they all must run thirty miles to Wahoo swamp, near the military road from Fort Brooke. They were to join Jumper and Alligator in an ambush on a column marching to relieve the beleaguered garrison here.

They melted into the palmettos before the sporadic fire from the palisades could have any effect. They had just vanished when Colonel Crane galloped up. He had heard the shots from the forest, where he was hunting to augment the miserable army rations. He loaded his pistols as he rode.

He arrived in time to hear the rustling of the war party's hasty flight. Then he heard Osceola's distinctive cry. It was a chilling echo of the one he'd heard the day Osceola was released from the guardhouse. Crane leaped from his horse.

"My God." He stared down at Wiley Thompson's blood-soaked clothes. His mangled scalp looked as if some beast had taken a bite from it. "My God."

CHAPTER 37

Naked, Mikanopee was not a pretty sight. Lumps of flesh seemed to flow toward his groin. His small, purple penis and scrotum were hidden in the soft brown waves. His pendulous jowls dangled like saddlebags on either side of his broad nose and lips.

His bulk was not keeping him warm as he crouched behind the fringed fans of the huge palmetto. He shivered in the cold wind. The icy drizzle had soaked his plumes. They hung, limp and sodden, off the side of his wet turban. He wheezed so loudly with each steamy breath that Alligator feared he'd alert the approaching soldiers.

Mikanopee was trapped in a role for which he was unsuited, just as he was trapped in his body. Major Dade had been a friend to him, and he had few friends. The tall, mustachioed soldier had shared tobacco with him, had joked with him, had been kind to him. Now Mikanopee would have to kill him.

"I say we wait for Talasee *Tastanagee*." The cold was affecting Mikanopee's sinuses, and he snuffled wetly.

"We've waited as long as we can. Osceola must have been delayed killing Sense-Maker Tahm-sahn." In council Jumper was courteous to his king. In private he wasn't. "For three days we've passed up every chance to attack. This is our last one. We'll not let a year's preparations go to waste for your cowardice."

"They're coming." Alligator brought up his musket and tensed. He and the hundred and eighty other warriors had danced up the dawn in an effort to stay warm. Then they had filed into the palmettos and tall grass of the pine forest. Each had chosen his cover near the military road and hunkered down to wait.

Alligator had been positioned here in the rain, behind this pine for two hours. His particular medicine made him impervious to bullets, so he wore his finest shirt and leggings, but he was still cold. The glow of the dancing had long since died and been replaced by a wet chill. Alligator was ready to fight. Fighting could warm a man as effectively as dancing.

Yea, though I walk through the valley of the shadow of death, I will fear no evil. Private Joseph Taylor wasn't a religious man, but that line had repeated itself in his head for three days. *I will fear no evil.* It murmured under the racket of the nightly bivouac and the daily march. The rhythm of the words was as constant as the drums that set the pace for the long column of men.

Private Taylor was intimately familiar with the valley of the shadow of death. It stretched sixty miles, from Fort Brooke to just about here, two-thirds of the way to Fort King.

It was dense jungle growth where Seminole could hide within arm's length of their prey. It was a labyrinth of columnar cypresses so tall that Private Taylor's tall, stiff collar prevented him from laying his head back far enough to see their tops. Moss hung from the bare branches like ancient, dusty cobwebs.

The valley of the shadow of death was miles of sulfurous water, black as pitch. It was where mud bogged men to the waist and poisonous snakes dropped from trees. Where a half-submerged log might surge upward and an alligator's jaw gape and hiss. Stinging insects swarmed in tenacious clouds, even now, in late December. In the valley of the shadow of death, birds screamed like women in agony, and the air was too thick with evil and decay to breathe without gagging.

The army road skirted the worst of the swampy country around the head of the Hillsborough River; but Private Taylor had spent plenty of time with his shoulder to the huge, mud-plastered wheels of the Dearborns. Rain had fallen for two days and flooded miles of the trail. Where it wasn't flooded, deep sand made the going just as difficult. Clearing fallen trees was so exhausting that those at the front of the column rotated to the back every two hours.

Swamps and jungles and mud didn't make this the valley of death. The Seminole did. Rumor said a thousand or more of them were out there. Every man in the column heard birds the old Florida hands said shouldn't be calling this time of the year. They felt the unseen eyes. They smelled the odor of damp, charred wood before they saw the half-burned bridges at each river crossing.

With their muskets and new rifles over their heads, the soldiers had waded the cold streams and waited for the enemy's gunfire to cut them down. At one crossing the cannon had fallen off its crude raft, and they'd spent Christmas Day dragging it out of the river. But in spite of the opportunities for ambush, no attack came. The mystery of it plagued them.

The Seminole could find them easily. Only one narrow road existed between Fort Brooke and Fort King. The two files of men wound out of sight around the curves. The double line of black forage caps looked like stripes on a huge, reticulated blue snake. One hundred men in bright blue uniforms with drums and fifes, horse and wagons, and a lumbering cannon and carriage were impossible to conceal.

Even so, Taylor wished the men wouldn't talk so loudly and the drummers wouldn't beat cadence. He wished the axles on the Dearborns and the carriage for the stout little six-pounder didn't screech like all the damned souls in purgatory. He wished the chains on the harness shafts didn't clank so. Mostly he wished he were back home.

Taylor was a musician. He was thirty-six years old. Not a young man. Certainly not a bright-eyed adventurer.

"Do you know what the recruiter told me?" he asked the man walking in the file across from him.

Twenty-three-year-old Ransom Clarke grinned and pulled his knee-length wool greatcoat tighter around him. Like most of the soldiers, he had stoppered the vent of his musket and buttoned the coat over it to keep it from the drizzle. The bayonet stuck up from his lapels and caressed the dark stubble on his cheek.

From a distance the soldiers looked natty in their dark blue coats and capes and their light blue trousers. But the uniforms were torn. They were stained brown by the swamp water. The matted, damp wool chafed terribly.

"The bastard said, 'Florida is a land with a climate so healthy folks have to shoot someone to start a graveyard,' " Joseph Taylor grumbled.

"I'd rather not speak of shooting and filling graveyards, thank you, Joseph," said Ransom.

"I never expected weather this cold." Taylor pulled the fur flaps of his tall cap farther down over his red ears. The men had slept in rain-soaked grass as high as their chests, and they were still wet to the skin.

" 'Tain't the cold," said a man from Vermont. " 'Tis the damp."

"We smell like a pack of wet spaniels," grumbled the soldier ahead of Clarke. "My feet have been marinating in these boots so long, they might as well be corned beef."

"Leave it to the army to issue low-topped boots for fighting in swamps," said Taylor.

"At least we'll not be entertaining any of Osceola's yaller naiggurs," said Private Neeley.

The road sloped upward, into the pine forest that would surround them the rest of the trip. Mud churned up by the wagons became less deep. The palmettos and high grass still provided cover for an ambush, but the pine woods were much more open than the country through which they'd passed. An army could maneuver in pine woods.

The gray-green fingers of the palmetto fronds poked through the ground fog that pooled around the trees. When the rain stopped, shafts of sunlight knifed through the dove-colored clouds. The tissue of frost covering the bushes began to shrink. Someone at the head of the line began to sing, "God rest ye, merry gentlemen, let nothing you dismay." Others joined in.

Captain George Washington Gardiner of the Second Artillery cantered up alongside his men in Company C. His small dog trotted beside his horse. Gardiner was barely five feet tall and as round and solid as the cannon he cherished.

"Now aren't you glad you came along, Captain?" sang out Private Clarke.

"Wouldn't have missed it." Gardiner was to have led the troops, but his wife had become ill, so Major Dade took command. Gardiner could have boarded the steamship that was taking his wife to the navy hospital in Key West. Instead, still wearing his black frock coat, he hurried to catch up with his men and his cannon. He had insisted, as a military courtesy, that Major Dade remain in charge.

Almost half the men in the column were foreigners. Few of them were professional soldiers. They were hatters and farmers, clerks, spinners, weavers, tailors, shoemakers, and one Irish hairdresser. Major Francis Langhorn Dade, however, was the image of the perfect soldier.

He was as tall as Gardiner was short. Heavily fringed gold epaulets widened his already broad shoulders. His boots were blacked. His slender hands in their white gloves held the reins casually. His double-barreled shotgun rode snugly in a boot slung from his saddle. His long, curved saber hung at his side.

Besides looks, he had a full measure of courage. He had boasted that he would march one hundred men through hostile territory with impunity. His men were relieved to see he was about to make good on his boast. He had all the qualifications of the perfect soldier but one. Judgment. He neglected to post flankers to scout the countryside. He allowed his men to button their rifles and muskets into their coats.

The tail end of the column entered the pine woods and wound through the thick palmettos. At the head of it, Dade stood in his stirrups. His strong voice carried to the men in back.

"Have a good heart," he shouted. "Our difficulties and dangers are over now. As soon as we arrive at Fort King you'll have three days' rest, and keep Christmas gaily!"

The soldiers's huzzahs almost drowned out the solitary rifle report. Major Dade sagged slowly in his polished saddle. His head bowed forward and brushed his horse's neatly combed mane as he fell to one side. With Jumper's bullet in his heart, he was dead before he touched the ground.

The warriors stood up in the palmettos and opened fire. The crack of their guns and their ululating cries filled the quiet woods. Blue smoke mixed with the fog. The warriors had painted their naked bodies red. They look like red peppers on a string of light, Private Taylor thought with a brief, curious sense of detachment.

The first volley cut down the soldiers as they tried to get their muskets out of their greatcoats. Through the acrid blue clouds of smoke, Taylor smelled feces and urine and realized he'd bewrayed himself. He sobbed as he clawed with stiff, cold fingers at the cumbersome buttons of his cape and coat.

When Taylor finally undid both courses of buttons, he cursed his piece, caught in the tails of his coat. The strap of his cartridge box tangled with the white crossbelt. Taylor dropped to one knee and, with shaking hands, tried to load. When he bit off the twisted paper from the end of the two-inch cartridge, powder spilled into the mud.

"Oh, shit," he sobbed. "Oh, shit. Oh, shit." If only they would all stop screaming. If only the guns would stop roaring, maybe he could think.

"Unlimber the cannon, God damn you!" Captain Gardiner waved his saber so hard it whistled around his ears. Salting his instructions with curses, he wheeled his horse up and down the ragged line. "Find cover, God damn it! Move!"

Gardiner slowly rallied the men as they fumbled for their weapons. Half the command lay dead or writhing in the mud. The first volley from the palmettos lessened, then broke into solitary pops as Jumper's men reloaded.

"They're no better shots on the second volley than a pack of Spaniards," Gardiner shouted. "Load and aim with care. Shoot to the right of the muzzle's blast."

Gardiner knew that before a battle the Seminole had time to load carefully. After that they often measured haphazardly, pouring the powder into sweaty hands. Or they didn't bother to patch, and the balls rolled loose in the barrels of their muskets.

Taylor and the other survivors slowly fell back to the cover of the trees. As Taylor aimed and fired, he strained to hear a scream, some indication that his ball had found a target. The Seminole's return fire splattered like gravel into the trunks of the pines. Wounded soldiers crawled to cover or dragged bodies into piles to form barricades. They fired from behind the dead.

The double team of horses pulled the half-ton cannon and carriage careening down the trail. The big wheels rolled over fallen men until the Seminole's second volley brought the horses down. Taylor helped lift the carriage trail off the two-wheeled cart still hitched to the thrashing animals. The men fitted the handspike into the trail's eyebolts and heaved it around.

"Sponge!" Gardiner shouted. "Ram! Point! Point, God damn it! No time to aim. Fire level." The explosion and the ball's deadly trajectory scattered the Seminole in its path, but Jumper and Alligator had trained their men well. Their ranks held.

When the smoke cleared the Seminole concentrated their fire on the gun crew, but as fast as they killed one soldier another took his place. The artillerymen worked methodically—sponging, pricking, ramming, firing—loading four times a minute.

While the six-pounder kept the Seminole pinned down, Captain Gardiner rushed back and forth, impervious to the lead rain. He was obviously *hadjo*, crazy. He impressed the

Seminole. He was about to become the stuff of their stories, but Gardiner didn't know that. He wouldn't have cared if he had.

"God *damn*! Take cover!" he screamed. "Shoot to the right, you whoresons! God *damn*!" all of which calmed his men and kept them loading and firing steadily.

Jumper and Alligator knew if they didn't do something soon, their own warriors would grow restless and refuse to obey them, so they signalled a withdrawal. After all, they had killed most of the white men, and they had lost three men themselves. They didn't want to risk more deaths. They could pick off the blue-jacket survivors as they fled through the woods.

The firing slowed, then stopped. The warriors melted into the palmettos. They regrouped on high ground, out of range but within sight of the desperate soldiers.

Silence pulsed in Taylor's ears a few moments before he realized he only thought he heard nothing. All around him men were moaning and crying for help. Captain Gardiner was shouting instructions generously laced with oaths.

Stooping below the cover of the grass, those who could walk moved along the line of march. They stripped the gun and leather cartridge boxes from the dead and helped the more severely wounded struggle toward shelter. The gun crew hauled water from a nearby pond. They would need it to sponge the piece.

Gardiner directed twenty of the more able-bodied to cut trees for a barricade. The steady *toc* of their blades was a comfort. The rest laid the logs on top of each other, as though building a three-sided cabin. Desperation gave extra bite to the axes, and the wall rose quickly. The soldiers had no time to notch the ends, so wide spaces were left between them. The wounded hobbled or crawled or were carried inside.

Of the thirty men still alive, many were like the lieutenant, who sat unconscious against the wall. His broken arms dangled at his sides. With handkerchiefs or pieces of their uniforms, men staunched the bleeding. Ransom Clarke rested his rifle against the barricade and began rubbing dirt into his white crossbelt.

"What are you doing?" Taylor asked.

"Blacking this damned thing." With a filthy finger Clarke jabbed the upper-left quadrant of his chest, sectioned off by the belt. "Aim here and I'm a dead man. Might as well paint a bull's-eye on my chest."

The barricade was slightly over two feet high when Jumper, Alligator, and their men walked boldly toward it through the palmettos. They loaded as they came, spitting their lead balls into the barrels and tapping the gun butts to settle them. They aimed almost casually.

Their plumes waved gaily. Their silver gorgets flashed in the sun. Their bare bodies gleamed with fish oil. The palmettos seemed alive with them as they fanned out to surround the breastworks. Private Taylor thought they moved with disconcerting discipline for naked, untrained savages.

The triangular barricade suddenly seemed a cage to the men inside it. The spaces between the logs looked wide enough for a cannonball to pass through. "My God, there are a lot of those devils," Taylor breathed.

"More than sufficient, I would say." Clarke didn't say more than sufficient for what.

Joseph Taylor envied the unconscious lieutenant. He would likely never wake up. Taylor knew with terrible certainty that the lieutenant was the lucky one.

"Steady, men." Captain Gardiner strolled around the barricade. He tapped his saber on the top logs and swore at the red shadows gliding silently through the palmettos. Gardiner's little dog bustled behind him, barking with excitement and wagging his tail furiously. Gardiner didn't flinch when the warriors began firing, popping up from cover, whooping, then disappearing.

Outside the walls, the six-pounder roared and a gout of smoke rose. It bucked on its carriage and rolled backwards with each shot. When one of the gun crew fell, another man leaped the barricade and ran crouching to take his place. He dragged the body away and piled it on the heap of dead and near dead. If men refused to leave the barricade, Gardiner swore and waved his sword in their faces.

"You will die discharging your duty, God damn you," he shouted. "Or you will die by my hand."

The cannon became too hot to touch. The crew's faces and

hands were black with powder and covered with burns. The cannon's roar made it impossible to hear each other, much less the battle.

Taylor and the others sat or lay at the barricade and shot through the cracks. Most of the dead lay parallel to each other where they had fallen at their posts along the wall. The odor of blood, sweat, and viscera was cut by the smell of fresh pine resin released by the balls splintering into the logs.

By late afternoon the barricade was so full of lead the balls often hit with a dull clink. The last of the cannon rounds was fired, and the gun crew stumbled back into the barricade. They joined the few remaining survivors, who lay in puddles of blood. Their uniforms were soaked with it. Their red-rimmed eyes peered from blackened faces.

Joseph Taylor's right shoulder throbbed with the lead buried there. His right arm no longer answered his muscle's commands. He propped his carbine against the barricade and loaded and fired with his left hand. The ammunition was almost gone from the heap of cartridge boxes and powder horns around him.

"I would give . . ." Taylor paused. He had nothing to give. Surely his life was no longer his. "I would give my soul's salvation for a drink of water."

A ball hit Ransom Clarke's shoulder and punctured his lung. Clarke rolled onto his face and lay still. A crimson pool formed near his mouth. Taylor bade him silent farewell.

Captain Gardiner had been hit four times. "I can give you no more orders, my lads." He leaned against a pine as he tried to load. "Do your best." He slid down the trunk and collapsed. His dog whined and licked the powder and dust from his face.

Private Taylor saw a small, painted Indian raise his rifle and aim it at him. Small as a boy, he thought. Too weary to move, he stared at the barrel in fascination. He almost welcomed Alligator's ball as it tore into his chest.

He was among the last to fall, but he wasn't dead. Through the opening between the bottom logs he saw the Seminole approach. He heard the rustle of their bare feet coming closer, until their legs filled the long, narrow frame of the opening.

As they looked down into the pen, Taylor could see the taut curves of their calves and the scars and scratches and insect bites.

He held his breath as Jumper and Alligator and a few others stepped over the low wall. He heard them talking in their strange, trilling language while they collected weapons. They gently lifted the straps of cartridge boxes and powder horns from the dead. Alligator hunkered beside Captain Gardiner's body, communing with his spirit and wishing him a safe journey. He took Gardiner's jacket as a keepsake, a symbol of the man's mad courage.

Sweat broke out on Taylor's forehead as he waited for them to find him. He decided he wouldn't die under a scalping knife. With blood spurting from his wounds, he surged to his feet. He jerked the rifle from a warrior's hand and caved in the man's skull with it. Then he vaulted the wall and ran. He didn't get far, but at least he died quickly.

The Seminole didn't mutilate the dead. They didn't even loot the bodies. Obeying Abihka and Osceola's orders, they took the weapons and left the soldiers where they lay.

Not long afterward, a party of blacks arrived. They were too late to fight, but early enough to take revenge. In spite of General Clinch's objections, Andrew Jackson's policies and territorial laws had turned the army into a tool for slave hunters. The blacks had even more reason to hate the soldiers than the Seminole did.

The black warriors killed anyone who showed life. They rifled pockets and pouches and stripped the bodies. Splattered with blood and brains, they cheerfully bartered for pocket watches and jewelry.

When they set fire to the cannon's carriage, the flames spread through the tall grass. As they were leaving, two of them shot Ransom Clarke again, for good measure. Then they mounted and rode away, laughing and singing. Vultures began to wheel silently overhead.

When Ransom Clarke woke up, it was night. He was wounded in the back, the shoulder, and the chest. His clavicle, his arm, and his leg were broken. He sucked air into his one lung and began to crawl over the bodies of his comrades, then across the charred landscape. Three days later he dragged himself into Fort Brooke, sixty miles away. He was one of two from Dade's command to survive, and the only one to live longer than a year afterward.

CHAPTER 38

Little Warrior walked between Alligator and Osceola as they strolled through the huge encampment. The evening was still early, but the camp was quiet. Everyone was waiting for the latest white war leader, General Edmund Gaines, to arrive with his soldiers at the nearby ford of the Withlacoochee. Victory depended on surprise. In this camp, no one beat drums or whooped or fired weapons.

Hundreds of thatched shelters blended with the palmettos and scrub oak of the pine forest. Two thousand people camped here. Fires were small. None would have been allowed at all except that lead had to be melted for bullets. Little Warrior liked to go with her father on his daily progress.

Osceola wore Major Dade's blue uniform jacket. Jumper had given the jacket to him when he arrived, mud-stained and weary and too late for the attack on Dade's command. Morning Dew had patched the hole over the heart.

"It goes well, *Tastanagee*." The people of Talasee had camped together, and they called their greetings as Osceola passed.

"It goes well," Osceola answered. "*Che'hahn tah-mo*—how are you?" "When's your daughter's wedding?" "Did Yellow Coat return the kettle she borrowed?" He admired each new baby. He remembered every name and every problem.

Alligator's exchanges were of an earthier sort, but everyone would have been disappointed if they weren't. Women's stifled laughter followed him through the camp. *"Shta,"* they said. "Be quiet." But they didn't mean it.

"Talasee *Tastanagee . . ."* The scout must have been about eighteen. He was naked except for a tattered breechclout, quantities of mud, and cracked red-and-black war paint. Now that he had stopped running he felt the chill of the night air on his sweaty body. He shivered.

"What news do you bring, Heartless Lye-Drip?"

The boy crouched in the fire's light. With the sharpened end of a palmetto rib he drew thirty-four crosses, each representing ten men. He pointed to them with the stick. "They're approaching with this many, three times. They're marching in three groups. They're about four sleeps from here. As usual their big gun slows them down."

"Someone smells like a singed possum." Alligator sniffed the air.

"One of the soldiers pissed on me." Heartless Lye-Drip looked sheepish. "He was so close he pissed on my breechclout. He didn't see me."

Osceola almost laughed out loud. His grin was more carefree than Little Warrior had seen in a long time.

The scout cleared a place in the sand and sketched a detailed map of the terrain. He added the three columns into which General Gaines had divided his one thousand men. He drew the placement of the infantry, the mounted troops, the officers, the supply wagons, and the six-pounder with its cans of deadly grapeshot.

"They're armed with the new rifles that load in the middle," Heartless Lye-Drip added.

"The ones that explode in the middle," Osceola said.

"Nephew . . ." Alligator picked up a piece of charcoal. "How do you know if a man has a breechloader, even if you don't see it?"

"How, Uncle?" The *tasikaya* was terribly earnest. He was eager for any wisdom the *tastanagee* was willing to share.

With the charcoal Alligator blackened the area under the generous overhang of his nose. "The ones armed with breechloaders have singed upper lips."

The boy looked unsure if this was useful information or

more of Alligator's foolery. "One more thing, *tastanagee*," he said. "Heartless Snake is guiding them. He says they have little food. Their three wagons are almost empty."

"You've done well." Alligator drew himself up to the peak of his five feet and touched the brim of his nonexistent forage cap in salute. Heartless Lye-Drip waved his hand vaguely, again unsure how to respond. Osceola smiled his approval, and the boy hurried off to give his report to Abihka.

"When the blue-jackets shit, we know what color it is." Alligator threw his arms out as though to welcome war into them. "A battle makes me three hands taller. It makes Baldy swell with pride."

His high spirits were contagious. He did a few steps of the white man's jig, and Little Warrior and Osceola laughed soundlessly with him.

Alligator wandered off, probably to importune both his wives. Tomorrow would begin three days of fasting and purification in preparation for the war trail. Alligator would make the most of tonight.

Osceola and Little Warrior walked away from the camp and the pine forest, into the night song of the nearby swamp. In front of them lay the dark expanse of the Withlacoochee, changeless in the face of so much death and pain and rancor.

Osceola felt himself shrink under the sparkling vault of the sky. He liked the feeling of being small and insignificant. Little Warrior stood in front of him and leaned against him. Osceola put his arms around her. For a few moments he was relieved to know nothing. To be responsible for nothing. The endurance that had kept him going for the past months with little food and less sleep finally had been exhausted.

He had no sooner reached Jumper and Alligator's camp after their defeat of Dade's column when they received word that General Clinch was marching toward them with seven hundred and fifty men. Clinch was planning to attack the camps in the Cove of the Withlacoochee.

Osceola and Alligator had ambushed the soldiers as they rested with stacked arms, one-third on one bank of the swollen river and two-thirds on the other. The warriors had killed four of them, wounded over fifty, and sent the rest fleeing in disorder. Wild Cat had made the east coast uninhabitable for his enemies. The planters and settlers huddled in Saint Augustine or in the disease-ridden forts of the interior.

The Seminole had won every battle. By the war leaders' calculations they had won the war, but the soldiers wouldn't admit it. They wouldn't leave the country that didn't belong to them and that they couldn't hold by force of arms. They were on their way to attack again, this time with even more men.

"Has the Panther spirit visited you again, daughter?" In the darkness, Osceola's voice seemed to come from far away.

"No. But you'll win. You have a thousand warriors." Little Warrior wanted this moment to extend indefinitely into the night. She almost never saw her father alone anymore. She cherished the warm protection of his arms. Whatever happened, she knew his strength and magic would protect them all.

Mist rose from the water's surface. The dawn cries of egrets and herons echoed hauntingly across the tranquil face of the land. Flocks of migrating ducks darkened the sky. Awakened by the birds, the earth itself seemed to stir sleepily.

The sky was brightening when a thousand warriors moved silently through the trees and brush toward the high sand banks at the Withlacoochee ford. About a hundred of them were black. As they walked each held a hand on his ammunition pouch so the balls wouldn't clink. The pale light and swirling ground fog gave them the look of ghosts.

The women and older girls followed. Their long skirts hid the motion of their legs, so they seemed to glide through the fog. Most of the older women stayed in camp with the young children, but Fighting in a Line insisted on coming along. She was the grandmother of Osceola, *Tastanagee Thloko*. She was an honored ancient one. She had outwitted Old Mad Jackson. And she wanted to watch her man go into battle.

The stripes of yellow paint had dried and cracked on Mad Dog's face and chest. He had knotted a faded rag of blue silk around his neck. His breechclout hung low on his withered hips. Vertebrae ran like a knotted cord down the center of his back. His leathery skin hung slack on the basket of his ribs. Fighting in a Line had never seen a man so handsome.

Mad Dog lifted his feet high, like a cat trying to keep his paws dry. His elbows flapped at his side as he hurried to keep up with the younger men. But he remembered the great Red Stick War. He could tell the young men how much better this war was than that one. He had been *tasikaya*, an ordinary warrior, when the British and the Americans had fought so bitterly sixty years ago. He had weathered war and adversity. Mad Dog was one of the wise ones. Some of the young men veered over to ask his advice and perhaps attract some of his magic.

Most of the men were almost naked, but the women wore their finest clothes. They had appliquéd geometric designs on their skirts and added more ruffles to their blouses. They wore all their beads. Their fringed shawls protected them from the cool February wind. If they hadn't been so heavily burdened, they would have looked as if they were on their way to a dance.

They carried the extra rifles and water gourds, cloth for bandages, hatchets, *sofkee* pots and ladles, and tinder, flint, and steel for starting fires. At their waists and tied to straps across their chests, they wore pouches of lead balls and patches of cotton sacking. Several pair of them carried fifty-pound kegs of powder on blanket litters.

Mink wore a wooden back frame with bags of parched corn, *koontee* cakes, and dried venison tied to it. Between her breasts were crossed the straps of powder flask, ammunition pouch, water gourds, a medicine bag, and a sack with pipe and tobacco.

Little Warrior had to trot to keep up with her. She carried the old fusil Osceola had given Mink. Like Mink she wore her skirt tied up at her waist so it looped in folds around her knees. She carried the snake arrow stuck into her belt. It would bring her luck.

When the women stopped in the stunted blackjack oaks at the base of the sand ridge, Morning Dew stayed with them. She and the others made a hurried camp. They hung the gourds on low limbs so the wind would cool them. They pried open the lids of the powder kegs. They laid the weapons, cleaning rods, patches, and balls on blankets and loaded the extra guns. They built brush lean-tos to shelter the wounded. They brought water to clean the rifles and cool them.

Morning Dew was happy to be on the war trail. She hated the waiting when Osceola set out on a raid. She hated the dread that lodged in her heart until he returned. Today they would either beat the blue-jackets or die together.

While the warriors took up positions just below the top of the high ridge, Mink settled into the grass at the end of the line.

"Child . . ." Mink took the fusil. "Wait behind that palmetto." She pointed down the hill. "When I give the signal, run, tell the women the enemy is here."

"Let me stay." Little Warrior had never been so close to a battle. She was quivering with excitement.

Mink just looked at her. With an angry sigh Little Warrior moved away from the ridgeline and lay down behind the palmetto. The fronds curved up and over her in sweeping, symmetrical plumes. They gathered her into the busy world in the fibrous bark at the palmetto's base.

She watched the insects and lizards scurry over her arms. With a twig she teased a scorpion into stinging itself. She imagined the ants were blue-jacket soldiers as she dropped them into the funnel-shaped ant lion's trap in the sand. She watched the ants struggle as the insect dug the sand from under them, then dragged them down.

She was so engrossed she almost didn't notice the coo of mourning doves, the signal. With heart pounding, she crawled backward, then hiked her skirt up higher and pelted down the slope. The first shots and war cries were sounding when, screaming her own warbling call, she raced into the women's camp. The women set up a high, mournful cry of their own.

"I'll take water to Father." Little Warrior made a grab for the gourds, and Morning Dew caught her arm. She held it tight while she counted the number of volleys from the ridgeline.

"He's fired twice. His gun will be fouled after the next volley. Take this." Morning Dew handed her the second rifle. "Listen to me," she said. "Hold the gun so the powder doesn't fall into the hole."

"I know." Little Warrior could barely contain her impatience.

"Bring back the first one so I can clean it. Look about you," she called at Little Warrior's heels.

Little Warrior labored up the hill with the women who were carrying loaded guns and water to their men. Just below the ridge she dropped into a crouch. Osceola jerked the rifle from her and handed her his other one.

"No," he said without even looking at her.

"Just one look."

A cannonball flew across the ridge at ground level. It sent sprays of sand into her eyes.

"Go."

All day Little Warrior and the women carried supplies up the steep hill. They carried a few wounded men down. Mink's powder and bullets gave out soon; but she had fought in battle with the men. When she joined the other women Little Warrior greeted her gravely and handed her a ladle of *sofkee*. Both Little Warrior and Mink were black with powder, streaked with sweat, and terribly thirsty.

"Did you kill some of them, Mother?"

Mink laughed ruefully. "I don't know." She took a long drink. "They flit though the trees like blue birds. They're falling, though."

The sun was low on the horizon when the firing from the other side of the river slowed, then stopped. It was replaced by the sound of axes. When Little Warrior crawled up beside her father she found him conferring with Alligator. He didn't send her away.

"What are they doing?" She peered over the top of the ridge. She could see flashes of blue among the pine trees on the other side of the river.

"Building a wall," Osceola said.

"They're building their tomb, niece." Alligator grinned. "We shall kill them all, just as we did before."

That night Little Warrior fell asleep in the open, between Mink and Morning Dew. She was exhausted and aching, but she awoke a few times and looked up at the top of the ridgeline. When she did, she saw her father, a dark form against the starry sky, keeping watch.

CHAPTER 39

Five days later the stench inside Major General Gaines's log breastwork made breathing an ordeal. Many of the soldiers wore handkerchiefs over their noses and mouths. Almost a thousand men, plus horses and mules, were crowded into a chest-high log pen fifty feet on a side. A few men waited until nightfall to sneak outside and answer nature's demands. Not many were willing to risk it.

The Seminole had set fire to the dry grass and brush. The wind had shifted, blowing the flames away from the barricade, but they left the ground around it black and barren. It offered no place to hide. Most soldiers figured having their scalps taken while their trousers were around their ankles was too high a price to pay for hygiene. They used the hole near a corner of the breastwork. Many suffered from dysentery and couldn't get there in time. Some urinated where they lay. Some knelt and tried to aim through the chinks in the logs. The walls stank of urine.

In the center of the barricade a small spring bubbled out of limestone rock. Its water had sustained them so far, but just barely. Three hundred and fifty feet away flowed a wide curve of the Withlacoochee.

As the long days wore on, the able-bodied took to passing by the rear wall of the barricade. In spite of the effluvium from the latrine hole, they stopped to stare out at the river. The cypress trees along its swampy margins had dyed it the color of strong tea. It teemed with snapping turtles and water moccasins and alligators two or three times the length of a man. No matter. The soldiers dreamed of submerging themselves to the neck in it.

Like the others, nineteen-year-old Samuel had gleaned corn dropped from the horses' feed sacks until not another mud-caked kernel could be found. The hungry horses neighed continually.

"What do you suppose alligator tastes like?" Sam asked.

"Like chicken, I hear. Not as good as dog, though." Sergeant O'Reilly was whittling his nails with his knife. "Shawnessy had some horse guts for sale for six bucks, but I prefer dog myself. How about you, son?"

Sam crouched protectively over his puppy. His was the last dog. The flayed hindquarters of the next-to-the-last dog lay on a bandana. It was stakes for a very serious game of seven and eleven. The sound of the dice in a tin pannikin was getting on Sam's nerves.

Flies formed a thick crust on the dog meat. Flies formed a crust on everything that didn't shake them off. There were those who wondered how flies would taste.

"Five dollars for a quarter of a dog," said O'Reilly. "Your'n is so small, I reckon it'd only bring a few bucks."

Sam glanced at the small knot of officers around a body under a canvas lean-to. Five days earlier a bullet had caught Lieutenant Izard on the first volley, as he tried to lead the advance guard across the river. The ball had pierced his nose, passed behind his left eye, and exited from his temple, leaving two neat, purple holes. Blow flies had laid eggs under the bloody bandage.

"Looks like Lieutenant Izard finally cashed in."

"Hope they bury him soon." O'Reilly squinted at the sun glaring like a polished brass button in a faded blue serge sky. "We don't need nothin' else rottin' in here."

Sam shuddered. The knot of fear and hunger tightened in his belly. He had been in Florida less than a week when he and the others in General Gaines's command found the remains of Major Dade's men. For six weeks the bodies had lain where they had fallen, in orderly firing position along the low barricade.

They had swelled until they'd burst their uniforms. They had turned yellow, then red, then purple, green, and finally black. By the time Sam saw them the blue jackets and trousers clothed identical skeletons, as though Death's army demanded absolute uniformity.

Sam had helped collect the bones of hands and bootless feet

and the skulls scattered by predators that considered brains a delicacy. The new recruits stopped joking about killing off all the redskins in a week. Sam had helped dig the mass grave for the officers. The noncoms were buried in another hole and the enlisted men in a third. The army was careful to preserve rank beyond the grave. Sam wondered if he and his comrades would end up in a similar hole.

"How many hostiles you think are out there?" Sam peered through the chinks.

"Thousand, maybe."

"We have that many. I'd rather charge than sit here and watch flies suck shit."

"I hear Gaines is waiting for reinforcements from Clinch. Sent 'im a note inviting him to the party. Wants to keep the hostiles busy so Clinch can sneak up behind 'em. Then the party's over. We all go home and eat and fuck till our brains squirt out our cocks."

"Do you think a messenger could get through?"

"Doesn't matter. The bastards at Fort Drane can hear our cannons."

"Look at this!" Sam waved O'Reilly to the barricade. "They told us them savages was no more'n rabble."

"They was wrong."

Out of range, Osceola formed the six hundred warriors into ragged ranks and files. While a bugle blared tunelessly and someone beat a drum tattoo, Alligator strutted across the field. He was bare-legged and bare-arsed. He wore a black forage cap and a blue uniform coat, and he waved a large red banner.

The warriors wheeled promptly, if not precisely, when Osceola shouted commands. While the men at the barricade watched, the Seminole performed a parody of the white man's close-order drill. Then they marched into the palmettos and out of sight, back to their comfortable camp along the river, and to the food cooked by their wives. Only Alligator's mocking laugh remained.

The soldiers had no way of knowing the drill was as much an act of desperation as defiance. After laying siege for five days, the warriors were bored and restless. They didn't mind fighting, but they couldn't abide waiting. Many of them were threatening to go home, and Osceola had staged the drill to distract and amuse them. Besides, this walking in step, in lines, must be powerful war magic, even if it wasn't helping the blue-jackets very much right now.

"Get down!" General Gaines roared. He neglected to follow his own orders. A single shot hit him in the mouth, and he spit out two teeth.

By the eighth day the soldiers had eaten the last of the horses, except for Gaines's gaunt gray. There was no wood for cooking the meat. The last wood detail had returned with two men dead and several wounded. No more went out.

When Sam crawled back from the latrine hole, O'Reilly had killed the puppy and was skinning him. Sam cried as he ate his half, raw. He had just finished when word of the truce rippled along the line of men at the barricade.

Carrying a white flag, Jumper, Alligator, and Osceola walked to the breastwork. General Gaines's envoy was saying he had no authority to promise them anything when they heard distant gunfire. General Clinch had finally arrived with reinforcements. Unaware of the truce, he opened fire on the Seminole's rear guard. Within seconds the Seminole army disappeared into the underbrush.

The soldiers cheered. As General Clinch's men approached, the shaggy survivors leaned over the walls and begged for food. Clinch's men dug into their haversacks and shared their bacon and biscuits. Gaines's men ate until they vomited.

Major General Winfield "Fuss and Feathers" Scott, Major General Edmund Pendleton Gaines, and Brevet Brigadier General Duncan Lamont Clinch arrived at Fort Drane about the same time. They didn't arrive in the same manner, however; and they proved that three generals in the territory were two too many.

After being relieved at the barricade on the Withlacoochee, General Gaines insisted his exhausted troops precede Clinch's through Fort Drane's gates. Even though his men were bearded and starving and their smell made a few people recoil, they entered with fifes and drums playing and flags snapping in the March wind. Gaines sat his steel-dust stallion like a piece of monumental statuary. His craggy face was expressionless. His bristling shock of hair was as gray as granite.

While the soldiers dispersed wearily to find shelter and food where they could, Gaines set off in search of General Scott. General Clinch let him go. In the four days since he and his men had come to Gaines's rescue, he had had quite enough of the man. In his long military service, Clinch had never met anyone so contentious.

Clinch gave orders to distribute rations to the men in Gaines's command. He saw that barrels of biscuit and bacon were rolled out for his own troops. He noted how few barrels were left. He made sure the horses and mules were taken care of. He accompanied the sick to the hospital and found each one a bed, which was no mean feat.

He nodded wearily while Colonel Crane briefed him on problems that had arisen in his absence. Fort Drane was still overflowing with frightened settlers. That meant a gracious plenty of problems, as Lieutenant John Goode would say.

As for Goode himself, his arm was still in a sling. The wound he'd received in the first battle of the Withlacoochee two months earlier had become infected and was just healing.

"What do you suppose they all will eat?" John watched the soldiers, the horses, and the wagons milling about among the refugee tents and lean-tos.

"They'll eat old Fuss and Feathers' caviar, I expect." Jacob Motte pushed his clumsy velocipede through the crowd. He and the fort's blacksmith had contrived it out of wood and wagon parts.

Jacob and John sauntered outside for a closer look at Winfield Scott's baggage train. The wagons had been driven outside the fort to a grassy knoll shaded by massive oaks. The few refugees bold enough to camp out there were ordered to move.

A haggard mob of civilians surrounded the mud-crusted Dearborns. Sentries looked askance at them, as though they expected them to try to set up housekeeping in the big wagons. The settlers would have if they could. The Dearborns' deep wagon boxes and osnaburg covers stretched over hooped ribs were luxurious compared with the refugees' accommodations.

While soldiers unloaded the wagons, the civilians jostled for a better view. Fathers put their children on their shoulders, and mothers lifted the little ones so they could see. They stared as though they expected to see ostriches and zebras prance down the loading ramp.

Their amazement wasn't all that farfetched. Three blue-and-white-striped marquees rose on the hillside as though the children of Israel were setting up camp. Scalloped flaps with scarlet trim decorated the lower edges of the peaked roofs. Brass rods shaped like spears slanted outward to hold up the front awnings. Bright pennants clapped in the breeze. Soldiers unloaded massive, ornate furniture and iron trunks big enough to hold a zebra. They trundled crates of vintage wine and tinned food into the general's marquee.

General Scott's newly arrived musicians unbuttoned the collars of their scarlet tunics and pushed their tall black hats back on their heads. In the midst of the confusion, they began to tune up their trombones, trumpets, and one stubby tuba. The settler women wistfully studied the polished brass buttons and gold braid on the musician's gaudy uniforms. The desire to finger the tinsel was evident in their sad, faded eyes. They brushed nervously at their own patched dresses. They hunched their shoulders and cradled their arms across their chests as though to make themselves less conspicuous.

"When we were on bivouac," Jacob said around his pipe, "I saw a farmer bring his wife seven miles to hear the drum and see the men stand in a straight line. It was a phenomenon she was as unacquainted with as a sucking dove. Imagine what they will make of this."

"Ahem." The young captain clasped his hands behind his back and cleared his throat. "Is one of you Lieutenant John Goode?"

"I am, sir." John briskly touched the brim of his hat. He could always recognize another West Point graduate. Alligator had been right when he once said they walked like they had ramrods stuck up their arseholes. "This is Assistant Surgeon Jacob Rhett Motte."

"I'm Captain John Lane, Second Dragoons. Temporarily with General Gaines's command. I have a message for you." In spite of the ordeal at the Withlacoochee barricade, Lane looked neat and nonchalant. He acted as though danger, starvation, and death were inconveniences at most.

"A message for me, sir?"

"Yes. From the chief they call Osceola. He asked about you when we were discussing the terms of his surrender. He seemed distressed to hear you'd been wounded. He said he'd told his men not to harm you."

"Osceola offered to surrender?"

"Not exactly." When the captain grinned, two rows of orderly white teeth flashed, as though on parade in his handsome, sunburned face. He couldn't have been much older than twenty-five. His curly hair was as dark as Goode's was light.

"What Osceola actually said was he was sorry the white people forced him to fight. He said we had oppressed his people, and they couldn't bear it. He said they wouldn't leave their land. Frankly, he was dictating terms to us when General Clinch arrived." The captain shook his head. "You have to admire them, you know."

"Yes, you do." Lieutenant Goode's voice took a bitter edge. "This war is a damned rascally business."

"Florida is certainly the poorest country that ever two people quarreled for." Jacob spoke quickly, to cover his friend's impertinence. "Osceola has all the advantage of this damned terrain. I wouldn't give one swamp for forty forts."

"Osceola seemed distressed?" The second part of Lane's surprising news finally penetrated, and Goode was skeptical. "Forgive my boldness, sir, but I can't imagine Osceola showing anything like distress in front of pale-eyes . . . white people."

"It wasn't evident to the untrained eye," Lane said. "But I've commanded Creek troops. I've learned to read them. By the way, how does one acquire the protection of Chief Osceola himself?"

"One treats with him honestly," Jacob said.

"Considering the ordeal you've been through, this may be a ridiculous question." John Goode smiled sheepishly. "You wouldn't have brought cologne with you from the North, would you?"

"You're the fourth man to ask me that. And the other three hardly seemed fastidious."

"We've found only two remedies for chiggers. Cologne and whiskey." Jacob leaned his velocipede against an oak. "Not many men will squander their whiskey ration to inconvenience chiggers."

"And some of them would drink the cologne if they had it," John muttered.

The wagons were finally emptied and driven off in a great rattle and clatter. The crowd drifted away to watch the band rehearse under the oaks. A few boys gathered around Jacob's velocipede and studied it. He could tell they had the fever. No bit of metal or wire would be safe from them until they had built their own.

The volume of the conversation in Winfield Scott's circus-striped marquee rose considerably. The three officers sauntered closer to eavesdrop. They would have enjoyed the generals' feud more if so many lives weren't at stake, but it was still entertaining. Many of the general officers had been commissioned in the field. They suspected the academy graduates disparaged them behind their backs. Their suspicions were usually well founded.

"The enemy had been met, beaten, and forced to sue for peace, General Scott." If Gaines had any doubts about that preposterous claim, his voice didn't hint of it.

"Clinch says when he arrived you had not a shot in the lockers." Scott's voice boomed so loudly he startled the three eavesdroppers into moving back a step. General Scott was pacing. At six feet four inches, his head brushed the lower perimeter of the marquee's roof.

"You made not the first sortie to extricate yourself," he said. "One more day and Osceola's rabble would have overrun your position and murdered you in your own excrement."

"One more day! Indeed, sir!" roared Gaines. "Why did we wait eight days for reinforcement? General Clinch tells me *you* ordered him to abandon men under siege." Gaines's rage gathered a good head of steam. "And so close you were within sound of our cannons! Only when Clinch's good judgment persuaded him to disregard *your* orders did he come to our aid. We had the enemy concentrated in unprecedented numbers. Clinch could have destroyed the entire force if you hadn't interfered."

"Don't speak to me of interference. You have no business in Florida. This is my command. Now you've bungled everything."

The ensuing silence was like a flintlock hanging fire.

"Damn you!" Gaines finally shouted. "Damn you to eternal perdition!"

General Scott's band was playing a sprightly rendition of "Gary Owen" as Gaines whirled and stomped from the tent.

"In less than twelve days from the time I leave here," General Scott shouted after him, "I shall have the pleasure of disbanding Osceola's army and shipping off the hostiles!"

Osceola and Alligator returned together to the abandoned barricade. They leaned on the top log and surveyed the reeking morass inside. We came so close, Osceola thought.

"We should have killed Caesar," said Alligator. "We shouldn't have talked to the white men."

"The warriors were tired of waiting. More soldiers were coming. We were almost out of lead." Osceola sighed. How much longer would this war go on? "We had beaten them. I thought we could demand they leave us in peace." Actually, if Osceola hadn't stopped them, the warriors would have killed Mikanopee's slave, Caesar. Fighting in a Line had graciously offered to do it herself with her skinning knife.

Probably at Mikanopee's order, but without consulting the war leaders, Caesar had approached the breastworks. He had told the white men the Seminole wanted to talk peace. Then Clinch, unaware of the truce, had attacked.

The army Jumper and Alligator and Osceola had so carefully gathered and held together by sheer will had dissolved. Standing there, looking into the pit from which a thousand helpless enemies had escaped, Osceola determined to continue the struggle. He and his people would win. No matter how long it took.

CHAPTER 40

The white men think they can catch water in a net, Osceola thought. Scott's plan to attack the Seminole camps in the swamps was so ridiculous, Osceola wondered if the American *Tastanagee* were insane. He and Alligator had left their dugout camouflaged not far away. Now they were watching two thousand blue-jackets make dogged, arduous progress through the labyrinth of deadfalls, vines, briars, trees, bushes, cypress knees, and bogs. Most country had underbrush, but in Florida the underbrush was a hundred feet tall. In Florida the underbrush blocked the sun.

Osceola almost felt sorry for the soldiers. They were too exhausted to swear, and he had never seen white men too tired to swear. With their swords they hacked at the resilient green wall. Whenever one of them stopped flailing, the rangy, long-legged mosquitoes settled on him like a black mantle.

Osceola and Alligator lay comfortably in the thick nap of resurrection ferns on the broad oak limbs. No rain had fallen in weeks, and the ferns were brown and tightly curled. The men's lean brown bodies blended with them.

The shrinking ponds from which the soldiers drank were fouled. The water caused flux and fevers. Because their supplies had almost run out and Scott's carefully planned provisioning system had failed completely, the soldiers were hungry as well as thirsty.

The supply wagons now carried only the band's instruments. The sick crowded in around the trombones and trumpets and the tuba. They lay packed together like salt cod in a barrel. From the smell that wafted upward as the wagons were pushed and hauled under Osceola's tree, he figured he'd rather crawl if he were a sick blue-jacket.

This was the central section of General Scott's celebrated

three-wing spring offensive. His plan was to surround the camps hidden deep in the swamps around the Withlacoochee. He intended to surprise the Seminole, capture them, and ship them west. Scott's plan wasn't working.

The fourteen hundred men of the eastern wing traveled a total of seven miles the first two days, and Wild Cat's warriors harassed them the entire way. Several of their dray animals died of exhaustion before the column finally bogged down. They were much too late to rendezvous with Scott.

The western wing, under Colonel William Lindsay, was lost somewhere to the south. In an attempt to locate the other two groups, Lindsay was firing his six-pounder every so often. So much for the element of surprise.

Over half the one thousand two hundred and fifty men in the western wing were Alabama volunteers. They were their own worst enemy. They disliked taking orders from a regular army man. They became so enraged when Colonel Lindsay refused them whiskey that they docked his horse's mane and tail.

They complained bitterly about having to carry their own duffel. They shot at everything that moved and wounded one of their own men. They blamed the accident on the friendly Seminole guides and tied them up. When Lindsay ordered the guides' release, the Alabamans threatened his life. Lindsay took a detachment of marines with him whenever he went into their camp. Finally he gave up and marched to Fort Brooke without finding Scott at all.

Scott and Clinch's center wing wasn't doing much better. Because Seminole scouts watched the military road, Scott had struck out through the wilderness. His column had taken three days to travel the twenty-five miles of cypress swamps from Fort Drane to the Withlacoochee.

When he planned his supply routes, Scott had seriously underestimated the treachery of the terrain; but supply problems had started before he ever left Fort Drane. The Seminole had destroyed his steamboats on the Oklawaha. The boats had breached and now prevented others from getting past.

General Scott's exit from Fort Drane had been impressive. He had insisted on the full panoply of war—parades, a band concert, speeches, flags, and an artillery salute. Unfortunately the summer uniforms had gone down with the boats on the Oklawaha. At the end of March and the beginning of the hot season, most of the men in his command were wearing their heavy blue wool jackets and trousers.

They were still wearing them as Osceola watched them slog and hack through the sweltering jungle. The uniforms must have been cooking the men inside them. Usually soldiers contrived to lose the bothersome parts of their uniforms or render them unwearable. But not here. Not with these mosquitoes. Most had even attached the fur earflaps to their forage caps.

The men passed so close under Osceola, the stench of sweat and fear and mildewed wool washed over him. Like a mink's den, he thought. He glanced over at Alligator. Alligator pinched his nose shut and grimaced. Actually neither of them smelled very good, either. The fish oil on them wasn't fresh, but it did discourage the insects. The white men weren't in any condition to notice the odor.

A company of Clinch's old-timers passed. They wore summer tunics and trousers, although the white linen was stained the color of molasses by the swamp water. Osceola inspected each man who passed under him until he saw Nakita approaching.

You are come, beloved friend. Osceola sent his silent greeting down like a fine, cool mist. *I wish I could join you at your fire tonight.* He studied John's face until the top of the forage cap passed under him and disappeared from sight.

At the end of the column the two six-mule teams heaved and complained. They dragged the cannon carriages onto the higher ground of the hardwood hammock. Behind them, teams of oxen hauled two enormous flatboats on trucks. Men flanked the boats and cannons, ready to push them when they bogged down, which they did every few feet. When they finally passed, Osceola and Alligator slid from their perches.

They kept the massive, furrowed trunks of the oaks between them and the soldiers as they ghosted through the snarl of uprooted trees, moss-covered logs, and tangled vines. They froze when two enlisted men carrying a third passed near them.

"We found him!" one of them shouted.

As soon as they passed, Osceola and Alligator moved on. They were soon swallowed up by the undergrowth. They found their dugout and poled silently away.

"Where did you find him?" Jacob Motte hunkered to check the man the two soldiers laid on the ground.

"Back a ways. Must have wandered off and got lost."

"Is he dead, Jacob?" asked John Goode.

"Dead as dust."

"Snakes? Hostiles?"

"Mosquitoes."

"Mosquitoes?" Captain Lane stared down at the body. "Did they drain his body of blood?"

"They suffocated him." Jacob closed the man's mouth. "The swarm grows so dense it flies into the victim's nose and mouth and interferes with respiration."

A detail of men buried the body as best they could. As fast as they dug, black water filled the hole. The rest set up camp.

Goode and Lane supervised their companies as they stacked arms. The stacking had to be done right so men could find their own weapons quickly in case of attack. The crack of snapping branches rang through the hammock like rifle reports as men gathered wood for their fires.

Drivers unpacked the mules. The dragoons unsaddled and picketed their horses on lines stretched between trees. Lane's hammer-headed, rawboned pony Neamathla didn't suffer that indignity. He trailed behind Lane as he went about his work. Neamathla was a veteran. What he lacked in size and looks he made up for in personality and stamina.

When Jacob finished his rounds of the sick, he came back to the fire Jack Lane had started. He and Lane mixed their ration of flour with a little muddy water in their big tin cups. They molded the mess around green palmetto ribs. As they held the sticks over the fire, they tried to sit in the smoke where there were fewer mosquitoes. When the doughboys were charred on the outside and gluey inside, he and Lane choked them down with rancid fried pork.

"Try these." Without thinking John Goode hunkered by the fire in a most unmilitary way. He had been off foraging and was still thinking like a Seminole. His leather hat was full of turtle eggs. The decapitated end of a diamond back rattle-

snake dangled over his shoulder. It reached his belt in front
and back.

"Damn it, man, you must stop sneaking around like a
painted savage," said Jacob. "One day I shall blow your head
off by mistake."

"No need your acting the part of Patience on a pedestal any
longer, Jacob. I brought you some edible food, unlike the
kind the army provides." Goode poured more murky water
into a tinned pot enameled with grease and soot. He set it in
the flames to boil the eggs.

"I will say," Jacob confided to Jack, "you couldn't find a
better commissary officer than John. As long as you aren't
squeamish. Did you bring swamp cabbage, John?"

"I did." With the tip of his knife John poked a hole in one
of the raw eggs. He untied the knot in a corner of his bandanna and shook a bit of moist salt from the fold into the
palm of his hand. He licked it, then sucked the raw contents
of the leathery egg casing while Jack Lane looked on, appalled.

While they waited for the water to simmer, Jacob balanced
his tattered journal on his knee and made an entry with his
nub of a pencil. Jacob's journal had seen hard service. It was
beginning to resemble the old socks of which its paper was
made. John skinned the rattler, sectioned it, and threaded
each part onto palmetto ribs. As twilight approached, the
mosquitoes became even more insistent, and a few million
frogs tuned up.

"Damn this infernal country!"

It was the closest Goode or Motte had seen Jack Lane come
to passion.

"I would say it's already as damned as it can get," Jacob
said mildly.

They peeled the eggs and ate the firm, tasty yolks inside.
They impaled pieces of snake meat on the points of their
knives. After gingerly picking out the delicate bones, they
wolfed them down. When they'd eaten everything, John stood
and picked up his palmetto whisk.

"Come with me." He flicked at the mosquitoes as he sauntered off.

Jacob and Jack and Neamathla followed him away from

the noisy bivouac and along an alligator trail to the edge of the hammock. They stood where the opaque water of the Withlacoochee curved close.

"What are we looking for?" Jack Lane searched the treeline for signs of hostiles.

"A bit of postprandial entertainment." With his chin, John pointed upward to the thousands of water birds gliding by on their way to their rookeries. They swirled into the sunset, into fiery heaps of gold and pink and lavender. Golden light poured from the lower edge of a V-shaped opening in the clouds, as though escaping from a box.

"This happens every night, whether we're here to enjoy it or not," said John in a soft voice. "It happens whether we're killing each other or not. It happened before we arrived. It will go on happening after we're gone." And it keeps me sane, he thought. "Singer says when we view nature with the inner eye it will always treat us kindly."

"Singer?"

"Black Drink Singer. Osceola. Powell."

"I say, John." Jacob had a sudden suspicion. "You must know where Powell's camp is."

"No, I don't." John sensed his friend's disbelief. "Truly, I don't, Jacob."

At first John had been wounded by Osceola's lack of trust in not taking him to the camps in the swamp. Now he was relieved. If he had known where the camps were, he would have been duty-bound to report the information. Osceola understood duty. And he had known there would be war long before John did.

The night sounds had started when the men returned to the bivouac. A panther screeched. The calls of frogs and owls, whooping cranes and limpkins, combined with grunts and cries no one could ascribe to any earthly source.

The nights were the worst. The nights had been known to paralyze men with terror. An eldritch chorale of wolves wreaked havoc with morale that was already at an ebb. To cheer his men Scott ordered the band to play.

When they struck up, thousands of bull alligators answered, then cruised closer to investigate. Their hisses and roars and booming grunts almost drowned out the music. As a finale Osceola and Alligator's war party opened fire.

The musicians retired in disorder, using their instruments as shields, while their comrades shot at the tongue-shaped flares from the Seminole's rifle barrels. The skirmish lasted long enough to kill one soldier and mortally wound another. Jacob Motte was making the wounded man's last moments as comfortable as he could when he heard Oseola's final yodeling cry and Alligator's laughter, then silence.

In five minutes the frogs and birds and wolves took up where they had left off. The limpkins, so demure and unassuming in daylight, resumed screaming like damsels on the rack. Not many men settled down to sleep. They rested their rifles on their knees and stared into the noisy blackness.

"Everything happens at midnight in a well-ordered camp," muttered Jacob.

John Goode checked his scratchy blankets for lizards, snakes, scorpions, frogs, and spiders. He lay on his back and slid under the edge of his mosquito bar. The mosquitoes were so thick on it, they looked like black fur. Goode believed the old adage, "He is the best soldier who takes the best care of himself." He had painstakingly mended the gauze of his mosquito bar with blue wool yarn raveled from an old uniform.

"They won't be back," he said.

"How do you know?" Jack continued to scan the trees.

"Too many ghosts abroad at night. The Seminole prefer to be safe at home with their sweethearts." John's heart suddenly constricted with grief as the image of Third Sister's face flashed onto his closed eyelids. He heard her terrified scream in the cry of the limpkins. He knew he probably would dream of her again.

Osceola had said that to sleep was to hunt dreams. John sometimes wondered if in his own dream hunting he found Third Sister or her spirit found him.

"Do you think we'll find Osceola, John?" Jack asked.

"Not unless he wants us to." John Goode was soon breathing deeply.

General Scott began fording the Withlacoochee at four o'clock the next morning. Osceola, Alligator, Jumper, and their men waited until the blue-jackets, with their boots slung over their shoulders, were slogging through the muck at the shoreline. Then they screamed their cries and began picking them off. Thousands of startled birds exploded from the trees in a roar of flapping wings.

John Goode listened intently, trying to distinguish Osceola's distinctive call from the din. The war cries still raised gooseflesh on his skin and stirred the hair at the nape of his neck. He could almost sympathize with the men who were on the verge of panic. "Remember to aim low and to the right of the hostiles' discharge."

From his right, Goode heard the drawn-out howl of men in a bayonet charge. They might as well try to bayonet smoke, he thought. Then the gun crews finished unlimbering and aiming the cannons. The roar of them drowned out everything else.

When the noise of the scattershot died, Winfield Scott and his men heard laughter. The laughing and shouting diminished as the Seminole retreated into the depths of the cypress head. They left the blue-jackets to a far worse enemy, the very land they were fighting to take.

The land defeated General Scott handily. After a few skirmishes in the cypress swamps, he marched his sick, demoralized troops to Fort Brooke. When he returned north he was called before a court of inquiry. He blamed the terrain, the climate, transportation, and General Gaines for his failure. He was acquitted.

CHAPTER 41

Little Warrior crouched at the edge of the cypress pond and searched the water for Sharp Ears. Besides being ugly, the supernatural creatures caused sickness. Witches and Little

People and Sharp Ears were among the very few things Little Warrior feared.

When she was sure the area was safe, she lay on her stomach in the soft sand. With the palm of her hand she splashed the water. The small waves washed away most of the striders, the gator fleas, and mosquito larvae, the whirligigs, water beetles, duckweed, and algae.

She sipped the tea-colored water, then scooped some up to cool her arms. This was the end of June 1836. It was hot here, even among the cypress. If a turtle were to stand too long in the open, the sun would render its fat to oil in the shell.

Little Warrior picked up her frog gig, hitched her skirt higher under her belt, and resumed her cautious stalk. With the flowing motion of a hunter she moved along the edge of the limestone basin that contained the pond. *Take advantage of the shadows,* Osceola whispered in her thoughts.

Her passing set up undulations in the mats of duckweed floating along the shore. The duckweed also covered the pond's crooked fingers reaching back among the trees and cypress knees. A glistening water moccasin slithered by like an extension of the pond itself.

Little Warrior had skewered eight pair of bullfrog legs onto a whittled-down palmetto rib. Some of them were as big as chicken drumsticks. She had tied a palm fiber cord to each end of the rib and now wore it over her shoulder, next to her bow. Her snake arrow was stuck with the other shafts into the back of her belt, next to her palm whisk. Slowly she lifted each foot high out of the water to create as little disturbance as possible.

"Look!" Five-year-old Crying Bird held up a box turtle for inspection. The struggling turtle was as large as the child's head, and she was having trouble holding it.

"I'm busy, younger sister." Little Warrior had patience for most living creatures, but not much for her sister. "Kill it."

"You kill it."

"Watch me, then, so you can do it next time." Little Warrior pinched the top of the turtle's craning neck and sliced off the head. She and Crying Bird took turns drinking the warm blood that spurted out. With the heel of her hand Little Warrior wiped the blood off her sister's chin.

Little Warrior quartered the plastron with her knife and removed the entrails. The job was harder than usual because the turtle hadn't been scalded. Nor would it be. Blue-jacket soldiers might be nearby, and a fire would attract them.

Little Warrior put the entrails into a sack. She could use them to lure herons into range of her arrows or to fish for the whiskered cats hovering in the freshets.

"Did you find any arrowroots?" Little Warrior tied the corners of her bandana over the turtle's remains and added it to the bundles at her side.

Crying Bird half turned to show the small carrying basket on her back. Six or eight muck-smeared tubers lay in the bottom of it. The child's hands were black from digging.

"I found an alligator nest." Little Warrior braced the butt of her cypress gig into the dirt and leaned on it. "I'll distract the mother while you collect the eggs."

Crying Bird looked dubious. She didn't like the sound of the plan; but she followed Little Warrior through the green well of foliage around the pond. Little Warrior stationed Crying Bird behind the flaring buttress of a strangler fig. Then she circled to approach the alligator's hillock from the other side. She peered around the gray trunk of another fig that had enveloped a bay tree.

The alligator was basking in the sunlight filtering through the pale green cypress canopy and the swags of Spanish moss. She was half again as long as Little Warrior.

Little Warrior pressed her lips together tightly and sucked air, drawing her mouth inward. She made a series of abrupt, high-pitched squeaks, the distress call of a baby alligator. The female reared up on her short legs and hissed. She trundled down the side of her nest and, with a curious rocking gait, hustled toward the call. Little Warrior grabbed one of the fig's roots, dangling from an upper branch, braced her feet against the trunk, and pulled herself up, hand over hand. Hissing and grunting, the alligator ranged back and forth under her.

Little Warrior kept up the call while Crying Bird raced to

the mound and dug frantically. Her small hands sent sprays of decaying forest litter arcing out behind her. The child shrugged out of her carrying basket. She dumped out the roots, put some humus in the bottom, and set a twenty of the small round eggs in it. She covered the eggs with more nest material, then stuffed a few into her breechclout.

"Run!" Little Warrior called. "Take the eggs to Mother."

But for once Crying Bird disobeyed. She couldn't leave her sister stranded. She picked up handfuls of mud and began pelting the alligator with it.

"Don't tease her."

Crying Bird stubbornly kept chucking mud. The alligator lunged and the child feinted, barely ahead of the snapping jaws. She threw more mud into the alligator's eyes.

"Mother will scratch you." Little Warrior pushed off from the tree with her feet, swung out on a vine, and dropped behind the alligator. She picked up a thick stick and hit the back of the alligator's head so hard the club broke. The blow didn't stop the animal, but it got her attention. She whirled and hissed. Little Warrior found a longer stick and held it in front of her as a prod.

"I'll race you to camp," Little Warrior called. She knew the magic words. Her sister loved footraces.

Without looking back the child ran off as fast as she could. She ran with a clumsy, stiff-legged gait to keep from jostling the eggs out of her basket or crushing the ones in her breechclout. Little Warrior started after her, then changed her mind. She took a deep breath, circled around, and tagged the alligator's tail. Then she ran. She was grinning broadly as she trotted to her family's camp at the the far end of the pond.

The ground was higher there and sandy and clear. The air smelled of smoke from the grass fire that had burned for days out on the prairie. Its glow had illuminated the horizon at night. Its smoke stained the daytime sky. The fire ate down into the fifteen-foot-deep layer of peat and burned underneath the grass. At night dim light shone from the crevices. Little Warrior and her family had lain awake listening to the grass's air cells explode in the heat. The distant popping sounded like gunfire.

Old Squat was supposed to be keeping watch, but he had

fallen asleep sitting against a tree. His withered legs were sprawled in front of him. His head was thrown back, and his toothless mouth was open. He made little clicks and whiffles, like beetles in a rotten log. He wore the same old hunting shirt he had had on for months.

Mink and Morning Dew and Fighting in a Line, fully clothed, were submerged to the chest in the pond. They were picking yellowish, heart-shaped pond apples from the trees growing in the dark water and dropping them into shallow baskets. They had stirred up the spongy layer of leaves and muck on the pond's bottom, and wading was difficult. A dugout would have made the task easier, but the usual watercourses to this pond had dried up from lack of rain. The pond itself was spring fed.

Besides, the men had all the dugouts. The men had most of the guns and ammunition, too. Mink had three lead balls and a fistful of powder for her fusil. Fighting occupied so much of the warriors' time that they had little left for hunting. Few crops had been planted, and fewer had been harvested. Once again famine was a familiar visitor.

Scott's three-wing offensive had failed to surround the camps in the Cove of the Withlacoochee; but his less ambitious campaigns had scattered the Seminole and kept them on the run. Villages had dissolved into small bands, usually made up of sisters and their husbands and children. The bands were moving farther south, deeper into the swamps there.

Old Squat woke up as soon as Morning Dew started dividing the pond apples, the turtle, the frog legs, and the alligator eggs. He piled dried moss and twigs under pieces of kindling. Then he began to strike sparks from his flint and knife blade.

"We can't light a fire, Grandfather." Patiently Little Warrior scattered the wood and tinder. Putting out Old Squat's fires was her latest responsibility. "The blue-jackets will see the smoke."

With gnarled, shaky fingers, Old Squat began reassembling his fire. While he was occupied at it, Little Warrior sneaked his flint into her pouch.

Everyone ate the raw food quietly, to the steady swish of their palmetto whisks. The heat soon dried the women's soaked dresses. Mink's patched fusil lay across her knees, under her swollen belly. Her child was due in three months. Her usual grace had a languid, dreamy quality about it, as though her thoughts were centered on her womb.

"Do you know the way back, daughter?" asked Morning Dew.

Crying Bird studied the motionless water and the wall of vegetation surrounding it. When she shook her head, her fine black hair whipped into her face. Morning Dew tossed a crumpled eggshell toward the center of the pond. After a few moments' hesitation the shell began to drift, almost imperceptibly, downstream.

"Still water often has a current," Morning Dew said. "We came from that way." She pointed upstream, toward the east.

"Listen," said Mink.

From the east came the sound of shots.

Fighting in a Line began scattering the remains of the meal. When she finished no trace was left that a white man would recognize. Old Squat creaked to his feet and stood a moment, bewildered. Then he held his shirt hem out and remonstrated peevishly with it. Little Warrior threw a ragged blanket over his head and the torn half of another over her own. She grabbed his other hand and pulled him after her. Morning Dew tugged a dress over Crying Bird's head before giving her a piece of blanket. With the blankets hooding their faces and shielding their bodies from the sawgrass, they all followed Fighting in a Line down the narrow deer trail toward the prairie. Mink and her fusil brought up the rear.

No one mentioned the fire that had raged here. When the men were away Fighting in a Line was the family's leader. She was their healer and storyteller and oracle. If she decided on this route, this was the one they would take.

They left the cover of the trees cautiously. To the east they could see a dark smudge against the sky. The soldiers were burning Abihka's camp. To the west the grass fire had died out aboveground, leaving large patches of blackened, open country mingled with the tall stands of sawgrass. Belowground was another matter.

Fighting in a Line stayed in the cover of the grass even though it plucked constantly at the blankets and at their skin and clothes. As they walked across the spongy, fibrous mat of roots and debris at the base of the grass, they concentrated on the temperature under their bare feet. When it became too warm Fighting in a Line backtracked. She veered onto another trail rather than risk having the ground give way and dump them into a pit of fiery ash.

The grass stood high over their heads. Even if they hadn't been shrouded in blankets, they couldn't see beyond a body length in any direction. Once into it they had to trust the thread of a deer trail to lead them to safety.

"Crying Bird," Morning Dew whispered. "Crying Bird."

Everyone stopped.

"Is Crying Bird with you?" Morning Dew called softly to Fighting in a Line.

"No."

They all listened intently for the sound of a child moving through the grass. Even Old Squat stopped murmuring. They knew that even if she were lost, Crying Bird wouldn't call out to them. She had been taught that raising her voice was a signal to enemies.

"Crying Bird." Morning Dew called softly, but her voice was ragged with fear.

"Younger sister." Little Warrior clutched her blanket tightly and moved a little way off the path. "Younger sister."

"Each of you keep sight of the one in front of her," Fighting in a Line whispered.

Little Warrior crouched low to expose as little of herself as possible to the sharp edges of the grass and crept forward, straining to see beyond the nearest stems. She thought she heard a rustle that wasn't the wind.

"Elder sister . . ." It was Crying Bird's quiet voice.

Little Warrior saw a spot of pink, the faded, much patched red dress Nakita had given her and that now her sister wore. She caught Crying Bird just as the ground gave way in a billow of ash. She pulled her back from the edge of the glowing hole and hugged the child to her as Crying Bird sobbed against her chest. Little Warrior silently vowed never to tease or scold her sister again.

CHAPTER 42

John Goode sat in front of his tent. He had rolled the flaps up in the unlikely event a breeze should happen by. A patchwork of leno gauze hung like a tattered, muddy petticoat in the doorway. It only slowed the mosquitoes down. It didn't affect the chiggers or sand gnats at all.

John could have slept in one of the airless rooms labeled "officers' quarter." Most of them were vacant; but he preferred the tent. The rooms were alive with fleas. And a month ago Major Heilman had put his pistol in his mouth and blown the top of his head off in one of them. John had found the body, and frankly he now gave the dreary row of dilapidated quarters a wide berth.

To shade his shabby domicile he had built an arbor of palm thatch laid across a palm log frame. It wasn't regulation, but no one was left to object. All the able-bodied soldiers had left for the safety of Fort Brooke and the west coast. They had joined the exodus of whites from the central part of the territory. Lieutenant Goode had volunteered to stay behind with Jacob Motte and a hundred sick and wounded men.

No trees shaded John from the July sun. Wood details couldn't venture far from Fort Drane's palisades, even if the soldiers had been well enough to work, which they weren't. All the trees and underbrush had been cut within rifle range. If they hadn't, the hostiles would have climbed the trees and fired down into the palisades.

With the cover gone, attackers had nowhere to hide. However, the belief was growing among the more superstitious soldiers that the Seminole didn't need to hide. They were beginning to believe they had the power to make themselves invisible.

In the dim, predawn light John was trying to salvage his

last pair of shoes. He sat on an upended section of a log with his legs straddling the stump he was using as a workbench. His bare toes and heels stuck out of the holes in his dingy, cotton-knit socks. The blackened hems of his summer whites were frayed to narrow fringes. They had shrunk, revealing two inches of the golden down on his ankles.

The shoes were less than a year old, but they looked like ancient artifacts recently unearthed. The black leather was webbed with cracks from being wet and muddied and baked in the sun. The thong lacings were knotted in several places. John had put leather inside each one to plug the holes in the soles.

"Give it up, John," said Jack Lane. "You have only to make one more march in them, then you can grow a dashing mustache and ride with me."

Lane had arrived with the escort of dragoons and militia the night before and had bunked with John. He had brought the approval of John's request for a transfer to the Second Dragoons. Today he and the others would load the sick into wagons and abandon Fort Drane to summer and the Seminole.

"A soldier's boots are his best friends." John shook his low-topped bootees for emphasis. The loose soles flapped in agreement.

"If those are your best friends, I'd rather not meet your enemies." Jack leaned against one of the arbor's corner posts and crossed his own natty boots. They were made from the stomach sections of matched alligator hides. The smallest scales from the alligators' chins were placed at the toes and grew larger toward the tops.

With a thumbnail Jack idly turned the pivot screw in his carbine. He removed the lock mechanism and aimed it south, toward the Withlacoochee. The lock made an effective pistol, which Jack was in the habit of concealing under his coat when he visited taverns off post. The practice was strictly against army regulations, but Jack had been known as a brawler before he'd come to Florida.

"Anyway," Jack said, "a man's weapon is his best friend."

"Easy for you to say." John used the butt of his pistol to hammer pegs into the edge of the sole. "You're mounted. If you had to walk even an hour in midday on that damnable, broiling sand, you'd sing a different tune."

"At the rate the horses are wearing out we'll all be walking soon enough. Have you seen what that hell-fired sawgrass does to their legs?"

"I've seen what it does to *my* legs."

"We had barely enough tackies to make the trip here."

"Mounted or afoot, we're glad to see you, Jack. The hostiles have attacked almost every day. Everyone who isn't unconscious or raving has manned the pickets."

"This should cheer you." Jack reached into his valise and pulled out a rumpled roll. Like a magician performing his best trick, he shook it into a new pair of wrinkled cotton uniform trousers. They were pristine and blindingly white. So white, in fact, they made John a trifle nervous. They would flash like a signal flare in the jungle. Still, they were handsome.

"Thanks." John grinned like a boy at Christmas.

"I tried to get you shoes. Not a pair to be had for any price." Jack surveyed his friend's uniform. "Take off those loathsome trousers. I'm ashamed to be seen with you."

In his clean white trousers and short jacket, with his polished shoes and saber, Jack Lane looked out of place here. John regarded him strangely for a moment. He tried to imagine a garrison where everyone wore clean uniforms and ate as much as they wanted. He had a sudden longing for collard greens fried with onions. He tried to remember what life had been like when supplies could be more or less counted on and messenger duty wasn't almost certain death. When a man could walk into the woods for a day of hunting and not be hunted himself.

The bugle's assembly call roused him. The bugle had arrived with the dragoons. It would be as effective as the cannon for informing the hostiles of the army's whereabouts. The dragoons and militia began to line up for roll on the parade ground. John quickly changed trousers. He was embarrassed that his friend could see his drawers, crudely sewn from a mill sack.

"Let's go help Jacob." John said it reluctantly. The hospital was the last place he wanted to be.

The civilian refugees had left with the ambulatory portion of the garrison. Fort Drane looked abandoned. The two men walked through the encroaching weeds and vines and the discarded debris of the settlers' shanties.

"I suggest you cover your face." John folded his kerchief into a triangle and tied it over his nose and mouth.

The hospital was in General Clinch's sturdy log plantation house. The vines growing across the roof of its wide piazza made it look tranquil and homey. Jack almost gagged as he walked through the front door. The stench hit him in the face like the flat of a hand.

The two main rooms and the wide hall between them were full of half-naked men on low camp beds or piles of palmettos. Many of them were moaning or sobbing or raving with fever. A few sat propped against the wall, but most lay on their backs. Anyone well enough to walk had made walking out of the hospital the first order of business.

The tiny orderly, Bemrose, was shoveling out the blood-and-vomit-soaked Spanish moss covering the floor. The chiggers in the moss made the men's lives more miserable, but it was slightly more sanitary than the bare floor would have been. A small mountain of soiled clothes and linens loomed by the door. The thick air in the rooms vibrated with the steady buzz of flies.

The voice of war is not cannons or rifle reports or the screams of the dying, John thought. It's the drone of flies.

"Good God!" Lane murmured.

"The devil, more like it." Bemrose's broad cockney accent made everything he said sound droll.

Jacob Motte stood at his oak operating table under the front window. He wore a stable frock, a rough, knee-length coat that once had been white. Now it was splashed with dried blood and substances Jack didn't want to try to identify.

"Welcome to my little kingdom, Jack." Jacob raised his bloody saw in salute. His eyes were pools of fatigue sunken into dark hollows. He went back to the grim task of amputating the leg. The sound of metal scraping on bone made John's skin crawl.

"I'm taking it off at the gartering place, Sergeant O'Reilly."

"Just leave my jewels intact, Doc." O'Reilly reached over

and pinched out the guttering flame of the stubby candle on the windowsill.

The sawgrass cuts had become infected, and O'Reilly's leg had swollen to twice its normal size. The green-and-purple-and-black skin was puffy and soft. The smell from the striped, pus-filled wound was terrible. Jacob dropped the leg into the moss on the floor. He took up the spurting arteries and, with string from a feed bag, sewed the flap of skin over the wound.

"We'll be back for you shortly, O'Reilly. Drink up." Jacob handed the sergeant another flask of whiskey and watched him upend it and drink it dry. O'Reilly was singing when Jacob steered his friends toward the door. Jacob waited while Jack vomited over the piazza railing.

"Proud flesh," Jacob said. "He wouldn't have survived the trip to Fort Brooke. An old Florida hand, too. Been here since twenty-four. Imagine going to war and losing your leg to sedge."

Jacob stripped off the stable frock and laid it over the piazza's railing. He washed his hands and arms as best he could in the dirty basin. "Did you perchance bring laudanum, Jack?"

"None to be had at Tampa."

"Pity. It tranquilizes the fever patients during the bad spells, although I hear a surgeon in Saint Augustine has been having some success with sugar and lead." Jacob put his pipe, unlit, in his mouth. "And of course there's no Peruvian bark at Brooke."

"No."

The Dragoons serving as teamsters were chivvying their mule teams into line in front of the hospital. They seemed able to do it only with a lot of swearing. The bugle blew general, and the men began striking the tents and loading the supply wagons.

A militia lieutenant slouched onto the piazza. His oily blond hair stuck in spikes from under his wide hat. Flecks of dandruff salted the shoulders of his rusty black coat. "We're ready to load, Doc." He shifted his quid. His teeth were the color of thin molasses.

"Thank you, Lieutenant Elkins," Jacob said. He pointed at two men manhandling a patient through the door. "Have a care! Gently, goddamn you."

"Lieutenant Elkins," said Lane, "don't you acknowledge superior officers?"

"Naw." Elkins ambled off the porch muttering about upstart, foppish army officers who thought it a great favor to speak to a common man. As he walked away he expanded his criticism to include the set of sons of whores who had sent him here.

"I think Elkins and his kind enlisted under the banner of Bacchus, mistaking it for the banner of Mars." Jacob watched him go. "But we're glad enough to have them. We were beginning to think we'd been forgotten."

The Tennessee volunteers and the small company of dragoons finished loading the sick by seven-thirty. Already the sun was glaring down with the ferocity of a tar kiln. Jacob tied a square piece of board on top of the folded tents and other baggage.

"Watch this." With his elbow, John nudged Jack.

Motte tethered Hog and Hominy, his angular red rooster and his molting black hen, onto the board. "Patients have offered me ducks and turkeys, but I felt compelled to decline any further extension of my affections," Jacob said.

"Why don't you eat them?"

"They provide me much more entertainment than they would nourishment." Jacob looked a bit shocked at the suggestion.

He was right. As the wagon jolted into motions, the chickens slid and flapped and whirled on the board. Jacob clapped time and called a reel.

"Why are *they* still here?" John nodded toward the five children standing in a row at the perimeter of the weed-grown parade ground. The eldest was Nimrod, the boy Jacob had treated for hookworm.

"Their parents died of measles." Jacob looked distracted, as though the children's plight were his fault. "They've been following one of the officers around. They must have stayed behind with him."

"I imagine they'll be making their way to Newnansville now," said John.

"Newnansville's a pesthole," said Jacob. "Six hundred and

fifty people crowded into hovels. Fifty-two died of measles and diarrhea there last month."

They watched as the captain who had befriended the children knelt in the dust to talk to them. He searched his pockets but could find only a religious tract to give them. Then he stood and walked away. When he got out of sight behind a wagon he wiped his eyes with his sleeve.

The children watched silently as the wagons started up with a jangle of harnesses and a creak of axles. They didn't wave. One of their mongrels tilted his muzzle upward and made a sound that was more a moan than a howl.

"Master Nimrod!" Jacob waved.

"Orders said no civilians," Jack reminded Jacob.

"Come here, children." Jacob and John boosted them onto the top of the overloaded wagon. "If the hostiles fire on us, get under the canvas," he told them. The children nodded. The dogs trotted behind the wagon.

Jack Lane stood on a stump to mount Neamathla. "It makes him cocky." Jack patted the pony's neck. "He acts eighteen hands when I do it."

He rode Neamathla at a walk beside John and Jacob as they passed through General Clinch's fields. Neamathla and Jack settled into a silent struggle. Neamathla was determined to eat the corn, and Jack was determined not to allow it.

"Twelve thousand bushels, in the milk." Jacob waved an arm toward the hills covered with glossy green plants, higher than a man's head. The golden tassels hung limp and thick.

"We could use twelve thousand bushels of corn," said John.

"Do you want to wait another two weeks to harvest it?"

"Hellfire, I feel cooked to a crackling." Jack Lane wiped his face with his handkerchief. "Is it always this hot?"

"I suppose so," said John. "We usually take leave in the summer."

"General Call scotched that." Jacob was irate that President Jackson had given a militia general the command of all the forces in Florida and appointed him governor of the territory into the bargain. "Brilliant plan, a summer campaign. Our enemies will be insects and fever and heat prostration."

"Call's a Floridian. He must know what he's doing," said Jack.

"You've never met Richard Keith Call." Motte shook his head. "He's the most cross-grained, self-willed, greedy churl I've had the hard luck to meet."

This whole affair is based on treachery and greed, John Goode thought. Perhaps Richard Keith Call is just the man to conduct it.

"Still, I'll not be sorry to see the war end that much sooner." Jack became suddenly animated. He flashed what John had come to think of as his magic smile, diffidence and supreme confidence all in one. "The problem's the terrain, don't you see? The hostiles burn our bridges. We come to a swamp or a river, and we must put in like so many spaniels."

"You don't say!" Jacob and John laughed. Jack was off on one of his enthusiasms. He had many enthusiasms. India rubber bridges and selling Florida land to consumptive northerners were a couple of the crazier ones.

"We've made large bags of India rubber cloth and filled them with air from a bellows. We attach them sideways." Jack tried to demonstrate with two wooden canteens and his powder flask, but John and Jacob were laughing too hard to pay much attention. The relief of finally being on the move made them almost giddy.

The laughter stopped as they entered the palmetto and pine barren a mile from the fort. The column that left Fort Drane two weeks earlier had been ambushed there, and five soldiers had been killed. Osceola and two hundred warriors had lined the road and maintained fire for an hour before disappearing.

John wondered if Osceola was there now, watching him pass. His skin prickled with dread. Was Osceola looking at him along the barrel of his rifle? John remembered gentle evenings around the *sofkee* pot. He remembered the hidden glade with the ghost orchids. He remembered Third Sister.

Lately, in his dreams, he was usually charging into a village with his company of soldiers. Women and children were screaming. Over and over John dreamed he was aiming his carbine at Third Sister and pulling the trigger.

Hidden in the palmettos, Osceola and Alligator and a hundred men watched the column pass so close that Osceola could hear Nakita's conversation. Nineteen of Osceola's warriors were black. Most of the rest were Mikasukee. The young

Mikasukee were the hardest to restrain. Osceola's will alone kept them in check.

"Let the blue-jackets pass," he had told them as they slipped in with the morning mist among the palmettos. "They're beaten already. They're dead men walking. We need their corn more than we need their scalps. Our families can't eat scalps."

CHAPTER 43

In spite of Richard Call's ambitious plans, with the onset of summer attacks by the soldiers slowed. Most of the men of the Alabama, Tennessee, and Georgia militias went home. Their three-month enlistments were up, and nothing could persuade them to stay. This was, after all, the sickly season. The men of the regular army weren't sorry to see them pack their belligerence and go. Enmity between the regular army forces and the militia volunteers ran so deep it made cooperation almost impossible.

In May General Clinch had resigned his commission and returned to Alabama. None of Andrew Jackson's blandishments could persuade him to assume control of the forces in Florida. Especially not after the humiliation of having the command taken from him earlier and given to Winfield Scott.

General Eustis, who had led the eastern wing of Scott's spring offensive, respectfully declined the honor of taking charge. General Eustis was no fool. The situation was disastrous. Food, ammunition, clothing, and medicine were in short supply. The thousands of frightened settlers who clustered around the small, fortified outposts made the shortages more acute.

When the sickly season arrived, many of the company-grade officers found reasons to take extended leave. More than half the soldiers still in Florida were ill with dystentery, malaria, measles, blackwater fever, or a dozen other maladies. The able-bodied rarely even saw the Seminole, much less engaged them.

Now it seemed the sickly season would do what men couldn't. It was suspending the war for the summer months. Weary warriors and their families began to gather again in their camps in the Cove of the Withlacoochee. The dugouts nosed their way through the wet prairies to beach on the hammocks' higher ground. The women and children helped the men heave the canoes onto shore. Then they reunited with friends and relatives to mourn those who had died.

This war was changing their way of life as no other had. It had divided and scattered and isolated them in a land more formidable than the one their ancestors had known. It was forcing them to rely only on the family and clan members who shared their tiny camps. But now they were free to gather in large groups and visit. Once again they could light their fires.

The women told stories and gossiped while they pounded *koontee* roots into flour. The boys refought battles, ambushing the girls who went to the spring for water. The children laughed again. In the evenings, after the day's hunting, the men lounged on blankets and smoked and bragged. When darkness fell, Mad Dog's stories conjured up magical beings and animals from the smoke of the fires. After everyone retired for the night, people called their conversations softly from shelter to shelter.

After bathing at dawn, the women blew into the embers of their families' hearths and rekindled the flames. They continued the cycle of life and rebirth the flames represented. Fish dried on racks near the hearths. Cranes and egrets and herons turned on spits. Garfish baked in the coals. No one went to bed hungry.

Abihka's village was on a large pine hammock set in the heart of miles of palmetto prairie underwater most of the year. The monotony of the pines was broken by guava and orange trees, cabbage palms and bays. It was accessible by boat or by alligator trails. Each morning Abihka convened the older warriors and the Beloved Men. They sat in their clan groups on palm logs laid out under arbors at the center of the camp. They discussed problems and suggested solutions.

When the councils ended, Abihka and Swamp Singer and Mad Dog would linger, sipping from the bowl of *sofkee* Morning Dew sent with Crying Bird. The old men wondered what to do with the problems that were always left over when all the solutions had been proposed.

When the dugout arrived with Osceola lying unconscious on a pile of dirty mill sacks in the bottom of it, they were taking a break from their worries. Swamp Singer was entertaining them for the thousandth time with the story of the scatological origin of Old Squat's name. His voice shook so badly he took a while finishing a story. He suspended his narration in midsentence as Alligator poled the dugout into the mud of the landing. Alligator and Jumper and Aury's Black stepped out.

Black lifted Osceola and carried him through the camp and into the square.

"How goes it with him?" Abihka stared anxiously into the pain-wracked face of the man he loved as a nephew.

"It goes badly, *Alektcha*, Doctor," Alligator said. "His soul travels far from his body. He has very bad dreams."

Word that Talasee *Tastanagee Thloko* had arrived traveled quickly through the camp. A small crowd of people gathered to escort him. Holding her swollen belly, Mink ran into the square. She stopped abruptly when she saw Black.

"You are come, Father," she said.

"I am."

Morning Dew and Mink walked on either side of Black as he carried Osceola to the small *chikee* set aside for his family's use. A shiny new scar formed a narrow elipse on his chin. Mink saw more white in his hair than she remembered. A piece of his left ear was missing.

"You didn't find her." Mink spoke in a low voice as she walked.

"No, daughter, I didn't," Black said.

"I'm happy you returned."

"I came as soon as I could." He gave her an enigmatic smile. In time Mink would ask him where he had been for the past year. But she probably would never hear all of what had happened to him.

When Black laid Osceola gently onto the blankets, Little Warrior took his hand. She could feel the fever burning through his skin.

Osceola, Jumper, Alligator, and their men had been harrying the soldiers at Fort Drane. They had been attacking the supply wagons that rumbled along the military roads. Osceola hadn't seen his loved ones in almost a month. He didn't see them now. He had malaria.

Mad Dog collected his medicine bag, retrieved his *sabia* from its hiding place, and disappeared. People who went to the far end of the hammock heard him chanting his curing song among the palmettos.

For days Abihka worked to cure Osceola, too. He simmered an infusion of catfoot and everlasting. He blew through the medicine tube, bubbling his magic into the brew. He chanted through the night. Dawn found him in earnest conference with the spirits.

When Abihka saw the perspiration on Osceola's face, he knew the fever spirit had gone. He accepted the presents Morning Dew and Mink and Little Warrior gave him. A doctor's medicine always worked better when it was paid for. Abihka left, shuffling off toward his *chikee* and sleep. Abihka hoped he wouldn't be needed again, but he feared he would.

"How long?" Osceola asked that each time the fever retreated and the sweating began.

"Two days," Morning Dew said.

While Morning Dew bathed his face and body with cool water, Mink brought a ladleful of *sofkee*. Osceola was always ravenously hungry when the fever left. Mink held the ladle for him. His hands trembled too much to hold it himself. The sores on his lips made even drinking a torture.

"I feel like a leaf after the storm has passed." He tried to smile but shuddered instead. He rolled onto his side, retched, and vomited the *sofkee* over the side of the platform. He lay back, waiting for the waves of nausea to recede.

"Mad New Town took me to the Horseshoe," he panted.

"The same dream?"

"No." Osceola winced. The usual dream was a horrible one. In it he was being smothered in a mass of warm, slippery viscera. He tried to climb out, but he kept sliding back, unable to get a foothold.

"This time Uncle flew with me over the battlefield. It was wonderful."

Along with the fever's pain came vertigo. When it swept over Osceola it made him weightless. It reminded him of the dream's exhilaration, of the ground rushing by far below him, the wind blowing in his face. He closed his eyes to experience it again.

"What does it mean?" Mink helped him take another sip of *sofkee*.

"Our way of fighting is the right one." He spoke so softly they both had to lean closer to hear. "We mustn't try to fight in the open like the white men. That's what destroyed the Red Sticks at the Horseshoe."

Morning Dew and Mink supported him when he climbed down from the platform and staggered into the bushes to take care of his needs. The diarrhea was worse now, and the result was bloody. He returned from the short walk as though he'd made a forced march of a hundred miles.

The agony in his head was relentless and disorienting. When he returned to his blankets he felt as though he were floating on a lake of pain. The pulse in his temples rocked him to and fro in it. He could feel the pressure of each hair tugging at his scalp. *Pain is your friend,* he reminded himself. *It tells you you're alive when you might have been dead.*

Morning Dew and Mink took turns sitting with Osceola. They talked to him when he had strength to answer and sang softly to him when he didn't. For several hours in the afternoon Black sat silently in a far corner, as though waiting for something.

Though no one said much about it, they all felt his sudden appearance was an omen. Black would only say he had come to help Osceola in the struggle against the white men. But his dark, scarred, brooding face seemed to contain secret knowledge. As though he knew how the war would end.

As the day went by they all dared hope Osceola had come through the worst of the fever. Fighting in a Line reassured the people who passed in a continuous procession to ask after his welfare and deliver gifts of food. She had taken over most of the chores, cooking and mending and keeping an eagle's eye on Crying Bird.

Little Warrior sat for hours by her father's bed. She told him stories when he was awake. When his eyes were closed in restive sleep, she stared into his ravaged face. She searched for the lithe, golden-brown warrior who had always stood between his family and death. Where had his spirit and his laughter gone? Who was this gaunt, pallid stranger?

At sunset Osceola seemed to rally. He turned his head to watch the families gathering around their fires for the evening meal and talk. From the depths of his fatigue and pain he looked out at the world of healthy people as though he already had passed to the land of the spirits.

"The women look tired," he said. "The children are so thin. We have to get to the fort. The corn is ready for picking there."

"We're well, beloved," said Morning Dew. "We've beaten the white men. Jumper says they're leaving our country. Only a few are left. You've won."

"All white men are like my great-grandfather. They don't quit." Osceola tried to laugh and failed. "Sometimes I think my great-grandfather's blood is very strong in me." This was the first time Morning Dew had heard Osceola refer to his white blood. "He was a stubborn old white man. He lived more than a hundred years. I'm like him. I'm too stubborn to die."

In spite of his pain, Osceola smiled up at her. She took his hand and caressed the ugly scar that circled his wrist. Osceola began to shudder violently.

"No, beloved," Morning Dew said.

"So cold."

"No." Morning Dew heaped blankets on him, and still he shuddered until his teeth chattered. Blood gushed from his nose.

"The children. I'm killing the children." He raved and thrashed and sobbed.

"Hush, dearest." Morning Dew threw herself across him to keep him from rolling off the platform. "Daughter!" she shouted. Little Warrior jerked awake. She had been dozing sitting upright on one of the hearth logs.

"Run to Abihka. Tell him to come quickly!"

Mink wiped the sweat from her forehead with her arm and left a track in the dust on her face. The dust would be washed away soon, though. She glanced up at the darkening sky. Swollen clouds were piling up from their flat base into the usual towering anvil shape of a thunderhead.

The clouds darkened to a purplish black. Their spreading, shifting colors were beautiful and eerie. A crash followed a skittish streak of lightning. Thunder Man was firing his arrows at Thunder Snake. The air was so hot it burned Mink's nose when she breathed, but she could smell the rain.

She could barely see Morning Dew's skirt, faded from red to pale pink, moving down the row of corn next to hers. Morning Dew was humming to herself. The plants closed in over Mink's head, making her feel hidden and safe. They provided food and cover and shade. Their glossy leaves were cool to the touch.

Three hundred Seminole, mostly men, were harvesting corn in General Clinch's fields, but Mink couldn't see them through the thick foliage. Mink twisted each juicy ear, yanked it loose, and dropped it into the big basket at her feet. When it was full she arched her back and squeezed her shoulders together to ease the ache. She stroked the wonderful bulge of her womb. She had begun to fear she was barren.

She moved to the next basket, leaving the full one for the boys to drag away. When they had picked all the corn they could and shelled it, they would load it onto the packhorses. They would have almost enough to make it through the winter. After a week of work, they were almost finished. Abihka had already presided over the Green Corn ceremony.

Mink could hear Alligator and Osceola and Wild Cat talking and laughing softly. She picked faster to keep up with them. She wanted to hear Wild Cat's story, but she also listened intently for Osceola. He was still frail from the fever, and the exhaustion in his voice made her heart ache. He was so thin Mink could feel the bumpy ridge of his backbone when she held him at night. She knew he was driving himself relentlessly, ignoring the terrible pains in his head, the nausea and the dizziness.

Wild Cat had arrived from a successful raid two hundred and fifty miles down the east coast. He had returned to find most of the whites gone from the center of the peninsula. He had reason to be cheerful.

"We attacked a round brick house on the coast." Wild Cat was trying to describe the Cape Florida lighthouse. "It's taller than six, seven houses stacked on top of each other. The whites build a fire on top to signal to their big canoes."

Mink imagined Wild Cat telling his story while the others worked. Wild Cat disdained physical labor. That he would consent to pick corn was a measure of his people's need.

"Two men shot at us from the narrow ledge at the very top. They burned the steps inside to keep us from reaching them. We could hear the fire roaring inside the house. Flames came out of the windows. We watched the men hopping around on the iron ledge like chickens in hot sand."

Mink heard a rustle of leaves. Wild Cat must have been imitating the dance of the two men slowly being roasted alive.

"The next morning the men were dead, but we couldn't get their scalps. The stairs were all burned up. Singed hair smells bad anyway."

Punctually at two o'clock that afternoon the thunderstorm announced itself with a blast of chill air. Mink joined Morning Dew, and the two worked faster, throwing the corn into a heap on a blanket. They worked on, even after the cold drops began to splatter in their hair and on their shoulders.

Lightning blazed and thunder crashed. The corn bent under the driving rain before they gave up. Mink and Morning Dew each grabbed two corners of the blanket and carried it between them. The cool rain felt so good they laughed as the wind shoved them from behind. They had almost reached the storage shelters the men had built in the shadow of Fort Drane's palisades when the shower stopped as suddenly as it had begun.

"Sister, look!" Mink dropped her edge of the blanket. Corn spilled out in a lumpy green flood around her bare feet. She stared at the peculiar cavalry galloping toward them.

Some of Major Benjamin Pierce's infantrymen managed to

ride their clumsy draft horses and shoot, too. After the first volley they drew their sabers, cutting off parts of their mounts' ears in the process. To keep from falling off, most simply clung desperately to their horses' manes. Major Pierce had borrowed the horses from the baggage wagons and improvised the charge to catch the Seminole by surprise. It did that, although it was more a stampede than a charge.

It carried the soldiers straight into the gathered Seminole. Gunfire so close to the unschooled horses' ears panicked them. They reared and squealed and tried to keep their footing among the tumbling corn. Their riders fell off. Guns fired into the air. Mink screamed as the hoofs of a plunging horse barely missed her stomach and the unborn baby curled underneath it.

"Run for the hammock!" Osceola formed his warriors into a ragged line to cover the women's retreat. They fell back slowly toward the cover of the hardwood jungle.

In the confusion, Mink grabbed her fusil, her ammunition pouch, and her gourd powder flask in one hand and Morning Dew's arm with the other. Her legs were several inches longer than Morning Dew's, and she dragged her bodily into the undergrowth. Working around her bulging belly, Mink loaded and fired until her ammunition ran out. Along with the warriors she retreated steadily deeper into the tangled growth while canister shot rattled around her.

With one soldier dead and sixteen wounded, Major Pierce called his troops back. Even with the cannon to back him, he hadn't the men to risk following his shadowy prey into the choking maze of the hammock. He ordered the Seminole's shelters torn down and took most of the corn. Then he and his men left.

Mink and the others waited until nightfall. They crept back to the ruins of their camp and salvaged as much of the scattered, trampled corn as they could. Not much was left. They set fire to the buildings and palisades and abandoned Fort Drane, too.

CHAPTER 44

Neamathla poked his knobby head between the front flaps of John Goode's tent and whickered.

"I have nothing for you, old friend." John looked up from his cot.

Neamathla stood, mute and hopeful. His oversized head drooped until his slack lower lip almost dragged in the dust, but his eyes never left John's face.

"Shoo!" John snapped his greatcoat at the pony. Neamathla snorted and tossed his cropped mane. He waited several beats before he withdrew, just to let John know he wasn't intimidated. Out of habit John turned his greatcoat inside out, rolled it neatly, according to regulation, and stuffed it into his haversack. Even though the November wind was chill, the coat would be an impossible hindrance where he was going.

The Seminole had been leading Richard Call's army deeper into the watery expanse called Wahoo swamp. The guides said this was where Osceola, Alligator, and Jumper had chosen to make their stand. Call planned a frontal attack.

The buglers had blown reveille. Soon they would call general, and orderlies would begin striking the tent around John's head, but he delayed going outside. He could hear the horses neighing piteously. He dreaded seeing the corpses of those that had died during the night.

There was no grain for them, and they had been turned loose to forage for themselves. The starving animals wandered the bivouac area devouring shoes, hats, saddles, harnesses, and wagon covers. They ate the cowhide wrapped around their legs to protect them from the sawgrass. They gnawed the tent stakes. Anyone who left a coat out overnight found a heap of brass buttons in the morning.

Watching a thousand horses die slowly of infections and glanders and starvation was bad enough, but John was haunted by another specter. In his mind he entered Jack Lane's tent again. He saw Jack lying facedown on the dirt floor with his head strangely elevated. The graceful crimson curve of his saber blade projected from the back of his skull. Old Wristbreaker was imbedded to the hilt guard in Jack's right eye socket. The image of the misplaced sword persisted, clear and fixed.

"Brain fever caused him to commit suicide," Jacob Motte said. "Brain fever disorders the intellect."

John disagreed. Jack was twenty-six years old. He'd just been promoted to colonel. Everyone predicted a brilliant military career for him. Jack couldn't have committed suicide.

John insisted that Jack had been cleaning Old Wristbreaker, had fainted from the heat and fallen onto it. For John's own peace of mind he had to believe it was an accident. A man could guard against an accident, but fevers struck indiscriminately. A fever that compelled a man to run his sword through his eye was too terrible to contemplate.

An hour later John was part of the blue line that stretched a mile across the half-submerged prairie. The line faced a hammock of cabbage palms, willows, pines, and thick underbrush. A deep blue sky vaulted above the silver-bright sheet of water. Light from the rising sun stained the wispy clouds red. Red-and-white guidons snapped in a rising breeze. Sunlight glinted on the barrels and fixed bayonets.

When Osceola's eerie, solitary war cry came, John's flesh crawled. "Boys, that opens the ball," he shouted to his men. "Throw away everything except your pieces and ammunition." But the soldiers probably didn't hear him over the war cries and gunfire.

Shouting, the horseless Second Dragoons broke into a run across the savanna. The charge slowed as the water grew deeper. John's men lifted their rifles to their chests, then over their heads. Bubbles of sulfurous gas rose to the surface and broke, and they gagged at the odor. They tripped on submerged stumps and logs. Some went under and fouled their pieces.

"Snakes!" The private nearest John began to shake and scan

the muddy water around him. "I feel them between my legs. Hundreds of snakes. Must be a nest of them."

"It's grass. Keep going." John had seen it before. Men who could face any human enemy panicked at snakes. He grabbed the man by his baggy tunic and shook him until his teeth rattled. "Advance, man!"

Everyone was jittery already, and fear had a way of spreading. The young soldier pushed on, but he whimpered softly. Around them the wounded and slain splashed into the water.

John listened for Osceola's call, signaling each volley. He knew Osceola now as a disembodied voice. A high, ululating, feral howl. Osceola's was a cry soldiers sometimes tried to imitate when they'd had too much whiskey.

When the dragoons struggled out of the mud and onto the hammock, they found it deserted. John wasn't surprised. The generals talked of sweeping the swamp. They were *hadjo*. They were crazy. They might as well try to surround the wind.

As John trotted his company through the palmettos, he noted the notches hacked into the tree trunks at chest level. The Seminole had cut them to steady their weapons while they aimed. They had prepared for this battle. John stooped and picked up a broken strand of blue glass beads. Their women were with them.

On the other side of the hammock the sea of head-high sawgrass looked unbroken, but John knew it was interlaced with narrow trails made by deer and alligators along higher ground. He knew Osceola and his people were fleeing silently along those trails. Or they were poling their dugouts through the deeper channels that were invisible to a white man in the grass.

Osceola's people were probably converging on the distant hammock. Its tousled cabbage palms were clearly visible in the featureless landscape. The slender trunks leaned toward each other as though the palms were sharing a secret.

John wasn't surprised when General Call gave orders to start after the enemy. He cast along the shore until he found the thread of an alligator trail almost invisible in the grass. He motioned his men toward it.

All day they chased the Seminole and never saw them. All

day they slogged through a succession of cypress heads and saw palmetto thickets and sawgrass ponds dotted with rafts of alligators. At night they slept crowded together on a tiny palmetto island, after they'd crashed around to chase away rattlesnakes. They slept in several inches of water. They had nothing to eat. Call's elaborate plan to float supplies down the Withlacoochee and build depots at strategic points had failed.

The wiser enlisted men had begged, bribed, and cajoled to be assigned to Captain Goode's company. The legend was that he had Chief Osceola's protection, and maybe that protection would extend to his men. Even if it didn't, Goode knew how to survive in this country. He knew how to take care of his troops. Now even John's men grumbled and swore. John didn't blame them.

Richard Call finally gave up and turned his army around. The starving, exhausted soldiers had to retrace their route across the swamp. As he swung his carbine in front of him to fend off the serrated blades of the sawgrass, John pondered the rumors about Osceola.

The army's Seminole guides said he had malaria. They said he had had several bouts of it. They said he had almost died. They said he was weak and thin.

The army's guides were no friends of Osceola. Most of them had been followers of Trout Leader. John knew they had taken this job in hopes of being able to kill him themselves. Yet John heard the amusement in their voices when they solemnly repeated the stories. A weak, sick Indian was leading two thousand soldiers on a merry chase.

In his thoughts John tracked his friend through the endless miles of sawgrass and water. He tried to imagine Osceola moving through the maze of tawny grass that stretched from horizon to horizon. He wondered what Osceola was thinking. If he was really ill. If he ever thought of his friend Nakita.

Osceola had taught John to think like his quarry, to picture the animal he was hunting. Now John found it easier to visualize Osceola and his family as prey rather than as friends. He imagined Morning Dew holding the hem of her long skirt up with one hand as she waded. With the other arm she supported Crying Bird on her hip. He pictured Little Warrior stepping in her mother's footprints.

While the warriors fired on the blue-jacket soldiers, were Morning Dew's gentle fingers loading rifles? John remembered those fingers brushing the bangs from her daughter's eyes and feeling the child's forehead for a fever. He tried to remember Third Sister, but her face was indistinct now. He could only catch glimpses of her through the fog of time.

Osceola said a man's soul could leave his body and travel, in dreams and awake. John knew if his soul didn't leave his body, his heart certainly did. He knew where his heart went when it deserted him.

He hummed the song Jack had always sung as he urged Neamathla into a reluctant, bumpy canter.

> Then cheer, boys, cheer for the girls afar,
> We'll all go home at the close of the war;
> And, sadly tanned by the southern sun,
> We'll spin long yarns of the deeds we've done.

*   *   *

"Forward by the front!" Someone in the Mosquito Fleet was determined to make a proper naval show, or else he had quite a sense of humor. The sailors and marines were overboard. They were heaving the fleet's seven cypress dugouts and its flagship, a long, narrow-nosed sailboat, through the mud. Even in December they were drenched with sweat.

Jacob and John slogged out to help them. They sank to their knees in the muck. Their motives weren't purely selfless. The navy was bringing supplies. As John strained to inch the canoe forward, he pulled back the tarred canvas and studied the prickly muddle of rifles, axes, shovels, and ramrods, stowed with the boxes and barrels. "My God, didn't you leave anything behind?"

"Dry land, 'bout fourteen hours back." The sailor flashed a toothy smile. Even under the mud his ebony skin made his white teeth startling. "The lead coquetted with us all day."

The men stumbled wearily onto the hammock and collapsed. Most of the island was covered with palmettos too dense to tent in and too tough to clear, although their fronds did make fine shelter. The thin shade of the stunted pines in the middle of the island wasn't worth struggling through the palmettos and rattlesnakes to reach. The soldiers' tents and lean-tos and the horse pickets covered what little space was left.

Colonel Archibald Henderson left his beached flagship, the gaff-rigged sharpie, and swaggered through the mud. "Attention, you leathernecks!" he shouted.

His weary men formed a ragged line among their packs and stacked arms on the narrow beach. The infantrymen and mustachioed dragoons joined them. Colonel Henderson was now the ranking officer on the hammock.

His command was a variegated lot. Like the keys on a pianoforte, Jacob thought. The navy had recruited white sailors and black ones. The sailors wore once-white uniforms with dark blue scarves and natty straw hats. The marines wore short, dark blue jackets; blue trousers; flat, tarpaulin hats; and leather neck stocks. Except for the mud, they looked dressed for a Sunday concert in the park.

As Henderson lavished instructions on his men, John regretted that the hammock was so small. Colonel Henderson needed a lot more room than this to operate. John wasn't bothered at being under the command of a marine. Men from all three services had been working together for a year or more. Nor was he surprised to see the commander of the marine corps on this godforsaken carbuncle in the middle of a swamp.

The colonel had left a sign on the door of his office in Washington City:

> Gone to Florida.
> Will be back when the war is over.
>
> A. Henderson
> Col. Comdt.

He had gathered four hundred and sixty-two marines, more than half the entire force, and headed south.

While the Mosquito Fleet rested, John directed the unloading of the dugouts. The pork and beef and beans, the rice and molasses and vinegar and powdery bread, were certainly welcome. The whiskey was a godsend.

Muttering about being reduced to horse leechery, Jacob left the mounts whose torn legs he was doctoring and had the sailors line up in front of his tent. Their legs were badly cut. Their feet were covered with blisters and raw spots from being wet days on end.

"That grass is the devil's own invention." Henderson watched Jacob dress a cut that had become inflamed and ulcerated. "We'll burn the hellfired stuff tomorrow. Be damned easier to travel through, and the hostiles'll have no cover."

"I wouldn't recommend that, sir."

"I'm not asking for recommendations, son." Henderson thumped off to supervise the clearing of the palmettos. The marines hacked at them for hours, their sabers bouncing off the resilient, fibrous trunks.

Colonel Henderson could always find something for his men to do, even on this sandpit, but Jacob and John had learned to relax. They savored their turtle and egret stew and became besotted with the aroma of coffee beans browning in a skillet. With the butt of his pistol, John pounded the beans in a shot bag and boiled them in the tin mugs. He and Jacob added their whiskey ration to the coffee and sipped it as they watched the sunset.

"*Omnem crede diem tibi diluxisse supremum.*" John fell easily into their favorite pastime of capping verses. "Think to yourself that every day is your last."

Jacob pondered a moment before he came up with one beginning with the last letter of John's. "*Me pinguem et nitidum bene curata cute vises.* As for me, when you want a good laugh, you will find me." Jacob lifted his tin mug in toast to the mass of lavender-and-rose clouds against a mauve sky. "The colonel intends to burn the prairie tomorrow," he said.

"Does he know a fire might burn underground for weeks?"

"Apparently not." Jacob brooded a bit. "I once treated a man who fell into one of those subterranean fires," he said. "The ground collapsed, dropped him into a hellish pit of ash and embers. Hot as a forge."

"Did he live?"

"No."

"Sailor," John called softly, "shake your bedding."

"Sir?" The sailor paused with one foot under his blanket.

"I said shake your bedding."

When he did a scorpion and a small black snake hurried into the underbrush. The sailor rolled his blanket and walked to the canoes. The men already bedded down in the bilge made room for him. They had spent so many nights slumped over the thwarts, one more made little difference.

Quiet descended on the bivouac. The fires burned low, although the glow could be seen for miles across the immense black loneliness.

CHAPTER 45

Under the huge, moss-and-vine-draped oak in the center of the hammock, the morning shadows were as dark as twilight. A crescent of light lay like a necklace on Mink's slender brown throat as she crouched, motionless, behind one of the oak's buttressed roots. She stayed there long enough for the crescent to slide down her neck, into the dark hollow at its base.

Hunger and the difficult birth of her child had left Mink gaunt and exhausted. Dark circles, like bruises, framed her wide green eyes. She exerted all her will to keep her legs from trembling in their uncomfortable position. She shivered in the cold wind.

The curved twin ridges of Mink's collarbone pushed against the worn fabric of her blouse. Her skin had the dusty look of malnutrition. Her wiry black hair had lost its sheen. Like the legs of a spider curled in death, her thin fingers gripped a stout, forked pole. But appearances were deceiving. Mink was like a piece of lighter pine, weathered a dull gray outside but a bright, resinous golden inside, capable of intense heat and light.

The long gauze ruffle on her blouse reached almost to her

waist. It formed a cape that protected her shoulders and arms
from mosquitoes. She had pieced it together from a dead soldier's mosquito bar. The ruffle near the hem of her skirt had
"Sperry's New Process Patent Roller Flour" printed in faded
pink letters along it.

It had been part of a mill sack scavenged from an abandoned bivouac. Mink and Morning Dew had been gleaning
cracked corn spilled where the soldiers picketed their horses;
but they had found little besides the empty sack. The horses
were starving, too. They had gnawed the bark off the pine
trees as high as they could reach.

Mink's anxiety made her restless. Her tiny son had to be
nursed every two hours. He would be fretting now, and
Fighting in a Line had only the last of the thin *sofkee* to quiet
him. Mink worried too that her breasts were drying up. She
no longer felt the pressure of the milk in them. When it was
gone she would have nothing to feed him.

Just when she thought she could wait no longer, the raccoon lumbered into the tiny clearing. Mink drew in her breath
and held it. The raccoon rustled in the palmettos for a few
last withered berries before he disappeared into the opening
at the base of the strangler fig. He had had a good summer
and fall. The fat rolled and quivered under his fur as he
moved. Saliva flooded Mink's dry mouth. She imagined him
as a nourishing broth for her baby.

When she thought the raccoon had settled down for his
day's sleep, she stood slowly to ease the pain in her legs and
crept forward. She stood downwind and to one side of the
opening. She jabbed the forked pole into it. The raccoon
grunted when the pole pinned him against the back wall of
his burrow.

Mink pushed hard, twisting to wind his loose fur on the
fork. He growled and shrieked and fought, but Mink hung
on. She dragged him into the open, pinning him in the angle
where the tree met the ground. Killing him wouldn't be easy.
He weighed forty pounds, and he seemed to have more than
his fair share of teeth and claws.

She held him down with the weight of her body on the pole
and fumbled with the long knife at her waist. He bucked and
squirmed and almost escaped before she drove the knife point

into his eye, through his skull, and into the ground. He thrashed once, digging his claws into the dirt and turning on the axis of the knife. He shuddered, twitched, then lay still. Mink wiped the sweat off her forehead with the hem of her skirt. She lashed the raccoon's feet together, shouldered him, and started home.

She found Fighting in a Line crooning her endless chant. She had woven a palmetto shoot into a rounded box with pebbles in it. She kept time with the rattle as she swung the little one in his palm fiber sling. The panther fur lining his hammock was supposed to make him grow up strong and agile. Mink doubted it would have much effect, no matter how often Abihka chanted over it. The little one had arrived early. He was small and weak. Mink loved him helplessly.

"He doesn't like my acorn teat." Fighting in a Line grinned toothlessly and patted the flat front of her blouse.

"How's Uncle, Mother?" Mink laid the raccoon on the ground, and Fighting in a Line pinched it, testing its plumpness.

"A bad spirit has invaded Swamp Singer's bowels. His water is black. Abihka's working for him. My old man is working for him; but he won't see the dawn."

"Tell Mad Dog my heart grieves."

"I will, daughter." Fighting in a Line squeezed the baby's hand and tickled his taut, swollen belly. She heaved the raccoon onto her shoulder. "We've lit a fire in a cave," she said. "We're taking turns cooking."

The baby began to hiccup, then cry weakly. Mink took him from the hammock and held him to her bared breast, but the milk was almost gone. He hadn't the strength to suck what was left. She coaxed him and caressed him, astonished as always that this tiny creature had come from her. She sat in front of the thatched lean-to and sang to him in a voice as sweet and piercing as a psaltery.

> It will go to sleep,
> That is what we say.
> Your mother, the turtle,
> Went hunting.
> Sleep. Sleep.

"Is he sucking?" Osceola supported himself with a hand on the lean-to frame as he looked down at them.

"No. But Grandmother's making a broth. He'll eat that." She stood so Osceola could see his son more closely. "He's not crying so much. I think he's getting better." Mink almost believed it.

Osceola took the baby from her and rocked him in his arms.

"He's glad to see you," Mink said.

Osceola had just returned from a raid on a supply train commanded by his old opponent at whist, Colonel Ichabod Crane. The raid had been successful, but a disappointment. One of the wagons was full of horseshoes. The captured goods hadn't gone far when Osceola shared with everyone.

Holding the baby in one arm, Osceola drew Mink to him with the other. He held her tighter and longer than usual before letting her go. If malaria had sapped his strength, it had given him in return an intense relish for life and a recklessness with his affection. Every breath had always been important to him. Now it was precious beyond calculating.

Carrying the baby, he walked with her to the small, makeshift kitchen yard where no fire burned. He handed the baby to her.

"It's returning." He shivered and almost fell.

Mink hugged the child to her and watched him walk slowly toward the sleeping shelter.

That night Mink sat next to the cold fire, as though to draw warmth and comfort from the memory of its flames. She cradled her son in her arms. He lay inert and silent. He had drunk some of the raccoon broth and then spit it back up.

Mad Dog and his unlit pipe kept Mink company. He had pulled his frayed shawl over his thin gray hair and withdrawn into its folds until only the pinnacle of his nose showed. He snuffled behind the shawl's slouched opening like a bear trying to hibernate in a cave much too small for it.

This was the village of Abraham, Mikanopee's black adviser. Over a hundred blacks lived there, but they weren't much in evidence. No cheerful fires formed golden globes of light around the hearths. An icy wind drove a mass of sooty clouds across the moon.

The woman who approached the hearth was the color of the Withlacoochee where tannin stained it almost black. On one wide hip she balanced a bone-thin, owl-eyed child.

"This is for Talasee *Tastanagee*." She laid a shallow basket on one of the palm log spokes of the cold hearth. "He'll be hungry when the fever passes."

"Thank you, sister." Mink poured the contents into one of her own baskets and returned the woman's to her.

"Is he better?"

"Abihka is working for him."

"I pray he gets better." The woman shifted the child, clutched a feed sack shawl tighter around her bulky shoulders, and walked slowly into the cold January night.

A few handfuls of corn lay mixed with the sand and leaf mold in the bottom of Mink's basket. Mink knew the woman had gleaned it from the soldiers' campsites.

In December of 1836, when General Thomas Jesup took over command of the forces in Florida, he continued to send forays into the swamps. He sent out smaller units to find the hidden camps and destroy the food supplies. They were more effective than the large operations of Scott and Call.

Abraham's village was one of the few so well hidden it hadn't been attacked. Black and Osceola and his family had come here when they'd returned to their own camp and found it a charred ruin.

Mink left Mad Dog to his contemplations and walked warily past the small hut Little Warrior and Crying Bird shared with Fighting in a Line, Mad Dog, and Old Squat. She could hear the two girls whispering together as they usually did before they fell asleep. She could hear Old Squat coughing and Fighting in a Line snoring.

When she came to the second shelter she whispered, "How is he?"

"The fever spirit's attacking again." Morning Dew's soft voice seemed to float in the darkness, like a leaf on still black water. The chills set Osceola to shaking so badly that the palmettos of his bed rustled loudly.

"I'll sit with him," said Mink. "Sleep, sister."

An hour or two before dawn, with the baby still in her arms, Mink fell asleep herself, leaning against a corner post.

She dreamed of pale-eyes storming through the village streets. She dreamed of gunfire and shouting. At first she thought the screams were part of the dream. Then she realized hands were shaking her.

She was pulled back and forth between those insistent little hands and the fatigue that numbed her. She felt as though she were at the bottom of a flooded, underground cavern. She was trying to swim to the small disk of light and air far above her.

"Mother! Mother! They're here!" Little Warrior tugged at her again. From the other side of the village came the report of rifles, women's screams, and the wailing of babies.

Mink handed the sleeping infant to Little Warrior. Then she and Morning Dew struggled to get their shoulders under Osceola's arms and lift him. They walked with him through the dim light of dawn. Little Warrior carried the baby and herded Crying Bird in front of her. Mad Dog and Fighting in a Line limped after them as fast as their arthritis allowed.

"Uncle," Mink called to Old Squat, who was scolding the hem of the shirt he wore, waking and sleeping. "Uncle, hurry!"

Old Squat started across the trampled yard. He reminded Mink of a tortoise, deliberate and imperturable. When a bullet severed his spine, he fell over a low garden paling fence, vomited, and died.

"Come." With her free hand Mink shoved Little Warrior between the shoulder blades. The woods were full of the rustling and shouting of the blue-jackets. Black crossed the village square at a run. He put Osceola's arm around his neck and half dragged, half carried him. They ran toward the river and the labyrinth of cypress trees along its banks.

"I know where we can hide." Little Warrior waded through the shallows along the riverbank. She clambered over the exposed roots and fallen logs and held vines out of her sister's way.

"The abandoned den?" asked Osceola weakly.

"Yes." Neither Little Warrior nor anyone else spoke of the fact that the alligator den might have been reoccupied.

Little Warrior searched around in the forest litter on top of the bank until she found the den's airhole. She enlarged it with a stick and camouflaged it with brush. Then she climbed down the exposed roots of a willow and joined her family standing in the icy black water in front of the hole.

The entrance to the den was almost hidden by the stream and the overhanging brush. Osceola paused there, trying to control the ringing in his head, trying to focus his eyes and keep the darkness from washing over him again. The gorge rose into his mouth, and he choked it back. He picked up a sturdy stick and held it in front of him as he belly-crawled into the watery tunnel.

Little Warrior went next. Morning Dew followed with Crying Bird. Mink lay on her back and put her whimpering baby on her chest. She held him with one arm and cupped her other hand over his mouth and nose to keep the water out. She took a deep breath herself and wriggled her shoulders and hips through the mud. The tunnel sloped gradually upward until the water stood only a few inches deep in it.

Black waited for Fighting in a Line and Mad Dog. When they arrived he helped Fighting in a Line kneel down and creep into the opening. Her swollen joints pained her, and she moved slowly these days. When she was inside Black splashed away loudly, drawing attention from the den. As Mad Dog wriggled after Fighting in a Line's bare heels, he wondered if the pale-eyes would see his muddy legs and feet disappearing into the hole. He expected to feel the hard pinch of fingers around his ankles.

Osceola breathed shallowly as he crawled along the fifty-foot long passage. The alligator had dragged large prey into the den to rot until it was soft enough to tear apart and eat. The stench of decay filled his nose and mouth and lungs. The water at the entrance blocked most of the air. What little entered from the hole the alligator had dug to the surface didn't help much.

Points of light winked and swooped like fireflies around his head. He squeezed his eyes shut to clear them. Then he doggedly pulled himself through the slime. Under his hands he felt the bones of the alligator's meals scattered the length of the tunnel. He felt as though he were crawling into death, not away from it. He had waked from his hallucinatory dreams into something far worse. He fought back the feeling that he was being buried alive.

The tunnel led to a hole big enough to sit up in. The five adults and two older children sat bunched shoulder to shoulder, with knees touching in total darkness. They all listened to the muffled shouting and gunfire and footsteps approaching overhead.

A shudder passed through the baby. He stiffened briefly, then went limp. Mink laid a finger lightly on his neck, but she could feel no flutter there. She hugged the tiny body to her as though she could transfer her own life and breath to it. She took Osceola's hand and put the tips of his fingers on the infant's neck. When he realized the child was dead, he put an arm around Mink and drew her close. He could feel her silent, shuddering sobs.

She laid the body gently in the center of the den. She couldn't even grieve aloud for him to send him on his way. The worst horror was that the child's soul might not be able to find its way out. They were trapped with a corpse and a lost spirit hovering about them.

On the bank above the den, John Goode and his men looked for tracks. John may have been a novice at tracking by Seminole standards, but his men were awed by his ability. A prisoner captured in the village told them Osceola had barely escaped. He had pointed in this direction.

John volunteered for every raid he could. He feared some militiaman would kill Osceola and his family for scalps to display as souvenirs. He had known men to do it. And Osceola's hair would be an especially valuable prize.

He saw the small print of a bare foot in the mud. It was as familiar as Little Warrior's face. When Osceola was teaching Nakita to track, they had practiced on the family. Osceola had taught him how to tell not only what species of animal he was tracking, but which individual. This individual was unmistakably Little Warrior. John didn't have to look hard to discover the den's airhole.

"Have you found any sign, sir?"

"No." John put his boot squarely on the track and swiveled it, obliterating all trace of the slender footprint.

CHAPTER 46

One fine May morning in 1837, General Thomas Jesup sat enshrouded in sheeting tucked into the high collar of his tunic. As usual the black barber was having difficulty shaving him. The general's large, square jaw was a prominent target, but a moving one. He was talking to John Goode.

Jesup was sitting on a wooden chair on the piazza of the officers' quarters. The chair rested on a small platform of empty crates so the slave could stand comfortably while he worked. The piazza gave the general an elevated view of Fort Mellon's morning activity.

Besides the usual commotion, a construction detail was hammering on a shaded platform for the surrender of the Seminole leaders. General Jesup was in an understandably good mood.

"Get rid of them, Captain." Jesup pointed his lathered chin at two civilians approaching from the dust raised by the close-order drill on the parade ground. "It's too beautiful a day to besmirch myself with the likes of them."

John moved off to intercept them. After a brief, contentious exchange, they left.

"They represent planters in South Carolina, sir." John kept his anger in check. "They said recapturing slaves was an object of scarcely less moment than peace to the country. They said they'd be back."

"Oh, they'll surely be back!" Jesup's good mood soured. He turned in his chair to watch the men go. His barber did a fancy twist of the wrist to avoid slitting the general's throat with the paper-thin edge of his razor. Then he continued his skillful minuet around Jesup's agitation.

"We're overrun with that sort of scum," Jesup said. "Have you read the latest *Charleston Courier*, Captain Goode?"

"Yes, sir."

"You saw the letters from the good citizens there?"

"Yes, sir." The steam packet could now deliver mail from Washington City via Charleston in five days. While it was a great boon to men hungry for the written word, the news in the northern papers was disheartening to say the least.

"Men who are unwilling to trust their persons nearer the Seminole than Charleston are denouncing my measures. I can only say that I will not convert the army into slave catchers. Particularly not for those who're afraid to come after their property themselves." General Jesup sighed. "If I were permitted, I would allow the Seminole to remain here."

"That would be an honorable solution, sir."

Jesup had cajoled the Seminole into coming to Fort Mellon by promising them their black people would be guaranteed them. The newspapers in Saint Augustine and Tallahassee were vilifying him for it. Now slave hunters were threatening to shatter his fragile negotiations.

Thomas Jesup knew he had to end the war soon. Word of the terrible conditions in Florida had reached the North. Men were becoming increasingly difficult to recruit. A hundred army officers in Florida had resigned in the past year. Many more had quit rather than accept duty here in the first place. Northern newspapers were very critical of the government's motives in starting the war and the army's method of waging it.

"Knowing the country as I do now . . ." Jesup poked his finger from under the sheeting and shook it at Washington City. "If I have ever said aught to disparage others' operations in this damnable place, I consider myself duty-bound, as a man of honor, to retract it."

"If you'd put that in writing, sir . . ." John smiled to blunt the impertinence to a senior officer. "I'm sure there are general officers who'd be grateful."

"We know who they are, don't we?" Thomas Jesup winked. As one of his first acts in office, President Martin Van Buren had recalled General Richard Keith Call. In a rage, Call had left for Washington City. Now he was demanding a court of inquiry to clear himself of the charge that he'd bungled his command. The feud between Generals Winfield Scott and Edmund Gaines still simmered.

"The difficulties are so great that the best reputations may be lost without a fault." At least, Jesup thought, I will be spared that indignity. I shall be the one to end this wasteful, frustrating conflict. "But then I don't have to tell you that, do I, Captain? You've seen generals come and you've seen them go."

"Yes, sir." Mostly, I've seen them go.

"But that's all past now. Alligator, Mikanopee, and Jumper have turned themselves in at Fort Brooke. King Philip and his arrogant twig Wild Cat, and that pair of great rascals, Powell and Sam Jones, are coming in to surrender."

"Yes, sir." John knew that. He also knew the leaders were coming in mainly to redeem the women and children captured in Jesup's raids.

He should have been relieved Osceola had agreed to talk and that the killing would stop, but he wasn't. He would be terribly disappointed if it ended like this. If Osceola's proud spirit were broken by the treachery of the United States government. If he submitted meekly to being herded into the internment camp at Fort Brooke, where seven hundred of Mikanopee's people were now. John couldn't imagine Osceola walking voluntarily onto a boat and leaving his beloved country.

He doubted the armistice meant an end to the war. He doubted Osceola would surrender. But he hoped the leaders would be offered an honorable treaty allowing them to stay in the country for which they had fought so hard and so well.

"Sir." The messenger was so excited he almost forgot to touch his hat in salute. "They're here, sir. They brought their womenfolk and young'-uns. Hundreds of 'em."

The barber made one last swipe with his towel at General Jesup's cheek, then gave a leap backward. He was familiar with the general's style. Jesup tore the sheeting from his collar. He threw it with a broad sweep of his hand and bolted from his chair. The barber balanced his shaving mug, brush, and razor in one hand. He caught the sheet in the air with the other and wound it around his arm before it touched the piazza floor.

"Can't let them see me like this." Jesup rubbed his smooth cheeks. "I have to bedeck myself with military baubles and tinsel. The savages like a show. Stall them for me, Captain."

"Yes, sir."

John tried not to appear hurried as he strode back to the tent that had been his home, off and on, here and there, for four years. The rest of the garrison wasn't as self-possessed. John could sense the excitement, from the youngest drummer to the oldest sergeant. They would finally see the men who for many of them had never been more than a scream from the jungle or a waving plume in the palmettos. Or a flash of fire from a musket barrel.

John wet down and smoothed his unruly blond hair. He twisted the ends of his mustache and inspected himself in the scrap of mirror hanging from the tent's center pole. He rifled his valise until he found his last packet of tobacco. He turned around nervously several times, trying to think of something else to take Osceola as a present.

"Che'hahn tah-mo? How are you, brother?" Osceola smiled at John's alarm when he whirled around. He realized he'd forgotten the pale-eyes' strange habit of scratching at a tent flap, like a dog begging for admittance. He realized he'd forgotten many of the bewildering customs of white people. He breathed in the odor of hot, musty canvas and the memories it called up.

For a moment John couldn't force words past the tightening of his throat. He took Osceola's outstretched palm with one hand and his elbow with the other in the Seminole greeting. Osceola had always been lean and tightly muscled, but now, through his shirt, John could feel the bones under the muscle. Osceola gave John's forearm the customary hard, downward jerk.

They gripped each other's hands and arms a long time, as though if they broke contact, circumstances might separate them again. They struggled to recall the words they knew of each other's languages, although they didn't need many words. Sadness. Joy. Loss. Death. Regret. Regret was the hard one. John decided not to speak of regrets.

He found the small bottle of brandy squirreled away in his locker and poured some into two tin mugs. Osceola sipped his slowly. John sat in a canvas folding chair, but Osceola preferred a crate. A folding chair was too comfortable. A man could be lulled, then trapped in a folding chair.

Osceola was much like Jack Lane, John realized with a start. And not just because of the proud defiance in the eyes and the silky black curls that fell from under his bright turban. The main similarity was their smiles, open and guileless and enigmatic. Osceola's smile was brilliant sunlight illuminating the mouth of a deep, absolutely dark cave.

Osceola smiled, and the power of his personality flooded the tent. In his thin brown face his dark eyes seemed much larger than John remembered them. The fire in them was more intense than he remembered, and he remembered it as being very intense indeed. The thick black lashes were so long they brushed his cheeks when he closed them. The curves of his mouth were sensual. At first glance Osceola hardly looked like a fierce warrior. On closer inspection, he certainly did.

No matter how straitened the circumstances, Osceola always looked regal on occasions like these. John knew that for him to look otherwise would shame his people. Black-and-white plumes dangled from the rear of his ornate silk turban. A broad, beaded sash and three large, silver crescents glittered on his chest.

John had to look closely to notice the neat, unobtrusive patches and the frayed collar of his faded calico hunting shirt. He had to look closely to see that inside his finery Osceola was very thin and very tired.

"Your wives and daughters, are they well?"

"They're well." Osceola paused. No purpose would be served by telling him about the son who died.

To give himself time to think, John poured another brandy. There were so many questions he wanted to ask. So many questions he dared not ask. He remembered the Seminole's penchant for frankness. "You look terrible," he said.

"I had the fever. The fever's an enemy, but it's also a friend. Like yourself." Osceola smiled sadly at him. "I had wondrous dreams, Nakita. Terrifying dreams. The fever took me on long journeys. I'm still tired from them."

"Did the dreams bring you here?"

"No. I came to play cards with you." Then he answered the question seriously. "You've earned your warrior's name. I came here to give it to you. I also agreed to talk with Chesup *Tastanagee* because the children cry from hunger. The women wear rags. They need food. They need rest." Osceola finished his brandy and held the cup out for more. John was surprised. Osceola never had approved of drinking.

"We've proved we can defend our land. We want Chesup *Tastanagee* to mark leaves that say it's ours forever."

"If he won't?"

"We'll fight until the last drop of our blood has soaked into the thirsty sand." Osceola savored the brandy and the lightness it created in his head. He thought how like the fever its effects were. "I once saw a cormorant surface with a fish in its mouth. A pelican swooped low. He whapped the cormorant on the head with his big feet to make him drop the fish."

"Did the pelican get it?"

"No. Neither bird ate the fish. This war is like that. The pale-eyes won't let us have what is ours. Yet they themselves don't belong here. They sicken, they die trying to wrest it from us. In the end, maybe none of us will have it while we live. Maybe our bones will finally share it in peace."

"Brother, my bones are weary of fighting."

"So are mine." Even the young men are tired of it, Osceola thought; but he didn't say it. Nakita was a friend, but his loyalties were to his own leaders. "It's time for you to go home to Pen-sil-way-nee-ya, Nakita. Find a woman. Make feet for children's moccasins."

Osceola saw the grief in his friend's eyes. "Third Sister loved you," he said gently. "Her spirit wants you to be happy."

Osceola took John by the arm, and together they strolled along Fort Mellon's tall, spiked walls. The drilling and drum signals, the rituals here, were alien to Osceola, but they made sense, too. War and hunting and love demanded powerful magic. Magic couldn't be attained haphazardly. It demanded ritual.

Talk stilled as they passed. Enlisted men turned to stare. Officers Osceola had known before the war called out greetings, and he smiled and answered in Seminole. John had the

feeling he was with an immensely popular politician, states-
man, and general all packed into one lean, brown frame
dressed in flowered calico and feathers.

"Hear, you, get outta there!" The sergeant leaned over the
low fence by the stables and shouted into the kennels. "Move
on, you heathen urchins!"

Osceola and John looked over the fence. Little Warrior and
Crying Bird stood surrounded by a dozen bloodhounds. The
deep folds of skin around the hounds' heads and necks
drooped in front of their eyes. Their sagging lower lids re-
vealed red, wet linings. Their dewlaps dragged the ground.
The dogs looked ravaged and serene. When they shook their
heads at the flies, long ropes of saliva caught on their ears
and hung in loops. They were falling over each other to position themselves under the girls' caressing hands.

"I have an old friend with me," Osceola called into the pen.

"Nakita, I came looking for you!" Little Warrior slipped
through the gate and stood, suddenly shy, in front of John.

"You thought to find me in the company of dogs, did you?"
Good Lord, she's a woman, John thought. A beautiful
woman, he amended.

Little Warrior was thirteen. She was slender and small and
delicately curved. Hunger had narrowed her lovely face and
matured it. She resembled her father strikingly. John found
himself suddenly blushing and short of breath.

"Sorry, sir." The sergeant snapped to attention and briskly
touched his hat brim. "I didn't know who they were."

"You're to treat all our guests with respect, Sergeant."

"Yes, sir."

Osceola picked up six-year-old Crying Bird and bounced
her in his arms. She laughed, then stopped short. Laughter
had become alien to her in the past two years. Laughter was
loud and careless and dangerous.

Crying Bird was frightened to find herself among the pale
demons who had tormented her in dreams and awake, but
Little Warrior wasn't. She understood that men fought because they had to. When one side won the white banner of
peace replaced the red one of war. The combatants smoked
together and discussed terms. Her father had won the war.

He had come here under a white flag to accept the capitulation of the blue-jackets. She was jubilant.

"Nakita, will you tell the story of Dah-nih-el in the panthers' den?" When Little Warrior took him by the hand, she was a disturbing combination of child and coquette. "May younger sister ring the bell? May she swim in the washerwomen's tubs?"

"We can do all of that," John said.

Like Crying Bird, Little Warrior wore a few strands of beads around her neck. Morning Dew had drilled holes in three silver ten-cent pieces and sewn them to Little Warrior's blouse. Both girls' skirts and ruffled blouses had been skillfully patched together from torn strips of worn-out clothes and feed sacks. Mink and Morning Dew and Little Warrior had appliquéed the strips into bands of geometrical patterns. The brave attempt at gaiety was even more touching than the girls' pinched faces.

The hounds set up a rumbling, disconsolate moan when the girls left. One of them pointed his muzzle skyward and bayed as though his heart would break.

"That's Preacher," said Little Warrior. "Father, will you ask the blue-jacket *tastanagee thloko* to give me one of his dogs?"

"Why are the dogs here, Nakita?" asked Osceola. "Does Chesup hunt with them?"

"They're to track slaves." John saw the anger in Osceola's eyes, and he hastened to explain. "They aren't vicious like bear hounds, I swear to you. A fugitive is only in danger of being licked to death by those dogs. Jesup promises he will detain only runaway slaves, not those belonging to the Seminole. Jesup seems a man of his word."

"To white men all black people look alike." Osceola sighed. It was as he had feared. No treaty would come of this meeting. The white men would make no concessions. The war would continue.

Osceola had heard former slaves tell stories of running through the night, heading south for Florida and freedom, with the dogs' eerie, moaning howls rising and falling behind them. One night a man had imitated the baying, and the entire black village had fallen silent in dread. It didn't matter that the bloodhounds were gentle creatures. They represented the lengths to which white men would go to hold on to what they considered theirs.

Osceola was busy the rest of the day. As *tastanagee thloko* he was in charge of arranging the ball play that started almost immediately. Little Warrior accompanied Crying Bird while she rang the big signal bell. She watched her splash in the huge washtub. She listened to the story of Daniel in the lion's den. But she was very quiet.

That night her family and friends gathered around the fire at Morning Dew's campsite. When John left, Morning Dew began shaving Osceola's head with her new razor, and Little Warrior spoke of what troubled her.

"If the white people are leaving this country, why do they talk of hunting black people with the sad dogs?"

"They'll not leave our country of their own accord, daughter," Osceola said.

"We'll have to drive out all the ones we don't kill," Wild Cat added.

"I thought they would mark leaves that say the country's ours." Little Warrior couldn't believe it. She heard a ringing in her ears as rage flared inside her. It wasn't fair. She was ready to storm through the pale-eyes' town and kill Chesup *Tastanagee* herself.

"Nakita says they will not give us our country."

"The Americans are taking the Creeks' land in the north." Wild Cat was pleased the Americans' Creek friends were suffering as badly as the Seminole. "The Creek scouts told me today they can get us ammunition. They're very angry. While they work for the blue-jackets here, the Americans are rounding up their families. White men are burning their homes. They're raping their women. They're forcing them to go to the west country."

"The rattlesnake has turned on the turtle whose hole it shares." Osceola laughed bitterly at the irony of it.

"We're better off as the blue-jackets' enemies." Along with the other leaders, Wild Cat had listened solemnly to General Jesup's blandishments luring them here. The latest blue-jacket *tastanagee* must have been very stupid indeed. "We sell Chesup *Tastanagee* the cattle we've stolen from the white people. With the pieces of paper he gives us we buy food, clothing, tools." Wild Cat evidently had been using his certificates to buy silver earrings and armbands, ostrich plumes and satin ribbon red as an opossum's eyes in firelight.

"We're all like Heartless Snake," Osceola said.

Everyone laughed. Heartless Snake had let the blue-jackets capture him several times. He received food, learned the soldiers' strength, then escaped.

"Brother, I propose a foray," Osceola said.

"Where?" Wild Cat was always eager to raid.

"Mikanopee's camp at Tampa Bay."

Wild Cat grinned. "As soon as we've exhausted the blue-jackets' generosity here."

"The women say smallpox has broken out among Mikan-opee's people." Morning Dew had finished shaving Osceola's skull and now was plaiting the three braids of his scalplock. "They say people are dying. They say once the pale-eyes have gotten all the black people from them, they'll load Mikano-pee's people onto boats. They'll drown them at sea."

The rumors about taking the black people were well founded. At Fort Brooke soldiers were separating out the blacks who could speak English and putting them in pens. Some Seminole had children by their black wives. Families were being split up. White men who claimed to have lost slaves were free to inspect them. The army wasn't very strict about demanding proof of the claims, and claimants were swarming thick as mosquitoes.

Osceola admitted what he had known for a long time. The war would go on, and it would be disastrous for his people. But he also knew he would go on fighting. Surrender didn't occur to him.

CHAPTER 47

Osceola stared down at the snoring, lumpy mound that was the revered hereditary leader of the Seminole nation. He reached out and yanked the hem of Mikanopee's ill-fitting homespun trousers.

"Don't tear the pantaloons," Alligator whispered. "We can use them as a tent." Alligator thought this a wonderful lark.

Wild Cat held his rifle leveled at Jumper. Jumper's opaque eyes masked his thoughts, although murder and relief probably figured prominently in them. That one of his *own* people, much less a Mikasukee, would hold him at gunpoint was an unforgivable affront. On the other hand, Jumper didn't want to accompany his king west. It seemed now that he wouldn't.

Mikanopee stirred and snorted like a porpoise surfacing. He rolled on his back and stared at the tip of Osceola's knife blade, poised a finger's length from his nose.

"Make no noise, Beloved Father," Osceola murmured.

"We should slit your throat," hissed Abihka. "We should leave your bones rotting like Chalo Emathla's." Abihka had no patience with those who surrendered to the white men. But Abihka knew that in order to coax Mikanopee's followers from here he would have to let the Great King live.

"I promised to go west in the pale-eyes' big canoes." Mikanopee stared groggily at the blade glittering in the moonlight. "Don't make me go back on my word. Kill me instead."

Mikanopee almost meant it. He had been humiliated many times in his life. He knew he was about to be humiliated again.

Osceola helped him to his feet. The six men ducked under the low-hanging thatch and into the clearing in front of Mikanopee's hut. In the moon's faint light dark figures darted in and out of the lean-tos. The two hundred warriors who had come with Osceola and Abihka were waking the camp's inhabitants.

"We have them all, *Tastanagee*." Black blended so thoroughly into the night, his voice startled Osceola. He and John Horse had freed the black people locked in a small stockade nearby.

Soon the camp swarmed with Seminole and their blacks, all absolutely silent. They carried huge bundles on their backs. General Jesup had made sure everyone who volunteered for removal received new clothes and utensils. No one wanted to leave anything behind. They knew they were in for more times of deprivation.

Small children rode on their mothers' hips or clung to their skirts so as not to be separated in the darkness and confusion. Warriors carried the sick on their backs or in their arms. They rigged blanket litters for the seriously ill. A virulent form of measles was responsible for the rumors about smallpox. Many were sick.

A hundred yards away the sentry snored loudly at his post. He didn't stop snoring as the long column disappeared into the night. Osceola led the escapees in the direction of the swamps around the Withlacoochee. The most difficult part, aside from transporting so many sick through the swamps at night, was keeping Alligator from laughing out loud.

Several hours later, in the pink light of dawn, General Thomas Jesup stared in disbelief at the empty camp. Osceola and Sam Jones had lied to him. They never had intended to surrender or to take their people west.

Even while Jesup was coming to terms with the abduction of seven hundred people from under his nose, various alibis occurred to him in double-time succession. The Creek allies had done this in retaliation for the mistreatment of their families in Alabama. The captain in charge of the camp was incompetent. Vindictive underlings were trying to ruin him. The slavers had stampeded everyone. Cuban agents were fomenting trouble. British agents were fomenting trouble. Whig agents were fomenting trouble.

Jesup burned with rage. He saw his career in the shambles of the abandoned camp. He had been so sure this war was over that he had discharged the volunteers and militia. He'd sent the marines back north. Settlers were leaving the shelter of the forts and returning to their farms.

In spite of the ringing in his ears and the churning in his stomach, Jesup began wording his resignation to the secretary of war. He felt as though a band were tightening around his heart and lungs.

He realized his mistake was in being too lenient, too trusting, and too honorable. And he knew who was responsible for this humiliation. Because Osceola spoke for Abihka, he had become the symbol for the most intransigent of the Seminole resistance.

Jesup looked forlorn, standing there amidst the drab, empty lean-tos, the pigs rooting in the middens, and the debris that blew in the morning breeze. But he was conceiving a deep, abiding, personal hatred for his nemesis, the quarter-breed Powell. The treacherous devil they called Osceola.

The country can be rid of them only by exterminating them, he thought as he stalked back to his office. He began a letter to the new commander of Fort Mellon.

If you see Powell again, I wish you to tell him that I intend to send exploring parties into every part of the country during the summer, and that I shall take all Negroes who belong to the white people. I have bloodhounds to trail them, and I intend to hang every one who does not come in.

He would end this war, by God. One way or another, he would end it.

Mad Dog and Fighting in a Line should have been able to enjoy their old age. Mad Dog should have been spending his days in the council square gossiping with his cronies. Fighting in a Line should have had a flock of great-grandchildren around her. But as Fighting in a Line watched Mad Dog play with Crying Bird and her friends, youth, not age, occupied her mind. The children had been robbed of the most important part of their childhood. Laughter had been stolen from them.

The five who played with Crying Bird and Mad Dog were black, as were most of the people in this small camp. The children wore masks plaited of palmetto fronds, with faces drawn in charcoal. They leaped and whirled in a war dance around a cold hearth. In the old days, Fighting in a Line thought, they would have been shouting and whooping to the beat of a drum. Now the game was silent.

Wearing a grotesque mask with a long, hooked nose, Mad Dog hobbled into the clearing. The children kept dancing as he swooped down on Crying Bird. When he began to tickle her, she fell grimacing and writhing in the warm sand. She brought her knees to her chest and clamped her elbows to her sides to fend off his bony fingers; but aside from one or two squeaks, she made no sound. Mad Dog finally got Crying Bird's mask off, sending her out of the game. She sat on a log and watched him attack each child in turn.

When Mad Dog had unmasked the last child he sat next to Fighting in a Line. He was chuckling to himself, but he was wheezing and panting in the August heat. Fighting in a Line wet a bandana and knotted it around his neck to cool him. As she tied it she placed her fingers, as though by accident, against his chest. His heart was pounding erratically.

Mad Dog and Fighting in a Line looked more like brother and sister than husband and wife. As the years went by the planes and angles of their cheeks and jaws and noses sharpened. The bones of their skulls became more prominent, as though to remind them they carried death as well as life inside them.

Morning Dew had raveled thread from the hem of her skirt and was trying to mend a tear with it. Mink sat Crying Bird on her lap and used the tip of her knife blade to dig three large ticks from the child's shoulders.

"They drop on you from the bushes, child. Look out for them." She stroked Crying Bird's hair and put her arms around her.

"Here, Grandfather." Little Warrior finished dressing out the squirrel she had killed with a rock. She served Mad Dog the head on a small palm basket. The sweetest meat was along the jaw. Mad Dog cracked the skull with the heavy bone handle of his knife and shared the brains with Fighting

in a Line. Fighting in a Line refused to think about how much
better the brains would taste roasted.

"I saw the comical birds with the black stripes across their
eyes," Little Warrior said. "Six of them were sitting in a row.
They must have eaten fermented berries. They were having
trouble staying on the branch. When one tried to fly he
crashed into a tree."

"I saw a drunken bear once." Mad Dog's chuckle ended in
a savage fit of coughing. "He ate the mash from the pale-eyes'
still. He staggered, he grunted like a man."

"Grandmother, tell us the story of the first time Father
drank bitter water." Whenever Osceola left on the war trail
Little Warrior missed him so badly her heart ached with loneliness. She often begged her grandmother to tell stories about
him. Fighting in a Line had a way of bringing his spirit among
them.

"Wococoi Clark gave him the bitter water," Fighting in a
Line said. "Old Crane's Nest always had bitter water with
him. This was after the battle at the Horseshoe when we left
the old country to come to this one. We were traveling the
swept road to Pensacola to ask the *Espanee* for guns. My
brother planned to fight Old Mad Jackson's blue-jackets with
them. He planned to win back our country."

Fighting in a Line was quiet a few moments. She contem-
plated the fact that the past twenty-five years of her life had
been a struggle to keep from being driven from her home.

"Your father was almost as old as you are, granddaughter.
His uncle knew he was drunk. I knew he was drunk, but we
didn't say anything. Mistakes are the best teachers."

"How did he act?"

"Foolishly." Fighting in a Line remembered the look on
Cricket's face when he woke up. He had passed out in the
dilapidated warehouse that under the Spanish had also served
as Pensacola's Catholic church and billiard hall. After their
evening of billiards, Mad New Town and the men had gone
outside to smoke in the relative cool of the night.

When they left, Fighting in a Line had pulled a box up to
the billiard table so she could reach it. She played by the light
of several stubby candles set in a tipsy row on the wide ma-
hogany rim of Governor's Manrique's felt-covered table. She

was studying the next shot when Cricket's loud moan startled her. Holding his hand over his mouth, he had stumbled across the room and out the door.

Fighting in a Line wondered how to describe the magnificence of Pensacola to children who had never seen such splendor. But she didn't get a chance to try. Her story was interrupted by the long, mournful note of a distant cow horn. Someone on another hammock was signaling the approach of enemies. A bloodhound bayed faintly in chorus with the horn.

Soldiers, slavers, it didn't matter. Mothers scooped up their children on the run. Older children tried to round up their pigs or catch their chickens in a storm of squeals and feathers.

"Sit down, girls." Mink crouched in front of Crying Bird, who held her legs out straight. Mink smeared her soles with alligator grease.

Little Warrior rubbed the grease into her own feet, then turned to do the same for her grandmother.

"Don't bother, child." Fighting in a Line gently pushed her hand away.

"You must." Little Warrior wondered if her grandmother was getting forgetful, as Old Squat had been. "The dogs won't come after you if they smell the grease."

"We're not going." Mad Dog seemed unperturbed by the panic around him.

"Mother." Little Warrior ran after Morning Dew, who was throwing their few belongings into blankets and tying them into bundles. "Mother, they say they won't come."

"Come with us, beloved ancient ones," Morning Dew said quietly.

"No." Mad Dog put his arm around Fighting in a Line. It was an unprecedented public display of love. "We slow you down. We endanger everyone."

"The pale-eyes will take you prisoner." Little Warrior was horrified at the idea of someone in her family giving up. "They'll send you to the west country."

"They can't take our spirits prisoner. Our spirits will be gone." Fighting in a Line took her pipe from her mouth and looked at it. "Anyway, I've smoked the last of my tobacco. Life isn't worth living without tobacco."

"You must come!" Little Warrior looked from Mink to Morning Dew. "Make them come!" She began to cry.

Crying Bird crossed her arms in front of her, clutched the collar of her dress, and sobbed. The baying of the dogs grew louder.

"Remember the flock of birds we once saw in a hurricane on the coast?" Fighting in a Line asked.

"The ones that hovered in the calm center of the storm?"

"Yes." Fighting in a Line rubbed the misshapen knobs of her arthritic knees. Her feet were cut and swollen and raw from walking for days in water. "My old man and I are like those birds. The war storm can't hurt us." Fighting in a Line pushed Little Warrior gently but firmly away.

"Come, daughter." Mink beckoned with her fusil. A large bundle was already tied to her back.

Morning Dew knelt in front of Fighting in a Line. "I shall mourn for you, Grandmother," she said. "I shall mourn as if you were a member of my clan."

"My heart thanks you, granddaughter."

Then Morning Dew turned, and taking the sobbing Crying Bird and Little Warrior by the hands, she dragged them toward the trail. Mink and her musket brought up the rear. The danger usually came from the rear.

Mink didn't follow right away, though. She squatted and rocked back on her heels in front of Mad Dog and Fighting in a Line. Fighting in a Line and Mad Dog both held their knives in their laps.

"Do you want me to shoot you?" Mink asked softly.

"No, daughter," Mad Dog said. "You need the ammunition. The noise would bring the soldiers sooner."

"May you live in peace someday." Fighting in a Line laid a hand on Mink's wild hair. "Give my love to Black Drink Singer. Tell him I say the white men will never take his land from him while he lives."

"I'll tell him, Grandmother." Then, with tears blurring the path under her bare feet, Mink hurried after the others. When she reached the edge of the clearing, she turned and raised her musket in salute.

The line of refugees wrapped blankets around their heads

and shoulders and moved along a faint deer track in the tall sawgrass.

Little Warrior's feet sank into the muck. The mat of decayed vegetation shifted under her feet. The jagged limestone underneath cut her. Mosquitoes rose in clouds and settled on her. She held one arm in front of her face, and soon it was slashed with long, diagonal cuts.

"Look." Mink had come up behind her and now pointed her musket into the setting sun. A dugout with several people in it was drifting on the sluggish current of a meandering lead. Morning Dew moved faster, trying to catch up with it.

They chased it for an hour until it stopped, snagged in the grass. As they approached they saw it was a dead alligator with a row of buzzards roosting on its back. When the buzzards rose heavily, their wings made a crackling sound, like distant gunfire.

The sun had almost set when they dragged themselves onto the next hammock. Little Warrior turned to look across the flat landscape to the island they'd left. Thick black smoke hung like a storm cloud over the burning village.

Little Warrior knew her great-grandparents were dead. She looked for their spirits, circling in the smoke like the terns she had once seen in the eye of a hurricane.

CHAPTER 48

Has there ever been a conflict where the combatants were on such good terms with each other? Jacob Motte thought as he watched Wild Cat, John Horse, and Heartless Snake ride down the wide avenue of live oaks toward the soldiers' bivouac.

The oaks were the only standing, flourishing remnant of John Joachim von Bulow's once proud estate. John never reclaimed it. He had died in Paris three months before, at the age of twenty-six.

The sodden beards of Spanish moss hung from the trees like solidified portions of the rain that had fallen continuously for a week. The massive, crumbling tabby walls of the destroyed sugar factory loomed like a vertical reef behind the gray curtain of rain.

Wild Cat's big white flag flapped in the high wind. He didn't seem in the least worried that he was riding into the lion's mouth. But then Wild Cat was the type who, on finding himself in the lion's mouth, would tweak the beast's whiskers for the fun of it. When being pursued by soldiers he'd been known to stop and wait for them to catch up before laughing and outpacing them again.

Solemnly he greeted General Hernandez in the customary way. As Wild Cat touched Hernandez lightly on the head with a bedraggled egret feather, Jacob thought how well matched the two leaders were. Both were dark and handsome. Both had more than a touch of arrogance. Both had piercing black eyes. Wild Cat, however, was twenty-eight. Hernandez was close to fifty.

"My friend!" Wild Cat spied Jacob. He cantered to where Motte stood, soaked and aching and tired and irritable. "My beloved friend, have you more of that fine medicine?" When John Horse translated Wild Cat's request, it was a form of defiance. On Jesup's orders, English-speaking blacks were being detained as runaways.

"I wish to God I did." Jacob sighed. A gill of Wild Cat's favorite mulled port wine would have slid down very nicely right about then.

Jacob wondered how Wild Cat could look so cheerful after two years of this hellish conflict. How could he be so sanguine when his father and uncle and brothers were captives in Saint Augustine? John Goode said the Seminole spoke of war sickness, of a man being overtaken by an all-consuming passion for battle. Jacob figured Wild Cat had war sickness. But if he did, it was a disease that made a man look more alert and alive than those who didn't suffer from it.

Wild Cat was three days late for this meeting. For three savage nights Hernandez's detachment had camped here.

Their bivouac fires, hissing like a thousand snakes in the rain, had cast dancing shadows on the splendid, ghostly ruins of the plantation around them. The men were beginning to grumble that Wild Cat wasn't fool enough to come; but he was here now, and they could leave. In two days' march they'd at least have a dry bed.

The soldiers collected their haversacks and greatcoats, their canteens and their carbines stacked in pyramids under whatever shelter they could find or construct. They crawled into the leaky palmetto lean-tos that had been home for the past three days and rolled up their boggy blankets. Thunder still rolled and crashed overhead, and the gusts of rain hit with stinging explosions.

"Ride with us, *Alektcha*, Doctor," Wild Cat shouted over the storm's clamor. "Tell us how my father was captured."

Jacob chuckled. He swung into the saddle and fell in with Wild Cat, John Horse, and Heartless Snake. Behind them the column formed for the fifty-mile ride back to Saint Augustine. It was already five in the afternoon, but no one wanted to stay here another night. At least they didn't have to make this journey on foot. Jacob was grateful for the slick warmth of the horse under him.

"Our horses bogged to their bellies getting to your father's lair." Jacob figured he might as well entertain Wild Cat with the story. He seemed the sort to enjoy a joke, even at his own expense. "We charged at daybreak and caught everyone by surprise.

"We soon found ourselves in the presence of royalty. There stood King Philip, your father, naked as the day he was born. He was compelled to cut diverse, involuntary somersets when a lieutenant's horse bowled him over. He was covered with dirt, I'm sorry to report."

The trail Jacob had helped clear with his sword after the battle at Philip's camp was obstructed again, this time by trees felled by the storm. More trees crashed in the forest around them. The wind flapped the capes of their greatcoats and blew their horses' tails and manes straight forward. They had to tie their hats on. They couldn't see their own horses' heads in the darkness.

The column struggled on until midnight, when a raging

river finally stopped them. Wild Cat and John Horse climbed into the broad crotches of the live oaks. They poked and thrashed with the barrels of their rifles until they had cleared out the snakes. Then they pulled blankets over them, curled up, and slept.

Most of the soldiers crawled under the single baggage wagon, and Jacob slept in a heap with them. Heartless Snake, who had taken a liking to Jacob, spread his blanket next to him. He lay on his back, looking up at the mud-caked boards of the wagon axles and bed, and thrummed his fingers on his bare chest. For several hours he hummed a plaintive love charm which Jacob was surprised to find he rather liked.

Toward morning the river overflowed its banks. Routed by the flood rushing under the wagon, Jacob and Heartless Snake trudged to the nearest bonfire. The soldiers might have trouble lighting a lucifer in this rain, but they could always build an enormous conflagration of pine trees. Jacob thought of it as some particular soldier magic. He once had seen bivouac fires so bright that confused geese thought day had come and circled above them for hours.

He and heartless Snake joined one of the shivering groups of men huddled around the blaze. The heat was so fierce the rain evaporated with angry hisses when it hit. The men sang until the sun rose.

Wild Cat held the damp, scarlet silk hose up to his waist to check the length. The two legs ended in pointy feet and were joined at the crotch like trousers. A drawstring gathered them to fit at the waist.

Wild Cat tried to jam one of his muddy feet into a leg, but his callused heel caught in the gossamer material. The silk stretched while the empty bottom half of the stocking dangled limply. Wild Cat could neither force his foot farther in nor pull it out.

He hopped around trying to keep the hose out of the puddles. With a hand on John Horse's shoulder he finally extricated his foot from the silken meshes. Then he tried to wind the flimsy hose into a turban. He studied the result in his mirror and decided he didn't like it.

He wound his old shawl around his head instead and covered it with the hose. He knotted the feet and let them dangle nattily down his back. He fitted his broad silver band down over the whole imposing structure and stuck three plumes into it.

"Chesup *Tastanagee* might try to capture you, too." John Horse spoke as softly as he could. The soldiers's Creek spies might be listening.

"My father sent for me. I can't deny his request." Wild Cat held up a pair of short, purple, Elizabethan trunk hose. The legs were cut to gather just below the groin. They were padded with straw to make them stand out around the hips. "These look like toadstools," Wild Cat said. "How are they worn?"

John Horse looked at the breeches' elaborate slashings lined with green satin and shrugged. "They're torn," he said.

"Chesup sent Heartless Snake with white cloth for a peace flag." Wild Cat continued with the business at hand, dressing for his entry into Saint Augustine. "We ride under truce. No harm will come to us." Wild Cat reluctantly threw the padded purple-and-green breeches back into the trunk and began sorting through the crimson and purple and gold sashes.

The clothes were the unwitting gift of an unfortunate Shakespearean company, ambushed a week earlier. Wild Cat and his war party killed three actors and made off with eighteen trunks of costumes, gaudy beyond their wildest imaginings. Wild Cat's toilet usually took a couple of hours. This embarrassment of riches had taken much longer to put on. General Joseph Hernandez, Jacob Motte, and the rest of the military escort waited impatiently beyond the grove of oaks.

General Hernandez owned three huge plantations on the Matanzas River. He had been a luminary of Saint Augustine's social life and the planters' aristocracy for twenty-six years. He had posted handbills with details of King Philip's capture, and the past three weeks had seen a series of balls and parties in celebration.

Hernandez knew what a stir Wild Cat would make. He knew how excited the town's inhabitants were to see the infamous young war chief. So he was prepared to wait for as long as Wild Cat took to dress for the occasion.

"I don't trust Chesup," John Horse said. "He promised

black people their freedom if they turned themselves in. But slavers are claiming those who do. Chesup does nothing to protect them."

"Good. The black people will see how worthless Chesup's promises are. They're cowards to desert the cause. They're fools to surrender."

"Those who turn themselves in are country niggers, only recently escaped from the plantations. They're used to the pale-eyes taking care of them, like children. They can't stand the hardships of war." John Horse and Wild Cat both knew one of Wild Cat's father's own slaves had led the soldiers to his camp.

"I don't care if Chesup captures me." Wild Cat finished fastening his crimson stroud leggings to his breechclout belt. The leggings were decorated with beads and bells and tassels. He tied tasseled and beaded garters just below the knees and put on his best moccasins.

He pulled on a voluminous blue satin shirt from the Shakespearean company's trunk and belted it. He slipped silver armbands over his elbows. He dropped the various sashes and silver gorgets and necklaces of hammered coins over his head. "If the pale-eyes capture me, I'll escape," he said cheerfully. "No prison can hold me."

Wild Cat put on a green-and-yellow satin skirted doublet over the shirt. He tugged the shirt's commodious sleeves down to their full length. With John Horse's help he fastened some of the metal hooks and eyes running up the front of the doublet. The shirt's tail hung well below the vest, but the effect was striking nonetheless. Wild Cat's fierce, dark beauty made the clothes stunning.

He painted black circles around his eyes and took a last look in the mirror. He looked like royalty in masque as he rode out of the grove. Saint Augustine was a stage, and Wild Cat was about to make an entrance.

The old town's narrow, winding streets were walled in by the blank facades of the two-story houses. The second-story balconies almost met over the streets, forming tunnels. The shell-paved lanes were hardly wide enough for Wild Cat and John Horse to ride side by side.

Spectators lined the main thoroughfare. John Horse carried the white flag and stared ahead stoically. Wild Cat nodded and bowed and smiled up at the women leaning over the wrought-iron balcony railings. Some of them threw flowers.

Many of the massive houses fronting directly on the street were two hundred and fifty years old. Where the weathered plaster had fallen off, the slabs of pink shell rock showed. The wooden doors and shutters sagged. The paint was faded and chipped, but the houses were draped with climbing rose bushes and great hanks of fishnets.

If Wild Cat's father's well-being hadn't been inducement enough to come here for talks, the city itself was. When he was young Wild Cat had never tired of exploring Saint Augustine. He had wandered its quays and markets. He'd peeked into its bathhouses and billiard parlors, its shops and bawdy houses and taverns.

The parade moved across the open plaza, bordered by ancient orange trees. They rode past the rambling, dilapidated governor's palace and the quaint cathedral with its Moorish belfry. Wild Cat once had climbed up into the belfry and looked out over the town, the azure waters of the harbor, and Anastasia Island to the blue-green ocean beyond. Wild Cat had been born in Florida. Except for the trees he'd climbed, he'd never been that high nor seen that far. The experience had been more thrilling than any dream or drunk he'd had.

Slowly the procession approached the squat hulk of the Castillo de San Marcos, now called Fort Marion. For a century the fort had changed and grown as more walls and earthworks, living quarters and bastions, were added to the star-shaped outline. The fort had grown by accretion, like the coquina shell rock that made up its thirty-foot-high walls.

The horses's hooves clattered across the wooden drawbridge, through the sally port formed by the ten-foot-thick walls, and into the coolness of the fort. A hundred blue-coated soldiers stepped from the shadows. Their carbines were primed and cocked and their bayonets fixed.

They took the white flag away from John Horse. Then they

marched Wild Cat, John Horse, and Heartless Snake at bayonet point into a high-ceilinged, dank stone cell. The foot-thick slab of a door slammed behind them with a hollow, reverberating boom.

CHAPTER 49

Hundreds of candles and whale-oil lamps flickered in the ballroom of General Hernandez's town house. The dancing light and shadows were having a ball of their own while the cream of Saint Augustine society celebrated the engagement of Joseph Hernandez's daughter Louisa. Louisa was marrying George Washington, a surveyor like his famous relative.

Hernandez couldn't have been happier. He had made a fine match for his eldest, and he had captured Philip and Wild Cat, the scourges of the entire east coast. He hovered near the washtub-sized crystal bowl of fish house punch. He was getting pleasantly drunk in the company of King Philip's younger brother. Philip's brother was enchanted by the forest of bottles and decanters on the white linen tablecloth. He was sampling them all.

A group of Cherokee stood in a corner. At the government's request, they had traveled from North Carolina. They were here to treat with the Seminole, to convince them to come in for talks.

On a small dais, a slave from Hernandez's cotton plantation Mala Compra—"Bad Bargain"—coaxed exquisite music from his cracked violin. The fiddle keened a lament of great yearning and passion in three-quarter time. The fiddler's small, jet-dark son tapped and jiggled a tambourine in rhythm.

Straining their tight gowns, dour dueñas were wedged onto the straight-backed wooden chairs lining the plastered walls. Their chins rested on Promethean bosoms that seemed to be keeping their heads from sinking out of sight. Their feet bulged from their tiny satin slipper. Looking at them, Jacob Motte was reminded of the stepsisters in the fairy tale of Cinderella.

Most of the matrons were in mourning for some relative or another. Black taffeta dresses and black lace mantillas heightened their formidable appearance. Like cats watched caged finches, they kept vigil over the young unmarried women who skimmed past in a sensuous rustle of silks. From a position near the punch bowl, Jacob Motte and John Goode watched them, too.

Jacob was slightly tipsy. For the past two weeks he had been comfortably quartered at Saint Francis's barracks, an old nunnery with a view of the sapphire waters of Matanzas Bay. He was rested and relaxed, clean and dry and totally infatuated with the women of Saint Augustine.

He could hardly be blamed. A few fair-haired Americans graced the floor, but most of the women were of Spanish-Minorcan descent. Decked in bright, elegant ball gowns, their sultry beauty was bewitching. "Fair flowers on the breeze of music." Jacob held up his glass to them.

"Indeed." John Goode was preoccupied. He had just returned from a long scout through the swamps of Mosquito Inlet. He found he had been assigned as aide-de-camp to General Hernandez.

"Difficult to imagine being cold and muddy, drenched, starving, and exhausted, isn't it?" Jacob mused.

"Not so difficult." In the midst of the kaleidoscope of light and music and pure, delicate colors, the memory of war in the swamps disoriented John as much as General Hernandez's fine brandy.

"Don't get down in the mouth, John. Did you encounter hostiles this trip?"

"They dusted. We found their camp deserted." John was haunted by the pathetic conditions of that camp. The only shelters had been the remains of palmetto lean-tos destroyed by the hurricane that had just passed through.

The inhabitants had left so quickly they hadn't been able to take their belongings. John had found clothing in rags and dust and chaff in the food baskets. He had found a baby wrapped in an old skirt. The tiny corpse had been disfigured by measles.

"General Hernandez sent a messenger asking Osceola to come in for talks," John said. "Hernandez gave me his word he'd be treated honorably. And I gave my word."

"Your conscience has been made tender by repeated applications of Shorter catechism." Jacob refilled John's glass. "Even if Jesup were to capture Powell by less-than-honorable means . . ." He held up a hand to stave off John's objections. "At least the war would be over. Your friends, the Seminole, are suffering more than anyone. It would be a mercy to end their trials."

John said nothing. The northern newspapers were still shrilly condemning the war. Taking Wild Cat under a white flag had stirred them up again. John assumed General Jesup wouldn't make that mistake a second time. But he continued to brood as he watched the dancers. He hardly brightened when Wild Cat came to stand next to him.

Jacob may have been infatuated with the young women, but they were smitten with Wild Cat. They peered at him over their luckless partners's shoulders. With their eyes they followed his barbaric splendor as he strolled between Jacob and John. Between dances he walked along the receiving line. The sloe-eyed damsels peered from behind woven palmetto fans that fluttered nervously, like an anhinga's wings in mating season.

Lord Byron's poetry and style were still the rage with young women, even here in this last ditch of culture. No one was more Byronesque than Wild Cat.

"Are they married?" Wild Cat nodded at the only woman who was staring at her partner instead of him.

"Yes. Only recently," said John.

"She's very pretty now." Wild Cat appraised her as he would a brood mare or milch cow. "I guess her husband enjoys her very much. But after she's had a few children she won't be worth the bother."

John looked around to make sure no one overheard. For obvious reasons, John Horse hadn't been invited to this affair. Wild Cat was making use of John's Mikasukee and his own rudimentary English, most of it obscenities picked up from the soldiers. He was also drinking a lot; but unlike his uncle, he was concentrating on General Hernandez's best brandy. As the evening progressed he leaned more and more heavily on John's arm.

"I saw Osceola," he said. Wild Cat had been released to take a message to him. Wild Cat's father and uncle had been held as hostages to make sure he returned. "I told him to come in to enjoy all this." He waved his glass at the spectacle whirling around him and spilled brandy on his red silk shirt.

Jesup and Hernandez may have thought Wild Cat a prisoner, but he obviously didn't consider himself one. Prisoners weren't released to deliver messages. They weren't treated to brandy and women and parties like this.

There were two real disappointments. One was that General Hernandez had politely turned down Wild Cat's proposal of marriage to his daughter Louisa. He'd rejected the proposal even though Wild Cat had magnanimously offered to treat Louisa like a queen and make his other wives do all the work. The other was that Wild Cat missed his daughter.

"What did Talasee *Tastanagee* say?" John asked.

"He said his heart was white, peaceful. He said he'd come in to talk, to arrange a ball play."

"He must intend to collect more rations from us," Jacob murmured.

"Do you think he'll come?"

"Of course." Wild Cat looked at John as though he were deficient in intellect. "He said he would. Black Drink Singer always does what he says he'll do."

The bell in the cathedral tolled midnight. Wild Cat and John and Jacob joined the laughing crowd trailing the aroma of food toward the sagging table boards in the other room. Two men struggled against the current. One carried Wild Cat's uncle's feet, and the other grasped him under the arms. Wild Cat's uncle was unconscious, but smiling.

When everyone had found a place at the long table, General Hernandez tapped his saber blade on the side of a glass tureen. "A toast. Who'll propose a toast?"

"To Andrew Jackson!" someone said. It was an injudicious choice. The ladies hissed and booed.

Impatient with the way the war was being conducted, Jackson had lost his temper. He'd boasted that he would take fifty women and whip every Indian who crossed the Suwanee. He said the Indians should shoot the men of Florida so the women could find new husbands of courage. Now not only the Seminole hated Old Mad Jackson.

"To the great untaken and still unconquered . . ."

Everyone turned to look at the dashing young dragoon captain who held his glass high. "To Osceola!" he shouted.

"To Osceola!" they all chorused.

CHAPTER 50

Chills shuddered through Osceola as he pulled his blue-flowered calico shirt over his newly shaved head. Malaria was toying with him again. Just standing demanded great effort. Objects wavered in and out of focus.

He remembered looking through a glass window in General Clinch's plantation house long ago. The window had been Clinch's pride. The ripples and bubbles in the small panes had distorted the view outside. They caused the moon to change shape whenever Osceola shifted position slightly. When the wind blew the trees outside, the glass made them appear to dance, as though in a hurricane. Now the fever was playing the same tricks with his vision.

"A woman dreams while awake." Morning Dew's fingers shook as she tacked down a few loose beads on Osceola's good moccasins. She was more frightened now than she ever had been. "Ghosts, omens, whisper to us in voices even we can't hear distinctly."

"The bones predict evil." Mink shook the small leather bag at her waist. Her ivory divining dice clicked inside as though discussing Osceola's fate in the dark there.

Neither Mink nor Morning Dew had ever tried to dissuade Osceola from anything he was determined to do. Now, while he dressed, they worked in shifts at persuading him to avoid the meeting with Jesup and Hernandez. Little Warrior was silent as she collected his clothes and jewelry from the baskets and pouches in the rafters. She shook the shawls and leggings and laid them out neatly. She smoothed wrinkles from them with the flat of her hand. Then she checked his rifle to make sure it was clean. When she finished that she began polishing the barrel and oiling the stock.

Osceola leaned against the *chikee*'s corner post as his women's bare feet padded back and forth on the resilient palm logs of the sleeping platform. *Remember this. Remember them this way.* He thought of his wives as his sun and moon. Morning Dew, open and cheerful, brightened his days. Mink, on the other hand, was dark and mysterious. She suffused his nights with a subtle radiance.

As for Little Warrior, he could not even describe what she was to him. She was the female aspect of himself. She understood what he was thinking without his speaking. He and she shared a single soul.

Abihka's wife had vacated her storage *chikee* for them. The people of Abihka's camp had brought whatever they could spare to replace a little of what Osceola and his family had lost. Even so, Mink and Morning Dew were hard-pressed to find suitable clothes for him to wear. Morning Dew handed him his scarlet leggings and belt. While Osceola rested from the exertion of putting on the leggings, Mink knelt to tie his tasseled garters under his knees.

So thin, she thought.

Osceola had been either away or too ill or exhausted to make love often during the past six months, but Mink remembered how their loving had been. If they never made love again, the memories of those times were enough. Mink could endure not joining with him in the slow, silken slide into ecstasy, but she couldn't bear the thought of never again falling asleep in his arms.

Crying Bird sat with her legs crossed under her long skirt amid the clutter of baskets and bags and clothing. Solemnly she watched her father's preparations. Osceola crouched and stroked her soft hair.

"You look gloomy as a pelican," he said. "I'll bring you a

present from the pale-eyes' town. I'll hold council with the blue-jacket *Tastanagalgee*. Then they'll give us presents."

"This might be a trick," said Mink.

"Red Eagle sent his word that it isn't. He says he'll be at the talks." Osceola had given John Goode as war title the name of the most famous leader of the Red Sticks.

"Then why can't we go with you?" asked Crying Bird.

Osceola rocked back on his heels to consider the question. He had never misled his family about the dangers or losses they would face as a result of his decisions. They had never let him down. They had never complained. They had never faltered in their determination to defend their country.

"I have to be free to concentrate on the talks. I have to be free to threaten war if necessary. If you're there, the white men might take you hostage."

"That's why you mustn't go." Morning Dew struggled to keep her voice steady. Osceola had always been stubborn, but he had never been foolish. Was the fever affecting his mind again?

"Listen to me. While the fever attacks I can't lead men well." He held up a trembling hand to stave off their objections. "Abihka can make the medicine that gives young men courage, makes them invisible. But he's old. He needs a strong arm to swing the tomahawk, to aim the rifle, to wield the knife. I was that arm. Now Wild Cat is our hope."

Little Warrior found her father's small tobacco pouch and gave it to him. He tucked it into his turban's folds. Osceola's bag of sacred objects hung on his belt. He would need all his *sabia*'s power for this trip.

"Alligator can lead the war parties," said Mink.

"Alligator, Jumper, are fine war leaders, but they turned themselves in with Mikanopee when he agreed to sail west. Abihka doesn't completely trust them. Wild Cat has never bent in the storm. Besides, his mother is Maskokee. She's related to the Great Kings. His father is *tastanagee thloko* of the Mikasukee. He can command loyalty from both Fires." He waited for his own voice to stop echoing in his head. He waited for the points of light to stop dancing in front of his eyes.

"No harm will come to me. Red Eagle swears it," he repeated. "We're all weary of this war. It grieves me to see the women, the children, dying of hunger. To see them in rags. I'll convince the pale-eyes to end the fighting, to grant us the right to our land. I'll bring Wild Cat back with me."

They watched silently while he wrapped his rifle carefully in blanketing. Like Mink, Morning Dew thought it would be easier to face life with her beloved Black Drink Singer dead than for him to be imprisoned, alive yet unreachable. And the possibility of his being taken prisoner was real.

Heartless Snake had brought the latest cajolery from Chesup *Tastanagee*. When he'd finished with the official message, he had other news. He said Wild Cat was free to roam Saint Augustine during the day, but at night he slept behind the heavy oaken doors in the stone fort. When he described Fort Marion Heartless Snake had stretched his hands as far apart as they would go to show the thickness of its walls. "The blue-jackets are thick as lice there," he had said.

Now, when Osceola flashed Little Warrior his smile, she thought of what he once had said. The fever was an enemy and it was a friend. It haunted him like a restless, malefic spirit. It sapped the strength that always had seemed superhuman to Little Warrior; but it also kept him home, where she could spend time with him.

With her fingers Morning Dew combed out the soft bangs and long curls that hung from under his turban. Osceola put the straps of his bullet pouch and powder horn over his head. He slung his rifle across his back.

He took Little Warrior's elbow and hand in a man's grasp of greeting and farewell. "When I return tell me the signs, the magic, you've seen while I was gone. Tell me your dreams."

"I will, Father." She was apprehensive, but not frightened. If her father said he would return, then he would.

Osceola saw Abihka approaching with a long, rawhide cylinder. It contained a white egret's plume, the symbol of peace. Heartless Snake carried the bolt of white cloth Jesup had given him for a truce flag. Black followed close behind them.

Osceola knelt and hugged Crying Bird, who clung to him, sobbing. Gently he loosed her fingers from around his neck. When he stood the ringing started in his ears again, and he touched a corner post to steady himself.

Mink reached out, her eyes glistening with tears. Osceola slid his arm around her shoulder and drew her to him. With his other arm he held Morning Dew. The three of them stood for a long moment intertwined, their eyes closed. They savored the feel of their bodies pressed together and the comfort and strength the touch imparted.

"Remember what your mother always said," Osceola murmured into the wiry black cloud of Mink's hair. " 'The destiny the One Who Lives Above has assigned you cannot be avoided.' "

"She also said, 'If one could know where death lived, one would never stop there.' " Mink looked into his face. "Death lives in the pale-eyes' towns, beloved."

"I'll return to you soon. Red Eagle swears it." Osceola stepped carefully down onto the upended log that served as a stair. He took the rawhide case from Abihka. And he murmured to Black, too low for his family to hear, "Take care of them for me."

On October 21, 1837, a breeze snapped the huge flags of the white cotton sheeting General Jesup had sent to Osceola. Osceola stood under the billowing flags of truce. He was flanked by seventy-one warriors and ten other leaders.

The irony of the meeting wasn't lost on Osceola. This was Moultrie Creek, where they had signed the first of the white man's lying leaves fourteen years earlier. The Moultrie Creek treaty guaranteed them their land for twenty years. The place had had a holiday air then. There had been dancing and feasting and boatloads of tourists with parasols.

Osceola's eye strayed to the mossy oak not far away. He and his new bride, Morning Dew, had camped there. He remembered what it had been like, locked in passion's grip, obsessed with his beloved. He remembered making love all night under the oak's sheltering branches. He remembered Morning Dew's firm young breasts, lying curved along the swell of her rib cage.

He remembered her wearing boy's clothes and jesting like a man with him and Wild Cat and Alligator. He and she had thought themselves so old, so experienced, so wise. Their world had been such a wondrous place, full of promise.

Now six blacks stood in a small group near the vine-covered ruins of the treaty platform. They were recent runaways Abihka had sent with Osceola to use in bargaining with General Jesup. He planned to try to exchange them for Wild Cat, for his father, brothers, and uncles, and for John Horse.

The blacks weren't sorry to be stakes in this game. They weren't longtime allies of the Seminole. They had enough of this kind of freedom. They were tired of the terrible privations of the camps hidden in the swamps. A return to slavery seemed better than slow starvation or a quick hanging if the soldiers caught them with the hostiles.

Osceola stood, straight and calm. In the crook of his arm he cradled Abihka's large white egret's wing. His rifle lay on a deer hide on the ground, with another thrown over it. Most of the warriors had hidden their weapons.

The warriors watched General Hernandez approach along the trail from Saint Augustine. Osceola felt them tense when the first of the dragoons appeared behind him. There were a lot of horse soldiers. Too many. General Jesup had sent two hundred and fifty armed, mounted men. But he wasn't among them.

Osceola relaxed when he saw John Goode riding just behind and to the left of Hernandez. Hernandez dismounted, and Osceola walked toward him, the egret's wing outstretched. They gripped arms and shook them. Hernandez was astonished at how exhausted and thin Osceola was. *Díos mío,* he thought. This is the creature who's led us such a chase.

Osceola smiled sadly. From the corner of his eye he saw the dragoons moving into a circle. Over the snapping of the truce flags he heard the faint jingle of their tack. He realized he could never get to his rifle in time. This was a trap, and he could do nothing about it.

He tried to speak, but his speaking magic deserted him. Red Eagle had betrayed him. The treachery, the realization that all this misery had been for nothing, overcame him. He motioned for Mad Partridge to do the talking.

"Have you come to give yourselves up to me as your friend?" asked Hernandez.

John gave a start. This wasn't what he'd been told would

happen. He opened his mouth, then closed it. He tried to catch Osceola's eyes. But Osceola wouldn't look at him.

"No," Mad Partridge said. "We did not understand so. We came to make peace."

"Are you ready to give up all the property you've captured?"

"Yes. We've brought a good many Negroes with us."

"I'm an old friend of Philip's. I wish the Seminole well."

Osceola saw the barely perceptible tightening of the ring of dragoons. The white men gave their hand in friendship, Osceola thought, but they held a snake in the other one.

"We have been deceived by you so often." Hernandez went doggedly on with his unpleasant duty. He consoled himself with the thought that capturing Osceola would end the bloodshed and terror. Saint Augustine's easygoing life of parties and dinners would resume, like a music box that had been wound up again. Everyone, including the Seminole, would be better off.

"You must come with me. You'll be treated well. Don't I speak the truth, Heartless Snake?"

"I thought Osceola, Mad Partridge, would go free." Heartless Snake looked at the ground.

With a clatter the dragoons raised their carbines and covered Osceola and the others. A few soldiers dismounted and collected the Seminole's weapons. Osceola ignored the man who drew the knife from his sheath. John burned with mortification. He knew he would never reconcile himself to this dishonor.

"Johnson," Hernandez said. "Unload the pack mule. Powell will ride it." Osceola looked so ill and exhausted that Hernandez couldn't bear to make him walk the fifteen miles to prison.

"He may use my mount, sir." John spurred his horse forward, to stand alongside Hernandez.

"I can't have my aide reduced to walking with the prisoners, Captain. The mule will do for him."

"May I speak with Powell, sir?"

"Be brief."

John dismounted and handed the reins to an orderly. He stood in front of Osceola. "Beloved friend, look in my eyes.

Know that I thought I was telling you the truth when I said your freedom was guaranteed."

Osceola studied John's clear blue eyes for what seemed a very long time while the dragoons' horses pranced and fidgeted. Finally he took John's arm and shook it slowly and firmly.

"I believe you, brother."

CHAPTER 51

John Horse watched Osceola and Wild Cat play roll the bullet in sand that had accumulated in one corner of the weed-grown courtyard. Around them loomed the weathered gray tabby walls of Fort Marion. Osceola pulled his frayed shawl tighter around his shoulders. This was the twenty-ninth of November, and the wind was cold. It moaned and circled endlessly, as though hunting for a way out of the high cliffs of massive shell-rock blocks surrounding the courtyard.

Osceola could have gone into his dank stone cell set into the wall, but it was not much warmer there, and he didn't want to miss any of the sun's wan light. Besides, Wild Cat was using the game to cover the fact that he was talking about an escape.

As Wild Cat squatted to shoot his lead ball, he looked like a mantis trying to disguise itself as a twig. He wasn't just thin, he was emaciated. John Horse wasn't much bigger.

Before Osceola's capture Wild Cat had been more an honored guest at Fort Marion than a prisoner. Now that Osceola was here and the pale-eyes had so many influential leaders of the resistance in their grasp, they weren't about to risk losing them.

To his dismay, Wild Cat found himself locked with twenty others in a small cell every night. He was confined to the great stone keep during the day. Being caged gnawed at him from the inside. Osceola didn't have to work hard to convince him to escape.

Once he decided on an escape plan, he began starving himself. He told Fort Marion's young commander, Captain Webster, that he was sick. He received permission to hunt for healing herbs, under a heavy guard, of course. Instead he brought back spurge, a purgative that could kill him if taken in too great a quantity. He doled it out to those who wanted to join his mad scheme. They kept Dr. Weedon busy prescribing for patients who were causing their own decline.

"Tomorrow will be the dark of the moon." Wild Cat squinted down the sand trough at the five holes gouged in the larger depression at its end. Osceola's ball was blocking the one worth the most points. "Will you come with us?"

"No."

"Why not?"

"Chesup has given permission for my family to join me." Osceola spoke casually, as though discussing the game. A few Creeks were billeted here as interpreters. He didn't want them overhearing him. "Heartless Snake has gone to fetch them. They may be on their way here. If I escape, the pale-eyes will hold them hostage."

Osceola was suddenly wistful, remembering the days when he was ready for any adventure. Now just walking across the courtyard made his head spin and his pulse pound in his temples. "I'll speak to my *sabia* about giving you success."

Wild Cat grinned at him. His face was so gaunt he looked like a death's-head, a mockery of his former beauty, but his eyes still burned with an audacious inner fire.

"If you change your mind, brother . . ." Wild Cat left the invitation unfinished. The less said the better.

The next night, the last in November, Osceola lay awake on his straw mattress covered with forage bags. He stared up into the blackness at the top of the cell. He couldn't see the high ceiling, discolored and scabrous from moisture, but he could feel its heavy presence hanging over him. He could feel the dampness from the walls. The *Espanee* built their warrior towns like underground caverns, he thought.

In 1671, using European craftsmen and the forced labor of Florida Indians, the Spanish built the first lime kilns and opened the coquina pits on Anastasia Island. They rafted the huge blocks of waterlogged shell rock across Matanzas Bay. Here, the stonecutters shaped it, and the kilns transformed oyster shells into quick-setting lime.

For years the fort had grown under their hands, and in the century and a half since then it had taken on life of its own. Now the ocean wind sighed through it like breath. The walls sweated salty water. Its cloaca stank as it excreted its daily wastes from the water closet under the wide stone stairway into Matanzas Bay. Osceola felt as though he were lying in the fort beast's bowels. He felt buried alive. He felt forgotten.

He listened to the ritual of the changing of the guard outside and to the footsteps echoing cavernously in the courtyard. The hollow reverberation was eerie, lonely, mocking. Osceola longed so for the touch of his women and daughters, for their sweet voices, that his eyes stung. The image of Mad Dog holding Fighting in a Line in his arms and cutting her throat intruded into his thoughts, and he cried for them, too.

Mad New Town kept him company for a while. He sat with his legs crossed and smoked and talked of the old days. But he didn't stay long. And he had no solutions.

Finally the fort grew silent, hunched and slumbering against the black sky. Osceola could hear the soft breathing and snoring of the men sleeping around him. He strained to hear signs of activity in Wild Cat's cell, separated from his own by the six-foot-thick stone wall. Instead he heard someone out in the corridor reciting the latest poem about Abihka.

> "The war is ended," comes the news.
> "We've caught them in our gin:
> The war is ended past a doubt,
> Sam Jones has just come in!"

Osceola tensed. The guard was tipsified again. When he got drunk he liked to socialize with his charges. Wild Cat had discussed this possibility. If the soldier persisted in his amiability, Wild Cat planned to tie him up and put a forage sack over his head. Escaping through the door of their cell wouldn't help them. They would still have to cross the open courtyard and pass the sentries posted along the terreplein.

Sure enough, the sentry rattled his large iron key in the lock of Wild Cat's cell door. Osceola could smell the burning lard and whale oil in his bull's-eye lantern.

"Any you boys awake?" When the guard shone his lantern around the room, gigantic shadows writhed on the plastered walls. None of the men moved or spoke from under their blankets. "I say," he whispered again. "Any you boys like a sip of coffin shellac?"

He waved a small flat bottle tantalizingly and waited for what seemed a very long time. When he got no response he backed out slowly and locked the door again. He figured if Indians didn't bite at whiskey, they must be asleep or dead. He continued reciting as he made his rounds.

> But hark! Next day the tune we change
> And sing a counter strain.
> "The war's not ended," for behold!
> Sam Jones is out again.

Wild Cat and the others waited until he finished the doggerel and started to sing. Judging by the sound, he was on the other side of the courtyard, near the laboratory where the ammunition was stored. Then they worked silently and quickly in the dark. From under their mattresses they took out the two long ropes plaited of strips torn from their bedding. Wild Cat tied them to his belt.

John Horse positioned himself on the wide low ledge under the cell's single window. The window was eighteen feet up, a slate-gray disk against the pitch-black wall. Wild Cat stripped naked. He put his knife in his teeth and climbed onto John's shoulders. While John Horse supported his legs, Wild Cat reached as high as he could and wedged his knife into a crack in the stonework.

Using the knife for leverage, he pulled himself up until he could grab one of the two iron bars. He had already worked the other one loose from the crumbling stonework around it. He removed it, tied it to one of the ropes, and lowered it gently. It wouldn't do to have it fall with a clatter onto the stone floor.

Wild Cat managed to tie the two ropes to the remaining

bar. He dropped the long one out the window and the shorter
one inside for the others to climb up. With his arms outstretched ahead of him, he began worming his way through
a hole that was far too small for him. The outside wall, dimly
lit by the few stars visible in the cloudy sky, swept away
below and around him.

The stone frame of the window scraped and tore the skin
from his chest and back, until he was slick with his own
blood. He feared he had miscalculated. He feared he was
stuck. He blew out his breath and pushed with his hands
against the outer wall. Blood flowed down his arms and
dripped off his fingers, leaving dark smudges on the rough
stone.

For a moment Wild Cat thought he wouldn't be able to
draw breath back into his constricted chest. He heaved himself a fraction of an inch farther out and gasped in a shallow
whiff of the night air, cold against his body. He held on to
the rope, hanging upside down as he worked to wriggle his
torso and legs free.

As he walked his hands down the braided rags and more
of his weight hung there, the rope stretched and creaked. He
knew it was going to break. He knew he was going to fall,
headfirst, to the bottom of the dry moat yawning twenty-five
feet below. He pictured his skull bursting like a melon.

He hung there with his bare toes hooked over the circular
windowsill. Then he took several deep breaths and pushed
away with his feet. His legs described a wide, downward arc.
The rope shuddered violently, and his arms wrenched in his
sockets when his full weight jerked at them. Wild Cat swung
like a lead plumb on a line. He bounced several times against
the wall and scoured the skin off his knees and elbows; but
the rope held.

He lowered himself into the slime covering the moat's bottom. He scrambled out and ran, crouching, into the palmettos. He lay there, listening to his heart pound and ignoring
the fact that every twig and thorn and stone made his flayed
skin burn. He could feel each fiery point of pain, delicately
intense. He thought of his body as a meadow of pain flowers,
stirred by the cold wind.

He heard voices nearby and held his breath while two soldiers strolled past. He could see their shadowy forms and the glowing dots of their cigars. Wild Cat glanced anxiously up to the dark disk high in the stone cliff face. He saw John Horse's arms and head appear, filling the circle. When the soldiers were gone Wild Cat walked into the open and waved at his friend.

"I can't make it," John called down softly. His broader shoulders were wedged tightly.

"Yes, you can, brother," said Wild Cat. "Let out all the breath in your body."

"It's no use."

"Gather yourself in, like a leaf shriveling in a fire."

John Horse slowly, painfully, emerged from the hole and lowered himself headfirst down the rope. When his feet swung free he lost his grip. He plummeted to the ground and crumpled. Wild Cat slid down the side of the moat and knelt beside him. With his fingertips he searched John's bloody neck for a heartbeat. He found it and dragged him to a lower place in the moat where water still stood. The cold water revived John, but when he tried to stand his ankle gave way.

"It's broken," he said. "Leave me."

Wild Cat put John Horse's arm around his shoulder, hoisted him up, and staggered into the palmettos with him. He found a mule someone had left tethered nearby. He helped John onto the mule's back and led him away.

He didn't stay to watch the others. They were to escape by twos and threes throughout the night. Such small groups would have an easier time eluding the patrols. When the corporal brought breakfast the next morning, he found no one in Wild Cat's cell. Eighteen men and two women had escaped.

Fort Marion and Saint Augustine tumbled into an uproar. Patrols left at a gallop, but they found no trace of the missing prisoners. Wild Cat was a principal war leader. The war they all had thought was at an end was obviously to be continued. At Fort Peyton, two miles south of town, General Jesup flew into a passion.

Jesup was sure Abihka was at the bottom of it. He ordered the remaining prisoners put in irons. He swore to dress Sam Jones in woman's clothes when he caught him. He swore he would turn the bloodhounds loose to track escapees, in spite of the criticism in the northern newspapers about the use of dogs. He swore he would have King Philip killed if his son didn't turn himself in.

As each post rider cantered in with Jesup's latest dispatch, the sentries passed the information to their expressionless charges. The whole garrison was in serious trouble, of course, but even the soldiers appreciated Wild Cat's feat. As for the stoic Seminole, the stone well of the courtyard echoed with their silent laughter.

By the time General Jesup got around to threatening Philip's life, Osceola knew he was like Little Warrior's friend the burrowing owl. He was a great display and little action. *It's the feathers on a fowl that make it big*, Mink always said. When the whites weren't looking, Osceola's mouth twitched into a mischievous smile. The game wasn't over yet.

CHAPTER 52

John Goode used all his pay and pawned his pocket watch to buy strings of beads. When he saw Mink and Morning Dew and their sad entourage approaching, he wasn't sorry he'd done it. His spare shirt and stockings, his gloves, handkerchief, overalls, and shaving case, had been evicted from his valise. The square leather bag was now stuffed with forty or fifty pounds of the brightest glass beads he could find.

In his saddlebags he carried ruffled skirts and blouses in almost-traditional Seminole style. He had bought the calico and commissioned a Saint Augustine seamstress to sew them. He hoped they would fit. When the seamstress had asked him about sizes, he could only blush and gesture with his hands, so tall, so wide.

A young warrior headed the small procession. John recognized him as one of the pack of boys who used to shadow

Osceola. He would wait patiently for a word or a smile from Talasee *Tastanagee* or for a message to carry or a service to perform. The boy had become *tasikaya* in the years since John visited Talasee. Now he was following his beloved Black Drink Singer into prison.

He rode one of the group's two jaded ponies, and he carried a large white flag on an eight-foot staff. Behind him walked Mink and Morning Dew and Crying Bird. Little Warrior led the bony, limping horse that carried their worldly possessions tied into a few small bundles.

Following them was a line of forty blacks. The blacks were thin and ill and barefoot. Their clothes hung in tatters on them. Abihka had collected those who had run away from their masters since the beginning of the war. He and Osceola's family hoped to buy his release with them, but they didn't hope much. For their part, the blacks weren't sorry to be returned to bondage. It was preferable to the life they'd been living.

John spurred his horse forward, away from Lieutenant Pickell and the fourteen-man escort. As he rode to meet Osceola's family he was appalled at how emaciated they were. He had expected them to be thin but not this thin. Not this tattered.

The army had set aside rations to take care of their hunger. John intended to do what he could for their pride. He patted the bags of beads and bright clothing to reassure himself they were still there.

Little Warrior didn't run to greet him as in the old days. She stood with her arms at her sides, the pony's reins held loosely in her right hand. She wore the neutral expression that was so eloquent, as silence can sometimes be more eloquent than words. She had always been graceful and poised. She had always had a spiritual quality about her. Now her eyes in her slender face were huge and dark and sparkling. She seemed ethereal.

"You have come," John said.

"We have." Morning Dew looked relieved to see the soldiers.

"How was your journey?"

"Bad." Mink almost spat the answer. Nakita was the cause

of Osceola's imprisonment. If he hadn't sworn safe conduct among the whites, Osceola would not have gone in for talks.

"Did soldiers harry you?"

"Our own people harried us, Nakita." Mink used John's foolish child's name instead of the war name Osceola had given him. She could not kill him or the blue-jackets with him, so she did the next best thing. She scorned him. "We had to hide," she said. "We had to travel through trackless territory. Has no one told you? Those who surrender are under sentence of death."

"Surely . . ." John started to protest. Surely the Seminole wouldn't kill the family of their most patriotic leader.

Surely they would. John thought of Third Sister. He despaired of his government ever realizing how determined these people were to keep their land.

"Talasee *Tastanagee* is eager to see you," he said a little stiffly.

"How is he?" Morning Dew's voice was still as soft as John remembered it.

"A doctor is caring for him."

"Will we see him soon?" asked Crying Bird.

"Yes, little one." John crouched to be on her level. "The streamboat will take you there."

For a man racked by malaria and chained to an iron ring sunk into a six-foot-thick stone wall, Osceola looked remarkably cheerful. He graciously thanked the sentry who unlocked the heavy iron bands. When the soldier released the men who shared Osceola's cell, they filed outside, blinking in the harsh winter sunlight.

A dozen armed soldiers waited for them. They would watch while the prisoners spent the morning smoking and talking and playing dice or roll the bullet in the courtyard. General Jesup had reconsidered his decision to keep the captives chained, but he was having them closely guarded.

"Let me check your heartbeat." Dr. Frederick Weedon bent over and held his stethoscope to Osceola's chest. The stethoscope looked like a six-penny toy trumpet. The Seminole interpreter, one of Trout Leader's band, stood behind him.

"Abominable treatment. Abominable," said Weedon.

"Jesup is being rightly condemned for his grab game. Capturing a man under a flag of truce. Then chaining him when he's sick." Neither Weedon nor Osceola ever mentioned the fact that the doctor's brother-in-law, Wiley Thompson, once put Osceola in irons and died for it.

"Chesup *Tastanagee* is being cautious," said Osceola. "We fierce Seminole might rise up. We might slaughter you all."

"I don't know how you manage to rise up from your miserable, flea-infested pallet each morning." Weedon was alarmed at how fast Osceola's heart was pounding. The malaria had a firm grip on him. He started to put his stethoscope back into his wooden medicine chest.

"Can you hear what's in my heart, *Alektcha*, Doctor?"

"I hear good in your heart."

Osceola's name had been anathema in the doctor's house for almost three years, ever since the post rider had arrived at Weedon's Saint Augustine plantation with the news of the brutal murder of his wife's brother. But Weedon found it impossible to hate this gentle, intelligent, mystical man. He preferred to think of Osceola as two different people, which in a way he was. The Osceola of three years ago never would have submitted to chains and imprisonment. But even Dr. Weedon recognized that although Osceola submitted serenely to prison, he did not submit meekly.

Osceola took the stethoscope and held it against the doctor's chest. With a small smile of discovery he listened intently through the starched white linen of Weedon's shirt.

"Can you hear what's in my heart?" the doctor asked.

Osceola nodded.

"Well, my friend, I have fewer patients since last night's escapade, but I had best see to them. I shall have the cook send you something special. We must put flesh back on your bones."

Dr. Weedon turned to leave and found John Goode standing in the doorway. "Captain Goode, nice to see you." As he brushed by he muttered, "He's very ill. All we can do is make him as comfortable as possible."

"Yes." John stared at the chains and heavy iron rings lying at Osceola's feet. "I see how comfortable Jesup has been making him." John waited until the doctor and the interpreter had left and shut the door behind them.

"Are you *hadjo*? Are you mad?" John asked. "Why are you grinning like an alligator?"

"I'm happy because my family's safe." Osceola gripped John's elbow and forearm and pumped it heartily. "I'm happy because Wild Cat played a wonderful joke on the blue-jackets last night. I'm happy to see you, old friend."

"How do you know your family's safe?" As far as John knew, no one had told Osceola about his family's arrival. John had asked to be permitted to deliver the news himself.

"My uncle told me."

"The uncle who's always telling you things? The one who's been dead fifteen years?"

"That's the one." Osceola rubbed his ankles, reddened by the irons. "Where are they?"

"Didn't your uncle tell you?" When John saw the sorrow flicker across Osceola's face, he felt mean and small. "Your uncle's right. Your family's here. They're safe. Captain Webster found a room the five of you can share. I've come to take you to them."

"Where's Heartless Snake?" Osceola knew the journey must have been dangerous. Heartless Snake had risked his life to bring the family through territory held by the antiremoval forces. He wanted to thank him.

"He's gone over."

"Gone over?"

"He's tracking for the army. *Really* tracking. Not just spying for you."

"Each man must follow his own path." Osceola began rummaging through the wooden box that held his clothes and jewelry.

John had expected Osceola to be in a rush to see his family. He'd forgotten that wasn't the Seminole way. Osceola washed in a big tin basin. John was pained by the way his ribs and hip bones protruded. While Osceola shaved his head and dressed, John sat on his straw mattress and shared a pipe with him.

"I miss greeting the sun each morning," Osceola said.

"That's my sun now." He nodded up toward the small round window near the high ceiling. "A pity it doesn't face east."

"The northern newspapers are full of articles condemning Chesup *Tastanagee* for his perfidy." John lowered his voice. This was an extremely touchy subject where Jesup was concerned.

"His reputation's in ruins," John went on. "If he were a Seminole *tastanagee thloko* or *emathla*, the council would probably depose him." John took a folded sheet of the *Niles Weekly Register* from inside his jacket. He shook out the creases and read aloud, squinting in the dim light.

" 'We disclaim all participation in the *glory* of this achievement of American generalship. If practiced toward a civilized foe, it would be characterized as a violation of all that is noble and generous in war.' " John grinned up at Osceola. "Outside of Florida you're a hero, my friend. Your name's on the lips of thousands."

"Then we're to be freed?"

"No." John refolded the paper. His jubilation vanished. "No, you're far too dangerous to be set at liberty."

"Do I look dangerous?" Osceola had finished dressing. In his faded finery he was pitifully thin and haggard. Against the dampness of the cell and the December chill he wore a fringed shawl over his bony shoulders. His hand trembled as he tamped a pinch of John's tobacco into his pipe. A casual observer would have said Osceola hardly looked dangerous. A casual observer wouldn't have noticed the defiance in his eyes.

"You're the most dangerous man in the country right now. Followed nose to nose by Wild Cat and Abihka, of course. By the way, when was old Sam Jones born, anyway?"

"In the summertime, I think."

"I mean how many seasons has he seen? His age is the subject of great speculation among the troops."

"Maybe ninety seasons. Maybe a hundred. I don't know."

John shook his head. "I hope when I'm his age I'm that full of piss and vinegar."

"Piss? Vinegar?"

John explained while the two men walked across the buckled pavement of the weed-choked courtyard. Even garrisoned, Fort Marion had an abandoned air about it. Bushes had taken root in the sand-filled cracks of the ramparts. The cannons were pitted by the salt that blew in on every passing breeze.

"Chesup *Tastanagee* is planning a winter campaign." John paused at the door of a smaller cell. "He's gathered nine thousand soldiers and militia against what? Two thousand warriors?"

Osceola wasn't impressed. "How will he feed nine thousand men, horses, mules, in the swamps? What will he do when half the men become sick?"

"Those are good questions." John shook his head at the relentless stupidity of his superiors. "But I'll be in the field with the troops. Your people are retreating southward, into Pahay-okee, The Everglades. We'll have to follow them, of course."

"Will you take your mountain gun?"

John laughed. The army, in its wisdom, had sent a stubby mountain howitzer in response to Jesup's request for artillery. The gun was almost useless in Florida's flat terrain, and it had become a joke.

"I may not see you for a while, so I wanted to tell you I'm resigning at the beginning of the year. I had always thought the army a noble calling, but I can no longer be associated with the kind of treachery visited on you and your people."

"A warrior can't resign."

"This one can."

"May it go well with you, brother." Osceola gripped his arm again, this time in farewell. "May the path you choose bring you happiness."

John touched his hat in salute. Then he turned on his heel and strode across the yard. He mounted his horse and disappeared through the high front gate.

Aware that the soldiers were watching, Osceola took a deep breath. With an expressionless face he pushed open the door to the cell, then closed it quietly behind him. Morning Dew and Mink had already spread woven palmetto mats and deerhides on the cold stone floor of the narrow, high-ceilinged room. The cell still echoed, but they were doing their best to make it into a home.

Mink was arranging a small fire in the center of the room

while Morning Dew unpacked the utensils. The girls were spreading blankets on the straw pallets. They all looked up, frozen for a moment by their grief and their joy.

"How will we see the stars at night, Father?" When Little Warrior finally spoke, the stone walls gave her voice a hollow quality.

"Will we have to stay here long?" asked Crying Bird.

Osceola couldn't speak. He knelt and gathered Crying Bird and Little Warrior into his arms and held them tightly.

The women had collected the roots of soapwort and powdered them. They had made Lieutenant Pickell stop at a river while they worked the powder into a lather and washed their hair. Now the children's hair was smooth and glossy. Osceola buried his face in the soft fragrance and sobbed.

CHAPTER 53

The young *tasikaya* had everyone's attention. Osceola, Philip, and two hundred captives lounged against the stone parapet or sat cross-legged on the terreplein as he told his story. A constant wind teased their ruffles and plumes and shredded the smoke from their pipes.

The new captive was tall and thin and wiry, and he wore only the breechclout in which he'd been captured. He crouched to get below the top of the parapet and out of the wind. He rested his forearms on his thighs. As he spoke his eyes narrowed, focusing on his memories of the battle. He stared past the rough stone wall and beyond the fishnets drying on the beach, past the houses of Saint Augustine. He stared toward the southwest, toward Lake Okeechobee, the Big Water.

In his imagination he was there again, sitting on a cypress uprooted in some past hurricane. With eyes half-shut he chanted his medicine song. His new caplock and his alligator club leaned against a log. On the wet prairie in front of him two hundred cattle grazed. From high overhead a hawk plummeted into the grass with a keening cry, and a marsh rabbit screamed.

The *tasikaya* imitated the hawk and the rabbit for his audience. A startled sentry slapped his shouldered piece and brought it halfway down to firing position. He was nervous about so many warriors being together. Many of them had been here only a few days. They were unpredictable.

The young man continued his story. He would not have chosen the duty of making sure the pale-eyes attacked the distant hammock; but he could hardly refuse when Abihka *Hobayee Tastanagee* selected him. He mostly regretted the certain loss of his wonderful new breechloader, taken from the stiff hand of a dead blue-jacket.

When the cows began to shuffle restlessly, the young man turned around, as though scanning for trouble. He pretended to be startled by the men of the Second Dragoons, who now had him in the sights of their carbines. He pretended to look for some place to hide, to run. Then, reluctantly, he held his rifle over his head and waited for the pale-eyes to take it from him.

He squatted, impassive, while the army scout questioned him. The scout was Heartless Snake. Heartless Snake wore a breechclout and a wool army jacket with dark, permanent perspiration stains under the arms. Sweat formed a beaded band in his sparse mustache. The weather was very hot for December 25, even this far south.

"Where are Abihka's forces?" Heartless Snake hunkered down to be closer to the captive, but he stared off across the prairie, toward the hammock. He pulled at a blade of grass as he talked. He was uncomfortable with this assignment. On the other hand, he knew the young warrior wasn't here by accident, but he kept that to himself. Let the pale-eyes figure out a few things themselves.

When the *tasikaya* on Fort Marion's terreplein pointed, his listeners could picture the pine and palm hammock about a mile away, lonely against the immense flatness of the sawgrass swamp.

"How many warriors?" asked Heartless Snake.

The young man sized up Colonel Zachery Taylor's exhausted troops. With a short chop of his hand he separated out a little more than a third of the one thousand horse and foot soldiers.

"Which *tastanagalgee* are leading them?"

The young *tasikaya* pointed to the left. "Abihka leads the Mikasukee there. Alligator is with the Maskokee in the center. Wild Cat with Mikasukee, John Horse with black warriors on the right. The big one they call Luhstee, Black, is with John Horse. Water in front." He was right to include the water. The swamp was part of the Seminole's forces.

"Horses no good." Heartless Snake threw in some advice to Colonel Taylor, who stood with hands on hips and glared down at him.

Heartless Snake stood. "Water, mud, this many deep." With the inner edge of his hand he tapped his belly. "Behind hammock, Okee-chobee, Big Water."

"Shit fire and piss nails." Zachary Taylor gnawed his lip as he studied the terrain between his men and the dense growth of the island. This was Taylor's first encounter with Seminole strategy. Before the first shot was fired he realized he had committed the gravest error a military man could. He had underestimated the enemy. He was scarcely consoled to know he wasn't the first.

Abihka was making a stand on his own terms. He had chosen a large hammock at the northern border of Lake Okeechobee, lying like a polished pewter platter forty miles long and twenty-five miles wide. The warriors could retreat along its sandy margins, and it made an encirclement impossible.

Taylor didn't doubt the Seminole were watching him from the branches of the oaks in the center of the hammock. With their long Spanish knives they had cleared a wide swath in the sawgrass to form a corridor for their fire. They had notched the trees so they could steady the gun barrels in them. Now they waited with the patience of hunters watching a deer run.

Heartless Snake stayed behind to guard the prisoner, but the young man paid no attention to him. Even a *tasikaya* was adept at registering scorn in an expressionless face.

The young man described for his amused listeners how the exhausted, waterlogged, hungry, ill, shoeless, tattered pale-eyes held their heavy carbines over their heads. He demonstrated how they splashed into the malodorous black water and slogged toward Abihka's trap.

The *tasikaya* didn't know the significance of December 25. Heartless Snake did, mainly because rum rations were doubled then. As he watched the troops march into the treacherous sawgrass, he murmured, "Me-lee Klis-mas."

"Tay-lo *Tastanagee Thloko* claims a big victory." Osceola spoke after everyone had had time to savor the story.

"The pale-eyes think we drag away our dead," said Jumper. "After each battle they count invisible corpses." Jumper restlessly prowled the parapet. Imprisonment was new to him. "Tay-lo carried more than a hundred thirty wounded men, dead men, out of the swamp. If he were a Seminole leader, he'd be in disgrace. No warrior would even follow him into the bushes to take a shit. Wild Cat has made a fool of him."

Philip stared south to where Wild Cat roamed, free and very troublesome for the pale-eyes. A smile played over the old man's lined face. His son's name was on everyone's lips. Philip knew he himself would die soon or be sent into exile to a far country. But he would live on in Wild Cat.

Tall, lean Jumper was flanked by his sixty-three warriors who also had surrendered to Colonel Taylor just before the fight at Lake Okeechobee.

"We saw the wounded blue-jackets carried through the swamp on litters," Jumper said. "They had a rough ride. We wagered on whether the pale-eyes would die of their wounds or the flux. We saw the pale-eyes horses falling dead by the sides of the trail."

"Sense-Maker." Mikanopee waved a languid hand from the custom-built, extra-wide canvas chair where he reclined. Jumper went to confer with him. Jesup had captured Mikanopee and his delegation under yet another white flag, which was why Jumper had surrendered. He was loyal to his king to the last. He had followed him into captivity. He would follow him into exile.

*   *   *

Osceola clutched his shawl tighter around his shoulders as another chill shuddered through him. On the last day of 1837 the temperature was eighty degrees, but the wind from the ocean was cool, and Osceola was rarely without the company of his old friend, malaria.

Osceola and his family and the other two hundred prisoners were waiting for the lighters that would transfer them to the steamer anchored across the bar. The *Poinsett* would take them to Fort Moultrie, South Carolina, safely away from any possibility of escape or mischief.

It was a clear, sparkling, sapphire-and-malachite morning. Sunlight glinted on the ocean. It gilded even the crumbling buildings and the rivulets of sewage running across the beach. It flashed on the silver scales of the heaps of rotting fish. Most of Saint Augustine's folk had come to take leave of the prisoners and their military escort. They formed a dark-eyed ribbon along the beach.

Among them were the hard individuals who presided at the weekly slave auctions. The auction was held in the garden of the government house, usually while the Bible Society met inside. If someone were to sit near the window, he could listen to the missionaries lecture, and he could bid on fieldhands at the same time. The men who traded in black flesh were always on the lookout for more wares.

One of the slavers eyed Mink greedily as he stepped out to intercept Captain Webster. Osceola watched him warily, and Morning Dew and Little Warrior moved closer to Mink. Little Warrior picked up a large beach stone, probably ship's ballast, and held it ready to throw. So far the army had kept its promise to protect the Seminole blacks who surrendered or were captured, but the slavers were aggressive and persistent.

Captain Webster dismissed the man with a curt wave of his hand. Six soldiers, with rifles at present arms, formed a blue barricade when the slaver tried to press his demand.

"Here comes *Alektcha*," Morning Dew murmured.

Osceola watched Dr. Weedon weave through the crowd. Two slaves followed him. They were struggling to carry an enormous footlocker.

"Ah, Powell!" Dr. Weedon waved. "I've settled things at the plantation. I'm coming with you."

"You make my heart happy, friend." Osceola shook his hand in the manner of white men.

"A bracing sea voyage, that's what I prescribe. Once you're away from this miasmic clime, your health will show marked improvement."

Probably Dr. Weedon decided to come with his charges out of friendship. Maybe he decided to come because he was now the personal physician of a national celebrity. Some people called Osceola a hero and a patriot. Some called him a murdering savage. But just about everyone knew who he was.

CHAPTER 54

In just a few days after his arrival on Sullivan's Island, Osceola became the spirit of Fort Moultrie. The soldiers grew used to seeing him, silent in his moccasins, as he wandered the brick maze of passages, stairways, and crannies around the parade ground. They nodded and spoke to him as they passed, and he smiled in return. Little Warrior was always with him. She shadowed him as though she feared he might slip away to the spirit world while she was absent.

Each day at dawn, before the excursion boats brought crowds of visitors to see the famous war chief, Osceola and Little Warrior went up to the terreplein to greet the Breath Maker. When the sun had risen they moved to the south wall. He wrapped in his shawl, she in an army coat, they would stand there for hours, silhouetted against the pale winter sky.

They watched the gulls and pelicans swoop over the restless water. They watched the shadows shift across the myrtles and oaks and cabbage palms on the distant mainland. The palms and the birds reminded them of home, and their souls traveled back to the verdant, radiant land they loved.

Cannons once had stood guard here on the tamped earthen platform of the terreplein. They were gone, leaving only the granite traverse circles of their emplacements. Weeds and small bushes had taken root. Fort Moultrie had been built fifty years earlier to protect Charleston harbor from the British. Now instead of keeping people out, its main function was to keep them in.

January 29 was gray and chill, but as usual Osceola and his family passed it on the terreplein. Morning Dew and Mink brought their sewing and basketry and sat in the shelter of the parapet. They unrolled a palmetto mat and laid out their rations of wheaten bread and bacon. They preferred to eat where they could feel the sea wind and hear the gulls' laughter.

They wanted to spend a quiet hour with Osceola, before his throng of admirers found him. Crying Bird played with the dolls the soldiers carved for her and her mothers had dressed. Little Warrior studied the new McGuffy's *Eclectic Reader* a young lieutenant had given her. Her lips moved silently as her fingers traced the words.

"Once, long ago, the One Who Lives Above decided to offer books to the red man as well as to the white man," Osceola said.

Little Warrior looked up from the primer, and Osceola smiled at her. She smiled back. His message was received and understood. He was proud of her for learning the white man's magic as well as her own people's.

"What happened?" asked Crying Bird.

"The One Who Lives Above let a wise old blind man choose who would receive the books," Osceola said. "The blind one gave the men a test. He told them each to bring back the biggest deer he could find.

"The red man traveled a long way to find a deer, deer being scarce in those days. The white man went only a short distance. He killed a cow. He gave it to the blind man. He told him it was a very big deer. The blind man believed the lying white man. When the red man came back with his deer, the white man already had the books. He had the knowledge in them. He's had it ever since."

"Your voice is hoarse, Old Man," said Morning Dew.

"My throat hurts."

"The blue-jacket cook has hominy. I'll make *sofkee* for

you." Mink already had struck a deal with the cook. He would give her half a peck of hominy if she would sew him a hunting shirt.

Osceola lifted Crying Bird onto the wooden banquette so she could see over the edge of the parapet.

"Will it be cloudy all day, daughter?"

Crying Bird studied the sky. "Yes."

"How do you know?"

Crying Bird held her arm out at an angle from her body. "The sun is this high, but the clouds still cover it. That means they'll stay all day."

"Excuse me." George Catlin stood at the head of the stone stairs. He was burdened with canvas, easel, palette, paint box, stool, brushes, and rags. Little Warrior closed the book and went to help him. She set up the easel and spread the paints out on the banquette.

"I had Dr. Weedon turn back the tourists," Catlin said. "Forgive me for intruding, but would you be willing to sit for me now? We're almost finished."

"I'm not wearing my good clothes."

"I'll be painting your face."

Osceola sat without moving while Catlin worked on his portrait. Little Warrior hovered nearby, to interpret if necessary and to watch. Catlin had spent some of his scant free time teaching her to sketch in charcoal. She was gifted at it.

George Catlin looked mild and shabbily effete in his high, frayed collar stock and dusty suit of brown domestic. But he was something of a celebrity himself. And he was a man driven by an obsession.

At forty-one he had traveled thousands of miles through the west. He had crossed prairies and mountains. He had gone into places where war and deadly plagues raged among the red man and the white. He had resolved, if cholera, smallpox, dysentery, and war should spare his life, to record the Indians' ways before they passed into oblivion.

He had drawn and painted hundreds of individuals from dozens of tribes. They had all, without exception, posed for him with great dignity. The man sitting in front of him now had something more. Catlin had seen the fiercest, the proudest, the most splendid of the western chiefs. But he had never seen such a look of gentleness and ferocity, sensuality and spirituality, in one face.

Catlin was terribly worried he wouldn't finish painting Black Drink Singer's eyes before death extinguished the light in them. He consulted with Dr. Weedon on a daily basis. Now, only when the dark clouds spread across the sky and rain was imminent, did he reluctantly pack up his equipment and retreat.

That evening Osceola joined Dr. Weedon and the captive leaders in George Catlin's large, comfortable room. He and the others usually gathered there in the evenings to share tobacco, play cards, and trade stories with Fort Moultrie's officers. Often the stories included accounts of battles where the officers and the warriors were on opposite ends of the muskets.

This night Catlin set a forest of precious candles on the mantel. He worked on the portrait by their light and the glow from the lanterns. He painted with a single-mindedness that was equaled only by Osceola's own. They were both oblivious to the good-natured banter and the laughter that went on around them. Osceola even ignored the spirited discussion of the officers' marvelous new repeating revolvers. He sat so still and looked so intense, he seemed to be willing his image onto the canvas.

"How do you feel tonight?" Catlin asked.

Osceola pointed to his throat. "Hurts." His voice was almost inaudible.

"Well, my friend, you don't have to talk, except to tell me if you approve." Catlin put the last strokes onto the picture, two tiny white dots that gave light and life and infinite sorrow to Osceola's eyes. Catlin stood back so the others could crowd around.

Osceola studied it a long time, looking into the eyes as if into his own soul. When he smiled it was reward enough.

"Here comes the heavenly messenger," said the young lieutenant. Little Warrior had pushed open the door and peered inside. Morning Dew usually sent Little Warrior when she thought Osceola might be tiring. She knew how insistent his friends could be. If they had their way, they would keep him awake all night, and he was too weak for that.

One night they had ferried him across the bay to a theater in Charleston. Little Warrior had been frantic with worry. She had wrapped a blanket around her and stayed up on the parapet in the frigid January wind until one in the morning, waiting for the launch to bring him back.

He had been too exhausted to get up the next morning. Dr. Weedon had raged at the commandant for allowing a dying man to be used to increase attendance at some frivolous farce.

"Come in, Little Soldier of the Panther clan. I have something for you." With an oiled cloth the lieutenant finished polishing the panther he had carved for her.

"Thank you." Little Warrior turned it over in her hands and thought of the panther that had visited her at night and stared at her once, long ago, in another lifetime.

"And have you considered my proposal of marriage?" The lieutenant was only half jesting. Little Warrior was almost fourteen and unequivocally a heartbreaker, the more so because she was unaware of it. She smiled shyly at him.

Osceola put his shawl around his shoulders and gathered his pipe and tobacco pouch. Little Warrior held her lissome panther in one hand and took her father's hand in the other. Dr. Weedon held Osceola's other arm and carried a candle. The three of them slowly walked in a bubble of light down the long, dark corridor toward the room Osceola and his family shared. Dr. Weedon bade them good night at the door.

In her bare feet Little Warrior could feel the coldness of the stone floor through the deer hides her mothers had laid down. Fully clothed, she crawled under the blankets and snuggled next to Crying Bird, who was sleeping soundly. Little Warrior lay, wide-eyed in the dark, listening to her father prepare for bed.

As Osceola undressed he began to shiver again. Morning Dew helped him onto the straw pallet and under the blankets. Mink lay curled with her soft breasts against his back and her arms around him. Morning Dew lay with her back to his chest. They often slept nested like that, keeping him warm when the malarial attacks came.

"I'm counting out my days on the drum of my heart." Osceola's voice was so hoarse Mink and Morning Dew could scarcely hear him in the echoing stone room. "Sometimes my soul flutters in my breast. It's as much a prisoner in this body as the body is in this stone house."

"We'll keep death from you, beloved," Mink murmured, her full lips brushing his neck. Against her cheek she felt the long, smooth tendrils of his unbraided scalplock.

"I don't fear death. I've carried it in my hand since I was a child." His fingers curved, without volition, as though holding the stock of his rifle. I've held death next to my cheek, he thought. I've heard it bark in my ear.

"Don't talk, Old Man." Morning Dew wound her arms around his and clasped his hands at her waist. Mink crooned to him in her husky voice until he finally fell into a restless sleep, full of bad dreams and omens.

It's time.

Little Warrior opened her eyes to darkness. The dream of her father, healthy and strong and laughing, vanished, but the words "It's time" lingered. Had Osceola said it, or had she dreamed it?

"Daughter," whispered Mink.

"I'm awake, Mother."

"Bring *Alektcha*, the doctor."

Little Warrior didn't stop to put on her moccasins or light a torch. She pushed open the heavy door, slipped out, and darted down the long, gloomy corridor. The lanterns used to illuminate the passageway had burned low. Every thirty feet one threw a tenuous wedge of light up the wall, leaving the area between it and the next one in darkness.

"Here, miss." When the sentry stepped from the shadows into Little Warrior's careening path, she almost screamed.

"My father." She dodged around him and ran on.

When she reached Philip's cell she wiped away her tears and composed her expression. She had to lift the hem of her skirt and batter the massive door with the sole of her foot to be heard. As she stood in the cold corridor she thought the men inside would never open it. Finally Philip poked his head out. His eyes were puffy with sleep. His gray hair stood in stiff disarray around his face.

"It's time. My father needs *Alektcha*." Little Warrior didn't wait for a reply. With her heart pounding in fear he'd gone already, she raced back.

She found Osceola dressed and huddled under a blanket. He unwrapped the small bundles of dried herbs and the sacred objects and laid them out. He touched each one lightly, lingeringly, with the tips of his long fingers.

In the past he could sometimes feel them move under his touch. He could sense the spirits that lived in them; but he hadn't felt them stir in a long time. The sacred objects looked shriveled and powerless against the cold stones of his prison.

Osceola wanted to slip away from life and be done with it. He wanted to end his long friendship with pain, but he couldn't die quietly, alone with his family. As Talasee *Tastanagee* he had a responsibility to die well.

He put away his medicine and lay down on the pallet near the fire. Little Warrior sat next to him. Mink piled blankets on top of him. Morning Dew bathed his neck with warm water in which the curer's herbs had been steeped. Crying Bird crouched in the corner with her arms across her knees and cried silently and inconsolably.

Footsteps and low voices sounded in the passageway, and the officers and Seminole leaders filed in. With his medicine tube the curer bubbled his breath through an herbal infusion. He waved his peacock feather over Osceola and chanted softly, hypnotically.

Dr. Weedon pushed his way to the front of the crowd and knelt to examine Osceola. While someone held up a lantern, he peered down Osceola's throat.

"The mucous membranes of the pharynx are in a high state of inflammation," he said. "If I don't scarify the tonsils, you may suffocate, my friend." He began sorting through the instruments in his box.

Osceola held his hand up as a shield.

Weedon turned to the curer, chanting under the hood of his blanket. "Let me at least give him some medicine and apply leeches."

The curer shook his head.

Sitting by his shoulder, Little Warrior didn't hear them. She was aware only of the suffering in Osceola's face. She was fixed so intently on him, she might as well have been alone in the crowded cell.

Osceola's throat was so swollen he couldn't swallow. The room swirled around him. He could feel death, a numbness spreading from his feet, but not blunting the terrible pain.

When he held out his hand Mink and Morning Dew and Little Warrior helped him sit up. Morning Dew held the mirror while he painted half his face and throat vermilion as though going into battle. He did the same for his wrists, the backs of his hands, and the handle of his knife. He would die a war leader.

When he finished he walked slowly around the room. No one spoke while he shook hands with every man there. They each bade him silent farewell, and he answered them with his gentle smile. Morning Dew held Crying Bird up so Osceola wouldn't have to kneel or bend down. He wiped the child's tears with his bandana, then held her small hand in his.

My heart is with you always, beloved, Morning Dew thought when he took her hand. She looked a little fierce. He must not think his family would be helpless without him. She felt his grip tighten. He understood.

"*Owa mwen*, my man." Mink murmured the Dahomeyan endearment too softly for anyone else to hear. "May you have a safe journey. Care for our son in the spirit world."

Little Warrior stood straight and self-controlled with her left hand at her side and her right hand out. When Osceola took it his fingers were cold as though death were already inside him. He stared into her eyes, bright with tears. *Carry the fire,* he said silently.

They helped him lie down and sat beside him. He laid his famous knife across his chest. He saw Mad New Town standing in the doorway with a bright light behind him.

I am come, Uncle.

You are, nephew.

Author's Note

After Osceola's death, Dr. Frederick Weedon cut his head off and carried it back to Saint Augustine. For years he kept the grisly memento, hanging it on his sons' bedsteads when they were disobedient.

King Philip died on the way to Oklahoma and was buried with full honors. Wild Cat was captured at a council with the army in 1841 and put in chains. He tried to convince others to surrender, but the remaining resistance leaders threatened to kill anyone who carried messages from the whites. Wild Cat and John Horse were shipped west, where they began a second career fighting Commanche.

Surgeon Jacob Rhett Motte's journal became *Journey into Wilderness*, edited by James L. Sunderman. It's one of the most entertaining accounts of the war.

By 1842 Alligator, Jumper, and most of the Seminole leaders and their people were captured and sent to Oklahoma. Abihka, then in his nineties, escaped with a few hundred of his followers. They fled deep into the Everglades and held out there.

Of the one thousand four hundred and sixty-six soldiers who died, three hundred twenty-eight were killed in action. The rest were victims of illnesses and infections. After seven long years of chasing the Seminole through forty-seven thousand square miles of territory, the United States gave up. The government declared the war over; but the Seminole never signed a capitulation treaty. Some older Seminole still refuse to sign anything official, out of fear the United States will send them away if they do.

The war broke out again in 1855 when a squad of engineers went into Big Cypress swamp. They destroyed the camp of Holata Miko, who was called Billy Bowlegs. Holata Miko retaliated. For three more years soldiers fought the Seminole. A bounty of a hundred dollars was offered for each warrior taken. Soldiers captured Holata Miko's small granddaughter, forcing him to come in. Then they sent him west, too.

About a hundred people still managed to hide and escape exile. Their descendants, members of the Seminole and Miccosukee nations, are still there.

The three conflicts known as the Seminole Wars lasted over forty years. The Second Seminole War prompted Thomas Hart Benton to write many years later:

> This was one of the most troublesome, expensive and unmanageable wars in which the United States had been engaged. . . . It cost some thirty millions of money and baffled the exertions of several generals; recommenced when supposed to be finished; and was finally terminated by changing military campaigns into an armed occupation. . . . All the opposition presses and orators took hold of it, and made its misfortunes the common theme of invective.

One of the reasons the war was so unpopular was because of Osceola.

The author found no records of the fate of Osceola's wives and daughters. In all probability they were sent west in the sad company of prisoners exiled there. Osceola's spirit stayed behind, a reproach to those who had treated him and his people so unjustly.

His struggle for his land made most of the public recognize the government's policy for what it was, an unjust war of greed and aggression. Until his death more than twenty years later, General Thomas Jesup tried vainly to defend his decision to capture Osceola under a flag of truce.

To many Americans Osceola became a symbol of courage, loyalty, and patriotism. His headless body was buried at Fort

Moultrie under a marble headstone donated by a Charlestonian. The inscription reads:

OSCEOLA

Patriot and Warrior
Died at Fort Moultrie
January 30th, 1838.

ABOUT THE AUTHOR

Lucia Robson was born in Baltimore, Maryland, and raised in South Florida. She has been a Peace Corps volunteer in Venezuela and a teacher in a disadvantaged neighborhood in Brooklyn, New York. She lived in Japan, South Carolina, and southern Arizona before moving to Tallahassee, Florida. After earning her Master's degree in Library Science at Florida State University, she worked as a public librarian in Annapolis, Maryland. She now lives near Annapolis in a wooded, eccentricly surveyed community on the Severn River.